HEAD OVER HEELS OVER WHEELS

With the last of his vehicle's momentum, Zeb slewed around leftward, putting the car across two lanes. He killed the engine and hopped out to stand on the driver's-side running board. He drew his pistols and aimed them across the roof at the oncoming car.

Muzzle flares erupted from its passenger side. He returned fire into the driver's-side windshield, emptying both pistols, hearing thumps and slams strike his own vehicle.

The oncoming car veered left and then right, as though the driver were indecisive about whether to pass Zeb on the right or the left. Then the car leveled off and steered straight at Zeb, and he realized the driver was probably already dead.

Zeb dove clear, hit the pavement with a bone-jarring thump, heard the shrieking collision as tons of metal met violently. . . .

heroes.

BAEN BOOKS by AARON ALLSTON

Doc Sidhe
Sidhe-Devil

Sidhe
Devil

Aaron Allston

BAEN

SIDHE-DEVIL

Copyright © 2001 by Aaron Allston

A Baen Books Original

Baen Publishing Enterprises
P.O. Box 1403
Riverdale, NY 10471
www.baen.com

ISBN: 0-671-31993-0

Cover art by Patrick Turner

First printing, June 2001

Distributed by Simon & Schuster
1230 Avenue of the Americas
New York, NY 10020

Production by Windhaven Press, Auburn, NH
Printed in the United States of America

Acknowledgments

I extend my thanks to:

The Eagle-Eyes, my advance readers, who make sure that I dot my eyes and cross my teas: A.T. Campbell, Kelly Frieders, Ruben Gamboa, Kali Hale, Steven S. Long, Beth Loubet, Matt Pinsonneault, Susan Pinsonneault, Bob Quinlan, Roxanne Quinlan, Luray Richmond, Sean Summers, and Lori Wolf.

The folks who volunteered technical answers in person and on-line, including Tobias Budke, Beverly Hale, Stefan Immel, Denis Loubet, Matt Pinsonneault, and Scott Ruggels. Any mistakes of detail that remain do so in spite of their involvement.

My agent, Russ Galen. His work lets me do more of the fun stuff.

Chapter One

Pistol in hand, Doc ran through the deserted streets of the city of Neckerdam.

The skyscrapers around him looked like the misaligned, broken teeth of some long-dead giant, spikes of black or gray or checkered white-and-green pointing accusingly at the sky.

At the stars. These weren't the stars Doc knew, not the ones that belonged above the true Neckerdam. That, and the fact that he had not seen one other living soul on the streets, told him he was dreaming.

But was he experiencing a true dream or a sending-dream? The second kind could be meaningful . . . and dangerous.

Ahead, on a street corner, he saw the wanted poster.

Above the text was a picture of Doc, but this was not the sort of picture normally posted on the walls of the city jails. In it, Doc stood in a heroic pose, gun in hand, wearing explorer garb better suited to exploration of the Dark Continent, his shirt ripped, his long snow-white hair flowing in a wind.

1

The words beneath the picture read, "Sought by the Crown, Doctor Desmond MaqqRee of the Sidhe Foundation. Also hight Doc, also hight Doc Sidhe."

There was something missing from the text. Doc shook his head; it was so hard to think in a dream. Then he knew: There should be some specification of charges, some indication of the reward being offered.

He looked up the street and now, where none had been before, his wanted poster was thickly plastered on every wall and light pole.

He heard and felt a grinding from beneath the pavement only a few steps away. Two large bronze plates set into the sidewalk clattered open and the elevator beneath them rose into view.

On it was a bed, a beautiful four-poster of ornately carved hardwood, draped in sheer bed-curtains, with a lavender canopy above. And lounging on the pillows lay Ixyail del Valle, Doc's lover.

She was a small woman, not just in comparison with Doc's generous height, but by any human standard; yet she was well and sleekly muscled like a panther in human form. Her features were delicate, the legacy of royal ancestry from the Old World, but her mouth was broad and generous. Her skin was a light brown, natural to her rather than the result of sunning. Her hair, flowing and glossily black, was far longer than Doc remembered it, as long as the silken nightdress that came barely to her thighs.

She gave him a smile that was all invitation and crooked a finger to summon him.

He took a last look around. There was no sign of an enemy. He felt nothing that indicated this was a sending-dream. He set his pistol down on the concrete and climbed in.

As he passed through the curtains his clothes disappeared. Ixyail seized him, pulling him atop her. This time, she had no need of love-play; she was ready for him, clutching, clawing, her skin hot to the touch. He tore her nightdress from her with a single yank and she drew him into her. She purred a true cat's purr and wrapped herself around him.

Too quickly, he spent. He held and kissed her, tried to form the words to soothe her, to appreciate her. But the words wouldn't come. He could see from her smile and her eyes that she'd understood his intent. Yet there was something odd to her eyes, an expression he had never seen in them before, an anxious expectation— she seemed to be asking a question he could not understand and could not answer.

She rolled over so that she was above and he beneath, and said, "I'll return when you are ready again." She slid from atop him and vanished as she passed through the curtains.

Doc tried to follow but found that his wrists and ankles were bound by heavy bronze shackles that held him, splayed, to the bed. He struggled but they were unyielding.

He tried to wake up. But above him the canopy of the four-poster bed remained stubbornly in place.

He looked around, but still there was no one to be seen on the streets of this phantom Neckerdam. Even his wanted posters were missing.

And he wondered if he were dead, gone to some place of afterlife punishment like the one the members of the Carpenter Cult described.

That's when the memory returned to him: the gun-man emerging from behind the pillar, his rifle rising into line, aiming at him, firing—

Zeb Watson wondered for the twelfth time where he'd seen the minister before. He also waited for words he'd once been certain he would never hear.

"I now pronounce you husband and wife," the minister said. He peered at the bride and groom over metal-rimmed glasses and waited. "Oh. You *may* kiss the bride."

Harris Greene, the groom, was a lean man, darkly handsome, with features best suited to a cheerful rogue on a TV show; he was dressed in a tuxedo the green of late-summer oak leaves. He took his new wife about the waist and drew her to him. The gesture was theatrical and dashing.

Gaby, the bride, Latina ancestry evident in her coloration and features, had a jaw that suggested stubbornness and alert eyes that spoke of keen intelligence. She wore a wedding dress in a matching green and a wreath of laurel leaves. She smiled at his display as she kissed him.

The crowd in the hotel ballroom applauded, the wedding party joining in.

The couple gave no sign that they were ready to break their clinch. The minister smiled as he stepped around them and past Zeb. He was a young man with a wispy brown beard and mustache and open features suggesting that stress, to him, was nothing but a word in the dictionary. He was dressed in the same style of green tuxedo as the groom's party. "Attention, please. As soon as we can pry Harris and Gaby apart and get the members of the immediate families up here, we'll start taking wedding pictures. If you can sort of gather in the open spaces, the hotel staff will be able to drag the chairs up against those two walls and get the buffet set up."

Zeb ignored him and kept his attention on Harris and Gaby. They were different from the last time he'd seen them. Six months ago, Harris had been an unsuccessful professional kickboxer, his career spiraling away to nothingness in New York. He and Gaby, a programming director for a UHF station, had been together for a while but signs had not looked good between them. Then something had happened—a neighbor had reported Gaby kidnapped, then she'd turned up again, then she and Harris had dropped out of sight.

There had been little word from them after the reported kidnapping. Zeb had received a note from Harris saying that all was well and that he'd explain later. The explanation had never come, but a wedding invitation had, eventually. Now Harris and Gaby looked confident, healthy, as happy as Zeb had ever seen them . . . and he still didn't know why.

Not that Zeb minded a happy ending. He just wished he knew how they'd gotten there.

At the back of the columned hall, in the last row of the seating devoted to the groom's guests, Rudi Bergmonk cupped his chin in his hand and decided that he needed a shave. On the other hand, he wasn't here to impress the wedding attendees with close-shaven elegance. He might have to shoot one of them, in fact. He might have to shoot several of them.

He and his four brothers stood as the rest of the audience did. That cut off their view to the head of the hall; the tallest of them was a head shorter than most of the men present. Rudi knew that this wasn't the only thing that set them apart, visually; the black suits they wore were badly fitted to their thick-chested, short-legged builds, and all five, unlike the genuine wedding guests, wore gloves.

Albin, the oldest and the only one whose beard was completely gray, said, "I still don't see him."

Jorg, the biggest of them, mopped a handkerchief that was as floridly red as his hair over his sweaty forehead. "Then he isn't here."

Albin fixed him with a look of contempt. "Have you even been looking among the crowd? He might be employing a disguise."

"Of course I have," Jorg said, his voice rising in protest. "We all have. Right, boys? No sign of him. Maybe he'll come later."

Albin still frowned. "I don't like it. I've done research on their weddings . . . but they're not doing it right."

Egon, the second oldest, though he still had some blond in his hair and beard, shrugged. His hands were in his pockets; Rudi knew that one hand would be on a knife hilt even now. "Perhaps you did your research wrong."

"Shut up," Albin said. "The part we've just seen, they're supposed to do in a temple. Then they have cameos taken. Then they have rice thrown at them as they leave the temple."

Otmar, youngest of the brothers except for Rudi, young enough not to have any silver decorating the brown in his beard, laughed—giggled, rather. "Messy."

Albin took a deep breath, an effort, Rudi knew, to keep his temper in check. "Dry rice, you idiot. Then they go to the hall where the food is—that's the best place we could have taken them, on the trip from temple to hall. But these cretins have cobbled together both parts of the ceremony. They do everything wrong." He looked around, directing his contempt against the other attendees instead of his brothers. "They actually let duskers into the hall." He gestured toward the head of the room, where, until the audience had stood, they'd been able to see the tall black man standing beside the groom. "They've got a dusker for the best man. I think the bride's a dusker passing for dark."

Rudi said, "That's not our problem. The fact that they're not doing things according to their own traditions is. So we'll have to improvise. Where do you want to do it?"

Albin curled a lip, still obviously distressed about the presence of the black man. "When they go to change their garments, I think. We'll follow them and catch them in their rooms, one by one or two by two."

The bride, the groom, and their families collected at the front of the room to endure the photographer's instructions. Zeb was far enough to one side to be out of camera range but close enough to hear the photographer's victims talk.

The bride's mother—small-boned, more than a trifle overweight, a frown seemingly a permanent feature of her face—leaned in to whisper, "That Minister Jones, is he a real minister?"

"Yes, Mother." Gaby kept her smile on for the camera.

"I think he's an actor. I think I recognize him from a peanut butter commercial."

"He *is* an actor from a peanut butter commercial. He and Harris studied theater together in college. But he's also a minister. He founded his own church. Government-recognized and everything."

"Well, it's not right. You should have been married by a real priest. A Catholic priest."

"Well, maybe we'll do it again with a real priest next time."

"How about next week?"

Minutes later, the families immortalized, the photographer maneuvered them away and had the wedding party step in.

Zeb put on his photographic face. He knew his close-cropped beard and mustache gave him a distinguished look, and his eyes were expressive—but only when he put on the right face. He had other faces for other situations. There was his war-face, developed and polished for the boxing ring, his I'm-not-to-be-messed-with face for walking certain neighborhoods in New York, his I'm-so-nice face for persuading people he was no threat to them. He had a face for every occasion. He sometimes wondered if any of them was his own.

While the photographer was changing cameras, Zeb leaned forward over Harris's shoulder. "Sorry I was so late."

"Don't worry about it," Harris said. "You got here, you didn't lose the ring, and in the original tradition of the best man, you're the most dangerous guy I know, so I had no worries that anyone would come and steal Gaby away."

The photographer said, "All right, bride only for a while." Harris and Zeb obligingly moved to one side and relaxed.

"We haven't had a lot of time to talk," Zeb said. He couldn't keep a trace of suspicion from his voice. "Months I don't hear from you or Gaby, and then boom! You're living in California, you're getting married, and you're doing what?"

"Freelance consultants. We're hotel reviewers and inspectors."

"Meaning what, exactly?"

"We're on the road most of the year, going from hotel to hotel under assumed names. We just look around, see how good the hotel staff is at doing its job, use all the hotel facilities we can without being obvious, cause a weird problem or two to see how they deal with it, and file reports to the companies that hire us. We might work for the corporation that owns the hotel, a corporation that owns rival hotels, a chain of travel agencies, a credit-card issuer, that sort of thing." Harris shrugged. "It's good work that pays well. And we like the travel."

A crowd of well-wishers descended upon Harris, shaking his hand, clapping his back, and then moved on to linger in a predatory fashion around the buffet table setup.

"Harris?" Zeb said.

"Yeah?"

"Where are the pictures?"

Harris gestured at the photographer, still posing Gaby and members of her family. "They won't be ready for weeks."

"No, not those. You've been travelling the last few months from hotel to hotel. The last time you and Gaby went anywhere, she came back with a lot of photographs. She was into photography and journalism in school, right? I remember she likes taking pictures when she's on vacation."

"You don't forget much."

"So where are they?"

"Hell if I know. I told her I don't like looking at pictures. She packs them away somewhere."

"Bullshit."

"What?"

"You heard me."

Harris frowned, but not at Zeb's remark. He watched someone toward one side of the hall. "Stay here a second. There's a guy I want to talk to."

"You're avoiding the question."

"No." Harris broke away and moved into the crowd.

The short, stocky man moved behind one of the columns on the long wall where chairs were stacked. Harris followed as closely as he dared. He peeked around the column, saw the man's broad back, saw over his shoulder as the man lit a pipe.

Harris moved out from behind the column and asked, "Pardon me, goodsir, what's the bell?"

The stocky man turned, revealing his bulbous nose and bushy brown beard; he automatically reached into the pocket of his vest and fetched out a large pocket watch whose lid was ornately engraved with the image of an apple tree. He opened it up. "Why, it's—" Then, guilt dawning on his features, he looked up.

He dropped the pipe, reached under his armpit. As he brushed his jacket lapel aside, Harris saw the gun butt and shoulder holster beneath.

Harris hit him, a knuckle-punch to the solar plexus. He stepped in even closer, slammed his forearm into the man's head, driving it back into the column, and followed through with a knee to the man's groin.

The stocky man let out a faint moan and slid, unconscious, to the floor. The plaster of the column was broken where his head had hit it.

Harris glanced around. With stacks of chairs all around them, no one appeared to have seen or heard their exchange. He bent and dragged the bearded gunman behind several tall stacks of chairs, an adequate place of concealment. Then he undid the man's bow tie and tied his wrists behind his back.

And cursed. The man's nose was a bloody mess, and so was the forearm of Harris's jacket.

He drew off the jacket as he emerged from behind the chairs. And Zeb was right there, waiting for him. "Dammit," Harris said.

"Man, why are you acting so strange?"

Harris sighed, then grabbed Zeb's tie and pulled him around to look behind the chairs. "That's why."

"What the hell happened to him?"

"I hit him."

"Why? What is he to you?"

"He's a fairy."

Zeb pulled back and looked appalled. "Harris, that's not like you at all. You've never been a gay-basher."

"No, no, no. He's not gay. Or maybe he is. I don't know. He's a fairy."

"You've lost me."

"In other words, he's someone from the fair world. Come on. We need to find out if there are more of them." He drew Zeb back around the column and into the crowd. "You see any guys about chest-high, built like bowling balls, point 'em out to me."

"So you can beat them up. Sure."

The photographer called, "Husband, please stand beside the bride again."

"Dammit! Zeb, give me your jacket."

Zeb watched Harris rejoin Gaby in front of the camera. Zeb could tell Harris's smile was forced. It looked genuine enough, but Zeb had known him long enough to distinguish between reality and acting where Harris was concerned. Zeb returned to the man Harris had slugged.

He didn't find an invitation among the man's effects. But he did find the man's gun. It was a strange piece, brassy in color, large for a revolver.

Okay. So someone had crashed the wedding with a gun. Harris might be crazy, with all this talk of fairies, but he wasn't paranoid. And he'd suggested there were more strange folk out there. Well, if there were potential enemies in the crowd with firearms, Zeb didn't intend to be unarmed. He wrapped the gun up in Harris's jacket and took it with him.

Zeb returned to the edges of the crowd and looked around. He immediately spotted men so like the one Harris had slugged that they had to be relatives: short, squat, thick-chested, most of them bulbous-nosed and bearded. They were wearing the worst off-the-rack suits Zeb had seen in a long while. All four stood at the main doors leading into the hall, but as he watched, three departed—leaving the tallest one behind.

A guard, Zeb decided.

Harris took Gaby in his arms and kissed her. Kissed her long past the point the photographer said he had the shot. Then he whispered, "There are fair folk here."

Gaby held her smile. "I thought you were acting strangely."

"Side by side, please," the photographer said.

They obliged. Gaby asked, "Someone Doc sent to guard us, maybe?"

"Nah. Son of a bitch wouldn't have drawn on me if he was guarding me. Is that another one? Over by your mother. Short, nose like a squashed avocado?"

"No, that's my uncle Ernesto."

"What's he doing out of jail?"

"Attending our wedding, silly. Wait, there's one, at the doors out. Oh, damn."

"What?"

"Zeb's headed right for him."

Zeb snagged a glass of champagne from a waiter's tray and added a drunken sway to his walk as he approached the door. *Convince him you're crippled,* he told himself, *and his guard will come down.*

On his way through the door he bumped into the squat red-headed man and sloshed champagne all over his chest. "Oh, man, I'm sorry. Here, hold this." He managed to get the glass into the man's hand and began mopping the stain with Harris's jacket. Beneath the man's suit coat he could clearly see the hard edges of the butt of another handgun.

"Stupid buggering dusker, see what you've done."

"Oh, man, I'm mortified. This jacket has to have set you back at least twenty bucks. I'll fix it right up." He grabbed the squat man's lapel and dragged him out into the empty corridor, mopping away at the stain. "Harris is a friend of mine. Friend of yours? You know he fights, right? I used to fight with him. Then I was his manager. What's a dusker?"

"That's you, lad. Dusky, stupid, and drunk, like all your kind—"

"That's what I figured." Zeb took a quick look up and down the corridor; sure that there was no one to see, he swung the gun wrapped in Harris's jacket and hit the man once in the side of the head, hard enough to jar his own arm. The man's eyes rolled up in his head and he fell.

Zeb looked around. Still no witnesses. He took several long moments to pull free the man's cheap tie and bind his hands with it, then stuffed him under one of the backless couches lining the hallway. Its shadow nearly hid the unconscious man.

The groom's party sweated under the photographer's lights. Zeb, lacking a jacket, stood behind Harris again. He leaned close and whispered, "There was another one, at the door. I got him."

Harris's eyes opened wider. "You *got* him? What does that mean?"

"I killed him and I ate him. What do you think it means? He's sleeping it off under some furniture."

"Hey, you! Straighten up, would you?"

Zeb glared at the photographer and did so. He stage-whispered, "There were originally four at the door. Three of them left. I don't know where they went."

"Great." Harris smiled and waved at Gaby, showing three fingers, then blew her a kiss. She caught it and ate it, then turned to her family. "Okay, she knows."

"Would the groom please quit waving and talking? We'll get this done a lot faster if everyone cooperates!"

Harris sighed and whispered, "The Donohues hired the photographer. Since we wouldn't let them arrange everything—"

"God, what a catastrophe that would have been."

"—they insisted on being helpful. Hey, watch Gaby. She's going to her uncle Pedro, the cop. I bet she lifts his piece."

"You're kidding." Zeb watched. Gaby hugged a middle-aged Latino man, talked sweetly to him, tucked something away in her flower bouquet as she was doing it. "Je-zus. What have you two really been up to the last six months?"

"Tell you later. Okay, she's got fire."

"Huh?"

"A gun. Time for us to take off. These guys can't be here for anyone else but us, so our departure will probably draw them off, keep everyone else safe."

"I'm with you."

"I meant, me and Gaby. Bye." Harris made a strangled noise loud enough for half the hall to hear. He tugged his tie free. "Enough! Time to change before this thing kills me." The crowd laughed. The photographer, plainly upset, tried to wave him back to his position, to no effect.

"Gaby and I will be back in fifteen minutes, dressed to gorge. We'll eat until the first guest blows up." More laughs. He moved through the crowd toward his wife.

Zeb caught up with him. "I meant it, man. You owe me some answers."

"I do. You want someone to shoot at you while you get them?"

They reached Gaby. Harris snagged her by the waist, pulling her from the embrace of her father. "I'm stealing her away again, Ted. Be back soon."

When they were a few steps away, Zeb continued,

his voice a growl, "I don't want them shooting at *you*, either, moron."

Gaby said, "I didn't spot any more in the crowd."

"They left," Harris said. "Probably not far."

"What do you want to bet they're either in our rooms or between here and there?"

Harris gave her an admonishing look. "Sucker bet." They reached the doors and the hall beyond.

"So, you're going to call the police on this?" Zeb asked.

Harris shook his head. "Nah. Too many complications already. What did you do with the door guard?"

Zeb pointed at the couch.

"Get his gun. If he doesn't have it when he wakes up, he can't use it."

Zeb stooped beside the couch and dragged the unconscious man's revolver out. He shoved it into Harris's jacket beside the one he'd taken earlier. "I do all this, I *do* get an answer, don't I?"

"Oh, I imagine," Gaby said. "Okay. You want to earn a hundred bucks the easy way?"

Zeb shook the concierge's hand and pressed the fifties into it. "My pal just got married down in the Catalina Suite. I want to play a little practical joke on him. I'd like to borrow a staff jacket and one of those rolling dinner trays . . . and to charge some champagne to my room."

Zeb knocked on the bride's door. There was no response. Gaby slid her card into the lock and Zeb opened the door, then pushed the cart ahead of him as he entered. He slowed the door's closing so it came to rest against the jamb without latching. "Room service," he called.

He didn't see them until he was almost through the

entry hall; beyond, two men, one whose blond beard was heavily tinged with gray and another who was clean-shaven, sat on the bed to the right, and a third, an older man, sat in a hotel chair dragged against the wall to the left.

All were squat and surly. The two on the bed had hands hovering near their armpits. The third, the one with the grayest beard, held something the size and shape of an egg but a gleaming black; this he rolled delicately around in his hand as he stared at Zeb. There was something unnatural about the little item; it didn't roll the way it should, but wobbled as though something alive were inside it. The man kept his other hand tucked into his jacket pocket.

Zeb managed a smile he didn't feel. "Champagne for the bride's party. Compliments of the house."

There was suspicion in the older man's voice: "What house?"

Zeb just stared for a moment. Was there anyone in the U.S. who didn't know what "compliments of the house" meant? "The hotel," Zeb said. "Compliments of the hotel. That means free."

The hands moved away from the concealed holsters, but Zeb didn't sense that the men's guards were lowering. "Put it there," said the grayest of them, pointing to the window.

"Yes, sir." Zeb positioned the rolling rack just so, then gestured like a game-show hostess at the bottle and the bucket of ice. "Shall I bring more glasses up?"

"No," said the graybeard. "Get out."

The door into the room widened. Silent, Harris entered. Zeb forced himself not to glance in that direction. "Yes, sir," he said.

He took a step as if to leave, then stopped and looked expectantly between them. He gestured at all of them, two fingers toward the men on the bed, one for the one in the chair. "Sirs, a gratuity is appropriate."

"What's that?" asked the graybeard.

Harris moved forward. Gaby entered behind him. She had Pedro's revolver in both hands, barrel raised toward the ceiling.

"A tip," Zeb explained patiently. "An informal reward of money for services rendered. At a hotel like this one, an appropriate tip is, well, too damned much."

They looked at each other, confused.

"Okay, forget it," Zeb said. "You look like some cheap bastards anyway." He lashed out with his left foot, hitting the beardless gunman in the side of the head, a gratifyingly solid connection.

Graybeard was fast. He lobbed the black egg toward Zeb. It hit Zeb in the chest and split open with a moist noise. Graybeard said something; Zeb thought the word was "beater."

And suddenly Zeb was wrapped up tight in a black sheet. It felt and smelled like rubber, constricting his arms and legs, holding him tight. He lost his balance and tipped over backward across the bed.

Someone was shouting in his ear, a wordless yammering, "Ya ya ya ya ya!" Zeb, wrestling with the black sheet, turned to look—right into the glowing eyes of a black rubber face. It was flat as a paper plate, approximately human in its arrangement of features, but looked like a cartoon image of a wild, buck-toothed native, and continued to shriek at Zeb.

"Goddammit, get this thing off me!"

Zeb heard a pair of thuds and a click that sounded like the cocking of a gun. He heard Gaby say, "Don't move. These are steel-jacketed slugs. You know what they do to you." Then hands were on him, rolling him over, yanking at the black sheet.

It seemed actually to struggle, but finally came away

from Zeb, and he could see Harris tugging at it. Harris gave it another yank and Zeb rolled free, off the bed and onto the floor.

What Harris held was something that looked like what would result if a large black cartoon man were squashed beneath a steamroller. It was sheet-thin and large enough to be a bedspread, but had definable limbs and head—a lolling head that continued to yammer. Its body now lay limp. Harris thoughtfully began rolling it up into a tube, starting with the head so the yammering was cut off.

Zeb sat up. Nearby, Gaby stood covering the graybeard, the one squat man who was still conscious; she held her gun in a two-handed grip, her wedding dress making it a curious picture. Zeb's gunman was unconscious, leaning against the bed's headboard; Harris's target lay flat on the bed, holding his throat and making choking noises. The graybeard was standing, gripping his right forearm in a way that reminded Zeb of hairline fractures.

Zeb asked mildly, "*Now* will you tell me what's going on?"

Harris smiled. "Nope."

"What do you mean, no police?" Zeb, tying the silent gunmen's hands with drawcords cut from the curtains, found time to glare at his friend. Harris stood easily, one of the brassy revolvers in his hands, while in the adjoining room Gaby shed her wedding dress in favor of a pullover sweater and slacks. Zeb tried not to be distracted.

"Police can't do anything about it," Harris said. "Gaby, ready?"

"Shoes," she said, and came in to sit on a chair and put them on.

"Police can get answers. Make them talk."

"No." Harris shook his head. "We could get some answers if we felt like employing torture. Which I don't. We could hand them over to the police and these poor sons of bitches would be dead in a day or two."

"L.A. cops aren't *that* bad."

"No, but these guys are likely to be dangerously allergic to ferrous metal. Put them in the wrong kind of handcuffs, in a cell, in an ordinary hospital room, they'll be poisoned to death before the doctors even figured out what was wrong." Harris looked from prisoner to prisoner. "You guys. I'm going to take you to the bottom of the stairwell and tie you up there. Eventually you'll get loose and can split. I'm doing this just 'cause I don't want your deaths on my conscience. You owe me your lives. Remember that sometime."

They just glared.

"Your red-headed pal is under a couch outside the Catalina Suite, and your other pal is under some chairs stacked at the side of the suite." Harris offered the squat men a mirthless smile. "Don't say I never gave you anything."

"Ready," Gaby said. She took up her uncle Pedro's gun and trained it on the three men.

Harris went into the adjoining room.

"Harris, are you going to write the note?"

"No, you do it, I'm changing."

"Well, I'm guarding."

Zeb sighed. "I'll guard." He took up one of the brass handguns, swung the cylinder open to assure himself it was loaded, and closed it again. He held it at the ready. "Just like a normal revolver?"

"Just like," she said. "Except that it's devisement-reinforced bronze, or maybe beryllium bronze, instead of steel. It fires a big, slow bullet, kind of like the original Webleys. In spite of its weight, expect a fair amount of kick." She set her own gun down and dug

around in the bedside table's drawer until she found
hotel stationery and a pen.

"Let's see," she said, and began writing as she
talked. " 'Dear Mama and Papa, and Mom and Dad
Greene, please tell everyone we know about what they
did to the Toyota, and you're not going to catch us
that easily.' "

"Good start," Harris said.

Zeb aimed at the silent, glowering gunmen. "This
is surreal. Gaby, I thought you hated guns."

"I do, pretty much," she said. "But if you're going
to shoot somebody, there's nothing better for it. 'By
the time you read this, we'll be gone, halfway to our
honeymoon, which isn't really in Toronto, despite what
Cousin Jane thinks. Fooled you.' Aren't you ready yet,
Harris?"

"Almost."

She smiled at Zeb and whispered, "I knew he
wouldn't be. But he was bothering me about it—"

"So you have to bother him. Right." Zeb gave
Graybeard his war-face. It was something to do that
fit the unreal mood of the situation, and he was gratified to see one of the other gunmen lean away from
his intensity, though Graybeard did not.

" 'And now you've fallen for our master plan. We're
gone, so you have to do everything. Jane can pack us
up and check us out; we're already paid up through
tomorrow. Mama and Papa and Minister Mike, if you'd
act as hosts at the party, we'd be grateful forever. Pedro
can throw everybody out when the time is right, and
if Mom and Dad Greene would pack up the presents
and have them shipped over to our apartment, we'd
really appreciate it. We love you all. Signed—' "

" 'P.S.,' " Harris called. " 'I think Uncle Pedro accidentally left his gun in my room; I've put it in the bedside table.' "

"Oh, good point." She scribbled that down.

Harris stepped back from the other room, now attired in blue jeans, dark T-shirt, and jeans jacket. "Ready."

"About time. You men, always slowing things down with your dressing and your makeup . . ."

"Well, I'm about to do it again," Zeb said. "I'm not dressed, I'm not packed, and I'm not checked out."

"Okay, you go down to your room and do that now," Harris said. "While we're disposing of our squat little friends. We'll meet you in the lobby in . . ." He checked his watch. "Ten minutes?"

"Done."

Chapter Two

On the walkway between the plane and the gate, Harris stretched. The plane had been packed, so he'd mostly sat in cramped discomfort on the long flight from L.A. to New York.

"He's going to be mad," Gaby said.

Harris nodded. "He sure is. But not as mad as if we took him there and got him killed. Then he'd *really* be mad."

They reached the gate. Beyond it they saw the main walkway between gates. It was thick with travelers.

Gaby said, "He *is* mad."

Harris looked. He sighed. "That doesn't begin to describe it."

Ahead of them, unmoving in the exact center of the walkway, straddling his suitcase, his expression one of glowering unhappiness, stood Zeb Watson. People walking by caught sight of his expression and circled around to keep well clear of him.

As they neared him, Harris put on a cheerful smile. "Would you believe we forgot?"

Zeb picked up his bag and fell in step beside them. "Nope. You ditched me." His voice was a low growl.

"How the hell did you find us, anyway?"

"Accident. After waiting around at the hotel, after checking your room, after making an idiot of myself, I took a cab to your address to see if I could figure out what the hell was going on. And when I found your address, it was a damned commercial mail-drop place. You don't even really live in L.A., do you?"

Gaby shook her head. "Our real apartment is here. Nice high-rise on the west side of the park."

Zeb glared. "How long have you been living in New York? And why didn't you tell me you were back?"

"We *don't* live in New York," Harris said. "So, technically, we're not back. We just have an apartment here. Again—how did you find us?"

"By giving up. My flight back home was tonight, remember? I gave up figuring out how or why you'd ditched me, headed to the airport to catch my flight, and spotted you at one of the gates. I thought about jumping on you right then and there, but I figured you'd have a harder time lying to me or ditching me again if I met you here. I checked and found out my plane would be arriving sooner—"

Gaby made a rueful face. "We couldn't get a direct flight at the last minute. Couldn't even get first class."

"So I just got here and waited."

"We should have just gone with him and helped him pack," Gaby said, her voice resigned.

Harris grinned. "Then you could have stared at him changing the way he was staring at you."

"Zeb! You weren't." She laughed.

"I wasn't! Okay, maybe a little. Get back to the point. Where are we going, and what are you up to?"

"Okay." Harris gave him an ingenuous look. "Here's the short form. For the last six months, we've been

living on another planet." He put his index finger up
to his forehead and wiggled it to suggest an antenna.
"We come back to visit occasionally, but we really live
there, and we shoot things for a living. Like monsters
and fairies with machine guns."

"We solve problems for a living," Gaby corrected.
"Which, to be truthful, sometimes does involve shooting
things."

"It's a dangerous job, and we don't like to drag other
people into it. But some of the trouble has obviously
spilled out into this world. Those guys at the wedding
were from the other world, and we need to find out,
fast, why they were here."

"So we're going back, tonight," Gaby said. "We're
going to step in a magic circle and disappear, and, poof,
reappear in the same place on the other world." She
gave him a smile. "Add it up, Zeb. Another planet."

"Monsters," Harris said.

"Magic circles."

"Monnnsters."

"We're crazy, Zeb."

Zeb fell silent, the brooding anger on his face suggesting that he didn't want to talk about it just yet.
Harris and Gaby left him in his silence until they were
outside, until they were in a cab headed toward Manhattan.

"I'm going to go there with you," Zeb said.

"No, no, no," Harris said. "Your line is, 'Harris, this
is complete bullshit. I don't want to talk to you for a
while.' And then we drop you off at home."

"But it's not bullshit, is it? I looked at those guns.
I didn't recognize the caliber of ammunition. I know
a fair amount about ammunition. One of those revolvers was a break-loader—as Gaby said, like the original Webleys. Large-caliber break-loaders are pretty rare,
and I don't remember seeing any like that one before.

Then there's that thing the old guy threw at me. That was no high-tech net weapon." He sighed. "Most of what you told me might be lies . . . but you *are* playing around with weird people using weird stuff. And I'm going with you so I can see the rest of it."

Harris said, "Not a good idea. It's a dangerous place, Zeb, especially if you don't know your way around."

"Harris, I'll just bet that when you went there, you didn't know your way around. And if I remember right, you weren't in the best of mental shape six months ago."

"That's right. I was depressed, I was a loser and didn't know why, and my brain just wasn't firing on all cylinders. But I fell in with the kind of people who could keep me alive while I learned the ropes."

"Well, you know the ropes now, and I'll be with you."

Harris shook his head. "Zeb, once upon a time I might have taken you across just so I could prove my story to you. But I'm not that insecure any more, and I'm not going to risk your life just so you'll believe me."

Zeb grinned at him. "Your brain still isn't firing right. Harris, I already do believe you. That is, I believe that either you're telling the truth, or you're covering up for something equally unlikely. I don't want to see it to assure myself that you're not crazy—I just want to *see* it. I mean, what an incredible thing! Like discovering a lost city from the Bible, except it's still full of people. It'll make the universe twice as big for me."

Gaby and Harris looked at one another again. Zeb wondered if they were somehow exchanging thoughts, but then he saw Gaby's faint nod.

Harris turned back to him, considering something; then he collapsed in silent laughter.

"What's with him?" Zeb asked.

Gaby shrugged. "Beats me."

Harris wiped his eyes. "Sorry, Zeb. I was going to give you the primer on life on the fair world. That's what they call where we're going. And the first thing I was going to tell you was that on the fair world, the duskies don't have all the advantages or respect of the lights and darks, so you're probably going to meet people who'll be nasty to you on account of your color . . . I was going to *introduce* this concept to you, see . . ."

Zeb gave him a pitying look. "Gaby, is there any place in town where we can buy this guy a clue?"

Zeb looked around. A twentieth-floor apartment, new furniture, framed prints on the walls, a glorious balcony view of nighttime Central Park immediately to the east. He whistled. "This must set you back a ton of money."

Harris unzipped his duffel bag and poured its contents out on the couch. "Yep. But we make plenty. We actually get paid in gold, which is pretty cool." He grabbed the roll of black rubber; it gave a little wiggle and resumed its faint yammering.

"You couldn't get back to the 'fair world' from L.A.? That would have been more convenient, wouldn't it?"

"No. We don't have a transference circle there. We could have set one up there if we'd known we were going to head right back to the fair world. But we were going on our honeymoon first."

Gaby, from inside the study, called, "Our now *abandoned* honeymoon. Are you going to help me with this?"

"Well, it was a second honeymoon anyway." Harris headed into the study.

Zeb followed. The study had a wood floor. Gaby stood on the large rug that dominated the center of the floor. Together she and Harris moved the table to the corner, off the rug.

"Second honeymoon?"

Gaby knelt to begin rolling up the rug. "We were actually married months ago in Neckerdam. That's the fair world's New York City. The L.A. wedding was for the families."

"So they'd shut the hell up," Harris said, his voice a growl.

"Well, they didn't want us to live in sin."

"Why not? I liked it. There's a lot of fun in sin."

"Harris, we have company."

Beneath the rug was a design painted on the floor. It consisted of two concentric rings of white paint; between them was a series of white symbols Zeb didn't recognize, markings that looked like half-finished stick people. Gaby and Harris bent, noses almost to the floor, and minutely examined the white circles all the way around.

"No breaks, no changes," Gaby said.

"Same here," Harris said. He dropped the black thing within the inner circle and then, from a cabinet, picked up something that looked like an ancient TV set: a carved wooden case that would have looked at home in Zeb's great-grandmother's attic, with a small, circular glass screen in the middle of it. Harris set it down in the middle of the circle and plugged it into an electrical socket that, incongruously, was set into the floor there. A pinpoint of light appeared at the center of the screen and began growing.

Gaby knelt in front of the set, put her hands on it, shut her eyes.

"What's she doing?" Zeb whispered.

Harris said, "She's projecting her mind into the Grid. Sort of like she had a direct brain-to-phone link to the fair world's Ma Bell and entertainment networks."

"Ah. You didn't mention you'd also become super-heroes."

"Slipped my mind." Harris kept his attention on Gaby. "Doing this from here is very hard for her, so let's be quiet."

After a minute of concentration, Gaby tilted her head. Static burst from the TV's speaker. She frowned, concentrating, and the static began to ebb and flow, almost as though it were the voice of some roaring beast of the airwaves. Zeb saw her mouthing words she did not speak.

Then she stopped and switched the set off. "Bad connection," she said. "But I got hold of Noriko. She and Alastair are coming to pick us up; he'll trip the circle in two chimes. She says Doc is missing and Ish is beside herself. Let's get ready."

"Right." Harris frowned. "Doc is missing. Gaby, if they were coming to grab us, why did they bring only one of those rubber grabby things?"

She shook her head. "Because they only wanted one of us?"

"Maybe. Or maybe they weren't after us. Maybe they were after Doc, figuring that he'd be at the wedding. Maybe they had two groups, and one of them got him back home."

Gaby's expression suggested that she didn't care for that idea.

Harris pulled out the contents of his pants pockets, set everything on the table. "Zeb, get rid of your wristwatch, put it here with my stuff. What've you got in your pockets?"

"Uh, loose change, keys, a pen, my wallet—"

"Dead weight, most of it. Dump it here. You can keep your pen if it's a fountain pen, otherwise chuck it."

Zeb obliged, then patted himself down. "I feel naked without my stuff. Why leave it?"

"We go through sort of a filter getting there. It

mangles anything that's too, well, technologically advanced for the fair world. Anything too mystically advanced gets wrecked on the way back." He grinned. "You haven't had a pacemaker installed recently? That would be bad."

"Get real." Zeb frowned. "Wait a second. If this filter wrecks mystical things, what about the rubber-sheet guy?"

Gaby said, "What Harris forgot to mention is that the filter is down for repairs."

"Yeah, but it could come up again at any time." Harris offered him an expression suggesting that one can't count on anything. "A bad guy named Duncan Blackletter cut the bonds holding the two worlds together. That also cut the filter and made it even trickier to go from world to world—it takes the most expert of the experts to set up the transference circles now. But the bonds are growing back together, and presumably the filter—we just don't know when it'll start up again."

Zeb gave him the sort of smile he normally reserved for small children. "Whether it's true or not, you know how this sounds."

"You can leave anytime."

"Nope."

"Then strip, soldier."

They dressed from a chest full of clothes that, to Zeb's eye, looked like well-preserved antiques. The men put on high-waisted suits with suspenders; Zeb's was brown with a matching vest, while Harris's was a two-piece green so dark it was almost black. Gaby returned in a painfully bright yellow skirt and blouse with a matching wide-brimmed felt hat.

"So, these museum pieces are what everyone's wearing?"

"You got it," Harris said. "How's it fit?"

"A little loose. You're gaining weight."

"I'm just broadening in the chest. That's what Gaby says."

"Yeah, but she has to put up with you. Hey, is that a fedora?"

Harris handed the hat to him. "Yeah, but on the fair world it's a merry, or merry-hat. Named after someone in a play."

Zeb tried it on, cocked it at a rakish angle. "Always wanted one of these. How does it look?"

Gaby said, "Great. But you two need to stop playing dress-up. We don't have much time."

"Right," Harris said. "Zeb, it's not certain how long we'll be gone. Do you need to make any arrangements?"

"Yeah, I'd better phone my partner. Ask him to deal with my apartment."

"Pets?"

"No pets."

A couple of minutes later, phone calls done, the three of them stood within the two white circles. Zeb looked at the other two, saw only a little concern, a little impatience. And for a moment the oddness of the situation got to him; he suddenly knew that his friends were playing him for a fool, that everything they'd said until now was part of an elaborate practical joke, that a roomful of people he knew would burst in through a side door with cameras and beer bottles.

He shoved those feelings aside. His gut told him otherwise, and when his gut and his brain disagreed, he tended to side with the former.

Then the world writhed around him.

It was as though the air outside the white circles had suddenly become a magnifying glass, distorting everything beyond, twisting the world into something huge and frightening. The twisting seemed to extend right into Zeb's stomach, bending him over with nausea, and continued as Zeb lost his balance and awkwardly sat down. The room around them flowed, the hardwood floor dropping away, the furniture fading into nothingness, the window becoming a wall covered in paisley wallpaper, two giant silhouettes standing before them. Then it all twisted its way back to more reasonable proportions.

"Oh, God." Zeb tried to control his stomach, which insisted that it needed to deposit his airplane meal on the floor.

On the tabletop, actually. Zeb found that he was lying atop a large, sturdy wooden dining table.

Harris said, "You get used to it." He hopped down and helped Zeb to slide off to stand, then turned to help Gaby down.

The room had somehow changed, too. It was larger, with a much higher ceiling than Gaby's and Harris's study. The furniture consisted of hardwood chairs and a wooden bench against the window. The table where the three of them had appeared had a circular top painted with the identical twin of the circle design from the study. Beside it stood a man and a woman.

The man was of average height and a little overweight; his features were cheerful and appeared European, but his skin was a nut-brown that no tan, natural or artificial, could produce; together they suggested someone from India, but then Zeb saw his eyes, which were a startling green. The man's trench coat gapped to reveal a stiff-starched white shirt and pants that reminded Zeb of old doctor movies.

The woman was short and very slender, with Asian coloration and features. She wore a black silk pantsuit with flowing sleeves and legs. In her hands she held a sheathed sword Zeb would have identified as a

Japanese katana if it had been curved, but it was ruler-straight. She was beautiful as the statue of a goddess suddenly come to life, but also as expressionless. She stared at Zeb with no emotion on her face, but he saw tension, suspicion in the stiffness of her body language.

"Quick introductions," Gaby said. "This is Zeb Watson; he manages fighters like Harris. This is Doctor Alastair Kornbock, the finest physician who ever slung a submachine gun, and Noriko Nomura Lamignac, princess—at least for the next few days—of the kingdom of Acadia."

"Glad to meet you," said Zeb. He leaned back against the table. His stomach still felt as though it were the midway point in a phantom Ping-Pong match. "Doctor, have you got a stomach powder?"

Alastair chuckled. "Yes. But wait a few ticks and the sensation will pass anyway, so I'd be out a stomach powder for nothing. Grace on you." His accent was not Indian—to Zeb, it sounded more English than anything.

"Grace upon you," Noriko echoed. "Harris, why have you brought him?"

"Some bullies came and I was scared, but Zeb came and beat them up, and now he's my friend forever. No, it's a long story. We'll talk about it in the car." He handed Alastair the rolled-up rubber thing. "See what you can make of this."

A cage-style elevator with ornately worked bars took them down. The skill and style of the hallway woodwork they descended past, visible even in the dim light of single naked bulbs, reminded Zeb of his long-dead grandmother's brownstone apartment building . . . but this building was in much better shape, much newer. He gulped a few more times and took a deep breath; his nausea was almost gone, as the doctor had predicted. But as the unreality of his surroundings hit him,

he almost wished he had the nausea back to distract
him. He tried to figure out some way this could have
been staged, but making him ill and then swapping his
surroundings would have required the use of
drugs . . . and Zeb couldn't imagine Harris drugging him
for a practical joke.

Yet despite everything Harris and Gaby had told
him, despite the fact that he had logically accepted part
of their story, he found he wasn't really prepared for
it to be true. Accepting it as a working hypothesis had
been one thing. But seeing that he was descending a
very different building from the one he'd ascended less
than an hour before hit him hard. He took in every
detail of the elevator, of the floors he saw passing
outside the cage door, trying to assure himself that he
could not be making a mistake, could not simply have
missed these details when arriving at Harris's and
Gaby's building.

The lobby had a lower ceiling and darker wall pan-
eling than the lobby by which he'd entered the building. Its doors were open to the outside and the
nighttime air was cool, autumn weather New York
should have been experiencing this year but hadn't yet.
They emerged from the lobby facing a broad brick
street with a tree-lined median.

Beside the near curb sat a car, a massive roadster
like many Zeb had seen at an automobile show featuring cars of the 1930s, all sleek boxiness with a hood
long and broad enough to contain a modern compact
car. The vehicle was black and gold, with a gold hood
ornament shaped like a flying dragon. It was parked
the wrong way, oriented leftward.

A woman stepped out of the rear passenger compartment and held the door open for the new arrivals. She was tiny and well-muscled, with raven-black
hair that fell to the small of her back. Incongruously,

she wore faded khaki shorts and shirt and a banded hat that reminded Zeb of Australian hunting wear. Around her neck was a gold-brown scarf decorated with jaguar spots.

"Ixyail del Valle," said Harris, "princess of the Hu'unal people, meet Zeb Watson, fighter and manager of fighters." He ducked into the passenger compartment, Gaby behind him.

"Hi," Zeb said, and followed.

Ixyail settled in beside him, staring. "Grace. I think you are the blackest dusky I have ever seen."

Zeb felt a flash of irritability. He hid it behind a mask of polite cheerfulness. "Why, thank you."

Noriko took the right-hand-side driver's seat. "To the Monarch Building?"

Alastair, studying the partially-unrolled rubbery creature, took the seat beside her. "No. Thirteen John's Son, Pataqqsit."

Noriko set the car into motion, merging into a sudden swell of traffic that, Zeb saw, stayed to the left side of the street. The cars were of various styles and colors, but, like this one, antiques. "What's there?" Noriko asked.

"Cars." The creature began yammering again; Alastair rapped its head several times against the car door and it shut up. "This is not a living thing," he said. "Just rubber imbued with a bit of mystical energy, a tiny amount of instinct."

Harris said, "What's going on with Doc?"

Ixyail crossed her arms as if against cold winds. "He rose before dawn this morning and said he had an errand to be about." Her accent sounded faintly Spanish, but a moment before, Zeb would have sworn she had none at all. "He did not return. Since noon, I have felt someone beneath my flesh."

Harris frowned. "Meaning precisely what?"

"I am not sure. That is the best way I can describe it." A patch of lustrous black hair sprouted on her forearm; distracted, she rubbed at it, and the hair fell away. "But I know somewhere there is devisement, and it involves me."

Zeb stared at the floor of the car, where the hair had fallen, and felt that sense of unreality cut through him again.

They headed east on a two-way boulevard that was thick with traffic. The cars continued to suggest a 1930s automobile show. All around Zeb saw brick-topped streets, buildings with antique neon and marquees, and fine-featured folk in brightly-colored clothes that, if not for their rainbow of hues, would have looked appropriate in his grandparents' closet.

But east from Harris's building should have been—

"Wait a second," said Zeb. "No Central Park?"

Gaby shook her head. "Neckerdam has parks all over, and hardly a street without big old trees. I guess they figured they didn't need a big park."

Harris stared at him expectantly, and finally said, "Well?"

"I already believed you, man."

"Yeah. But believing is one thing, seeing it is something else."

"True."

After the trip across what should have been the Brooklyn Bridge but wasn't, they pulled up in front of a large building whose green neon sign read BELLWEATHER. Behind its huge windows were bright new cars, squatter and rounder than the one Noriko drove, less ornamental.

The front door did not yield to Alastair's pull; he began banging on it.

Someone beyond yelled, "We're closed!"

Alastair said, "I need to see Fergus Bootblack."

Zeb saw the others exchange significant looks. "What's all this?"

"Fergus is a mechanic," Harris said. "Used to work for Doc. But he sold information to one of Doc's enemies and almost got me killed. He later sort of made up for it, so we're okay."

Ixyail looked disgusted. "So *you* say." Her Spanish accent was even stronger than before. "I think he should be gutted, his entrails tied off to a bumper while he screams for mercy—"

"Around to your right," called the voice from within.

They moved around to the side of the building, where a large sliding door stood open; light spilled out from within.

When they entered, they found themselves in the dealership's garage. Two cars were up on racks and two swearing men were working under one of them.

A man in green overalls and a plain red shirt, both grease-stained, approached. He was short, like most of the men Zeb had seen here, with black hair and skin that was closer to white than to pink. But he wasn't pale from worry; he seemed curious but not intimidated by this group of visitors. "Grace." He looked with special curiosity at Zeb.

Zeb found himself growing irritated. "What's the matter, do you have a special entrance for 'duskies'?"

"No. Light, dark, dusky, all welcome at Bellweather." Fergus made it sound like an ad slogan. "But you're not really a dusky, are you? You're a grimworlder."

Alastair stepped up. "You've got sharp eyes and a good memory, Fergus, and I need them both." He handed the mechanic the rolled tube of rubber. "See what you make of this."

Fergus unrolled it on a table not completely covered with tools and automotive parts. It immediately began yammering again. Harris whacked its head a couple of times and it shut up.

"Inner tube rubber, or something very like it," Fergus said. "Except inner tubes are not usually so noisy." He picked up something that looked like a miner's hat; he put the thing on and turned on the light, then peered intently at the surface of the rubber. "What do you want to know about it?"

"Anything. Whatever you can tell us."

"Your timing is very good," Fergus said. "Next week I'll not be here."

"New employment?" Alastair asked.

"In a manner of speaking. I've passed all my tests and rented a Neckerdam office. Next week I'll be a free eye."

Gaby stood on tiptoe to whisper in Zeb's ear: "Private eye."

Alastair's expression suggested that he was at least slightly impressed. "Truly? I didn't know you had it in you."

"That was always the problem, wasn't it? I study in a dozen fields for a dozen years and the Foundation associates can only ever think of me as a mechanic."

"Let's not get into that again, Fergus. The problem—"

"Here you are." Fergus peered closer. "Very interesting. See these numbers?"

Alastair leaned close. "Barely. Black ink on black rubber. What do they mean?"

"They're a maker's mark. And these numbers belong to Fairwings Tiring. Which is odd, as Fairwings went under just after the Fall. Six, seven years ago."

"Who bought them out?"

"No one. Who could afford to? Their plant has stood closed all these years." He looked up into Alastair's face; when the doctor winced away, he shut off the lamp on his hat. "Sorry. And what's especially interesting is that this rubber here is full of cracks of age. Whatever devisement has animated and given it a voice is preserving it; without that devisement, it would just come to pieces when stressed."

"How do we get there?"

"It's here on Long Island. Go east on Lancers' Lane about four destads. Just past Trolton you'll see the old Fairwings sign."

"What will you charge when you're a free eye?"

"A lib a day and expenses."

Alastair flipped him a coin, which he caught. "There's your first fee. Lady's luck to you on your new business."

"And to you on yours."

Chapter Three

"My grandmother," said Ish in a whisper, "had a special recipe for traitors like Fergus. She would boil them alive in lime juice, with cuts in their flesh so they would feel what was flavoring them—"

Alastair snorted. "First, I've met your grandmother, and she is a nice old lady who would never do something like that. Second, your people aren't cannibals—"

"Oh, no, we would never *eat* such a stew . . ."

They sat in Noriko's car with the lights out and stared at the Fairwings factory. It was a dark mound of brick, an irregular artificial hill whose windows had been replaced by brick of a lighter hue. Zeb couldn't detect any straight lines in its walls; everything was curved, rounded. The wooden fence surrounding the property had fallen in places and the grounds were overgrown.

Noriko returned to the car where it sat on Lancers' Lane a hundred yards away from the property. "I found fresh car tracks where one section of fence was down," she said. "Many tracks; someone has been driving back and forth. The front and side doors are nailed to, but the rear door is new; it has merely been painted to look old."

Harris said, "All the windows bricked up?"

"Yes."

"Okay," Harris said. "Gaby, I want you at an angle to cover the front and side doors. Alastair, Ish, Noriko and I will go in the back. Zeb, you want to wait here?"

"And let you get into trouble all alone? Nope."

"Then you stick close to me."

The car's trunk turned out to be a mobile armory; it was packed with cases and racks that yielded long arms, handguns, and ammunition. Alastair took what looked like a bronzed Thompson submachine gun and struggled into a barrel-like vest that Zeb assumed to be approximately bulletproof. Gaby selected a bolt-action rifle. Harris and Noriko took paired revolvers; Ixyail, a double-barreled shotgun.

Zeb, at Harris's gesture of invitation, took up a rifle like Gaby's and a large pistol shaped like an oversized Army-issue semiauto. He checked to see whether they were loaded and quickly familiarized himself with them.

Zeb saw Noriko whisper something to Harris. Harris nodded and murmured something about the Army. That rankled Zeb; Noriko was obviously checking to make sure he was fit to carry a weapon.

He decided to let it pass. He'd earned marksman's qualification in the Army. But it was true that when it actually came down to a live fire situation—the kind these people obviously expected they might face—he'd never been put to the test. Harris had no proof to offer Noriko about Zeb's reliability in such a situation.

Harris quietly closed the trunk. "Let's move out."

Noriko twisted the handful of picks inserted into the lock and was rewarded with a satisfying *clunk*. Quietly, she pocketed her tools and pulled the door open, sniffing.

She smelled old oil, aging rubber, freshly-spilled fuel, and something else: the faint odor of ozone, often given off by Doc's electrical devices. There was also something her grimworld friends could probably not detect, the disquieting smell of rusting steel; the fairworlders would need to be careful within. She gestured to the others, took a thin pair of gloves from her belt, and put them on. Alastair and Ish followed suit. The dusky grimworlder looked confused; she saw Harris lean in and whisper to him, mentioning the fairworlders' deadly allergy to ferrous metals.

Then, inside. She advanced cautiously into the darkness, letting her eyes adjust. But there was not even the faintest light for them to adjust to. She reluctantly brought out her torch and snapped it on, revealing her position to whomever might wait within.

The beam illuminated a huge open area; the light did not reach the far wall. The ceiling was supported by rusting steel framework. Everywhere were chains and hooks hanging from overhead winches, sagging conveyor belts, partially disassembled machinery lying in huge, collapsed piles. From the ceiling supports and their crossbeams hung tires and inner tubes ranging in size from those appropriate to cars to giant things suited to tractors.

Behind Noriko the others snapped on their torches and advanced. "Alastair with Noriko," said Harris. "Zeb, with me. Ish, stay at the door."

Ish grimaced. "I hate door duty."

"It's your turn."

Alastair joined Noriko and they moved straight ahead, along the main corridor between piles and supports, while Harris and Zeb circled around clockwise.

Noriko saw Alastair close his left eye, peering only through his right—his Gifted eye. "There's been devising hereabouts, recently," he said. "And something straight ahead—"

Noriko's torch beam fell on the massive table set up near the center of the factory—and on the pale figure atop it. A tingle of fear rose within her. She sprinted forward, knowing that Alastair would cover her advance.

On the table lay Doc. He stared straight up, unseeing, but moved a little as she reached him. His arms and legs were chained by links of bronze to the corners of the table. He was naked. "I have him!" she called. "Doc, are you well?"

"Noriko?" His eyes moved but he did not seem to be able to find her.

"Yes." She examined the cuffs on his wrists. Heavy, well-machined restraints. Their chains were bolted to the hardwood table's sides.

"Find Ish," Doc said. "She's here somewhere . . ."

"She's at the door. She is well."

Alastair joined her. "Good evening, Doc. I see you've been up to some fun."

Harris and Zeb heard Noriko's call. Harris shook his head and the two of them kept along their circular path, alert for other surprises the factory might have waiting for them. They moved along tight-packed aisles of junked machinery and piles of tires.

Zeb kept his voice low: "Was Ish serious about boiling Fergus?"

"No. She talks like a bomb-throwing anarchist, but it's really just part of her act. She's extremely recognizable the way you've seen her . . . but she can put on normal street clothes, drop that Castilian accent to zero, and when you run into her you'd never recognize her."

"Protective coloration."

"You got it."

"You've mentioned that steel thing twice now. Were you serious?"

"Oh, yeah." Harris nodded. "I've seen some fairworlders who, if they just touch ferrous metal, their skin blisters. If it's held to them for just a few minutes, they get sick, poisoned. It can kill them."

"Man."

They reached a wide cross-aisle. Their torch beams fell on scrapes on the floor, piles of small cuttings of rubber. "Something used to be set up here," Harris said. "Maybe where they made your rubber friend."

Zeb heard a rustle like a bird in the rafters; he shone his torch upward. The light played up a support beam and to the roof, but he could see nothing moving.

Now, that was odd. The light had crossed an unusual-looking lump, a shapeless brown mass about the size of a backpack, tied off to the support beam about a dozen feet up. Zeb returned the light to the lump. "What's that?"

Harris looked up. "Unknown," he said. "I hate unknowns. Here, hold this." He passed Zeb his torch and began climbing—a difficult task, since the support, shaped much like the I-beams Zeb was familiar with, offered little in the way of handholds. Harris had to climb through sheer grip strength. He made slow progress and began swearing.

"You're really out of shape, Harris."

"Shut up." Harris got his hands on the crossbeam directly above the brown lump. He pulled himself up to peer at the mass. "Some sort of rucksack. The flap's partly open." He wrapped his legs around the support beam and held out his hand. "Throw me the torch."

Zeb did so.

Harris shone his light into the partly-open back-pack and sucked in a breath. His voice, when he finally spoke, was quiet. "One regulation alarm clock and a lot of sticks of what look like dynamite." He swung free of the support beam, hanging for an instant by one hand, and then dropped to land in a crouch beside Zeb. "C'mon." He sprinted back the way they'd come.

Zeb kept up. "Shouldn't we do something about the bomb?"

"No. We have no bomb experts here. And that one bomb wouldn't necessarily bring down the ceiling or kill Doc. So there are bound to be more."

They reached Doc's table, where Alastair peered into Doc's eyes and Noriko worked with her picks at the cuff on one wrist. Their torches were tied off to support beams, aimed more or less at Doc's table, granting some dim light to the whole area, while Alastair used a much smaller torch to examine Doc.

Harris said, "We've got dynamite, uh, magnacendiaries here on a kitchen timer. Half a chime left! That's about five minutes, Zeb. Ish!"

Her voice came, faint and distant. "I hear you."

"Call 'fall back'!"

Zeb heard her cry out, an odd series of yips and yowls.

Harris continued, "And the timer has only been going four or five minutes. We've been on the property that long, so the guy who set it is still here, or set it and left when he first heard us. Noriko, can you get him out of those in a quarter chime?"

She shook her head, not looking up.

"Go on guard, then." Harris moved around to the table side opposite the door by which they'd entered the factory. He set his shoulder against it and heaved.

The massive table slid forward a couple of inches. "Zeb, give me a hand here."

"There's a big rolling cart back the way we came," Zeb said. "Under some sheet rubber."

"Get it!"

Zeb began to turn. Then he was hit, a blow from above as if someone had dropped a bowling ball on his shoulders from one floor up. The impact slammed him to the concrete floor; his face hit the floor hard. He saw tiny dots of light swirling before his eyes and felt blood run from his nose.

Then teeth, like a small animal trap whose edges were made up of needles and broken shards of glass, closed on his shoulder, cutting through his shirt, slicing through his skin.

Zeb roared, a noise made up of pain and sudden fear, and came upright, despite the weight hanging from his shoulder.

There were children around him, five or six of them, advancing on him—

No, not children. They were no more than three feet tall, but had squat and powerful builds. Their eyes were large, their mouths broad and half-open, revealing rows of teeth that were crooked but long and sharp. Their skins, in the dim light cast by Zeb's dropped flashlight, seemed to be blue or gray or some hue in between. They wore crude sleeveless shirts that hung to their knees, leather gloves protecting hands and forearms nearly to the elbow, and leather wrappings lashed to their feet and lower legs.

And they carried weapons—wooden handles with stone heads lashed to them by hide strips. They raised those weapons as they came at Zeb.

Zeb jammed his hand into the face of the one that had bit him, sought the eyes, shoved his thumb into an eye socket when he found it. He thought he hit eyelid rather than eyeball, but the creature cried out, a gratifying squawk, and dropped away from him—but carried Zeb's rifle away with it. There were other noises, now—curses from Zeb's other companions, sounds of struggle, words he did not understand from the attackers.

Zeb stood. The nearest attacker came at him, swinging its stone club at his groin. Zeb struck just as it began its attack, his knifehand blow hitting it just beneath the wrist. He didn't feel the wrist break, but the attacker dropped its club and withdrew, howling, holding its injured hand. As it dropped back into proper range, Zeb took it in the chest with a snapkick, his blow sending it tumbling back into the darkness.

The others—Zeb thought there were six, but couldn't afford the time to count—surged toward him. He spun and leaped clean over one charging him from behind, its stone club passing between his legs, and he landed on the lip of the table that held Doc.

Noriko, Alastair, and Harris were down, each with three or four of the attackers on them. Alastair's eyes were closed and a stream of red ran across his temple. Another club-wielder stood on the table with Zeb, straddling Doc's chest, his club held high, a moment from bringing its stone head down on Doc's skull.

And for Zeb, the world went red.

It had happened before, sometimes late in a fight, sometimes when he'd taken a shot to the nose. All the colors would change, as if someone had put a reddish filter across his eyes, and the ability to think—beyond figuring out what it took to break his opponent into pieces—was washed away by pure rage.

Zeb hit the dwarfish man, a spearhand blow that took him in the throat and crushed his trachea. The clubman staggered back, pain and fear crossing his features, and Zeb kicked him clean past Doc's feet and off the end of the table.

Zeb leaped across Doc to land on the far edge of the table. He felt the impacts of stone heads hitting where he'd just stood.

His tactical sense undiminished, Zeb knew he needed help. He couldn't kill every one of these little bastards himself, much as he wanted to. He dropped behind the ring of four clubmen that had Harris pinned down. Three of them saw him and hesitated, each trying to figure out whether to continue to hold Harris or to rise and deal with this new threat. The fourth, his back to Zeb, remained unaware of the danger long enough for Zeb to reach around him. Zeb took his chin in one hand, the back of his head with the other, and twisted. It was surprisingly simple, as one instructor had told him it would be. The clubman's neck made a gruesome snapping noise and it dropped to the floor, nerveless as a puppet.

And Zeb turned his war-face to the other three. These little men didn't surge toward him. Their eyes grew wide.

Harris, flat on his back, his arms held by two of the attackers but his legs now free, brought his right knee to his chest and then lashed out, taking one of the attackers beneath the chin. Zeb heard the attacker's teeth crack, saw its jaw deform. It staggered back. His left arm now free, Harris drove his fist into the crotch of his other holder.

Zeb's sense of timing told him he'd been unaware of events behind him for a second or two too long. He spun. One of the club-wielders was sailing through the air at him, its leap carrying it clean over Doc's body. Zeb pushed off from Doc's table, sending him backwards, and the attacker flew past him to land hard on the concrete floor. Zeb kicked, driving his heel into the back of his attacker's neck. He heard and felt vertebrae crack.

Harris was up now, and moving toward Alastair. Zeb turned the other way, toward the knot of creatures holding Noriko.

They had her up off the concrete, stretching her taut and thin, two of them holding her arms and two her legs, as they played tug of war with her. A fifth stood by, its club at the ready, as it watched the contest; there was a wide, uncomplicated smile on its face.

The macabre quality of the scene almost caused Zeb to hesitate, but redness still suffused everything he saw. He stepped up and threw a kidney-punch into the guard's unprotected back before any of them were aware of him. The guard fell, his strangled cry loud enough to hear. The other four dropped Noriko and tugged their clubs from their belts.

The first of them charged Zeb, swinging, a blow fast enough to bring home the fact that these little fellows had to be stronger than they looked. Zeb skipped backward, putting his body just outside the thing's swing, and grabbed his attacker's wrist when its arm was at extension. He twisted, bringing the thing's arm up behind its back, then yanked him into the path of the second clubman's attack. The stone club struck his temporary captive in the sternum. Zeb shoved his captive into that attacker, fouling them both temporarily.

The other two advanced more slowly, moving in tandem, too cautious to make the same mistakes their fellows had. Zeb backed away, glancing around, patting at himself, hoping to find a weapon with which he could block their potentially deadly clubs . . .

There was something metallic and heavy in his pocket. He drew it out. It was the pistol he'd been given, forgotten in the heat of the moment, forgotten because he never carried guns.

The clubmen's eyes widened as they realized their quarry was armed. They lunged forward.

Zeb switched the pistol's safety off and moved right-ward, firing as he went. His shot caught the rightmost clubman in the chest and his movement put the injured clubman between him and the other attacker. The uninjured attacker shoved his wounded comrade out of the way; Zeb shot him in the face. That clubman fell, a spray of red matter decorating the support beam behind him.

There were no attackers in front of him. Zeb spun. In addition to the clubmen he'd put down, there was another one on the floor, its head, shoulder, and right arm severed from the rest of his body; Zeb logged that one as no threat and kept going. His sights passed across Noriko, who was standing, her sword in her hands; she was looking at Zeb with an expression he couldn't read, some combination of dismay and caution. Zeb logged her as no immediate threat and kept turning.

Another clubman was coming over Doc's table at him. Zeb gave him a double-tap, a sloppy first shot that had to have taken out its right lung and a more accu-rate follow-up that was dead center in the chest; as that attacker fell, Zeb continued.

There was Doc, still chained, looking around as if blind and bewildered. No threat; Zeb kept going.

There were a lot of clubman bodies down. Most were utterly still. A few twitched. Zeb ignored them for the moment, though he'd have to look at the twitchers again in a second or two to make sure they weren't getting up.

Alastair was up, bleeding heavily from his scalp wound, the lean to his posture suggesting that he wasn't fully functional. He held his autogun in both hands but wasn't pointing it at Zeb. Potential threat. Zeb kept his aim on Alastair but continued turning his head.

And there was Harris beside him. Harris grabbed his wrist, raised it so Zeb's aim was off Alastair. He was talking. Zeb tried to focus, tried to understand the words.

"—right, Zeb?" Harris waited for a response. "Are you all right?"

The words didn't mean anything, so Zeb worked harder to interpret them. He shook his head and the redness that suffused his vision faded, returning the colors of his surroundings to normal. His hearing, dulled as if he'd been underwater, returned. "I'm fine, man. Let go."

Harris did so. Zeb flipped the pistol's safety and pocketed it again. He felt uneasy, as if there were something he should be remembering. "Who are these little bastards, anyway?"

"*Kobolde*," Alastair said. "Very primitive, too. From the Old Country. The kind you see only in books." He was stanching his scalp wound with a handkerchief. He looked pale and wobbly.

Harris caught his eye. "Zeb?"

"What?"

"Rolling tray?"

"Right." Zeb darted back into the darkness between stacks of supplies and equipment. He looked for more Kobolde, but nothing moved within his sight.

He reached the object he'd seen before and threw tires and sheet rubber off it, revealing the heavy rolling cart beneath, and began pushing it toward Doc's table.

He heard more gunfire, single shots from a handgun, and Harris's voice: "I've got him pinned down. Zeb, keep your eyes open. There are more of them out there."

But nothing sprang at Zeb out of the shadows, and he reached Doc's table and got the cart around in front of it. "C'mere, Harris. Help me lift."

Between them, they got the front end of the table up on the cart, then moved to the other side and strained to lift the other end.

Alastair stayed with them. The handkerchief was around his brow as a bandage now, and he kept his attention on their surroundings. He fired two shots out into the darkness as Zeb and Harris lifted the front of Doc's table, and smoke now rose from the barrel of his submachine gun. "I've seen at least three more," he said.

"Can you talk to them?" Harris asked.

"Maybe. With thousands of tribes you get thousands of dialects."

"When we get near the door, tell them this place is about to blow up, so they'd better run for the hills. For now, brace this cart."

Harris and Zeb returned to the foot end of Doc's table. They heaved and pushed, sliding the table until as much of it as would fit lay across the cart. Harris told Alastair to stand aside. When next they heaved, the table rolled awkwardly forward. Within moments they went from walking to trotting to running, barely keeping up with the table end they had to lift.

Zeb heard Noriko repeat the "fall back" signal, heard Alastair open up with his autogun. Then, in the light from Noriko's torch, he saw ahead the doorway out, saw that it was—

"Too narrow!" Zeb shouted.

Harris picked up his pace. "Push push push!"

They hit the doorway like an express train, more than half a ton of wood and metal and flesh travelling nearly as fast as a man can run, and the two corners of Doc's table blew through the doorjamb and adjacent brick wall as though they were plaster. Zeb felt the impact against his shoulder like the kick of a badly-held shotgun. And suddenly they were outside, their rolling table trying to grind to a halt and fall over as it plowed through gravel and overgrown grass—

The first explosion behind them didn't seem that loud, the rude cough of a giant, followed by shrieking metal within the factory and hammer blows all around them—bricks slamming into the ground. Then came the second explosion, louder, and the third.

Harris heaved against his corner of the table. The opposite corner slid off the cart, bit into gravel, and the table upended. Harris got around it, under it, kept the top side from smashing full into the ground, kept Doc from being crushed.

Zeb joined him, helped Harris strain against the table's massive weight. Alastair and Noriko got around as well. Zeb heard bricks crashing into the other side of their wooden shield. He looked down; Doc hung from his chains at full extension, his head inches from the ground, his expression dazed and quizzical, his eyes unfocused.

There were four more distinct explosions and a further hail of broken bricks. Then there was only the rising roar of fire and scream of bending metal.

Zeb looked around the edge of the table. What had once been a mountainous building was now a broken egg half, still collapsing, flames rising from its interior. There was no likelihood that any of the attackers could have escaped it.

Harris cried, "Gaby!"

No answer. Harris nodded at Alastair. The doctor thumbed the selector switch on the side of his submachine gun and fired two individual shots into the air. He was rewarded with the sound of a shot from the direction of the road. Zeb saw Harris sigh and relax. Closer by, Ixyail broke from a stand of tall grass and ran to the table, her attention on Doc.

As they carefully pushed the table over to set it back on its feet, Noriko said, "Zeb?"

"Yes?"

"You are a priest of Morrigan or Crow-Badb?"

"No."

"Of one of the other war-makers?"

He shook his head. "I'm a manager of fighters. I'm not a priest of anything."

She turned away, her features schooled once again into peaceful unreadability, but Zeb thought he caught for a second time some lingering worry in her eyes.

Harris said, "Zeb?"

"What?"

"Did I or did I not tell you this would be dangerous?"

Zeb reached around to touch his shoulder where it was throbbing. His fingers came away wet and he looked at the blood on them. "Yes, you did. But there's hearing it, and then there's experiencing it."

Police and firemen came from three surrounding towns to investigate the explosions. They looked at identification papers Alastair and Gaby offered and became very cooperative.

"That's a trip," said Zeb.

Harris asked, "What is?"

"Cop just asked if I wanted a cup of something. Shock." He moved his shoulder around. His jacket and shirt were now off, and Alastair had applied a bandage to the bite he'd received. It was starting to stiffen.

Gaby smiled. "It's *xioc*, ex-eye-oh-see. A chocolate drink. More bitter than coffee. What most people drink here instead of coffee."

"My point is, most of the times I've been approached by cops on the real world, they've asked me something

different, like whether I'd grope the wall while they
patted me down. Or else."

"Any time you're in Novimagos," said Harris, "which
is the north part of the Eastern Seaboard, you tell the
police—that is, the various city guards—that you're a
consultant with the Sidhe Foundation. You'll get cooperation. Maybe after they check out your credentials,
but soon."

Gaby shrugged. "At least, it's usually worth a cup
of xioc."

Doc, wrapped in a blanket from Noriko's trunk, sat
in the passenger seat of her car, the door open, his bare
feet on the ground. The movements of his eyes suggested that he could see again, and he seemed to be
talking coherently. He was flanked by Alastair and Ish
and had been talking to them and to the senior guardsman on site for some time.

Now, finally, Zeb had an opportunity to get a good
look at Doc. The man was tall, a couple of inches
over Zeb's six foot two, and very pale of complexion.
His eyes were sky-blue and his hair, nearly pure
white, fell below his shoulders; it was now bound back
in a tail. To Zeb's eye, his features and build were
a little odd: He seemed to have just a little too much
muscle for his swimmer's frame, while his features,
handsome and elegant, seemed to belong to a cruel
storybook prince somehow softened by experience and
compassion.

The senior guardsman finally nodded and withdrew.
Doc waved Gaby, Harris, Zeb and Noriko over.

Harris asked, "How're you doing, Doc?"

The tall man shook his head. "My mind is still wooly.
But I don't think I'm hurt. And I can focus now." He
held out his hand palm upward. A small flame, like one
from a cigarette lighter, sprouted from his palm, but
did no harm to his skin. Other flames ignited from the

tips of each of his fingers. He closed his hand into a fist and the flames were smothered.

Gaby gestured at the ruin of the factory, where firemen still trained water on flames licking through a collapsed wall. "How did you get here?"

"I'm not sure. I was—" Doc paused so long Zeb was sure he'd forgotten he was talking. "This morning, I went out on an errand. It's the anniversary of my father's death. Before dawn, I went to the temple of Longarm Lug to make my respects—my father was a priest of that order.

"As I was leaving, descending the steps, I saw a girl trip and I reached down to steady her. I didn't get a good look at her. Dark hair, worn short and tightly curled. She grabbed at me, I thought for balance—"

"No woman grabs at you just for balance."

"Thank you, Ish. And she had me wrapped up long enough for her confederate to shoot me. I think he was behind a column."

"*Shoot* you?" said Gaby. "I didn't see a gunshot wound. Alastair, is he—"

"It wasn't a normal gun," Doc said. "It sounded like a small-caliber rifle, but before I blacked out, I looked down and saw the missile. It had struck through my shirt into my chest. It looked like a tiny brass syringe. I have to conclude it was filled with a powerful narcotic."

"Dart-gun," said Harris. "They use them all the time on the grim world, mostly to drug wild animals so they can be tagged and tracked."

Doc managed a wry smile. "Am I tagged?"

Alastair, who had obviously heard this and more already, looked dissatisfied. "So they kidnap you, subject you to erotic dreams—"

"I'd better have been in them," said Ish, her voice a growl.

"You were, dear heart," Doc said.

"—and then leave you to die. I don't get it. Except," the doctor added, "it *is* the way I'd prefer to die. Perhaps someone thought he was doing you a favor."

"I'll have to thank him," said Doc. "Just before I realign all the bones in his skull."

"I think we're through here," said Harris. "If there are any more leads to be found, we'll have to find them tomorrow. Let's get back to Neckerdam and tuck Doc into bed."

On the drive back, Harris, Zeb and Gaby were piled into the driver's compartment with Noriko. Zeb marveled that with four people in it, it was still fairly comfortable. Even more than before, though, he missed having seat belts available. In the passenger compartment, Doc slumbered, his head in Ish's lap, Alastair on the opposite side of the seat. The window was down between the driver's compartment and passenger compartment.

Harris asked Zeb, "Seen enough?"

"You're joking. I haven't even had the nickel tour."

"Well, then, I'm going to treat you to the best hotel in Neckerdam. Arrange you a native guide so you can see all the sights."

"Wait, wait, wait. And what are you going to be up to?"

Harris shrugged. "Foundation business. My job."

"Yeah, let's talk about that. What is this 'She Foundation'?"

"Well, first," Gaby said, "though it's pronounced 'she,' it's spelled ess-eye-dee-aitch-ee. You don't hear the word much today on the grim world, except as part of the word 'banshee.' Anyway, the Sidhe Foundation solves problems."

Zeb nodded. "You mentioned that before. What sort

of problems? I've already gotten the impression you don't just fix flat tires."

Gaby smiled. "No, it's a little more involved than that. We look into strange events. Crimes that make no sense to city guards. Rituals that might do very nasty things to innocent people. Gangland activity that suggests big changes. Anything that could get very dangerous very fast."

"Who pays for all this?"

Harris jerked his thumb toward Doc. "The big guy. He's rich. Mostly from inventions and big engineering jobs. And sometimes grateful rulers will just dump loads of money on us when we've solved one of their little problems."

"But sometimes," Gaby said, "bad eamons—bad guys, I mean—will start something and then say to themselves, 'You know, as soon as news of this breaks, Doc Sidhe is going to come after us.' So they start things off by gunning for Doc."

"So that might have been what led to this attack on your boss?"

Gaby nodded. "It's worked that way before."

Zeb gave her a stern look. "So your punch-drunk husband thinks I'm going to let everyone get into trouble while I'm off eating filet mignon?"

"You ought to consider it," she said. "Sidhe Foundation business is sometimes nasty business. And inconvenient—there are times when we jump on a plane and go places for months at a time. Can your business back home stand for you to disappear like that? You don't want to get sucked into it, Zeb."

"Maybe not. But my partner can manage things without me. I chose one who could be independent."

Harris looked dissatisfied. "Just like you." He tried another tack. "Zeb, you insisted on coming tonight, and now you've had to kill men. Little nasty men, sure, but men. Has that dawned on you yet?"

"Yeah." Zeb let out a long, slow breath. "But that was a question I settled in my mind back when I first went into the army. Whether or not I could kill. I decided I could, under the right circumstances. Those circumstances came up tonight and I discovered I was right. If they come up again, I guess I'll do it again. For example, if I see someone using a stone axe to bash in what you laughingly refer to as your brains. You and Gaby are my friends. I don't have very many."

Harris gave him a cold stare. "Neither do I, and I buried two of them just a few months ago. I don't want to bury you, or have to inform your family."

With some heat to his voice, Zeb said, "Regardless of where I die, you don't *tell* my family. Let them read it in the newspaper. It's none of their business."

Ish said, "Harris, he shoots well and he thinks fast. And you said he was in the army, so he knows what it is to choose a path that he realizes might kill him. If he can follow orders, he is probably suitable."

Zeb offered Harris a victorious grin. "That's right, theater boy, listen to the lady."

Harris glared at Ish. "Thanks for the support. Okay, Zeb. If Ish is willing to have some sorry old fight manager tag along with us, you're in."

"Old, hell. I can whip your ass."

"In your dreams."

"Find us a ring."

They topped a hill and the glittering sea of lights that was Neckerdam rose into view before them.

Chapter Four

"So this guy Blackletter kidnaps Gaby because she's sort of a mystical anomaly," Zeb said.

Harris grinned. "Hey, you know the word 'anomaly.' Cool."

"Yeah, and I'm about to teach you the meaning of the word 'defenestration.'"

They sat in the lab room of the Sidhe Foundation headquarters. This was the ninety-first floor of the black-as-night Monarch Building—or "up ninety," as Zeb had learned the fairworlders called it. This room alone was as large as some sporting halls, and full of tables piled high with laboratory gear, bottles, boxes, tools, machines, and bookcases.

"Once he cuts the ties between the grim world and the fair world," Zeb continued, "and kills Gaby, he can set up a new filter between them. Make 'em both more the way he wants 'em."

"Right," Harris said. He returned his attention to the newspapers before him.

"But the Sidhe Foundation rescued Gaby and stopped Blackletter."

"Killed him deader than disco."

"Disco's back from the dead, man."

Harris grimaced. "Yeah, I guess that was a bad analogy."

"There's something I don't get."

"What?"

"Light, dark, dusky. I'm not clear on what these distinctions mean. Ixyail calls me a 'dusky'—why am I not a 'dark'?"

"Oh, boy. Zeb, you're just asking to open up a whole can of worms."

"I like worms. Out with it, Harris."

Harris sighed. "Okay. 'Light' and 'dark' both refer to what we'd call white people. 'Light' means fairer than fair, ancestry mostly from northern and western Europe. Blond, red-headed, even some white-haired guys like Doc."

"The Aryan ideal."

"Something like that. 'Darks' are white folk who tend to have dark eyes, dark hair. More Mediterranean. I'm classed as a dark. In Europe, the New World, and anywhere European countries have colonies, the lights and darks are in charge . . . and the lights always have the majority of top jobs."

"Why?"

"Tradition, conspiracy, stubbornness, that sort of thing. Way back when, the lights had the power in a very real sense. Their devisements kicked everybody else's devisements around the block."

"You're talking about magic now."

"Yeah, but nobody much uses that word here. Too primitive. Devisement is the science of mysticism; magic is the superstition."

Zeb snorted. "Like there's a difference."

"Anyway, the duskies are everyone else who isn't a light or a dark. You. Noriko. Alastair. Gaby and Ixyail are technically duskies, but since they're light-complected, and run around in the company of lights and darks, and have the mannerisms of the fairer folk—"

"You're telling me they pass for darks."

"Basically, yes. Anyway, 'dusky' is the proper term for them. When you hear 'dusker,' it's more like, well—" He looked uncomfortable.

Zeb didn't let him off the hook. "Like what?"

"Like nigger."

Zeb glowered at his friend. "Well, I can't say you didn't try to warn me."

"I did. Ready to go home now?"

"No. So, you comfortable with the status quo?"

It was Harris's turn to glare. "What do you think?"

"Well, I don't see you marching in the streets with signs in your hand. I see you hooked up with the whitest white guy I've ever seen, living in a nice place, hanging out in a skyscraper office—"

"Listen, Doc gives less of a damn about color than anyone I've met on either world. Look at who he's surrounded himself with. He sets an example. Some people appreciate what he's doing. Some people just call him a dusker-lover. I get called that, too."

"Aw, poor thing. My heart breaks for you."

Doc said, "Status?"

Both men jumped.

"Jesus, Doc," said Harris. "Don't sneak up on me like that."

"What you call sneaking, I call walking." Doc stood beside the table. He wore a sea-green robe. He looked hung over and blinked unhappily into the glare of morning sunlight. "What's our status?"

Harris said, "Well, we're in the news." He gestured

to the stack of folded newspapers on the tabletop. "Big explosion. Sidhe Foundation involved. Kobolde. One of the more rabid papers is talking about a new Kobolde threat and suggesting that the little guys will be breaking into every good light's house to bust up furniture and poop on the rugs."

Doc snorted, amused. "The associates?"

"Alastair is subjecting Mr. Rubber Man to some tests, trying to figure out how it was animated. Gaby's on the talk-box, looking into the front that rented the Fairwings factory from the town, and trying to find out how those Kobolde entered Novimagos, what part of the Old Country they're from, and so on. Ish is just back from tracking down some sort of shaman; she was hoping he could tell her more about those skin-crawling sensations she felt last night, but no luck. Noriko's waiting for me down in the gymnasium; we're going to take off and talk to craftsmen who might have built that dart-gun." A little frown crossed Harris's brow.

"What is it?"

"Doc, I have a bad feeling that the dart-gun is really important. Not because of what it is—because of what it represents."

"What does it represent?"

"Well, it could be that someone here on the fair world has just invented dart-guns out of the blue. It could happen. But I haven't heard of it, and I spent all morning on the talk-box with experts who've never heard of such a thing. Which could mean, since your captors were probably tied in with the guys who crashed my wedding, that they brought the idea of the dart-gun back from the grim world and built it using fairworld technology."

Doc considered. "Meaning they could have brought back more ideas."

"Right."

"I've thought of doing such a thing myself, from knowledge I gained during the brief time I spent on your world. I now know that rocket-propelled airwings are indeed possible. I've been longing to design one."

Harris sighed. "Today, rocket planes. Tomorrow, junk-food franchises. Anyway, I'm just about done with today's mail." He gave Doc a significant look. "We did get the official invitation from the Crown to send athletes to the Sonneheim Games."

"You and Gaby are awfully insistent about those games."

"We think they'll be important."

"Some of your future knowledge?"

Harris took on an expression Zeb construed to be deliberately blank.

"All right, Harris. We'll either get someone there to observe or ask someone from the Crown's espionage corps to do so."

"Thanks."

Doc turned his attention to Zeb. "Last evening, I did not properly thank you for participating in my rescue. I am in your debt."

"Don't worry about it."

"I won't worry. But if you have a need arise, don't hesitate to come to me." He turned away. "I'll be with Alastair in the lab, should you need me."

On the elevator, Zeb asked, "What did he mean about 'future knowledge'?"

"Elementary, my dear Watson—"

"Don't you *ever* say that again. You know what it's like to put up with that line all your life?"

Harris grinned. "Stop bitching. With me, it was 'It ain't easy being Greene.' Anyway, unless you've been hit in the head a lot since the last time I saw you,

you've probably noticed that everything in the fair world looks a little antiquated."

"I got that."

"There's a reason for it. Part of the tie between the fair world and the grim world. The clock on the fair world runs a little behind the grim world. Like about sixty or seventy years."

"And?"

"And their history does, too. It sort of mirrors ours. Lots of details different, but the overall structure the same. Gaby's been trying to figure out when it started— that might be a pointer as to when the split between the worlds happened. She's homing in on a date sometime in the Dark Ages. Anyway, the fair world had its own weird versions of the European colonization of the New World, the American revolution, World War One, lots of stuff."

Zeb considered that as floors slid past the elevator cage. "And if their present is like ours was sixty or seventy years ago—they're about to get to the Depression?"

"Been there, done that. They call it the Fall. Big economic collapse, happened a few years ago, still not fixed yet. No, we think they're looking at the Second World War. There's a guy in Europe, King Aevar of Weseria. His National Purification Party staged a coup d'etat a few years ago and put him on the throne. The Party is gaining power all through western and central Europe and the talk is that Aevar has imperial ambitions. And the big plank on his platform is kicking all the duskies out of Europe."

"Racial purity."

"Bingo."

"Je-zus. You're talking about Hitler."

Harris shook his head. "No, and that's the problem. He's an asshole, certainly, and he's going to cause trouble. But as loosely as the fair world follows grimworld history, we can't be sure that he's the kind of genocidal maniac Hitler was. There isn't a Jewish race on the fair world, as far as we can find, though there are what we think are gypsies, and the National Purificationists haven't singled out any specific races to vent against the way the Nazis did. So we don't know what precisely is going to happen."

"You've told Doc all this."

"Not exactly."

"Why not? I'd think you'd want him to know."

Harris glared. "Oh, thanks for stepping in with all the answers, Zeb. I hadn't considered any of this."

"Stuff the sarcasm."

"Stuff the advice. At least until you have some perspective on what Gaby and I have to deal with. What if we went to Doc and said, 'King Aevar is going to unite the people of Central Europe and start a war to take over the world, and the people of Wo will side with them, and millions of people will die—'"

"So what if you do?"

"What if it's not the truth? Aevar might not be the one; Weseria might not be the place where it starts; Wo might not come into it. Zeb, our preconceptions, if they're acted on, might screw things up completely. What Gaby and I have been doing is telling Doc to look at certain things, monitor specific situations. Like the expansion of Wo's military occupation throughout Asia, like events going on in Weseria. He can put two and two together."

"A lot of folks who could put two and two together in the Thirties still couldn't predict the Holocaust."

Harris's tone became exasperated. "Maybe when you've paid your dues on the fair world you can set up shop as Mr. Answer Man. Until then, just watch and learn, okay?"

"In your dreams."

✧   ✧   ✧

The city streets and sidewalks were busy but not crowded. Zeb watched the parade of humanity, if that was the correct word in the fair world, in their bright antiquated clothes and massive, new-yet-old automobiles.

There was a wider range to the sizes and shapes of people here than on the grim world, he saw. Some people could have passed for grimworlders without trouble, though the average person was a little shorter, a little leaner than his grimworld counterpart.

But there were a lot of folk who just looked strange. People with pointed ears, with noses that looked as though they'd been curved specifically to pop the tops off soda bottles, with spindly builds that would have suggested wasting illnesses had the people not been so energetic. There were men and women standing half Zeb's height who had barrel-shaped torsos. And he thought, though he caught only a glimpse of her, that he saw a woman whose backless dress revealed a hollow place where her back should be, a skin-lined depression large enough to fit a small backpack into.

He saw plenty of duskies that looked like Alastair— Caucasian features under nut-brown or earth-brown skin—but had only spotted a couple he thought were of African descent.

He saw men and women carrying rifles. These folk were not uniformed, though several were dressed for more rugged terrain, wearing heavy boots and durable clothes. He caught sight of several of them as they were going down into subway stations and wondered if they would be heading off to the country for hunting or some strange fairworld sport. No one paid them any attention.

Harris was in the center, Zeb and Noriko to

either side; Zeb wondered if Noriko had chosen the arrangement to keep some distance between her and the unknown quantity Zeb represented.

"Here's the drill," Harris said. "We're going to Wrightway—"

Zeb snorted. "I'm glad, I don't want to walk the wrong way."

"Wrightway is a street where a lot of wrights, metal craftsmen, including some of the world's best gun-smiths, have their shops set up. If I have it paced off right, it's approximately where New York's diamond district would be. I'm going to concentrate on the businesses where the proprietors are lights and darks, and Noriko on the duskies."

"And what am I supposed to do?"

"Accompany Noriko. Play the part of her bodyguard. See what goes on."

Noriko's expression didn't change, but Zeb thought he detected a new tension in her body language. She didn't like the idea.

"So I'm not good enough to go into the shops of the lights and darks?"

"Dammit, Zeb." Harris sighed and appeared to be collecting his thoughts. "We have a specific assignment. Find out what we can about this dart-gun. See if someone in the wrights' district made it. We can do it efficiently, or we can do it in such a way as to express our own political agendas. We don't know for sure, but lives may be at stake. So you call it."

Zeb walked in silence for a while. "Seems that during the last few months you've gotten better at making your point."

"Saves wear and tear on my fists."

"I don't have to like it."

"No, you don't."

❖   ❖   ❖

One westward turn and a few blocks later, Harris left them to enter the first of Wrightway's guncraft establishments. Zeb followed Noriko onward. They walked in a silence Zeb found uncomfortable.

Finally he asked, "Do we have a problem?"

It was several seconds before she answered. "Perhaps."

"What is it?"

"You must understand, I am not ungrateful. Last night, you were the first of us to get free. Lives hung on ticks of the clock, and you were fast enough to save those lives. I owe you my life."

"But?"

"But there is something wrong with you."

Zeb laughed. "You *do* go straight to the point. Something wrong with me? First I've heard of it."

"You gave yourself up to a war-bringer."

"That's a god, right? You were talking about priests last night."

"That's a god. A bringer of war. There are many, but like all the gods, they live on in drowsy slumber. The priests, and devisers like Doc, can sometimes bend their ears. Can sometimes give themselves up to one of the gods, to be imbued with some of the god's power."

"Noriko, where I come from, the gods are more than just drowsy. They're nothing more than legends. If they existed at all, which most people don't believe, they're probably dead now. But I sometimes fight that way there, too. What does that tell you?"

"That you brought your own demon with you from the grim world to the fair."

Zeb sighed. "It's not a demon. It's, uh, I don't know, a fugue state. A different state of mind. Very efficient for fighting, especially in the ring. When you're in that state, there's very little going on in your head that *isn't* fighting."

"It's fueled by anger. Hatred."

"Yeah, some of it, maybe."

She was silent long enough for them to cross another street and pass a cluster of wooden carts laden with fruit for sale. "When you're in the ring," she said, "there are no friends with you."

"True."

"Last night, when your gaze fell on Alastair, if his barrel had been oriented toward you, what would you have done?"

"Nothing." Zeb frowned, trying to recapture his mental state during last night's ambush. He was suddenly no longer so sure of his answer. "Besides, Alastair obviously knows what he's doing with firearms. He's not going to let his aim fall on a friend."

"He was hurt last night. Dazed. He might have. Zeb, you didn't see your face. The rage in it. The, I don't know, *appreciation* you showed when you destroyed one of those Kobolde."

"That's just my war-face, Noriko."

"Never mind," she said. "Ah—here is our first shop."

The sign read EAMON'S BALLISTERIUM and a piece of posterboard in the window said, LIGHT, DARK, DUSKY WELCOME.

They spent their morning and afternoon progressing down Wrightway, moving from shop to shop, sometimes doubling back to check out leads and recommendations given them by shop owners and craftsmen. Zeb and Noriko passed Harris several times as their research carried them along the craftsmen's district.

Most of the people they talked to admitted to no knowledge of dart-guns, though some described crossbows used by scientists on Dark Continent safaris that carried large, ungainly hypodermics.

"So the fair world already has a device that would do the same thing," Zeb said. "But these people had a gun made special for the purpose. Why?"

"I can only guess," said Noriko. "But it is probably for purposes of concealment. It is legal and common to carry rifles."

"I've noticed. It's kind of unsettling."

"My point is that no one notices rifles, but a crossbow would attract attention and be remembered. Long blades are also memorable, which is why I have my pistol and not my sword with me today."

"I am obviously not going to get used to fairworld logic anytime soon."

They stood near a vendor's wagon, having lunch. Zeb watched the traffic—youthful-looking fair folk in their garish, antiquated clothes and the brightly-painted cars for which he was quickly developing an appreciation—and dubiously ate at a tasteless, greasy mass wrapped in paper. It seemed to have been created from a potato-and-beef hash formed into a dense ball and refried. He decided that it would never replace the hot dog. He threw the last of it away.

Noriko, already finished with her sweet cakes, said, "Harris says our worlds are alike in an important way. You eat 'street cuisine' at your own risk."

"He's right." He turned with her and they began their return to the street of wrights. He ignored the frequent suspicious looks of lights and darks. "Mind if I ask you something?"

"No, you may ask."

"Last night they said you were a princess. Is that right?"

"In a manner of speaking. My husband was Jean-Pierre Lamignac, prince of Acadia. He used to do for Doc what Harris now does—arrange, coordinate. He died early this year. One of the friends Harris spoke of burying."

"I'm sorry."

"Thank you. But since his royal parents never cared for me, since I never bore Jean-Pierre a royal heir, since his estate is very valuable and they want me to have none of it, since circumstances demanded—"

Zeb heard a little catch in her voice, the first emotion he'd detected in her.

"—that I miss even his funeral, they are prevailing on the judge who wed us to annul the marriage. When that happens, not only will I no longer be a princess, I will never have been one. Or a citizen of Acadia."

It was startling to Zeb how that faint display of emotion humanized Noriko. He'd wondered, the previous night, if she were as dispassionate as she appeared; now, the pain in her words cut through the image she obviously worked hard to project. "That's a raw deal."

She managed a faint smile. "Another grimworld phrase that must mean something other than what it sounds like. I am not sad about losing the title, Zeb. I was never welcome there, never lived there. Doc is arranging for me to have citizenship in Novimagos; I will not be set adrift. I am only sad that the law chooses to pretend that I was never Jean-Pierre's wife."

"Why are you in Amer— I mean, in the New World instead of back in, uh, was it Wo?"

She nodded. "Wo."

"If that's too personal a question you can tell me to just go to hell."

She stared at the sidewalk and managed a slight frown. "Not too personal. Just rare. I am unaccustomed to speaking about it." She walked in silence for a long while. "Do you know the story of Cinder Ella? The girl with the fur slippers?"

"Glass slippers."

"No, fur."

"I'm sure it's glass."

"Perhaps on the grim world. Is that not a grim detail? Wearing slippers of hard, unforgiving glass instead of soft, comfortable fur? That seems like something grim folk would imagine. But you know the story."

"Sure."

"In the land of Wo, it is a somewhat different story than here in the west. There, Cinder Ella is a spoiled, selfish girl. Only when she begins to demonstrate proper gratitude to her stepmother and proper manners to her stepsisters does her guardian spirit come to help her become happy again, and to convince her stepmother to provide for harmony in the household."

"That's a pretty weird version."

"From a western perspective, perhaps. So. I was Cinder Ella. My father was very modern, very western. He was once an aide to our ambassador to the League of Ardree and was very well-travelled. As were we all; I learned the language of Lower Cretanis when he was posted in Verway."

From what Harris had insisted he learn of the maps of the League of Ardree, roughly the U.S., Zeb knew Verway to be a state-sized region including the city that was the counterpart of Washington, D.C. Like the U.S. capital, Verway was an important center of international politics. Zeb nodded.

Noriko continued, "I was indulged in most ways. When my brothers took up the study of the Sword of Wo, what we call ken-jutsu, I begged and insisted until I was allowed to, as well. Wrestling. Driving. I was allowed to see film plays from the League of Ardree, which we could see in the Foreign Sector after we returned to Wo. I was very spoiled.

"Until my parents and brothers died. Murdered by

an anarchist from Shanga; Wo had just invaded one of
their territories." She was silent a long moment. "I went
to live with my aunt and uncle."

"And had to abandon everything you'd done before?
All your interests and studies?"

She shook her head, eyes still downcast. "No. I had
to do them all more than before."

"That's not very Cinderella-ish. I don't get it."

Noriko managed a slight smile; Zeb could barely see
the curve of her lip. "My uncle was in the Foreign
Office, too. He clearly saw advantages in having a niece
who could speak Lower Cretanis, had lived among the
people of Ardree, who could fight . . ."

"You were trained to be a spy."

"Yes. All that had been enjoyable before became
work. Like Cinder Ella, I was selfish and resented this.
But I did it to retain my father's respect. Though he
was dead, I knew he would smile on a loyal daughter
of the Empire. But then, when they began to teach
me to assassinate rather than kill in honorable fashion, to use poisons and cutting garrotes and tiny, sharp
knives meant only for the throat, I knew I would lose
my father's respect. So I fled. Unlike Cinder Ella, I
remained selfish, and never met my guardian spirit. I
accepted help from diplomats my father had known and
I went back to Verway, where I met Doc and Jean-
Pierre."

"And the rest, as they say, is history."

She smiled again. "I have heard Harris say that, too.
It is a common phrase among the grimworlders?"

"Too common, maybe." He took a deep breath. "It
must be tough for you, being separated from your
whole nation."

"I am not simply separated from it, Zeb. I am
loathed by it. I am a traitor to all of Wo who know
of me . . . except my father and my mother. I would

not have it the other way around." She finally looked up and around, then abruptly turned and headed back the other way. "We have passed by our destination."

In the craftsmen's shops, Zeb saw an even wider variety of fairworld humanity than he had on the street. Some of these wrights were tiny, the size of midgets; some had skin that was as rough as tree bark and limbs as gnarled as branches. In some of these shops, the ones that displayed jewelry in glass cases, thick-bodied men stood as guards and traded flat, unfriendly stares with Zeb while Noriko did the talking.

One shop had a guard dog instead, an enormous brown beast that looked, Zeb decided, like a cross between a mastiff and the First National Bank. It lay stretched out beside the main counter as though it had lowered itself to be saddled. It kept friendly but close attention on all the customers. Zeb stayed on the far side of the shop from it, beside the windows, while Noriko talked to the proprietor.

Zeb saw a trio of black men talking out on the sidewalk. They were dressed in pinstriped suits and merry-hats, and they weren't just the European duskies he'd seen so often; their features were African, or the fairworld equivalent.

He glanced back at Noriko, who was still in deep conversation with the head craftsman. She didn't look like she'd need any help here. He headed out to the street.

The three men stopped their conversation and turned as he approached them. "Hallibo," said one.

Zeb blinked. "Sorry, I don't get you."

The three looked at one another. Zeb saw both amusement and suspicion in their eyes. The one who'd spoken said, "Can't down to trail?"

"Look, I'm from kind of a long way away. Could I get you to—"

The speaker smiled. "Lapbo of light 'n dark, can't down to trail." His accent seemed half-English, half-Caribbean lilt; pretty, but unfamiliar. "Sadbo, go back to lap." The others laughed. The speaker jerked his head and the three turned to walk away, still chuckling among themselves.

Zeb stood there feeling stupid. He was still there minutes later when Noriko emerged from the shop.

"I think we have something with this one," she said.

"Good."

"You sound angry."

"I am. Just with myself. What did you get?"

"Rospo, the owner, was asked by a light gunsmith to put together a set of four barrels. This gunsmith had too much work and had to spread some of it around, though he wasn't supposed to. Rospo was to make big, heavy-caliber barrels to very precise specifications. Unrifled. And not so heavily devised that they'd need to withstand the pressure of a normal hunting round of the same scale."

"So you're talking about a rifle that fires big rounds slowly and not too accurately. Meaning it's probably built for short-distance targets."

"Yes."

"That could be it."

"Let's find Harris."

Across town, the Bergmonk Boys assembled in the stairwell between up thirteen and up fourteen. Otmar wore a bandage across the bridge of his nose.

"Kerchiefs and gloves," said Albin.

All five took oversized red handkerchiefs from their pockets and tied them around their faces, then donned gloves.

"I suggest we not do this," Rudi said. "It's stupid."

Albin glared at him but did not reply. "Fire," he said.

The five men produced six handguns—four big revolvers and Rudi's twin semiautomatic pistols.

"I mean, we could just call him from a public talk-box. That's all it takes."

"No," Albin said, his voice rich with forced patience. "The whole city has to look to him for salvation, and he has to fail before all their eyes."

"How is he going to fail? We can't actually do what we're talking about, can we?"

Albin ignored him. "Script."

Otmar fumbled around in a coat pocket, then produced a folded and crumpled piece of paper. It was rough with tiny holes where the typewriter keys, especially punctuation symbols, had struck it too hard. He handed it to Rudi, who pocketed it.

"And why even bother with the kerchiefs?" Rudi asked. "They're going to know it was us. We might as well go out there with faces bare, singing and dancing."

"Shut *up*," Albin said, and drew back his gun hand as if to hammer Rudi with his revolver butt.

Rudi pressed the barrel of his own gun into Albin's cheek, beside his nose.

The other three tensed, looked at one another, and decided to stay out of it; they kept their weapons out of line.

Albin's face flushed red. Then his eyes crinkled and the cheeks beneath his kerchief rose. Rudi knew he was smiling. He knew which smile, too—the false one, the glad-handing political one. "There, now," Albin said. "You wouldn't be shooting your own brother, would you?"

"No more than me own brother would be hitting me," Rudi said, keeping his voice level. He took his barrel away from his brother's cheek and waved it toward the door out of the stairwell. "Albin, let's walk away from this. This isn't us, isn't the Bergmonk Boys. It's not about money and good living."

Albin lost his smile but nodded. "That's right. But we have a higher calling now—"

"What calling? You never say who this is for—"

"Can't, yet. But trust me. There'll be plenty of money and good living, and we're making the world a better place as we earn it. And never forget . . ." Albin leaned in close, his eyes brighter than Rudi could remember ever having seen them. "I run the Bergmonk Boys. As long as you wear the name Bergmonk, you stick with us and do as I say." He looked at Rudi's pistol. "I'll forget about that . . . because I was a wee bit out of line, too. Now you get *back* in line. We're on Bergmonk business. That's it, lads. Let's go." He pulled the door open and charged through.

Rudi swore to himself and brought up the end of the line.

They emerged onto the floor up fourteen. There were people in the hall, moving between offices; seeing the band of armed men, most threw up their hands and shrank away.

The Bergmonks ignored them and charged past to the doorway marked AETHER GOLD. Jorg charged through, gun at the ready, covering the secretary in the outer office, shouting over her shrieks, telling her to quiet down. The brothers moved past, through the side door, down the business' long corridor. Workers flattened against the hallway walls to let them pass and were kept in place by the unwavering attention of Egon, who remained behind.

Big glass windows let them see into some of the station's offices. In one, a man with a thin mustache, his coat off and sleeves rolled up, sat with a bulky

headset on. He looked alarmed as he spotted the
bearded men in the corridor, but continued talking into
his microphone. The lit sign over his door read
AETHERBOUND.

"That one," said Albin.

Jorg kicked that door in. He could have just turned
the knob and opened it, but that would not have been
as impressive. He stayed outside while the other three
men swept in. Otmar yanked the headset from the
announcer's head, then gave the man a push; the
announcer slid to the floor and scrambled back, away
from the gunmen. Albin kept his own gun trained on
the thickset technician in the next chamber—who was
protected from stray sounds, but not from bullets, by
the big window between the rooms.

Rudi donned the headset, sat, and unfolded his
paper, trying to quell his sense of unease. "We interrupt this broadcast for a special announcement," he
read, adjusting his voice to sound like an upper-class
light. That was one of his gifts, but this time he took
no pleasure in it. "In precisely two hundred beats,
we will have an announcement for Doctor Desmond
MaqqRee and the Sidhe Foundation. Lives are in the
balance. Please inform the Sidhe Foundation immediately." He kept his voice crisp. "In precisely one
hundred and eighty beats, we will have an announcement for Doctor Desmond MaqqRee and the Sidhe
Foundation. Please inform the Sidhe Foundation
immediately. In precisely one hundred and sixty
beats . . ."

The room's overhead lights were out, but Doc put
on a set of smoked-glass goggles before joining Alastair
at the table.

Set into the tabletop was a crystal disk nearly
Alastair's height in diameter. Nor was it ordinary crystal;

it glowed with bright, wavering light. Alastair also wore goggles against the glare.

Atop the crystal was the rubber man the grimworlders had brought from California. It still yammered mindlessly. Occasionally it would twitch. Though the material it was made of should have been thick enough to stop all light, the glow from the crystal disk shone through it. Tendrils of yellow, blue and red light played about on its surface.

"Anything new?" Doc asked.

"Yes. It's a puppet."

"In what sense?"

"It has strings." Alastair struck at the moving tendrils of color, mashing them into the rubber man's chest. Just for a moment, much finer tendrils of color, connected to the thing's limbs and head and stretching up into the sky, were illuminated. "It literally is a puppet. A very simple one, too. No sensory attachments, no self-will, and no outgoing flow of energy to the controller—thus he can't know what it's doing at a distance."

"So it's only for use in the presence of the controller."

"That's what I'm trying to find out now. Am I recording?"

Doc looked at the adjacent table, where a large box sat waiting. "No." He reached over to switch it on. "Yes."

Alastair looked at the clock on the wall. "Time, about a chime short of three bells. Subject, Milord Airtube. In this test, we'll detach some of the control tendrils and reattach them to organ samples." He indicated a jar in which floated a pair of eyes attached to what looked like a brain stem.

They heard a mechanical pop and crackle from behind them. They turned to see the talk-box in the

corner of the room activate itself. Gaby's face quickly
swam into focus. "Doc," she said, "something's up. The
broadcast from the Aether Gold station keeps mentioning you."

"Go ahead."

Her face did not disappear, but there was another
crackle over the speaker, and words spoken by someone unknown, a man with a pleasant Old World accent:
"Please inform the Sidhe Foundation immediately."

A silence of several beats followed, then the voice
returned. "This message is for Doctor Desmond
MaqqRee and the Sidhe Foundation. Yesterday we took
the criminal Doctor MaqqRee into our custody, but he
escaped the punishment to which he had been con-
demned. To retaliate for this gross transgression, we
will destroy the Danaan Heights Office Building and
everything in its vicinity at precisely four bells today.
We invite Doctor MaqqRee to try to stop us. Should
he die in the attempt, the rest of Neckerdam will no
longer have to fear any further justice on our part."

There was a faint clatter from the speaker, then a
long moment of silence.

"This is not good," said Alastair.

Another voice began speaking: "This is Red MacOam
returning to the air." His voice sounded hushed. "The
men who seized control of the Aether Gold offices have
left. There were three of them—four? Four of them,
with fire in their hands and fire in their eyes. I think
that—I'm getting reports that they're gone. Five? Five
men, all lights in ordinary street dress with red kerchiefs over their faces, they— I'm being told that our
offices are now trying to get in touch with the Sidhe
Foundation to get their reaction to this challenge—"

Alastair asked, "Garage, Doc?"

Doc didn't answer.

"Doc? Garage?"

He finally shook his head. "People will be fleeing the Danaan Heights Building by the time we get there. We might not be able to get in at ground level. We'll direct the Neckerdam Guard to try. As for us . . . Gaby, meet us in the hangar. We're taking the Outrigger."

"Oh, no," she said.

"Oh, no," said Alastair.

Chapter Five

Doc's hangar occupied the top floor of the Monarch Building. One large section of the ceiling was a hinged panel that would rise away to allow his special aircraft to take off and land; on the stained concrete floor beneath it usually rested Doc's primitive version of a helicopter, the diamond-shaped rotorkite. When Gaby reached the hangar, Doc and Alastair already had their shoulders set against the rotorkite's stern end and were rolling it out of the way.

Gaby apprehensively turned her attention to the Outrigger. It looked something like a long, sleek, green car with landing gear instead of ordinary wheels. From a cross brace that resembled stubby wings hung two large engines with wooden propellers. Atop the vehicle was tied a mass of heavy gray cloth.

Doc and Alastair trotted up and positioned themselves behind the vehicle. Doc said, "Gaby, ready the hose." Doc and Alastair set their shoulders to the Outrigger.

By the time they wheeled it into place beneath the

panel, Gaby had the hose ready. Before the Outrigger
was quite centered over the painted takeoff "X," she
had fastened it to the nozzle on the cloth mass and
tripped the catch at the end of the hose. With a great
hissing noise, the cloth began to inflate.

Doc ran chains bolted to the floor to hooks on the
vehicle's undercarriage, then climbed into the cockpit.
Alastair threw a switch against the wall. The hangar
lights dimmed. A vibration rattled the floor and walls;
the ceiling rose away, opening on its hinges, revealing
late afternoon sky above.

Gaby joined Doc in the cockpit, helped him count
off the items on the vehicle's brief checklist. She felt
the Outrigger wobble as the lozenge-shaped balloon
filled with helium and tried to carry the car into the
sky.

Alastair slid into the back seat and dogged the door
shut. "Fully inflated, and the timer's ticking on the
hatch."

"Ready to go." Doc flipped a switch on the console
and the port engine roared into life, filling the hangar with fumes. Another switch, and the starboard
engine added its own roar and stench. The Outrigger
vibrated with their power. "Gaby, set us free."

She pulled a wooden handle and felt a little shudder as the hooks on the underside rotated, heard a
metallic crash as the chains fell away. The Outrigger
lurched and rose a few inches into the air.

Doc throttled the engines back and the propellers
slowed. "We're too heavy. Gaby, drop some ballast." He
consulted the gauges before him. "Two talents."

Gaby pulled the ballast lever. Out the window to her
left, she saw water pouring out of the Outrigger's
underside. When the gauge indicated that a hundred
and twenty pounds of it had poured out, she restored
the lever.

The Outrigger lifted up and forward into the sky. Doc said, "Alastair, would you like to do the honors?"

The doctor nodded and closed his eyes. Over the roar of engines, Gaby barely heard the words he said—invocations in High Cretanis, the ancestral language of lights like Doc. Gaby knew that updrafts and bizarre wind conditions made it impossible to land aircraft on or take them off from Neckerdam skyscrapers like the Monarch Building . . . unless one could persuade greater powers to still those winds for brief periods. She hoped this would not be one of those times when the powers chose to ignore the requests of a mortal.

"So who commissioned the gun barrels?" asked Harris.

"Rospo didn't know who the original client was." Noriko looked east up the street. "The gunwright Francisc deCallac, up that way, gave him the assignment."

"I talked to him." Harris frowned. "He didn't say anything about this."

"Probably protecting his client." Zeb cocked his head. "That's the second siren I've heard in just the last couple of minutes."

"I'll call in to see what's up," Harris said. Then a third siren sounded, nearby and approaching. "Wait a second." Harris stepped out into the street and held up his open wallet.

The oncoming city guard car, a huge, lumbering Bellweather painted in blue and gold, squealed as it braked. The driver, a uniformed guardsman, leaned out the window and saluted. "Sir."

"What's happening?"

"Explosives threat at the Danaan Heights office tower. Your boss has been called out by the exploder."

"Get us there." Harris held the rear door open for his companions.

A side wind nearly blew the Outrigger into the Monarch Building's mooring tower, but Doc regained control and wrenched the vehicle around to the northeast. "Well, Alastair's invocation must have done some good; we're not being flung like a crackbat ball. But the winds are still bad," he said. "Updrafts."

Gaby grimaced. "I'm going to go in," she said. "It'll be better than feeling what you're about to put us through."

Doc smiled.

Gaby put on the radio headset, closed her eyes, and launched herself into the Grid. The world around her faded to grayness. Then she was somewhere else, her special room, a stone-walled bedroom with a mirror on the wall, her eight-legged horse doll on the bed before her.

The room, she knew, existed only in her own mind. Doc said it was a metaphor concealing the set of controls that allowed her to do what she did. That didn't make it any less comforting or less private.

She stared at the mirror, groped beyond it with her mind, and found the little eye she was looking for. She opened it. The reflection in the mirror faded, replaced by a view of a nice-looking young woman seated behind a telephone switchboard. The woman looked startled—as did most people when Gaby remotely turned on their talk-boxes without warning. "Goodlady Greene," the woman said.

"Sibyl, anything that comes in related to the Danaan Heights Building, and any call from one of the Foundation associates, forward directly to the Outrigger."

"I will."

"What's the number for the main switchboard at Danaan Heights?"

Sibyl turned to a large bound volume on the table beside her and opened it. She searched for a moment. "Brambleton South one naught four seven."

"Thanks, out." Gaby waved and the switchboard disappeared. Once again she felt beyond her mirror, this time looking for a specific eye by identity rather than by familiar location—a trickier prospect.

A moment later she had it, tried to open it. But she felt only pulses of noise.

She opened her eyes and the Outrigger cockpit swam back into reality around her. "Sibyl's alerted," she said. "And the Danaan Heights switchboard is busy."

"Not a surprise," said Doc. "Can you force yourself in?"

"Oh, yes."

"See if you can get to the building management office. I want someone standing by there with the building plans in hand." Doc kept the pitching, bobbing Outrigger oriented toward the distant rust-red Danaan Heights skyscraper.

The Outrigger was almost directly overhead when the Royal Guard car reached the vicinity of the Danaan Heights Building. Harris took note of the approach of the aircraft as he and the others piled out of the car a block away from the building.

They couldn't park closer. A steady stream of men and women flowed from the building doors, spreading out across the street, stopping traffic. Office workers from surrounding buildings joined them, all fleeing the vicinity of the Danaan Heights Building, most heading first toward the sprawling park that lay across the street from the building's east-facing main entrance.

Zeb said, "They take bomb threats pretty seriously around here."

"I don't think I've ever heard of a false call," Harris said. "Around here, bombers, or exploders, tend to be rare, but when they say there's going to be an explosion—"

"Got it. Hey, isn't that Ixyail?"

It was; she was on a clunky-looking motorcycle behind a begoggled man. Harris shouted, "Ish!" and waved.

As the cycle slowed, she dismounted with extraordinary agility and ran over to join them. "What's the task?" she asked.

"Get in, get to their main operations office, see what we can find out. The cops—Novimagos guards, I mean—will doubtless do a floor-by-floor to evacuate stragglers and look for explosives; they'll need all the help they can get." They headed toward the building, pushing their way through a panicky, ever-thickening crowd.

The Danaan Heights Building was about forty stories tall. The roof was peaked, with a radio tower pointing into the sky; there was no place to set down. Doc circled and thought about it.

"Do you have the building manager on the talk-box?" he asked.

"Better than that," Gaby said. "He snagged an architect from a firm whose offices are up thirteen. The architect is standing by to interpret the building plans for you."

"Excellent. Here's what we'll do. Alastair, you'll start from the top floor. Use your Good Eye to see if you can spot devisement residue that might relate to the explosives, just in case they're not wholly chemical. I'll hurry on down to the basement supports; if the explosives aren't there, I'll get on the talk-box with the architect. Between us, we'll figure out where the best placement of explosives is likely to be, and I'll look at those sites."

"Doc?"

"Yes, Gaby?"

"How do you and Alastair plan to get down there?"

"Line and winch."

"Ah." She shuddered. "Doc?"

"Yes, Gaby?"

"Who do you plan to have fly the Outrigger?"

"You."

"I don't think so. I haven't soloed in this gasbag. There are winds. You said so."

He smiled at her. "You're about to solo. By this time tomorrow, you'll have your license to fly liftships. With my signature on it."

"Oh, great."

Harris and company all picked up assorted bruises from the shoulders and elbows of fleeing office workers as they forced themselves into the building lobby. Zeb looked around and swore. Unending streams of frightened people poured out of the stairwells, crowding the lobby, clogging the exits.

Harris grabbed six people in succession before one could tell him where the building's main office was: ground floor, down a side hall. He and the others pushed their way through the crowd of escapees to get there.

Inside, the building's manager, a dumpy man who would have reminded Zeb of a stereotypical accountant if not for his long nose, pointed ears, and sharp one-inch fingernails, introduced himself. "Gwern Tunny," he said, and shook Harris's hand. He nodded at Ixyail, ignored Zeb and Noriko. "This is

Crimmal Hyde, of the building firm MacQuill, Tew, and Hyde."

A lean, mournful-looking man with dark hair rose from a chair and shook hands all around. "I don't run very fast," he said with a trace of apology. "I trust you'll give me at least a chime's head start before it's time."

"Count on it," Harris said. Also on hand were a lieutenant of the city guard and the office secretary. Harris turned to the guardsman. "Athelstane, good to see you again. Has anyone else from the Sidhe Foundation been in touch?"

The blond, bearded man gestured to the telephone handset lying on the desk. "Your lady's on the talk-box now."

"Great." Harris picked up the handset. "Gaby? Gaby?" After a moment he set it down, looking troubled. "No answer."

Gaby struggled to hold the Outrigger steady. She kept the liftship's nose into the wind, tried to apply just enough power to keep the vehicle from being blown away from the building. She leaned out of the window to take a look down.

Below, a cable hung from the liftship's passenger compartment. Twenty yards down, Doc was still descending hand over hand; Gaby had to lean out of her window to see him. Ten yards above him, Alastair, not quite so physically adept, struggled with his own descent.

Doc came abreast of the building's radio antenna— aether antenna, Gaby reminded herself. He was still a dozen yards from it. He took a look up.

She steeled herself and put on more power, forcing the little liftship forward into the wind. The line holding two of her dearest friends above a five-hundred-foot fall swung steadily closer to the antenna.

Closer, closer—then just past, as the wind died down and the Outrigger picked up speed.

Below, Doc twirled something in his hand, then released it. It was a hook on a line; she saw the hook wrap itself around the antenna and catch fast. Doc quickly tied its line off to the cable.

The wind redoubled its force. The Outrigger turned to starboard and drifted sideways. Gaby saw the cable and line attaching it to the antenna grow taut—saw the antenna bend as the Outrigger threatened to pull it clean off the top of the Danaan Heights Building. Doc looked up, aggravatingly patient. The Outrigger's nose swung toward the antenna as wind and the liftship's tether conspired to inconvenience Gaby.

Gaby swore and struggled with the controls. She increased power, moving toward the antenna to reduce tension on the line.

Finally Doc was able to shimmy across the fragile-looking line and get his hands on the now-bent antenna. Alastair, looking nowhere near as composed as Doc, followed suit more slowly; when he reached the antenna, he held on to it as though it were a long-lost lover. Doc flashed a knife and the line fell away from the antenna.

Freed of nearly four hundred pounds of weight, the Outrigger leaped upward. With the pull of a lever, Gaby quickly bled some pressure from the gasbag; should she need to retrieve Doc and Alastair from the roof, she could increase lift by dumping more ballast and replenishing gas with the bottled helium onboard.

By the time she got the Outrigger under control again and could lean out to look, Doc had pocketed the knife and the little grapnel. He gestured up at Gaby, raising his fist and twirling it: *Climb and stand by.* She nodded and finally began breathing again.

❖   ❖   ❖

"Any suspicious activity around the building?" Harris suggested.

Gwern Tunny shook his head. "Well, some vandalism."

"Tell me about it."

"Someone chiseled some gouges into the building's dedicatory plaque this afternoon," Tunney said.

"No, I'm looking for something like an opportunity to bring a lot of explosives, maybe dozens of talentweights, into the building."

"Nothing like that."

"New tenants? Has anyone rented an office on the first few floors in the last week or two?"

"Just one. Kymon's Cameos, a camera studio, up three."

"Do you have a master key? Give it to me." Harris passed it over to Noriko. She and Ixyail departed without a word; Zeb followed.

Tunney looked even more distressed. "Uh, Goodsir Greene . . ."

"Yes?"

"The Danaan Heights Building is lights and darks only."

Harris looked at him.

"Well, it is building policy."

Harris didn't answer.

Tunny tugged at his shirt collar. He seemed unable to turn away from Harris's emotionless stare. "I'm not responsible for establishing the policies of this company, sir, just for enforcing them."

Harris let him writhe a moment longer, then asked in a quiet, chill voice, "You're saying you no longer require the aid of the Sidhe Foundation?"

"Nothing like that, sir—"

"Then shut up."

"That sort of language is not appropriate—"

"It's very appropriate." Harris heard a tinny voice on the telephone handset; he picked it up. "Hello?"

Alastair walked slowly down the main corridor of up forty. Doors hung open, xioc still steamed on desktops, talk-boxes still blared with music, but there was no one to be seen. Doc would probably be ten floors down and descending fast.

Alastair held his left eye shut. His right eye saw more: little telltale traces of devisement would waver or glow under the gaze of his Good Eye. But he'd seen no unusual devisements walking around this floor, just improvements on the occasional lock, glows on the walls that probably heralded warded safes.

Down the hall, an elevator cage slid open and four uniformed royal guardsmen spilled out. One came directly for him: "Goodsir, the building is being evacuated, you need to get down to ground—"

Absently, Alastair held open his wallet, letting the enameled bronze shield of his Novimagos Guard commission show.

The guardsman saluted. "Sorry, sir."

"Don't fret about it. But if you find anything odd in the course of your evacuation, send someone up for me immediately. I'll be descending floor by floor, fairly slowly."

"Yes, sir." The guardsman left him alone. He and his fellows charged through the halls, shouting hellos for anyone who might somehow have missed the news.

Nothing here. Alastair headed for the stairwell down.

"Goodsir Tunny, can you hear me?" Gaby waited, then hissed in vexation. She wasn't in her special room now, but was still connected to the communications grid by her special gift; she maintained her link to the building manager's line and could feel that it was still open. So why wasn't anyone answering?

A new voice: "Hey, little girl, who's your daddy?"

"Harris! I was hoping you wouldn't even hear about all this."

"Next time we'll ask the bad guys not to advertise on the radio and panic the whole city."

In as few words as possible, she filled him in. "When Doc gets to the basement, he'll call in, and I'll patch him through to you. And Harris?"

"Yeah."

"I want you out of there two chimes before the deadline. More if possible."

"I'll see what I can do."

"I'll make every talk-box in the building ring and ring and ring. You hate that."

"Too true. I love you."

"I love you."

The locked door to Kymon's Cameos opened to the master key. Beyond, the offices were dim, the only illumination from sunlight filtering in through the Venetian blinds—blinds with, to Zeb's eye, archaically broad wooden vanes. Ixyail called out for anyone who might hear, then they searched the place with sloppy speed, knocking things off tables, opening closets and cabinets and spilling their contents out onto the wooden floors.

It looked like a photographic studio. Zeb saw tripod-mounted boxy cameras with lenses at the end of accordionated bellows, colorful backdrops, curved silvery light reflectors, positionable lights. He tore through filing cabinets filled with photos, many of them cheese-cake shots. He heard Noriko committing what sounded like acts of vandalism in the darkroom. Ixyail merely walked around, nostrils flared, sniffing.

Noriko emerged, looking frustrated. "Nothing."

"Place is a photo studio," Zeb said. "Ixyail?"

Ish shook her head. "Nothing."

Noriko picked up a telephone handset and spoke into it: "Gaby Gaby Gaby Gaby Gaby Gaby . . ." She kept it up for several long moments, then her expression cleared. "Tell Harris that the cameo studio is just that. No bombs. Yes, I will." She waited. Then: "Yes, I have it."

She hung up. "Doc reached the basement. No explosives there. He's in the building office now with Harris and Lieutenant Athelstane; they are about to ascend and look at support pillars farther up. Zeb and I are to look at specific places on the exterior walls; Ixyail, you have the liftshafts."

Ish nodded. "Ah, good. I adore climbing greasy metal ladders above long falls."

Gaby kept the Outrigger high above the building, where winds whipped into dangerous jets of air by the concrete confines of Neckerdam were much less likely to reach her. Updrafts still battered her, distracted her from what she needed to do: monitor the phones, route the information to her allies.

Doc reported in. No explosives found between ground and up six, but Harris had to chase an amorous young couple from a supply closet—in their preoccupation they'd managed to miss the noises of panic and evacuation.

Alastair reached her. He was up thirty-seven and still descending. No sign of devisement.

Zeb reached her. He and Noriko were checking out station after station Doc had sent them to investigate. No news. No bombs.

Gaby could see the evacuees from the Danaan Heights Building and surrounding skyscrapers fleeing

the site, a stream of ants now becoming just a trickle.
The Neckerdam Guards had set up roadblocks, with
their distinctive blue-and-gold wooden barricades,
blocks from the building.

She swore to herself. Maybe Harris was right and
their opponents had brought ideas from the grim
world—ideas like phoning in false bomb threats.

Far below, shadows lengthened across Neckerdam.
The sun was low on the horizon. Gaby, her arms sore
and weary from wrestling with the Outrigger's controls,
irritably checked the clock mounted on the console.

Two chimes short of four bells. Less than twenty
minutes until the big event—assuming it wasn't a false
alarm.

In her head, she felt the insistent push of an incoming call. It didn't feel like any of the connections she'd
been using, but had to be important, since it was being
relayed to the Outrigger. She let it reach her. "Sidhe
Foundation, Gaby Greene speaking, grace on you."

"It's me."

"Harris, where are you?"

"I'm out at Lieutenant Athelstane's car. It's equipped
with a talk-box. I've got Zeb, Noriko, and Ish with me."

"Doc and Alastair?"

"Still wrapping up. If they talk to you—"

"I'll set their ears on fire for being slow."

"Exactly what I was going to ask for. You stay way
up there, now."

"That's my plan. Bye." She broke connection, added
a little more thrust, opened the flow of helium from
tank to balloon, and began rising still more.

At one chime short of four bells, Doc and Alastair
joined their fellows at the guardsman's car. Behind it,
wooden barricades and nervous guardsmen held back

crowds of the curious, many of whom had come from the endangered building.

Ixyail, her clothes ruined and face marked by grease, wrapped her arms around Doc. "I need a bath."

He smiled down at her. "I'll give you one."

The Danaan Heights Building had turned nearly black in the shadows cast by taller buildings. The streets between it and the blockade were eerily empty. Suddenly, streetlights came on, illuminating the empty lane before the building and the broad park opposite it.

Doc turned to Athelstane. "Lieutenant, the surrounding buildings?"

"As empty as we could make them." The guardsman shrugged. "Anyone left behind is determined to die, or certain that he knows better than we that there won't be an explosion."

Noriko saw it first. She looked up into the eastern sky. "The goddess," she said.

The rest looked up.

It was a second sun, tiny and distant and in the wrong direction; the real sun was setting in the west, while this one was approaching from the east. They could see eruptions like solar flares on its surface.

And then it wasn't so distant any more. It grew as it arced toward them.

Harris lunged for the open window of the guardsman's car, dove halfway in, grabbed the talk-box handset from the dashboard. He shouted into it, "Gaby! Get out of there! Hard to port! Go go go go!"

The Outrigger hung suspended almost directly in the new sun's path.

Gaby heard Harris's voice over the chatter on the talk-box's police bands. The panic in his voice cut through her. She shoved the throttle forward, manipulated hand and foot controls, tried to bring the Outrigger around to port. But *why*—

Then, far below, she saw the late-afternoon shadows shortening, the building tops brightening.

A roar like a forest fire passed her stern and a blinding glow struck at her eyes from the pilot's side rearview mirror. Then the Outrigger was seized as if by a giant hand and stood on its tail.

Gaby's stomach lurched. She stared up into twilight sky . . . and her stomach coiled itself still tighter as the Outrigger continued over, turning upside down, continuing its helpless rotation. Suddenly Neckerdam *was* the sky—

Through the car window, Harris saw the sun come to earth.

It roared down from a slight angle, directly toward the Danaan Heights Building, coming to ground at the building's base. In the moment of collision, Harris saw the building face blacken and shrink away from the awesome heat of the fireball, saw the miniature sun eat its way into the ground and the building before it.

The fireball flattened from sphere to oval and spread out, its fiery mass filling the streets, flowing outward— and then, with a tremendous roar, burst, hurling balls and flares of fire in every direction.

Chapter Six

The Sidhe Foundation members ducked behind Athelstane's car as a small ball of fire with a curling tail of flame, ejected from the impact of the miniature sun against the building, roared toward them. They felt its heat pass overhead and watched the bright thing's passage. The crowd beside the barricade shrieked, ducked, pushed to get clear; flames trailing the fireball dropped among them, igniting clothes, and some of the victims yelled and slapped themselves or rolled on the street to put the fires out. The little fireball itself slammed into a skyscraper a block past the barricades, bursting across its face, raining fire down on the street below.

Almost in unison, the Sidhe Foundation members stood to look back at the Danaan Heights Building—all but Harris, who had eyes only for the sky.

The front of the Danaan Heights Building was gone, burned away to a height of eight stories, to a depth none of them could discern. Flames raged throughout the gaping hole and along the street below, greedily eating into building fronts, trees, and parked automobiles.

"God, she's on fire," Harris said.

Hundreds of feet above the ruined building, flame also licked atop the Outrigger.

The Danaan Heights Building made a cracking, rumbling noise like a god of the earth clearing its throat. Then, slowly, barely perceptibly, it began to lean forward.

The Outrigger's bottom-heavy design righted it. Gaby was slapped helplessly against the doorframe, felt a blow to the side of her head, and for long moments was helpless with dizziness. But her hands and feet automatically sought out the controls.

When she could again see, she leaned out the window and banked to look below.

Whatever fiery thing had grazed her had also eaten away the front of the Danaan Heights Building and set it and nearby buildings ablaze. Frantic, she scanned the street until she spotted police cars at barricades; it didn't look as though any of them had been destroyed by the impact or its aftermath. Good—it meant Harris was okay. It *had* to mean that.

Then a glow attracted her. She looked up to where the Outrigger's gasbag blazed.

Cold panic gripped her. In seconds, the fire would eat its way through the rubberized cloth and hit the gas—

Helium, not hydrogen. It wouldn't explode.

No, she wouldn't die by fire. All the gas would escape and she'd drop a thousand feet or more to a death on the streets below. She was already losing altitude.

How many individual gas cells did the Outrigger hold? Two, she thought; but if one went, the vehicle wouldn't fly. It would just plummet more slowly.

Gaby forced the panic back, held it at bay. She had to get down, fast. Not too fast. She pulled a lever to open the nozzle on the bottled helium to slow the vehicle's descent, then opened the engines wide and guided the Outrigger down.

She felt the vehicle's rate of descent increase. Her stomach lurched—in spite of the extra helium being pumped into the system, her descent was too fast. At least one of the gas-bags had to have given way. The Outrigger would not survive its fall to the street.

"Baby, pull up," Harris said. "Up, up—oh, God." As the burning Outrigger banked west and began its last descent, he took off after it on foot, charging across the street littered with flaming debris.

None of the others saw. Instead, they watched the Danaan Heights Building's lean become more pronounced. It teetered out toward the street; then, with a great trembling roar of noise, it sheared at the top of the crater made by the destructive sun. Upper stories leaned further as they dropped toward the street, and sheared again higher up, as the building frame, designed to hold up under the pull of gravity in its proper orientation but not in any other, gave way.

The great mass of the building poured into the street, an enormous man-made avalanche of stone and twisted metal. What had been upper floors smashed into the park beyond, obliterating benches and fountains and statues, burying them under tons of rubble. Fragments the size of cars and trucks rebounded, sliding and bouncing along the streets toward the barricades, followed by a thick cloud of dust and smoke.

"This is going to be bad," Zeb said, and ducked behind Athelstane's car to join the others. He found himself between Doc, who was sheltering Ixyail, and Noriko. Instinct prompted him to cover the woman of Wo, sheltering her.

Bricks rained down around them. Something struck Zeb on the shoulder like a blow from a baseball bat. Then darkness rolled across them.

The street climbed toward Gaby.

There were no parachutes on the Outrigger. She remembered Doc saying something about weight limitations, damn him.

Maybe if she projected her mind into the Grid, she wouldn't really die when her body did . . .

Then she saw the building ahead to starboard. It was a thirty-story skyscraper, and atop it, as with most tall buildings on Neckerdam, was a large cylinder-shaped construction made of cedar. She banked, the Outrigger responding sluggishly to the controls, and headed straight toward it.

No, she was losing altitude too fast to aim right for it. She had to aim to overshoot it and hope that her estimates were right, that her loss of lift would drop her right onto it. But if she was wrong, if the vehicle held enough lift too long, she'd sail right over it and then plummet more than three hundred feet into the street. She wailed, a noise of fear and anger, and aimed over the cedar cylinder.

A blow like a negligent kick from a giant-sized place kicker rocked Athelstane's car. It hammered the car door into Zeb's head and threw him onto the street with the others; he groaned and touched his temple, which throbbed under his fingers.

Doc was up, barely visible through the thick cloud of smoke and dust that now blanketed the area. Over the shriek of the crowds and roar of settling masonry, he shouted, "Bring the fire trucks up! Athelstane, get this car out of the way!"

"Can't, sir! There's a girder through the engine!"

"Well, put it in no-gear."

Zeb saw Doc move around to the back of the car and begin pushing. Zeb stood, dizzy, and joined him, if only to prove to himself that he was still functional. Joined by Alastair, they shoved the crippled automobile aside as fire engines, parked and silent for the last few minutes, started up their sirens.

Then the associates turned to the hours they knew lay before them of treating the injured, searching for the missing, looking for information.

Gaby woke up as the men in hospital white loaded her into the ambulance. Harris, his skin and clothes dark from dust and smoke, stood above her, worry in his eyes, and clambered into the ambulance with her. When she reached for him, he embraced her with tender care. "Shh, baby, you're all right. Don't talk."

"Can't shut me up that way . . ." She couldn't seem to talk above a whisper and it annoyed her. Experimentally, she moved her arms and legs, which told her they were bruised and battered and exceedingly unhappy with such experimentation. She was also damp, head to toe.

The rear doors slammed. A moment later, the ambulance lurched into motion.

"How long—?"

"You've been out for a couple of hours, I think. I found you an hour ago. It took a while to get the ambulance. You aimed for that water tank, didn't you?"

"Uh-huh." Try as she wanted to stay awake, Gaby felt herself growing sleepy.

"That's my smart, smart lady."

". . . Outrigger?"

"It's a wreck."

"Good. Won't have to fly it again." The recollection of what had set the Outrigger afire jolted her. "The building?"

"It's gone, baby. But we got everybody out. Now we're going to figure out who did it and decide just how badly to hurt them."

"Good." Her sense of propriety soothed, Gaby let herself be lulled into sleep.

Well into the wee hours of the night, freshly bathed and bandaged, Zeb lay down on the bed in the room they'd given him in the Monarch Building and stared out the window beside him.

Below was a sea of lights, a broader rainbow of hues than the lights of Manhattan and viewed through less hazy air, but still reassuringly familiar. Beside the window, a radiator hissed and sighed, another familiar sight and sound.

But sleep eluded him.

The universe *had* become twice as big for him. Now, with heart and soul as well as intellect, he believed in the fair world, in the wonders Gaby and Harris had hinted at.

But why hadn't he realized that with twice the wonder, twice the humanity, there would be twice the pettiness, twice the evil?

There were no atomic bombs here. Atomic fission was still just a theory; Harris had mentioned that to him. But any place where someone could drop a giant fireball on a skyscraper with pinpoint accuracy had to have its own slate of technological horrors.

And then there was the racist dogma that rivaled the worst armpit regions of the grim world. Of home.

For Zeb, it had always boiled down to expectation.

It was to look in someone's eye and see an expectation of laziness, of criminality, of sheer inferiority, and to feel lower, to be reduced, because of it. That was the heart of the experience.

In the last two days, he'd had that look from more people than he could count, from more people than any time in years.

He steeled himself against those expectations. *To let their opinions matter to you*, he told himself, *is to take a step toward becoming what they expect you to be*.

But try as he might to keep those feelings at a distance, the constant barrage of dark and suspicious looks he'd been experiencing wore on him, tired him. Tired him, and yet kept him from sleep.

And then there was Noriko.

Her comments about his—what should he call it? His blackout, his episode, his rage—at the Fairwings plant still nagged at him. Thinking and thinking about it, he couldn't be certain that he wouldn't have fired on Alastair if the doctor's autogun had been pointed at him.

There were no friends in the ring, only enemies to beat and referees to ignore. He wasn't certain he knew how to concentrate on fighting and yet be aware enough of his allies to protect them. That was disturbing.

And Noriko's sudden change of subject that afternoon had prevented him from telling her why he understood her exile. His family in Atlanta had expected him to grow up in their image. Yet he'd forced himself to learn to speak English with the midwestern, TV-blanded dialect that no one in the U.S. prejudged as too rural, too ethnic, too stupid—it helped keep business opportunities within his grasp, but his family said he was putting on airs, that he thought he was too good for them. Choosing to stay in New York to train and manage fighters as boss of his own business had been the final blow; his last visit home, years ago, after his father's death, had been a time of tension and unspoken recriminations. He wouldn't return until his own kin could let him be who he was.

It was not the same, he knew, as Noriko's situation. He was not in exile from his native country, not considered a traitor in the city of his birth. But he felt for her loneliness, her vulnerability. He was certain that her mask of emotionlessness, even the fighting skills the Sidhe Foundation held in such evident regard, could not really shield her; they could only keep people at bay.

He swore. He did *not* need to be getting interested in a woman from a world he hadn't even believed in a few days before. It was stupid. Soon enough, he'd go home and that would be it.

But not before the ones who'd launched that giant ball of fire were brought down. By effort and sheer chance, no one had died today when the building fell. Yet the weapon that had caused the destruction of Danaan Heights had to be taken from the men who'd used it. He was committed now, couldn't back away from a task when Harris, whom he'd always thought of as a man light on determination or resolve, remained so effortlessly a part of the mission.

Zeb turned his attention to the featureless ceiling and waited for sleep to come.

And waited.

At dawn the next morning, they were a cheerless group in the Foundation's main room.

Noriko looked almost as though the previous day's events had never happened; dressed in a red silk pantsuit, she could have stepped from the pages of a fashion magazine, had a bruise on her cheek not spoiled the illusion.

Doc and Ish had apparently had their bath, and perhaps a little sleep; they looked clean and rested.

Alastair had benefited from neither. He wore the smoke-saturated garments of the previous day and a night's worth of stubble. Dark rings under his eyes proclaimed that he'd been up all night—helping with the wounded, he explained. He smelled like something that dogs would like to roll in and the others insisted he sit at a separate table. He nursed a cup of xioc; the bitter chocolate drink was all that kept him awake.

Zeb had finally managed to get a couple of hours' sleep, but the mirror had shown him bags under his eyes that were a clear indication he needed more.

Harris was last to arrive. He emerged from the elevator hall in yesterday's dirty pants, a starched white shirt probably loaned him by the hospital, and a haggard expression. "She's going to be fine," he said before the others had time to do anything but look the question. "Bruised breastbone from hitting the controls. Lots of other bruises. No concussion, no burns. She's mostly been asleep since we got her to the hospital. Now she's in *that* sleep." He poured himself a cup of xioc. He joined Alastair, sniffed, thought the better of it and moved to the others' table. Alastair grinned.

Zeb asked, "What's *that* sleep?"

"It has to do with her Gift. Basically, it recharges her batteries. If she can get enough sleep, she can bounce back really fast from exertion or injury that would wipe me out." He sipped at the bitter brew and winced. "God, I hate mornings. So, what did you find out while I was off gallivanting?"

Doc stirred. "The Danaan Heights Building was destroyed by a powerful devisement of unknown type and origin."

"I'm shocked." Harris looked around at impassive faces. "That's sarcasm, guys. How 'unknown'?"

"Very unknown. The residual flavor of the energy didn't match any god or goddess I'm familiar with. The delivery mechanism is unknown. The launch site for the miniature sun is unknown; I didn't see any sort of aircraft at its point of origin, though it might not have been possible to see it behind the ball of fire."

Alastair mumbled something. He looked at them expectantly, as if waiting for an answer, then cleared his throat with another swallow of xioc and tried again. "The strings have been cut."

Harris asked, "What strings?"

Doc frowned. "You mean, on the rubber man?"

"Yes. That's almost the first thing I checked on when I got back. The rubber man is no longer connected to a human controller."

Doc looked as though he wanted to swear. "And now, a lead lost because of this event. That is something we did not need."

Harris straightened. "Jesus. What if that was the point?"

The others looked at him. Ixyail said, "Destroy a building just to have time to cut the ties between your rubber puppet and its puppeteer? That would be like swatting flies with an autogun."

"Yeah . . . if that's all they did." Harris moved to the nearest telephone-style talk-box and pulled a grimy, crumpled list of names, addresses and numbers from his pants pocket. "Give me a minute."

It didn't take Harris long to get the information he sought.

According to the city guard, yesterday, while most of Neckerdam's attention was glued to talk-box reports of the Danaan Heights situation, gunwright Rospo Platsmith, the man Noriko had spoken to about the making of four unusual gun barrels, was approached by a potential customer. The man, a gray-bearded light, opened a carrying case containing a shotgun, an old Gudson Model 1 in fair condition. He claimed that he needed the hardening devisements renewed on the weapon's metal. But as Platsmith reached for the weapon, the client took it by the grip and turned to shoot the shop's guard dog, firing both barrels. He then drew a revolver and shot Platsmith twice in the chest and once in the head. He then turned the gun on the other gunsmith and two customers in the shop, shooting each once in the head or the back as they fled. Both customers apparently died instantly; the second gunwright lingered long enough to give city guards the story before she, too, died.

Half a bell earlier, a few blocks up the street, gunwright Francisc deCallac and members of his staff had been murdered by a person or persons unknown. DeCallac's clerk and shop guard were found in a back room, lying upon the floor, shot in the back. DeCallac was found between the ground floor and up one on a back stairway, apparently shot in the back while fleeing.

No evidence was left behind to indicate why the two gunwright shops were attacked in this way. But Noriko confirmed that deCallac was the gunwright who had commissioned Platsmith to fabricate the four barrels.

Zeb listened to these accounts in a sort of haze. All those people murdered just to impede the Foundation's investigation—he knew they should be his chief concern, but the image of Rospo's dog as he'd last seen it, stretched out on the floor, body inert but eyes and ears attuned to every customer's movements, stayed fixed in his mind's eye. His throat felt tight.

"They're cleaning up after themselves," Doc said, his tone wondering, "and they may have knocked down

Danaan Heights just to give themselves uninterrupted time in which to do so."

"No," Harris said. "There's already talk on the street that the great Doc Sidhe couldn't stop this bombing. I heard it in the hospital. They were cleaning up after themselves *and* messing with Doc's reputation. A double victory."

Ixyail wrapped her arms around herself as if against a chill in the air. "I hope this does not mean the building was a casual demonstration of what they can do."

"For now, we have to presume it is," Doc said. "And take steps based on that presumption. None of the associates is to move alone—go in pairs at least. No one is to go unarmed. Spend as little time as possible in predictable locations, like the Monarch Building and your own homes. Harris, we might all find your makeup kit handy—"

"Right."

"Who is protecting Gaby?"

"Two of Lt. Athelstane's men. And as soon as I can get back over there, me. She'll probably check out later this morning."

"Good." For a moment, Doc's tired, discouraged expression reflected the years Harris knew he carried. "Milords and miladies, we appear to be at war. Conduct yourselves accordingly."

Chapter Seven

"Got one," Zeb said.

Harris moved around to Zeb's side of the table. He refrained from leaning over the book Zeb was looking at; the little windowless room in Neckerdam's main guard station was hot and he didn't want to drip sweat all over the cameos.

The book was the equivalent of an old-fashioned grimworld mugbook. It was large and leatherbound, with a half dozen photographs affixed to each page.

The photo Zeb pointed to showed a thick-necked, belligerent-looking man. Though the picture was a black-and-white, the man obviously had a lot of gray in his beard. It was the graybeard Zeb had met in Harris and Gaby's hotel room.

The text beneath the picture read:

CLAN Bergmonk NAME Albin
Plowmoon 17, RBG 23/SY 1430

"Taken five years ago," Harris said.

"What the hell is 'Plowmoon'?"

"Roughly the month of May."

Zeb shook his head. "Man, I hate their dating system."

"You and me both." Harris called out the door, "Sergeant, can you get us files on Albin Bergmonk and anyone you have who works with him?"

Doc pulled the top-down roadster out of the garage door a block from the Monarch Building. He'd driven from his underground garage along the side tunnel he called his "sally-port"; it gave him access to the street by way of this less conspicuous exit. Once he was on the street and a block from the garage, he pulled the green beret from his head and tossed it into the back seat; the wind whipped his hair into a trailing cloud of whiteness. Harris sat in the passenger seat. The other associates were in Noriko's lumbering luxury car, following.

Doc had to raise his voice to be heard over the wind. "Albin Bergmonk. 'The Bergmonk Boys'?"

"That's them. You've heard of them."

"Only a little. Tell me."

Harris started to open the file folder on his lap; as wind yanked at the corners of the papers within, he changed his mind and kept it closed. "Five of them. Actually, there were thirteen kids in his family, but only five of them turned out bad. They're a self-contained little gang, specializing in robberies, especially bank robberies. Professional, with family loyalty going for them.

"The oldest one is Albin, the leader. He's fifty, a graybeard both literally and socially in his clan. Plans their robberies. He's the one whose arm I kicked back on the grim world. Next is Egon. He's been up for dueling manslaughter two or three times, prefers the knife; he's in his mid-forties, still has some blond in his beard. Him I kicked in the throat."

"You're very good at making friends, Harris."

"I know. Then there's Jorg, the biggest of them; the sergeant said he'd been known to bench-press the front of a car so his brothers could change a tire. He's about forty, a big hairy redheaded thing. He's the one that Zeb, who also knows something about making friends, belted in the temple with a gun butt. Otmar's next. He's the one whose nose I broke. A bit of a whiner, according to the records, but he never ratted out his brothers."

" 'Ratted out'?"

"Sold them up the river?"

Doc gave him an admonishing look. "Speak the queen's Lower Cretanis, would you?"

"In spite of his perceived weakness, he never turned them in to the authorities. Never testified against them, never implicated them for any crime. Anyway, he's their driver. Competed in professional races before he entered the family business. Also their pickpocket. Last is Rudiger, or Rudi, the baby—about twenty-five, and beardless. Zeb kicked him in the head. Though they can all shoot competently, he's supposed to be the best of them, and a charmer."

Doc turned left up Lady Way; the business skyscrapers quickly gave way to residential towers and small private estates. "Robbers. Any variant on that?"

"Well, plenty of other crimes, but no *professional* crimes of other types. They've been sent up individually for brawling, dueling, nonpayment of debt, assaulting city guards, making of threats against the Crown, and so on . . . but when it comes to money, robbery only."

"I wonder what caused them to change careers." The private estates to the left abruptly ended. Next was an open field, upon it a sprawling four-story mansion, a graystone monster of bell towers, gargoyle-filled ledges, and wrought-bronze fences.

Harris looked the building up and down. "Dr. Frankenstein's mansion, I presume? Where's the storm cloud?"

"Neckerdam Civic Museum. A little bit of omen-reading this morning suggested that it might be a place to get questions answered. Which suggests that answers about the Danaan Heights Building will point us in the direction we need to go."

"Omen-reading. Doc, you really know how to build confidence in your associates."

Zeb kept his intimidation face on as he stared unblinking at the museum guard. The guard, talking to Doc, tried to ignore him, but his gaze kept being drawn back to Zeb. Beyond the guard, beyond the turnstiles, museum visitors were milling in and passing through the spacious foyers, looking at the first glass-case displays placed in their path.

"I am not saying you can't go in," the guard said. He was a tall man for the fair world, burly, wearing an ill-fitting uniform that was reminiscent of the Novimagos Guard but didn't incorporate the same crest that the true police uniform did. "I'm saying that it isn't the hour for duskies, and *they* can't go in." His nod took in Zeb, Noriko and Alastair.

Doc's voice was cold. "Call your curator."

"The rules—"

"Call your curator now, before I choose to become unpleasant."

Much put upon, the guard sighed, withdrew from the line of turnstiles to the little booth that was his personal domain, and dialed his phone. Zeb could hear his words: "Ma'am, the Sidhe Foundation is here. Well, yes, ma'am, but there's a problem. Three of them are duskies, and it's not the hour—" The guard was suddenly obliged to hold the earpiece a few inches from his head, and even at this distance Zeb could hear shrill noises of unhappiness emitting from it. Finally: "Yes, ma'am. Whatever you say, ma'am."

He hung up and returned, even less happy than when he withdrew. "Go right in," he said. "Goodlady Obeldon will be down immediately. If you'll wait over by the statue of Barrick Stelwright?"

As the associates belatedly moved through the turnstiles, Zeb caught the guard's eye again. "So, what changes around here when it's the duskies' hour?"

The guard's tone was dismissive. "We increase the guard, of course."

"Of course." Zeb shook his head and joined the others.

Barrick Stelwright, if the bronze statue were to be believed, was unusually tall, with a saturnine face and mocking expression, and wore clothes that, as far as Zeb could tell, were pretty close to contemporary Neckerdam styles. The inscription at the statue's base identified him as a Favorite Son of Neckerdam, essayist and critic.

"Actually," said Gaby, "he seems to have been a complete rat bastard. Movies, plays, novels, he'd rip them to shreds in his column regardless of whether they were any good. I've read a collection of his reviews: brilliant, but mean."

Zeb asked, "So, why would they put up a statue to him?"

A new voice, female and cheerful, answered: "He willed a *lot* of money to the Museum, of course."

The speaker, arriving from the direction of the staircase, was the whitest woman Zeb had ever seen, her skin having only the least amount of color necessary to impart it the semblance of life. She was

Gaby's height, tall for a fairworld woman, with hair that, though long and luxuriant, was just a shade too pale to be honey-blonde. Her dress, knee-length and cut in the practical fashion of downtown money-exchangers, was a pastel green. She wore gold-rimmed glasses just a little too large for her face, and beneath them her smile was both mischievous and infectious. She was beautiful.

She extended her hand to Doc. "Dr. MaqqRee, isn't it? I am Teleri Obeldon, curator of Neckerdam Civic Museum. Grace upon you."

Doc shook her hand, though Zeb suspected from the way the woman had presented it that she'd expected it to be kissed. "And on you," Doc said.

"Allow me to apologize for the guard. He's reliable and observant . . . but hasn't much sense for situations like this."

"What sort of situation would that be?" Zeb asked, his voice innocent.

Teleri's smile faded; she cleared her throat delicately before answering. At least she met his gaze. "Well, you must understand, it has only been in the last two years that we've even had hours for visitation by duskies. They were implemented by my predecessor, whose heart was much bigger than it was strong—he died when it failed him, not long after he added the dusky hours. It may be that all the letters and talk-box calls he received complaining about the new policy pushed him to that collapse." She shrugged. "So the guards have had to make some changes in the way they do things. Some are slower than others at it." She smiled brightly again at Doc. "Now, please, tell me how the lowly Civic Museum can be of help to the famous Sidhe Foundation."

"You're aware of the destruction of the Danaan Heights Building."

"Oh, yes."

"We'd like to find out if there is anything in the history or construction or location of the building that made it especially vulnerable to devisement attack."

"Of course. Well, our library is the place to start." She slipped her arm through Doc's and turned him toward the archway leading to the south wing. "It is also by appointment only. You now have an appointment, and you'll be the only ones today, so you won't be disturbed in your studies." She leaned close as she walked with Doc.

Zeb glanced at Ixyail, but her expression, watching the curator, was more a combination of amusement and pity than irritation. She noticed his look and whispered, "Plain, half-blind old maidens have to be *very* obvious to get anything. It's sad, really."

"Plain. Right."

"Of course, she will get nowhere with my Doc."

"Sure."

The library, closed off from the rest of the museum by imposing bronze-bound doors, was at the south end of the building. In the lobby before it was a scale model of the entire city, ten paces long by four wide, meticulously constructed, every skyscraper in its true colors. A heavy brass-reinforced glass lid protected the model buildings from straying hands.

Alastair whistled. "This wasn't here two years ago."

Beside the model was a dark wood door with a sign reading, BY APPOINTMENT. Teleri unlocked it. "It wasn't here two weeks ago," she said. "One of the uses to which we put Barrick Stelwright's money. And some of the budget set aside for the model is still available for annual corrections."

Doc stared at the model, found the little statue representing the Danaan Heights Office Tower. "By chance, do you have an overlay showing Neckerdam's ley lines?"

Teleri smiled. "Nothing so crude as an overlay." She returned to the model. "Stelwright," she said, "ley lines."

A dim glow manifested itself among the buildings of the model, two straight lines that crossed east-west and north-south in the vicinity of the model of the Monarch Building. Neither came near the Danaan Heights Building. "Very helpful," Doc said.

"It's nothing. Stelwright, underground." The ley lines disappeared, and a bewildering series of dotted lines, some in red, others in yellow or blue, manifested themselves at street level on the map, appearing to well up like wet paint from beneath the surface. At intervals, little stars appeared beside the lines. Subway stations, Zeb guessed.

"It took careful coordination between the model maker, Wenzel of House Daython, and a deviser with some artistic skill," Teleri said. "I think the effect is worth it."

The library turned out to be three stories of books with a central atrium. Dust was heavy in the air, and Alastair began sneezing almost at once.

Teleri pointed out the cabinet holding the catalogue of books, then the phone on one of the ground-floor tables. "The museum has its own switchboard; simply ask for my office if you need me. I'm also the resident expert on the settlement of Neckerdam, which nationalities contributed to the settlement, that sort of thing, so if you have questions along those lines you have merely to ask."

"You've been very helpful already," Doc said.

After Teleri left, Ixyail snorted. "Not as helpful as she wants to be."

Doc gave her an admonishing look. "Now, Ish."

"You are sometimes too appealing for your own good."

"I shall remember to complain when I'm old and withered. Very well, everyone, let's start looking."

Doc pulled books referring to the construction of the Danaan Heights Building and magazines showing its decor. Alastair found volumes on the settlement of the neighborhood around the building; he and Noriko looked for anything pertaining to unusual phenomena or events occurring there before the building was raised. Harris fetched city plans showing subway routes, sewers and other utility construction, while Ixyail and Gaby pored over business articles and financial reports on the consortium that had owned Danaan Heights.

Zeb, lacking enough knowledge of Neckerdam to feel particularly useful, found a recent travel guide to the city and settled in to learn what he could.

"It wasn't on the ley lines," said Alastair, "and I'm not finding any unusual stories related to the site. It was a hotel thirty years ago, a livery service a half century before that."

"Good construction," Doc said. "No sheathing on the steel supports, but a lower than usual incidence of iron poisoning because of good maintenance."

"The underground didn't come any nearer than a block," Harris said. "Normal sewer and utilities, but it'll be hell to find out if there was anything going on there; it collapsed when the building fell down."

"No indication of crime-family ties," Ish said. "Danaan-Gwernic Limited owns real estate from here to Nyrax. Very solid."

"I don't understand." That was Alastair, who, if anything, looked worse and more tired than he had earlier in the morning, despite a bath and change of clothing. "Why did the ball of fire hit the base of the building? There are two primary ways to get the ball to the building—aim, or plant a beacon and send it toward the beacon. Either way, assuming there's any skill involved, it's probably easier to hit the building a few floors up—and just as effective."

The talk-box chimed. Zeb, not taking his gaze from the book before him or much of his attention from the conversations going on all around him, picked up the handset. "Hello. Uh, I mean, grace."

"Is this the Sidhe Foundation?" The voice was low, raspy, and familiar.

Zeb covered the lower portion of the handset with his palm. "Doc, it's Albin Bergmonk."

Doc and the associates all scrambled toward Zeb. Zeb took his palm from the handset. "Yes, it is. To whom shall I direct your call?" He kept his voice light and pleasant, like a phone operator's, and saw Harris suppress a snicker. Doc leaned in close and Zeb held the handset so both of them could listen. Gaby sat at the table, grabbed the talk-box cradle with both hands, and closed her eyes.

"Shut up and listen. You saw what we could do at the Danaan Heights Tower. That was a free demonstration. Now it starts to cost. Fifty thousand silver libs in two bells' time or the Gwall-Hallyn Building comes down the same way. Do you understand?"

Doc nodded.

"Sure."

"If you start to evacuate the building, we bring it down ahead of schedule. Do you understand?"

Doc nodded again and mouthed the word "Where?"

"Where do you want the money?"

"We'll call the Monarch Building in a bell and a half with further instructions." Bergmonk disconnected.

Gaby jerked as though she'd been slapped and her eyes came open. "Not enough time," she said, apology in her voice. "Somewhere in this district, though. Very close."

Zeb set the handset down and blinked at her. "You were tracing the call? Just by concentrating?"

"One of my little gifts."

Alastair said, "Three possibilities. We were followed here, they had an observer here already, or they were tipped off by someone in our organization."

Noriko said, "We weren't followed."

Alastair's voice took on a soothing tone. "I have every confidence in your driving. But are you sure we weren't followed by anything? A bird? A little liftship like the Outrigger?"

She considered it and shook her head. "No, I'm not."

Harris said, "We vetted pretty carefully after Fergus turned out to be a traitor. It's unlikely they were tipped off by someone at the Monarch Building—especially as we didn't announce our destination, we just took off."

Ixyail nodded. "It is asking much to assume they had someone here watching for us. I think we can strike that choice from the list."

Gaby said, "I'm not so sure. This would be an obvious place for us to do research, obvious to someone who knows our methods. And they do—otherwise they wouldn't have known how to capture Doc. But why would they just call us here with a threat and not send in the Bergmonk Boys with autoguns?"

Doc waved the subject aside. "Not important right now. I'll have our office staff get the money. Alastair, what you and I need to do is find some way to put a devisement beacon on it. And since they'll be expecting that, and obviously are working with a deviser, we need to find a way to do it they won't easily find."

Harris caught the associates' eyes as he addressed them in turn. "Okay. Gaby, I want you on-station at the switchboard at the Monarch Building to get a trace on their call when they tell us where they want their money. Noriko, Zeb, you and Ish and I will go on over to this Gwall-Hallyn Building—"

"It's a residential tower," Doc said. "Very new, very forward-looking. The first few floors are offices and shops. Take both cars in case you have to split up. Alastair, Gaby and I will take a taxi back to the Monarch Building and pick up more transportation there."

"Right," said Harris. "We'll check Gwall-Hallyn out, see if we can spot any anomalies. Not try an evacuation; I feel like taking these guys seriously. Any questions?" There were none. "Let's go."

Chapter Eight

The wind attacked Ixyail's hair as though they were longtime enemies, mercilessly whipping and tangling it. Seated in the passenger seat beside Harris in Doc's two-seat roadster, Ish could only pull her safari-style hat tighter on her head and glare at Harris. "You chose Doc's car to torture me," she shouted.

He grinned and put the roadster through a hard right-hand turn that cut the vehicle ahead of two cars turning in a more leisurely fashion onto the same side street. He shouted back, "You could have ridden with Noriko and Zeb."

"You knew I wouldn't. I think she likes him. Though she is still tense in his presence. Perhaps it is *because* she likes him. But they should have some time together."

"How romantic. A high-speed drive to stop a building from being destroyed. That's where love blossoms, all right."

She merely sighed.

Harris pointed forward. "That's it ahead."

The Gwall-Hallyn Building was just coming into
view, thirty stories of gleaming chrome and brass,
with a pointed summit, curving lines and arch-topped
windows that suggested to Zeb a cross between the
Chrysler Building and a spaceship from a 1950s
movie.

Up two floors and left from the elevator was building
manager Eamon Inksel's well-appointed office. Inksel,
middle-aged and unamused, invited them all to sit,
though he made no eye contact with Zeb. After hearing
Harris's request, he said, "May I ask why you want to
know?"

Harris said, "It's better if you don't."

Inksel took off his wire-rimmed glasses and methodi-
cally polished them. "The Sidhe Foundation's activities
are widely reported, you know. The last news of you
concerned the Danaan Heights Building. Now you're
here asking if anything odd has taken place at *my*
building. Is Gwall-Hallyn in any danger?"

Harris kept his gaze steady. "Yes."

"Like the Danaan Heights Tower?"

"Yes."

"Then my first order of business is not answering
questions, but arranging for the building to be emp-
tied."

"No. If you do that, we go from it being a possibility that the building will be destroyed in a couple
of bells to a virtual certainty that it will be destroyed
right now."

"Ah. Well, then." Taking the news that he was under
a death sentence with the same imperturbable calm
he'd exhibited on their arrival, the building manager
took a moment to consider. "Odd incidents. In the last
two days, we've had a wallet lifted from a patron of
a ground floor restaurant—very upsetting for the restaurant, as the thief turned out to be one of their staff;

we've had some vandalism in the lobby; and we had
an expectant mother faint in the lift."

Harris sat up straight. "Vandalism in the lobby. Don't
tell me: Someone damaged the building's dedicatory
plaque."

Inksel's eyebrows rose toward his receding hairline.
"Yes. A single deep score. It happened this morning.
How did you—"

"Did anyone see the vandals?"

"Yes, the lobby guard. The vandals were two men
spending time reading the plaque. Both burly. You'd
have to ask the guard for more exact descriptions. He
didn't think anything of it until he heard a screech-
ing noise; that must have been the damage being done.
And then the men ran outside to a waiting car before
he could confront them."

"Is that guard still on duty?"

"Yes. I'll take you to him if you choose."

Harris nodded. "Ish, call Doc or Alastair and tell
them this. The vandalism he's talking about precisely
matches some that took place over at Danaan
Heights. This is our first procedural link between the
two sites, which is probably really important to
Devisers. Call Lieutenant Athelstane at the guardhouse and ask him to check into similar reports of
vandalism—top priority. Then join us downstairs. Zeb,
Noriko, let's go."

The lobby guard, a large dark named Lekkin,
described Jorg and Albin Bergmonk to Harris's satisfaction.

They looked over the dedicatory plaque. It was
bronze, some three feet by two, with upraised letters
describing the philanthropic qualities and financial
genius of the millionaires who'd erected this building
as a testimonial to their own worth. A deep gouge along

WALDENBOOKS

SALE	1486	102	2324	05-10-01
	REL	7.1	42	18:18:33

01 044100847X   6.99
02 0671319930   6.99
PREF NO. 506054808 EXP 05/02
PREF DISC   13.98 10% OFF   1.40-
             SUBTOTAL   12.58
CALIFORNIA 7.5% TAX   .94
             TOTAL   13.52
             CASH   15.52
             CHANGE   2.00-
             PV# 0022324

PREFERRED READERS SAVE EVERY DAY

===========CUSTOMER RECEIPT===========

one edge of the text marred the stately appearance of the plaque.

"What about the material cut from this gouge?" Zeb asked.

The guard shook his head. "There was nothing to sweep up. What they cut out, they took with them."

Harris frowned over that. "Okay, get a prybar. We're going to take this thing right off the wall."

The guard hesitated, but Inksel nodded permission and the man trotted off toward a side corridor.

"Let me guess," Zeb said. "This plaque is the 'beacon' Alastair was talking about?"

"I'm not sure." Harris scowled at the plaque. "I don't do devisements; I just keep running into them. But that would answer a question or two. Like, why the fireball hit Danaan Heights at ground level—"

"Because it was drawn to the plaque in its lobby."

"Right. I think."

Ish finished writing on her notepad. "Thank you, Lieutenant." Her Castilian accent was back in full force. "If you think of anything else, you will notify us? Yes? Grace." She hung up.

And immediately felt a blade point pressed against her back.

Her breath caught. *Did not hear anyone enter the office. Raise hands, present no menace. If I—*

The blade thrust home. She felt it enter her back, shearing through one of her vertebrae, angling down to pierce her stomach instead of her heart.

The pain was unimaginable, flashing out from the injury to burn through every cell of her body. She dimly heard the sound of her own scream. Then the wooden floor rose to slam against her body and darkness drowned her.

The guard was back in the lobby within minutes and pried the plaque free from the marble wall behind. His exertions bent the plaque out of shape and snapped the bronze pegs that held it to the wall. The way Harris held it told Zeb that it was heavy, forty or more pounds.

"Next," said Harris, "we go out a back way in case the front's being watched, take a cab over to the river, and hire a couple of boats to get us out into the center of the river."

"A *couple* of boats."

"Right. One we leave the plaque on. It'd be better yet if we could get a buoy to leave the plaque on, but I want it on the water as fast as possible. We don't throw it overboard because if the fireball doesn't come, Doc and Alastair are going to want to study it. Where the hell is Ish? She should be here by now."

Inksel said, "I'll find out," and headed off to the talk-box at the guard's station.

He was back a moment later, a touch of distress, or perhaps only regret, in his expression. "Goodsirs, my secretary informs me that the young lady has collapsed. She is unconscious. My secretary has summoned an ambulance."

Harris swore. He held up the plaque. "Zeb, can you get this out on the river? Take the roadster, a cab might not stop for you."

"No problem . . . Unless the cops hassle me for being a black man in an expensive car. Unless the people with boats to rent have objections to—"

"Point taken. You and Noriko take care of Ish. I'll deal with this. Goodsir Inksel, thanks."

"Thank *you*."

Despite his imperturbable manner, Inksel moved fast when he wanted to, leading Zeb and Noriko a quick trot up the stairs rather than waiting for the lift. In his office, secretaries crowded around Ixyail where she lay.

She was curled in fetal position, her chair lying toppled behind her. She twitched constantly as though she were undergoing electrocution. Zeb could see no sign of injury.

He swore and knelt beside her head. "Inksel, give me that cushion off your chair. And your jacket. Noriko, dial the Foundation for me."

He had Inksel's cushion beneath Ish's head and the jacket over her a moment later, and had Alastair on the line shortly after that. In few words he described Ish's condition.

Alastair's voice was strained with worry. "Have the ambulance take her to Thown Hospital. Keep her warm—"

"To reduce the chance of her going into shock. I'll get her there, Doctor."

"I'll be there before you." Alastair hung up.

Ish's eyes opened, unfocussed. She gave a full-body shudder, cringed from the pain it obviously caused her, and looked up without moving her head. "Zeb. Noriko." Her voice was a rasp.

"We're here. We're getting you to the hospital. Just hold yourself together."

"No, Zeb. I'm dying. Too deep a wound for Ixyail." A single tear escaped the corner of her eye. "Tell Doc. He knows I love him. Tell him he was all I thought of when my time came."

Zeb and Noriko exchanged a confused glance. "What wound?" asked Zeb. "Ish, you don't have a mark on you."

She coughed; maybe it was a laugh. "Do not patronize me. I'm run through. The blade is still in me. I'm almost there."

A chill of fear ran through Zeb; her voice was so

weak, so agonized. "Dammit, Ish, there's no blade. No blood." He carefully ran a hand across her back.

She jerked and bit back a shriek. Then he held his unblooded hand before her eyes and she stared at it in dull confusion.

"A devisement," she said. "Killed by devisement . . ." Her eyes closed.

Zeb's fear became a hard knot of panic. He heard Noriko cry out, a noise of helplessness and despair. He drew in a deep breath, then roared, "Open your goddammed eyes, sister!"

Ixyail's eyes snapped open. She stared at him in pain and surprise.

Inksel made a noise of protest. "Goodsir, your language is not appropriate—"

Zeb twisted to glare at him. Whatever was in his eyes was sufficient to convince the man to shut up, and more; Inksel drew back, to the far wall of the office, and stayed there.

Zeb returned his attention to Ish. He let no mercy, no sympathy creep into his expression. "Ish, repeat after me. I am not wounded. I will not die."

Ish shook her head helplessly. "The hurt—"

"The hurt is a *lie*. You have to fight through the pain. You're going to fight through the pain. Fight it. Hit me."

She shook her head.

"Hit me, by God, or I'm going to hit you, and you'll die with some grimworld asshole beating you!"

She slapped him. It stung. Her movement dislodged the jacket lying across her and caused her to cry out in more pain.

"Again. 'I am not wounded. I will not die.' "

She slapped him again, and cried out again. Then, the words forced past her teeth, "I am not wounded. I will not die."

"Again. 'I have to fight through the pain.'"

She struck him a third time, and he actually felt dizzy from the strength of her blow. Her voice was a moan. "I have to fight through the pain."

"You're getting stronger. Again." He tensed himself against the blow to come.

She didn't lash out this time. "It doesn't hurt as much."

"It should be getting worse. You thought you were dying a second ago. What's that mean?"

"The pain is a lie. I have to fight through the pain." She grimaced and Zeb felt another wave of agony ripple through her. "Ai . . . oh, that was bad. But it's just . . ."

"Pain. Just pain." As gently as he could, he pulled her up so that she leaned against him. He could tell it hurt her, but was just as sure she could stand to have arms around her. "Pain's a signal. It means something's wrong. But you can't let just the signal kill you. Distance yourself from it. Don't ignore it: Just understand it. Ish, I used to be boxing champ for my regiment. You know what that means? You have those on the fair world?"

She regained some focus, glanced up at him. "Yes. In an army. You fought unarmed for sport, boxing." Her voice wavered but was a little stronger.

"Right. And I won almost all the time. Not because I was better than everyone I fought; I wasn't. It was because," he leaned close to whisper in her ear, "I could really take a beating."

She managed a faint smile. "What?"

"I could take more damage than they could. More pain. Keep my mind sharp. Keep hitting. It discourages them when they beat the living hell out of you and you keep on hitting. To do that, you have to fight through the pain."

From the street below came the sound of a siren,

a more rapid cycle of noise than he was used to from the ambulances of his world. He managed a prayer to lend wings to the feet of the ambulance attendants.

"That's my name," she said.

"What is?"

"Ixyail. It means, 'the lady of pain' in the tongue of my people."

"Because you inflict pain or receive it?"

The faint smile returned. "Inflict, I think. Until today. Hush, now. I have to talk to someone." Her eyes closed.

"Ish, dammit, don't fade away on me!"

"Hush. I will be well. The pain cannot kill me." She relaxed against him.

Finally he looked up at Noriko. Her gaze was on him, not Ixyail, and her eyes were wide—whether with surprise or with revulsion he could not tell. Noriko wiped away a tear rolling down her cheek.

Two men in hospital whites were in the office a minute later. The dark-haired man, probably the ambulance driver, carried on his shoulder two poles wrapped with cloth; Zeb inferred a stretcher. The blond, whose bag indicated he was a doctor, checked Ish's pulse with an ungainly-looking stethoscope, carefully thumbed open her eyelids and pronounced her unconscious, and timed her breathing. Then he sat back a minute as Zeb described what Ish had said.

"Sounds like an arrow of the gods," he said.

"A what?"

"Just what it sounds like. A sudden piercing pain leading to collapse and quick death. Not a stroke; arrows of the gods leave a lingering residue of devisement. But this young lady is still with us and not, I think, fading, which is something new to me. Let's get her to Lord Reev's as fast as we can—"

"Thown Hospital. Special request of the Sidhe Foundation."

The doctor shrugged. "Sidhe Foundation paid for my medical education. I'd drive her to Lackderry if they asked." He gestured for the driver to set the stretcher down.

Zeb carefully handed Ish over to them. As he stood, he looked again at Noriko. Her imperturbable expression was still gone; she seemed troubled. Guilty. "What is it?" he asked.

"You just did something—something extraordinary. I wouldn't have known how. I would have let her die."

"I doubt that."

"I don't. You have no respect for the forces that attacked her. I do, and I would have doomed her." She turned to watch the doctor and driver transferring Ish to the stretcher. "I hope she forgives me."

There was almost a delay at the hospital as a large orderly tried to prevent Zeb from following the stretcher in. Zeb grabbed the man's outstretched hand, twisted, was rewarded with the sound of a bark of pain as the orderly went to one knee. Zeb brushed past him without altering pace or expression. Noriko walked around the kneeling man, not acknowledging him, as she followed. The next orderly read their eyes and didn't interfere.

Alastair was just inside, already in medical whites, and directed the stretcher, Zeb, and Noriko into an emergency theater.

"Where's Doc?" Zeb asked.

"Getting the money together. Waiting for their call." While the driver and the blond doctor arrayed Ish on the examination table, Alastair began taking instruments from his bag and laying them out on a silver tray. Some were medical instruments Zeb recognized; others, including gems, small musical pipes, leather bags and rattles, seemed less professional.

"Je-zus. He couldn't hand that off to somebody?"

"We needed a deviser to work with the money and then to look at the delivery site. That means him or me. I'm better with the injured." Alastair dismissed the ambulance crew with a wave and a thanks. "If you're wondering, it is eating Doc from within that he can't be here now. So tell me everything." He affixed a lavender-tinted monocle to his eye and bent over the unconscious woman.

Gaby depressed the button on the intercom-like device the fairworlders called a dicto. "Call coming in from the building switchboard. I'm told it's a rough voice."

Doc's voice, tight and weary, came back. "I have it."

Gaby touched the main panel of the switchboard serving the Sidhe Foundation floors. As she had six separate times since their return to the Monarch Building, she relaxed and let her consciousness be tugged into the Grid.

This time she did not invoke the imaginary bed-chamber that was her usual haven while navigating the Grid; time was at a premium. Now she floated in a black void, distant from her body, which she could no longer feel. Words jangled through her, both halves of Doc's conversation, and she oriented herself toward them.

Doc's voice first: "—as you demanded. Fifty thousand, silver."

Another voice, one Gaby recognized from the radio broadcast. "And no tricks. No beacons. No curses. We'll find them and make you pay."

Gaby broadened her perceptions, trying to find the same words being spoken elsewhere, slightly out of phase, at some odd angle or distance. Doc's voice and that of the other man were still loudest, but now beneath them was the buzz of an entire city's talk-box traffic.

Calls could be traced by mechanical means. That meant having an operative at the Grid company and running among towering blocks of relay equipment in order to physically trace the relays handling the call. That took many minutes, and no career criminal would be foolish enough to stay on the line that long.

But Gaby's Gift, though less reliable, let her conduct a call trace much more swiftly than the mechanical technique . . . when it worked.

"No tricks. But I still have to know where to bring it."

"King's Park on King's Road. You'll know where to put the coinage when you see it. You have exactly one chime to get it in place . . . or thousands of deaths fall on your shoulders."

" . . . on your shoulders." Gaby heard the distant echo of those words. She flew toward them.

Doc's voice lessened in volume as her attention moved; she could barely make out his words. "*One chime*. Impossible. This is twenty manweights of silver. I need more time."

"A pity. You do not have it. The timepiece is running."

Gaby swept toward the man's words, enfolded them, spread out from them in all directions. Even as the man hung up the talk-box she got an impression of his surroundings; then his disconnect thrust her back into her body.

She shook her head to clear dizziness away and again hit the dicto button for the garage. "Doc, I have them. I can find them, anyway. Morcymeath, near the docks, a six-story residential building. I can't visualize it but I'll know it when I see it."

Doc's voice came back, weary. "Just stake it out. Call the Novimagos Guard and let them lead the raid."

"And who's going with you?"

"No one."

"The hell you say. You need backup—"

"We're running low on associates." He disconnected.

Doc pulled out onto King's Road and headed north. He shifted gears, grudging the vehicle's sluggish performance. It was a big military truck painted in dull red, the back end covered by a reinforced bronze frame holding up a red cloth cover that flapped in the breeze. Its name was Deuce because Harris said it was like the "deuce and a half" trucks from his grim world, and it was more than adequate to haul the fortune in silver that rested in fifty heavy bags in the back . . . but it was not speedy.

He noticed that his knuckles were white on the wheel. It didn't surprise him. *Gods and goddesses, let Ixyail be well.*

As he got the truck up to speed he began honking nearly continuously to persuade slower drivers ahead that he was not going to slow for them. Vehicles pulled aside and pedestrians crossing the street scattered for him. If someone did linger in his path, he'd brake . . . but he preferred for no one to test him. Preferred not to lose the precious ticks of the clock such an action would cost him. *Time. Did Alastair get to her in time?*

When traffic allowed, he glanced at the coin bouncing around on the seat beside the passenger door. It was a worn, ordinary-looking silver lib . . . and the very sort of trick the Bergmonk brothers had warned him not to implement. The devisement he and Alastair had cast upon it would be almost invisible, undetectable by all but the most proficient of devisers. But a full chime after it was warmed by the touch of a hand, its devisement would become active, radiating a beacon he or Alastair might be able to detect.

If he decided to add it to the treasure in back, that is.

He swore, using an expletive his associates had never heard him voice. The coin was subtle, but his enemies knew so much about him. They knew his methods. If he dropped the coin in amongst the ransom and they detected it, thousands might die.

Two-thirds into the time he'd been allowed, King's Park, with its riotously colored flower gardens and Khemish pylons, came into view ahead. He blared his way through traffic, ignored the wave-off of a guardsman directing traffic, and headed straight toward the curb.

No time to search on foot. He hopped the curb, the truck's cargo weight sending a painful shudder through the vehicle, and drove right up on the grass and through the first long bed of yellow flowers. Hand-linked lovers and painters sitting before portable easels scattered before him.

The Bergmonk on the talk-box had been correct: His target was easy to spot. A transference circle was painted onto the grass toward the center of the park. It was on the broad lawn a hundred paces or so from the Greater Pylon from Khem, an ancient obelisk brought to Novimagos by treasure hunters long ago.

There wasn't enough time to unload the cargo of silver. He kept his hand on the horn and drove straight onto the white circle. He set the brake, then bailed out of the driver's seat to look at the damage he'd done to the white circle.

The paint was fresh. With his bare hands he smeared undried paint across the brown trenches his tires had made in the grass, restoring the circle to its unbroken state. This was the simplest sort of transference circle, meaning the corresponding circle, where the truck would arrive, was not far away.

Someone was shouting: "Goodsir, are you mad?"

He returned to the driver's door and, reluctantly, scooped up the special lib, sliding it into a shirt pocket, smearing both with paint as he did so. "Sidhe Foundation business," he shouted back. "Were you here when this was painted?"

Another voice, a boy's: "I was!"

Doc trotted over. The shouter was a round-cheeked boy of maybe twelve summers, dressed in a red playsuit that had until very recently been clean. Doc stood well away from him; if his opponents intended some extra assault, such as a sniper's attack, he wanted to avoid endangering innocents. "What did you see?"

"Three old men. Thick. They had beards. They had paint cans and shovels."

"How long ago?"

The boy shrugged. "Two or three chimes. I don't know. Are they bad eamons?"

Doc nodded absently. "I'm going to ask you to look at some cameos at—did you say shovels? Did they bury something?"

"At the center of the circle. They buried some of the paint cans."

Doc resisted the temptation to swear again. "All right, boy. I want you to run that way," he pointed toward the far end of the park, "as fast as you can, *right now*. Go!"

The boy hesitated a moment, as if trying to gauge whether Doc were joking, and ran. Doc himself ran around the truck, shouting "In the name of the Novimagos Guard I order everyone back! Get back! Bomb! Bomb!"

Some of the onlookers began moving back—a few steps, too slowly.

Doc sighed, then pulled his handgun from his shoulder holster and began firing—in all directions, but into the earth.

The onlookers began running.

The truck shimmered as though it alone were sitting under the desert sun. Doc began running, too.

"Interesting notion," Alastair said. "Arrow of the gods. Young Doctor Dermot may have been close to the truth." He continued making hand-waving passes over Ish, staring at her with his left eye closed.

Zeb and Noriko each kept a hand on Ish's, though she still exhibited no sign of consciousness. "What does that mean?"

"Just what it sounds like. A god decides he doesn't like a mortal and shoots him dead. The arrow isn't physical—at least, none has ever been found."

"You're saying that there's a real god who wants Ish dead."

"I doubt that." Alastair opened his eye and cupped his chin in his hand to stare down at Ixyail. "It takes a lot these days to make a god that angry at a mortal. And Ish, despite her sharp tongue, doesn't go out of her path to insult the gods."

Ish's lips twitched into a smile. "Sharp tongue." Her eyes opened. "I protest." Her voice was weak but steady.

Alastair breathed a sigh that sounded to Zeb like relief. He bent over her. "How do you feel?"

"Much better. Terrible."

"You fell unconscious and worried Zeb and Noriko unto death."

"No. I went to talk to the other me."

Zeb snorted. "The other you? Is she as bad-tempered as you are?"

"Worse."

Alastair bent over to examine her eyes. "And what did she tell you?"

"That she wasn't hurt. She didn't have a blade in her belly. So I knew Zeb was right. The injury was a lie." She smiled up at Zeb. "You saved my life, Zeb. Thank you."

"All part of the service, ma'am."

"Did you tell Doc?"

Zeb frowned. "About you? Of course. He couldn't come—"

"No, no, no. About the other—my notepad? Did you see my notes? About the other building. The building with the vandalism."

"Other building. Oh, God. Tell me."

She told him.

Doc ran. He didn't have to see the truck to know what was happening. The devisement of transference was preparing to move the truck to a circle some distance away. Now, to the eye of the observer, the truck would appear to be twisting, warping, shrinking—in a moment it would be gone with nothing but fresh ruts left behind to mark its presence.

He heard the pop of its disappearance. He didn't slow his run, but continued to catch up to the innocents he'd shooed away. Some of those before him looked over their shoulders, saw him coming on fast, and picked up the pace, sure that he was running them down.

Then there was light and heat on his back. He threw himself forward, skidding on the damp grass, and a fraction of a moment later the sound of the explosion and bow wave of displaced air hit him. He felt it sweep over him, a hot but not burning blast, and saw it catch up to those ahead of him—men and women suddenly felled by the impact.

✦   ✦   ✦

Half a chime later, Doc was still moving among the people who'd been knocked flat by the bomb, and among others farther away who'd been cut by glass falling from surrounding buildings. Though most of those windows had shattered inward, pieces of glass had sometimes clung to the window frames and then fallen out moments later. Fortunately, no one had been seriously hurt. His back still felt sunburned, and would for some time. Sirens screamed the approach of ambulances and guard vehicles.

He moved more slowly than usual, still rubber-legged with relief. It wasn't relief at his own survival, but at the results of his too-quick call to Thown Hospital, and news from a nurse that Ish would survive whatever had struck her down.

Even while helping the burned and injured, staring into their shocked and frightened faces, Doc had had a hard time keeping a smile from his face.

He stopped to help bandage an elderly man whose scalp had been slashed open by glass. The man perched on a stoop as Doc worked. "Thought you were supposed to be Daoine Sidhe," the man said in a tone that could have been taken as garrulous or argumentative.

Doc finished wrapping cloth torn from his shirt around the man's skull. "I am."

"Isn't this a bit beneath you? Patching the common man?"

"Are you common? I saw you comforting a young mother and her baby while others stood by and complained about their bad luck. That doesn't seem common to me."

"No, no, don't change the subject." Then the old man changed the subject. He stared up, past the summits of nearby skyscrapers. "What in the name of the gods is that?"

Doc looked up.

Another fireball raced across Neckerdam's sky and began its descent.

Chapter Nine

Knowing it was futile, Doc ran north along King's Road toward the descending ball of destruction. He had run no more than thirty paces before it dropped from sight behind the skyline.

Moments later, the fatal sound of explosion carried to him—much more distant, much more deadly than that which had endangered him minutes before.

He leaped onto the running board of the first Novimagos Guard car he saw. He didn't have to direct the driver to the proper location. Both men were grim and pale as the car raced north.

"What in Anoon was that?" The shouter was Rudi Bergmonk, and the target of his ire, Albin, was just hanging up the talk-box. They stood in the living room of their Morcymeath apartment, its wallpaper stained with rust from years of roof leaks. Seated respectively on a sagging sofa and a solid hardwood chair that looked as though it had seen decades of use were Jorg and Egon, turning their attention from speaker to speaker as they followed the exchange of words.

Albin smiled. "That was the *Kingston Guardian*, meeting their richly deserved fate. And, not incidentally, that was also Plan Two."

"That was *never* Plan Two! There was no Plan Two!" Rudi stared incredulously. "The deal was, we threaten, they pay, we find a new target to threaten. We got the money. Why did you do this?"

"Those were the orders." Albin shrugged. "Rudi, we have a chance to change the world. We're going to. Whatever the cost."

Rudi stepped up to him. Anger trembled in his voice. "That's not what we're about. We take banks and payrolls. Smart and fast. Only shoot those who're in our way. Those people weren't in our way!"

"Lad, it's time for you to shut up and start following ord—"

Rudi hit him, a fast hook that caught the surprised Albin full in the face. Albin staggered back, turning, and fell, smashing a low table into splinters.

He rose, pressing a finger to the blood welling from his lip, and smiled. "You always could throw a good punch, baby brother. But if you don't want me to have Jorg pound you into paste, you need to settle down so we can get on with the planning."

Rudi shook with the fury running through him. "I'm out, Albin."

"Are you? Are you giving up your share of all that silver downstairs?"

"I wouldn't take a penny of it, or anything else to do with you, you vomitous pile." Rudi turned and left through the front door, still shaking.

Albin shook his head sadly, turned to the other two. "Don't worry. He's just feeling his oats. I'll go talk him out of leaving."

But once in the hallway outside their quarters, he pulled his revolver from beneath his coat before hurrying after his brother.

From blocks away the damage was evident: burning rubble in the street, people running from the site of the impact, traffic snarling as drivers coped with panicky survivors of the fireball. Doc waited until the driver got to the point where traffic began to congeal and leaped from the running board to run the rest of the way.

Up close, the damage was worse. Where the old *Kingston Guardian* newspaper building, a rounded three-story mound, had once sat, there was now a heap of burning brick. Fire had spread to buildings on three sides of it and had spilled into the roadway before it; cars and bodies that had been charred to blackness lay on the street. The injured who were capable of thought and movement ran, walked, even crawled away from the spreading fire.

Others moved among the wreckage. A doctor, identifiable by his bag and stethoscope, the sleeve of his coat charred, moved from one still form to the next. A beat guardsman with a blanket put out flames on the bodies of the dead and injured.

And Zeb, a full-grown man across his back in a fireman's carry, moving at a half trot away from the wreckage, Noriko beside him, a child in her arms.

The heat from the burning wreckage finally reached Doc, a wave that caused him to break out in a sweat. He walked past the charred, lifeless form of a young woman and the still-burning perambulator she had been pushing. A coldness settled in his chest, and he knew that those who had caused this damage, should they ever fall under the sights of his gun or the point of his sword, could not expect mercy from him.

✧   ✧   ✧

Albin, creeping up the hall, heard the building's lift rising toward this floor. Ahead, Rudi stood before the door to the liftshaft, his pose one of stiffness and anger.

Albin stopped several paces back, lifted his revolver, and thumbed the hammer back.

Rudi straightened and turned at the sound. His expression became bitter. "So much for family loyalty," he said.

Albin shrugged. "You're not as important as the plan. Neither is the Bergmonk clan."

"Care to make it an even contest? I have my pistols right here."

Albin merely grinned.

"Albin Bergmonk, drop your gun!"

The voice was female, from paces behind the graybeard. Albin started and glanced over his shoulder. It was the woman whose wedding he'd attended on the grim world. She was several paces from him, holding a revolver in a two-handed grip.

Albin heard the whisper of metal on leather as Rudi's pistols cleared their holsters. He cursed to himself.

Then another voice, Egon's, from well behind the woman: "Albin! We have Otmar on the talk-box; he says there's—who's she?"

Albin shoved hard against the wall, throwing himself back, and shouted, "Trouble!"

Rudi's first shot hit the wall where Albin had been standing. Albin dove forward, into the hallway before the elevators, taking two steps toward Rudi. He returned fire against his brother, fast shots intended to force Rudi under cover, and they did; Rudi scrambled back around the corner of the elevator shaft, and Albin veered to head toward the stairs.

He'd almost reached the door to the stairs when he felt ripping pain and heat in his leg, knew that one of

Rudi's shots had clipped him. He hit the frail door hard, shattering it off its hinges. He tripped and rolled down half a flight of steps.

Trapped in the corridor between two Bergmonk brothers, one definitely armed and the other probably so, Gaby threw herself to one side, grabbing the knob of the closest door within reach, twisted, prayed—

It came open and she shoved her way through, slamming the door behind her.

It was an ordinary flat with a hardwood floor and dusty circular rugs. A surprised-looking man in boxer shorts and undershirt sat with a cereal bowl on the table before him. Music blared from a sound-only talk-box.

Gunfire sounded from the hallway. "Don't move," she told the man.

"I don't have anything—"

"Get on the floor." More gunfire, but not as loud. She dared to pull the door open, poked her nose out, glanced up and down the corridor.

Albin was gone. So was Rudi. So was the third Bergmonk, the one who'd emerged from the brothers' flat behind her. She swore to herself and, hoping that Lieutenant Athelstane and the city guards she'd summoned were close enough to hear the gunfire being exchanged, she slipped back into the hall and moved as quietly as she could toward the Bergmonks' door.

The pain is nothing. Suffer it later. Albin ran down the stairs. He forced himself up to his usual running speed; the flesh wound in his thigh and the sharp pains where his fall down the stairs had bruised his ribs threatened to slow him. He heard Rudi trotting down above him, but his baby brother was not exposing himself to fire.

This wasn't good. Albin carried one revolver, six shots, only two shots left until he reloaded. Rudi, the best shot of all the brothers, carried two Greenling semiautomatics: eighteen shots total, no more than three of them spent. Albin's chance of winning a gun-fight had disappeared with the advantage of ambush gone. He put on more speed.

Gaby slid up to stand, her back to the wall, just beside the Bergmonks' door. She listened, but her ears were still ringing from the gunfire; she might hear shouting, but nothing quieter.

She heard nothing at all.

She wished all these events hadn't scattered the associates across Neckerdam, wished she knew where Harris was right now.

Then she tapped on the doorway. "Novimagos Guard! Open up!"

No answer. At least they hadn't replied with gun-fire.

With her revolver at the ready, she twisted the doorknob and shoved. The door swung in easily. She leaned in for a fraction of a second and then yanked herself back, as much to force them to fire early as to catch a glimpse of the interior.

No gunfire. No one visible in the seedy living room.

She glanced again, took a moment longer this time. There was a talk-box on the table, the handset still off its cradle. Doors left and right were open. So was the window on the far wall, its curtains flapping.

Gaby took a moment to catch her breath and won-der where her saliva had gone. She kicked off her pumps, then moved in as noiselessly as she could, straining to hear, keeping her revolver pointed wher-ever she looked.

Door left—bedroom. Spartan and tidy. No

Bergmonks unless they were under the beds; with their thick torsos, she didn't think so.

Door right—kitchen. Also neat. One of the brothers had to be compulsive about cleaning. Still no Bergmonks unless they were hiding in the icebox . . . and since this kind had a door latch that made escape impossible, she doubted it.

There was a metallic clatter from the street below the window—more like metal bending than cars colliding. Then there was a crash. She ran over to look.

Two Bergmonk brothers were on the fire escape, two stories above the street and hurrying down. Halfway up along the building, a truck had come crashing through a garage doorway.

She knew the truck, Doc's rust-colored deuce-and-a-half, and she was momentarily confused. Then she saw the last Bergmonk brother through the windshield, saw the bandage across the nose her husband had broken, and knew this wasn't part of the Sidhe Foundation's efforts. She slid through the window and began trotting down the fire escape stairs.

The truck pulled to a halt beneath the fire escape. The Bergmonks didn't wait to reach the street; they threw themselves over the last rail, landing on the hardy cloth top over the cargo bed. One shouted, "Go, Otmar!"

She heard the reply, words she couldn't make out, and heard both brothers shout, "Go, go!" Then Otmar got the truck into gear and it began lumbering up the street.

As Gaby reached the midpoint of the fire escape, a pair of Novimagos Guard cars roared up the street. She waved frantically at them; one screeched to a stop just where the truck had rested a moment ago while the other continued in pursuit of the truck. The driver—Lieutenant Athelstane, with another officer to his left side—waved in return.

The rough bronze of the fire escape tearing at her hose and feet, Gaby continued down.

Albin raced through the building lobby and out onto the street, King's Road.

Luck was with him. The traffic signal's HALT sign was up, and waiting at the corner was a roadster with its canvas top down.

He ran across the street and jumped onto the back of the car. He winced as his weight came down hard on his injured leg, and again as he dropped into the left-hand passenger seat. The driver, a thin, mustachioed man in green-and-yellow tweed and a roadster's cap, stared at him in confusion.

Albin put the barrel of his gun against the man's forehead. "Drive or I kill you."

Then Rudi emerged from the building lobby. Albin shifted his aim, moving the barrel just behind the driver's head, and fired. Rudi must have seen the motion of Albin aiming; he was moving before the hammer fell, diving behind a mail box. The driver screeched and put a hand up to his ear.

One block over, the rust-red money truck roared southward. Albin shouted, "Follow that truck!" and again pointed the gun at the driver.

Athelstane set the car in motion, accelerating fast after the deuce-and-a-half and the other guard car. In the back seat, Gaby checked out the soles of her feet—scratched and a little bloodied, not bad, but the stockings were a loss.

Before their car reached the corner, a painfully yellow roadster turned from a side street to follow the red truck; Athelstane accelerated in its wake.

"Dammit." Gaby leaned forward. "That's Albin. Is that one of his brothers with him?"

The other officer, a guardsman whose name Gaby remembered as Paddaddin, shook his head, setting his red beard into wavy motion. "Bergmonk has a gun on him."

Athelstane said, "And he's too skinny to be a Bergmonk. Albin has a hostage."

A checkered-green taxi screeched into line behind Athelstane's car. Gaby looked back. "There's Rudi," she said.

Rudi, a mad grin or a rictus of pain on his face, was the sole occupant of the taxi. Gaby wondered what had become of the driver.

Ahead of them, the other guard car accelerated and drew abreast of the car Albin had commandeered. Gaby thought for a moment that the guardsmen were trying to force the yellow roadster off the road, then realized it was merely trying to pass. "They're just concentrating on the truck," she said. "They don't even know—"

Athelstane honked, trying to get the attention of the other guard car, and pointed frantically at the roadster. But it was too late. Albin merely leaned to the left, pointed his revolver at the guard car's right front tire, and fired.

Gaby saw the tire deform. The guard car weaved to the right, banging into the yellow roadster, then veered off to the left, up onto the sidewalk, crashing into the corner of a building at an alley mouth. Athelstane swore as they passed the wreck, then said, "Sorry, ma'am."

"Apology accepted. Now get that son of a bitch."

Albin's roadster tried to take advantage of an opening in traffic and whip past the truck, but a car turned onto the street and drove side by side with the truck, forestalling him. Gaby could see the two Bergmonks she'd chased in the back of the truck, kneeling by the rear panel, probably ready to fire . . . though their guns were not yet in sight. "What was the big boom a couple of minutes, I mean half a chime ago?" Gaby asked, though she suspected she knew.

"A fireball came down. But I think it landed north of the Gwall-Hallyn Building." Athelstane's tone was grim. "Two cars were all I could bring to support you. Everything else was being sent to the fireball."

Rudi's taxi pulled alongside Athelstane's car, to the left. Gaby brought her gun up, but Rudi merely tipped an imaginary hat at her. Then he surged ahead, the taxi's lighter mass giving Rudi more acceleration than Athelstane could summon. Rudi aimed a pistol out the window . . . at Albin.

Albin, not hampered by a window, pulled his trigger first. But nothing happened; Gaby didn't hear a gunshot. She saw Albin say something curt and break the gun open to reload. Rudi fired and blood blossomed high on Albin's left arm.

Athelstane said, "He's on our side?"

"No, but he's against Albin. Albin tried to ice him upstairs." Then the brothers in the back of the truck brought revolvers up and opened fire on Rudi's car; sparks flared off the radiator grill. "Dammit, stop firing, there are people all along the street!"

It didn't much matter. None of the brothers' shots missed to endanger innocents.

Then a shot found one of the taxi's front tires. The driver of the roadster braked, allowing the taxi to careen forward. Rudi wrestled with his wheel; the taxi slid forward and rightward in a skid across Athelstane's path and into the oncoming traffic lane . . . and he fired one last time through his driver's side window.

Albin jerked and redness sprayed from the back of his head. More blood poured down from his hairline. He turned back toward Rudi, his expression one of

surprise turning to blankness. His gun and a handful
of bullets tumbled from his hand, across the roadster's
rear, and into the street as he slumped backwards
against the car door. The roadster's driver braked
harder.

Gaby watched as the two cars in the northbound
lane missed Rudi's taxi, then the third, a longnose
roadster, smashed into it, spinning the checkered-green
car around like a top. Then Athelstane's car passed the
taxi and the roadster. In moments both cars were too
far behind them to worry about.

The brothers in the back of the truck might have
been confused about what to do about the gunplay
between their brothers, but with Rudi and Albin gone
they had no such problems concerning the Novimagos
Guard car. As soon as the car closed a few paces, they
opened fire.

Their shots were accurate; the windshield before
Athelstane starred and glass rained across the guardsmen in the front seat. Both men flinched, then came
upright again and shook glass out of their beards.
Guardsman Paddaddin aimed his own revolver through
the hole fortune had offered him, but held his fire:
There were still too many innocents ahead who might
act as backstops.

Athelstane continued gaining, then whipped up
beside the truck and passed it on the right. As he came
alongside, the truck's driver veered toward him, ram-
ming him into the oncoming traffic lane. He yielded
rather than be hit, and slid rightward an extra lane to
allow an oncoming taxi to roar by. Then he angled left
again and came back into the southbound lane ahead
of the truck.

Gaby and Paddaddin leaned half out of their pas-
senger-side windows and aimed. The driver flinched,
but as if by prearrangement both fired at the truck's

tires. On their third set of shots, the right front tire
rippled and tore itself to shreds, sending the truck's
front end into shudders.

The truck swerved left, toward the line of cars
parked alongside the street. The driver yanked his
wheel right, overcorrecting, and abruptly the truck was
skidding on its left front quarter, turning, rolling.

It performed a complete rotation and a little more,
then came to rest on its left side, its bed twisted further
than the cab. Athelstane braked. Before he got the
guard car turned around, they all saw the truck's driver
clamber out of the cab and go running back up the
street.

Athelstane pulled to a stop beside the truck's bed;
the car behind him screeched to a halt barely in time
and began honking for him to clear the lane. "You deal
with the men in back," Athelstane said. "I'll run down
the driver."

Gaby and Paddaddin hopped out. Gaby bit back a
curse as her bare foot came down on an irregularity
in the bricktop road. The honking driver saw her
handgun and stopped making noise. Athelstane roared
off after the driver. Gaby and the guardsman moved
to where they could see the opening into the bed.

The bed held bag after bag full of silver libs; mira-
culously, only a few had torn open.

There were no Bergmonk Boys, unless they were
buried out of sight under a ton and a half of silver and
canvas.

They gathered in the bar of the Sidhe Foundation's
suite in the Monarch Building. It was similar to any
streetside pub, one long bar with shelves of liquor
behind it, stools on the other side and small tables
beyond that, most of the furniture in dark hardwoods
and dark leather. But it was all dusty, little-used.

Gaby, her feet still bare and her stockings discarded, did the honors, silently pouring drinks for the assembly.

Harris, smelling of salt water and carrying a canvas bag with forty pounds of bronze plate inside, wouldn't sit. He paced beside the window, swinging the bag.

Doc, hair mussed and the front of his shirt and trousers dirty, with blood—not his—across his right shoulder and breast, took the stool at the end of the bar, the seat with the best view of the room.

Noriko, creases and sweat for once marring her clothes, as somber as the others, took one of the little tables.

At the next table over sat Zeb, slouching in his chair. There were burn marks on his shirt and bandages under them, a bandage on his brow, bandages on his arms, and bloodstains—some his—across his clothing. He glared into distant nothingness with the war-face expression Gaby had seen him wear when he still fought professionally. Since he wasn't facing off with an opponent now, she decided, with a shudder, that he had decided to kill someone.

They were not a happy-looking assembly.

Doc cleared his throat. "I think we've experienced a near total failure today. Please report." He looked at Harris.

Harris told of the events at the Gwall-Hallyn Building, of prying the dedicatory plaque free, of hearing of Ixyail's collapse, of leaving her in Zeb's and Noriko's care while he fled to the river. "Which seems to have been completely pointless," he said with bitterness in his voice, "as the fireball didn't follow the plaque."

"Did you get a good look at the fireball?"

"I sure did. It crossed overhead. Spectacular." He frowned, thinking. "Two things about it."

"Go ahead."

"First, I don't think it travelled all the way from wherever to Neckerdam. It was suddenly roaring overhead, but the smoke trail it left behind didn't extend very far—it just stopped, like it had appeared somewhere over Long Island out of nothing. Also, I don't know if this means anything, it did fly east to west like the first one."

"Interesting. In keeping with its solar character." Doc turned to Zeb, who didn't appear to notice him. "Zeb."

Zeb took a deep breath. "We got Ish to the hospital and Alastair checked her out. He's certain it was some sort of magical attack—"

"Devisement attack."

"Oh, shut up, Doc. Something like an 'arrow of the gods,' but he didn't recognize it. She woke up, a lot better, and remembered that she'd talked to Lieutenant Athelstane about other buildings whose plaques had been vandalized. One had been the *Kingston Guardian* newspaper building, at almost the same time as the Gwall-Hallyn Building."

"What did you do?"

"Called here. All the associates were gone. So I called the *Kingston Guardian*, got the publisher, told him I was with the Sidhe Foundation, told him to get everyone out of the building *now*. He said he'd do that. Noriko and I . . ." His voice choked off. He gulped down a shot of whisky and waited for it to do its work. He was silent long enough for Gaby to wonder if he was through. Then he continued, his voice tight, "Noriko and I took Alastair's car and drove to the building. We were coming up to it when we saw the fireball coming down, so we spun around and got some distance between us. There were people still coming out . . . You were there for the rest."

Doc nodded. "The *Guardian* takes a lot of unpopular

stands and publish editorials that make people mad. This morning's was a diatribe against the destroyers of the Danaan Heights Building and an essay on coward-ice; that may be why they were targeted. But they only have about one hundred employees. So loss of life was . . . not as considerable as it might have been else-where. And you cut down those numbers. No one is sure how many got out—fifty, maybe seventy or more. You saved those lives."

Zeb slammed his hand down on the table. "Not good enough! How many died? Thirty, forty, fifty? Because I forgot to pick up Ish's notebook? Maybe I precipi-tated the fireball by having them evacuate!"

"You did everything—"

"To hell with everything!" Zeb stood and slammed his table to one side, sending it crashing into a cluster of unoccupied tables. Noriko flinched. "I screwed up, and they're dead." He turned toward the wall, slammed his forearm into it; the boom echoed through the room.

Silence hung over them a long moment. Finally, his voice low, Doc said, "That's why I am still in this business, Zeb. The newspapers talk about the good we do. But when I dream, only the ones I failed to save come to visit me. And I think, 'Maybe next time. Maybe then I'll get everyone out. Maybe then I'll take the killer down in time.' I owe it to the ones I've failed."

Zeb leaned his forehead against the wall. "I'm sorry, Doc."

"Don't. It is the life I've chosen."

"Not about that." Zeb pressed his fists into his eyes for a moment. "Well, about that too, but that's not what I meant." He turned around to look at Doc. "Until today, even after Danaan Heights, I thought this place, the fair world, was, I don't know, some sort of amuse-ment park ride. Less real than where I come from. A couple of hours ago, a little girl died as I was carrying her to a doctor. Died of burns. Her smell is still all over me. I've had kind of a change of heart." He took a deep breath. "I'm going to kill those sons of bitches."

"I won't stand in your way." Doc turned to the bar. "Gaby?"

"I told you I'd traced the call to a place in Morcymeath," she said. "I was right. I found the building. I called Lieutenant Athelstane and then went upstairs just to look around. What I didn't know was that the Bergmonks had rented the ground-floor garage in that same building . . . and that was where the receiving end of the transference circle was. So your truck ended up there, with one of the Bergmonks, Otmar, tending it, while the rest were upstairs.

"I blundered into an attempt by Albin to kill, or maybe just intimidate, one of his brothers—Rudi. And then it got messy, with all the Bergmonks bailing out and Athelstane and me chasing them. I saw Rudi kill Albin; his body is in the hands of the Guard. The others got away, one into the Underground, the other two we don't know where." She shrugged. "They didn't get away with the money. Novimagos Guards are guarding it now."

"A small blessing, especially as Alastair and I weren't able to put a devisement beacon on the money. They would have gotten away with it cold."

Gaby said, "You ought to go see Ish."

"I will. In just a chime, we'll be through here—"

The talk-box under the bar rang. Gaby answered, "Guardhouse Liquory, you give us the crime, we give you the proof . . . Oh. Hold on." She looked startled and tucked the handset against her neck. "Doc, call from downstairs. Rudi Bergmonk is in the special elevator. He wants to come up."

Chapter Ten

In the main laboratory room, they crowded around the large talk-box, a quadruple—sound and picture, send and receive. It showed an overhead view of an elevator whose only occupant was Rudi Bergmonk. He had his arms crossed and was glaring at the closed door before him.

Harris consulted a viewscreen set into the wall beside the larger talk-box. This screen showed something like static, with several consistent patches of brightness moving slightly on it—three large, one smaller and dimmer. He gestured, three fingers and then one, to Doc.

Doc stood next to a wall panel of switches on the other side of the talk-box. He thumbed a switch. "Goodsir Bergmonk, grace on you. Might I ask you to pull open the handle behind you?"

On the main talk-box, Rudi started and looked up—toward the camera he could not see but the speaker he could hear. He glanced behind him and tugged at a brass handle on the wall, opening an inch-thick metal door inset in the wall. From the camera view, Zeb couldn't see what lay beyond the door.

Doc said, "Please place your fire in the box."

Rudi waited, shrugged, and pulled a pistol from beneath each arm, placing the weapons as Doc requested.

Doc thumbed the microphone again. "All of them, Goodsir Bergmonk."

Rudi scowled, then pulled a smaller pistol from his boot and added it to the collection.

"And your clasp-knife."

Rudi shut the wall-box with the guns still within, then glared up in the direction of the camera. "If you want me to be tame and safe as a housecat, you'll just have to shoot me," he said. "I always have me fists with me. I might as well keep the knife. I might have to clean me nails."

Doc considered, then pressed two more switches on the panel. The elevator interior wobbled a bit as it began to move.

They stood in a semicircle before the elevator as Rudi emerged. He seemed little the worse for wear, smiling, charming, as he looked between them. "Goodsirs MaqqRee, Greene; Goodladies Lamignac and Greene. Grace on you. I don't know the dusky. No, I do! From the wedding. You knocked me brains loose, a futtering good kick."

"Language, please," Doc said.

"Zeb Watson," Zeb said.

"Goodsir Watson. Well-met. I don't suppose any of you would have a spot of liquor on you. I've had a bit of a day."

They conducted him into the bar, surrounding him like a detachment of guards. "Why are you here?" Doc said. "In coming here, you have turned yourself in."

"Well, there's turning yourself in, and there's turning yourself in." Rudi took one of the smaller tables. "A brandy would be nice. And I'm here for something like turning myself in, but first I wanted to give thanks to Goodlady Greene. But for her I'd be dead." He tipped an imaginary cap at her as she poured his drink. "I appreciate it."

"You're welcome. So long as you don't give me any cause to regret it. Or to shoot you myself."

"I doubt I will." He accepted the glass from her, drank half its contents. "Not bad." He turned his attention to Doc. "Yes, I'm turning myself in. You can have me one of two ways. You can have my silence and try me in court . . . for a few crimes I might have something to do with and a lot I don't. Or you can have my knowledge and grant me immunity from prosecution."

Doc sat opposite him. "You're very confident I'll accept. Otherwise you'd be negotiating from a talk-box."

"True."

"But I think someone needs to pay for what happened to the *Kingston Guardian*, the Danaan Heights Building, for everything else you've been doing. You might as well be the first to pay."

Rudi knocked back the rest of his drink and stared levelly at Doc. "Well, then, I tell you this. Make of it what you may.

"On my honor—and I have honor, else I'd not be here—I had nothing to do with the *Kingston Guardian*. Didn't know it was to happen. Since this all began, I've killed no one—excepting Albin, who was trying to kill me." A bleak look crossed his face. "I've killed me own brother. He taught me to play ball and to shoot, and now I've put a bullet in his brain. But there was no bringing him back from where he'd gone. The fireball today was all Albin and his master."

Gaby refilled his glass. He took a solemn sip before continuing. "I want immunity from any charges related to this whole plan. Conspiracy, blackmail, smash-and-enter, smash-and-grab, the works. Oh, yes, and for Albin's death. Self-defense, that was. For it, I'll tell you everything I know. Without it, you can find out for yourself. Certainly, you don't have any reason for haste; I'm sure Albin's master will happily wait for you to track him down."

"There's no need for sarcasm." Doc considered. "I accept."

"In the name of the Novimagos Guard, as well as your Foundation?"

"Yes."

"Good." Rudi slouched back and put his hands behind his head, but the pain in his eyes belied his casual pose. "Just set the bottle down, would you, dear? I'd appreciate it. This will take some time.

"The story goes back, oh, three years or so. That was the first time I went to the grim world."

"How did you get there?" Doc asked.

"My brothers and I were sent by a man you used to know. Duncan Blackletter."

Harris swore, feelingly. Duncan Blackletter, like Doc one of the rare full-blooded Daoine Sidhe, had been a criminal mastermind on the fair world decades ago. Later, he'd found a way to transport himself to the grim world, using his devisement arts to steal a human baby there and replace himself with it . . . and convince the baby's hapless parents that he was their child. After years of work, he'd built up a fortune in the grim world and commenced a plan to cut the existing links between the two worlds, a measure that would have allowed him to bring modern tools of warfare from the grim world to the fair.

Many people on the fair world knew of Duncan

Blackletter and his crimes. A few knew of his plan to conquer the fair world with grimworld weaponry. A very few, most of them now in this room, also knew that he was Doc's son—the powerful devisements he'd wielded throughout his life not allowing him to retain youth as Doc had, so that he appeared to be many years Doc's senior.

"Go on," Doc said. His expression had not changed, but Harris saw that his shoulders were tight. Nor had Doc seen fit to caution Harris about bad language.

"Duncan was working with some lads in Europe. Our Europe, not the grim Europe. Helping them get information. We Bergmonks—you'd have been proud of us! No crimes, no taking of scores. We just took gold from Duncan and went to grimworld libraries, book vendors, some special shops, that sort of thing." He frowned for a moment. "No, there was a bit of sticky-fingering. We stole some library volumes. I suppose that's a crime. Trip after trip, we did the same thing."

"What were you researching?"

"Devisement. They call it magic and witchcraft and new age and a lot of names."

Doc shook his head. "The grimworlders don't have a tradition of successful devisement."

Rudi grinned. "Oh, there you're wrong. They have dozens, hundreds of traditions. Most of them are dunderheaded and wrong, too many details lost over the centuries. Some of them are sheerest fiction. But there's truth in others. We recorded them all and brought them back for Duncan's correspondents."

"Who are . . . ?"

"I don't know. We handed the information off to his golden boy, the Changeling; he passed them on. Maybe Albin knew."

Harris nodded. The so-called Changeling, Darig MacDuncan, was the human child with whom Duncan had traded places. Raised by Duncan's subordinates on the fair world, he had grown up a competent criminal lieutenant . . . and had died minutes before Duncan had, killed by Harris.

Rudi continued, "So. We did all that, and then they didn't need us any more. We went back to, oh, other lines of work. Work I won't be discussing. Not relevant. When Duncan died, we figured we couldn't ever go back to the grim world; the Changeling had always said their European friends did not know how to do that.

"Then, just a few moons back, Albin gets word from his old employers and goes to talk to them. He comes back breathless, with eyes gleaming. He says they've learned a lot from the texts we brought them. Tried every technique in all those books, most of them dead wrong or even harmful, a few of them useful.

"He says they can make puppets that walk or grab. You saw one, Goodsir Watson. Make dolls in the likeness of people so whatever harm befalls the doll befalls the people as well."

"Voodoo," Harris said.

Gaby shook her head. "That's not real voodoo, that's movie voodoo. When I was still at the TV station I interviewed a real voodoo priestess. She—"

"Gaby, relevance?"

"Sorry, Doc."

Rudi continued, "And they figured out how to get back to the grim world. They sent us back through once, just to be sure they were right . . . risking our lives instead of their own. But we got the impression they didn't need any more missions there for the time being.

"Until a few days ago, when we were supposed to go through, see if we could find *you* there," he nodded to Doc, "because there was no sign of you here."

Harris said, "How did you track us down?"

"We had your names and those of some of your

friends, information Blackletter had dug up in his final days there. We used that and spread a lot of money about. Albin's master gave him lots of money. 'I'm Daffyd Greene from the old country,' I'd say, 'and I want to throw a big party for Harris and my other American relatives. But I don't have his address.' You were living out of a little mailbox, it seemed. And one of them said, 'Party? Before or after the wedding?'" Rudi grinned. "After that, finding out where and when was inevitable."

"Who told you about the wedding?"

"A cousin of yours. Sheila, was it? Redhead? Loves parties, or so she said, but she likes her men taller than me."

Harris's voice turned cold. "Did you hurt her?"

"No. I'd never hurt a woman who wasn't pointing fire at me. I paid her hush money."

Doc regarded him levelly. "And you were to kill me?"

"No. Albin was adamant. We were supposed to capture you. Anyone who hurt you would be hurt, anyone who killed you would be worse than killed. He really wanted you alive. Wanted something from you." Rudi shrugged. "What, I don't know. I do know we weren't the only crew looking for you. Albin let on that there were other groups, some here in Neckerdam, trying to track you. Since you weren't at their wedding, we were to grab the Greenes and bring them back. I suppose they were to be made to talk."

"You're sure you don't know who Albin's contact was?"

"I'm sure."

"So far, your information isn't that useful."

Rudi smiled. "I think it is. Ask more, maybe I'll recall more. Here's something else. Since my brothers don't know who Albin's contact is, they can't call

him to let him know how badly things went today. He
may, in fact, think they've run off with all that silver.
Until he tracks them down, you may have a little time
to breathe."

"Good point. I retract the 'isn't that useful' allega-
tion." Doc turned to Harris. "How does this so-called
'movie voodoo' work?"

Harris considered. "Well, you make a doll in the likeness of the person you're going to screw up. Then you
get some pins . . . no, that's not right. You get stuff
belonging to the person and put it on the doll. Then
there's chanting and incense and snakes and Lord
knows what."

Doc snorted, amused in spite of himself. "'Chanting and incense . . .' Harris, the part you're glossing over
here is the most important one. The very art of the
deviser."

"Sorry. Anyway, when you stick pins into the doll,
the real person hurts. But that's just movie magic."

"Perhaps . . . but it follows certain fundamental
requirements of the laws of similarity and contagion."

Zeb asked, "What are those?"

"Similarity. An action enacted on an object or location may be replicated in an object or location that is
very similar. Contagion. An object associated with a
person remains so even when separated from that person, even across a great distance or for a great amount
of time—the more personal the object, the better."

Zeb said, "Well, voodoo dolls and pins sounds a lot
like what happened to Ixyail."

Doc straightened, looking surprised. He nodded.
"Yes, it does. But Ish is very knowledgeable about
devisement. She's as meticulous as any deviser about
not leaving personal items, hair, nail clippings, anything
behind where a deviser could get at them and identify them with her."

Gaby said, "I'll bet a bucket of libs they used her hair to do it, and I know where they got her hair."

"Where?"

"From you."

Doc opened his mouth to protest, then closed it and gestured for her to continue.

"You were with her the night before you were kidnapped?"

"Yes."

"Slept with her?"

"Yes."

Zeb gave Gaby an I-can't-believe-you're-asking-that look. She ignored him. "When you got up in the morning, did you shower or bathe as though you'd been contaminated? Did you avoid her like the plague, or embrace her?"

"I washed. But of course I didn't avoid her."

"Then odds are good, very good, that you had some of her hair on you. And then you were captured. And no one would mistake her hair for yours."

"A good point. But would they know that stray strands of black hair were hers? They could have been yours, or Noriko's."

"Not mine; her hair is longer. And, yes, they'd have to know you and Ish were lovers, I guess."

"Knowledge that is limited to Foundation associates and a few other confidants."

Gaby nodded. "But you already know that someone told them about your annual devotion to honor your father—something *I* didn't even know about! Doc, someone has sold you out."

Doc's jaw tightened. "Yes. You're correct."

Harris stood abruptly and began pacing again. He looked off into the middle distance, beyond the walls of the Monarch Building.

"Harris?"

"Give me a second. A few beats."

He paced in silence for several moments, then turned back to Doc, his eyes bright. "I know how they did the fireballs."

"Tell me."

"No. I'm going to make some talk-box calls to confirm a couple of facts first. You take that time and visit Ixyail."

Doc managed a smile. "Is that an order? I thought I was the boss here."

"No, you just pay the salaries. Git."

Doc returned three chimes, less than half an hour, later. Hours of weariness and worry seemed to have fallen away from him.

The associates were still in the bar, though most had taken time to change. Gaby was no longer barefoot, and though Zeb's skin was still covered in small bandages, his clothes were clean . . . and he no longer stank of burned flesh.

Harris was on the talk-box. "But what I really need is to know where it was delivered . . . Yes, I've seen your work. And I'd really like to commission you for an assignment . . . Yes." He began scribbling on a notepad.

Doc stood over Zeb. "Might I have a few ticks of your time?"

"Sure."

Zeb accompanied Doc to the far side of the room, away from Harris. They sat on high stools at the bar.

Doc said, "Ixyail told me what you did for her. I do not know how to express my gratitude."

"Just give me a few minutes in a small room with Bergmonk's boss."

"You might just get it."

"How's Ish?"

"Much better. Alastair says she can be moved, so

she'll be here in her own quarters within the bell. He'll see what he can do to defend her from this 'movie voodoo doll' while we're gone."

"Listen, since what we've got here is a sort of war going on, there's something else I'd like to know."

"Ask."

"A little while ago, you said you did this sort of thing to help make up for the people you'd failed. But you didn't say why you did it in the first place. Whenever I hear people outside the Foundation mention you, they talk about how spooky the Daoine Sidhe are ... and then a lot of them say, 'Except for Doc Sidhe.' I don't get it."

Doc considered the question in silence; he looked into the long mirror behind the bar as though his reflection might offer to answer. "Daoine Sidhe aren't human, Zeb. We're related; humans and Daoine Sidhe and most other tribes can have children together. But we're different. And I can remember when I was young, well before mechanical carriages were invented, out riding in the countryside on my horse, reveling in those differences, so apart was I from the people I'd see."

"What differences?"

"It's not easy to express." Doc shook his head, trying to find the correct words. "On those rides, I'd often forget my name. I'd forget language. I didn't need them. If I crossed the path of one of my kind, we could exchange a look, and with it, an entire conversation. If I crossed the path of a member of one of the lesser tribes—and among the Daoine Sidhe, all other tribes were considered lesser—their fear of us would compel silence and obedience. I could be out for days, never once thinking in words. Never once knowing empathy. Just appreciation for beauty or pleasure.

"But one day I found workmen repairing a little

bridge on my mother's estate. I had to force myself to remember speech so I could tell them they were doing something wrong. I intuitively knew how to improve on their design, and I made them do it my way. Then I grew curious about the art of engineering and studied it. I built things all over that estate—more bridges, stables, a temple—and later I found that whenever I came across something I'd built, language and names and all those human things returned to me, as though memories were imbued in the things I'd made.

"I studied with engineers and architects who were not sidhe. And as I grew to know them, I found, for the first time, that they, that the continued existence of people who were not my kin, had meaning for me. This distanced me from my kin, most of whom did not understand." Doc shrugged. "But I found that I was at my best when I was infected with these human traits. And that meant it was impossible just to ignore matters when people chose to deprive others of their loved ones, of their futures. So if there's an answer to your question, that is it."

"Thanks. I'm sorry to have pried. But I had to know . . ."

"What sort of man you were working with?"

"Basically, yeah."

"I'm not offended. Even if I were, you saved me from a monstrous injury today. Much of what I am is because of the associates, but most of all because of Ish. What would I be tomorrow if I lost her?" Doc was now staring well past the mirror, into a future Zeb couldn't begin to speculate about.

"Got it!" That was Harris, hanging up, tearing the top sheet from his notepad. He waved the sheet. "Here's the name of Bergmonk's immediate boss, the deviser. And here's where the deviser's lab is."

The others joined him. Doc took the sheet, read it, and whistled.

"And one more piece of bad news, Doc," Harris said. "We got a call from Lieutenant Athelstane. They've had another report of lobby vandalism. Dedicatory plaque vandalism. It happened earlier today, but the report was delayed because of all the commotion over the fireball."

"Where?"

"Across the street, the Montgris Building."

"That makes sense. It would be impossible to score the Monarch Building's plaque, with the guards we keep in the lobby. Destroy the building next door, though . . ."

"And it may bring down the Monarch Building as it falls."

Doc nodded. "Arm up. Let's go."

In the elevator down, Rudi said, "Do I get me guns back?"

Doc considered. "No."

"Well, of course you don't trust me. But believe me, I have no love of Albin's boss. He offered rewards that turned Albin from us. If not for him, I would not have had to shoot me own brother." Rudi gestured as though his words were the height of reasonableness.

"No."

"Well, damn it all, pay me something. I've never turned on an employer. You'll be safe from me then."

"You've just turned on your employer. You confessed all against him."

"That was Albin's employer. I never received a penny from him. Albin was *my* employer, and I stayed with him until he fired me. Fired *at* me."

Doc considered that. "On your honor?"

"On my honor."

From his vest, Doc pulled a single lib piece and handed it over. It was smeared with white paint.

Rudi burst into laughter. "Oh, the shame! Lawful employ just does not pay. But I'll take it, and serve your ends today. On me honor." Chuckling, he pocketed the coin.

"Keep that as a lucky piece," Doc said. "Your first honest pay."

"If it turns out to be lucky, keep it I will."

Minutes later they piled out of Noriko's touring car and Doc's roadster a block from their objective—an office building in the neighborhood of Drakshire; Zeb calculated that if this were Manhattan they'd be a few blocks east of Central Park's southern end. The day was ending and the sun had set beyond the city's skyscrapers, casting deep shadows along the streets.

"Our objective," Harris said, "is the west-side basement of Number One Seventeen. There will probably be access from the lobby by stairs and maybe lift, and stairs down from the sidewalk to an exterior door. There's no way to tell which accesses they may have blocked off or booby-trapped, so be very careful."

Doc said, "Rudi and I, the lift. Gaby, Harris, interior stairs. Noriko, Zeb, exterior stairs."

They moved out.

Number 117 was four stories tall and half a century old, with sagging courses of red brick reflecting its age and tired condition. A sign in front advertised the business occupying much of the ground floor, a firm manufacturing sporting equipment for the game of crackbat.

Most of the associates went around the block and approached the building from the north so as not to pass the southern basement windows looking out on the sidewalk. Noriko and Zeb waited until the other four were inside the building before creeping up to the stairs descending to the southern basement. Here, the sign above the door read STORAGE, BY APPOINTMENT ONLY, and the barred windows were an opaque green, painted from within.

Passersby who noticed, in spite of the dim light, the odd movement of the two duskies, then the firearms in their hands and the sword sheath across the woman's back, went from a walk to a trot in order to get clear of the area. Zeb knew that guard sirens would eventually approach—brought by reports of the two armed duskies.

"I'm not an idiot," said Rudi as they entered the lift.

"I never claimed you were," Doc said.

"I mean, I know why I've been tapped to go down the most visible way."

"Why is that?" The lift doors closed and the car descended.

"Because I might get admission into their quarters just by knocking."

"Correct. You might also get shot."

"I've been shot before."

The doors opened; Doc pressed himself against the side of the car so as not to be immediately obvious to anyone outside.

Rudi leaned out. "Doors to the south basement left and north right. Stairway door just to the right."

"Eyeholes?"

"Left door."

"Go stand in front and block it."

Rudi did as he was told. As soon as his face was directly in front of the door's peephole, Doc slid out and moved to situate himself beside the south-side door. A slight movement drew his eye; the stairway door had opened a couple of fingerspans and he saw Harris was ready beyond it.

Doc gestured as if knocking. Rudi knocked, an aggressive pounding.

A voice from beyond, male: "We're closed at this bell."

Rudi raised his voice to a bellow. "Open up, you daft eamon! It's Rudi Bergmonk. I need to talk to your boss."

A long delay. Then, from within: "Where's Albin?"

"Dead! I need instructions!"

Another protracted delay. Then: "Step back from the door and put up your hands."

Rudi cheerfully complied. He and Doc heard bolts being snapped back on the other side of the door, saw the knob turn and the door begin to open—

Doc hit the door with all his considerable speed and mass, felt it slam into a moving body, and followed through into a dimly-lit storeroom. He glimpsed shelves and boxes, naked bulbs hanging from the ceiling. The door guard, a tall dark with a revolver, was flat on his back. The man shook his head and tried to bring his weapon to bear on Doc. Doc leaned over and slapped it from his hand, the force of his blow sending the weapon into the wall.

Ahead, a door on the left wall slammed shut . . . and suddenly the air was filled with the roar of a Klapper autogun pumping out deadly streams of rounds.

Chapter Eleven

Doc went flat, falling onto the man who'd tried to shoot him; he grabbed the man by the jaw and slammed his head into the floor, an impact audible even over the sound of the autogun fire. The guard went limp, his jaw skewed at an unhealthy angle. Doc glanced back; Rudi was on the ground, elbow-crawling forward, and Doc could see Harris and Gaby emerge from the stairwell, keeping to the left of the doorway, out of direct line of fire.

Ahead, wooden crates on shelves and stacked atop one another shuddered and disintegrated under the assault of the autogun.

Zeb and Noriko heard an impact from within, and then the opening fire from the autogun. They exchanged a glance.

Zeb stepped in front of the door and lashed out with a side kick. The blow smashed in the wood beside the doorjamb, shattering the door open.

Beyond was a small, well-lit office: desk, chairs, floor

lamp. Opposite was another doorway, this one with a redheaded gunman in it, turning to see what had become of the exterior door, aiming a large pistol. Zeb, off-balance, struggled to bring his own gun in line—

Noriko's handgun boomed and the redhead spun and dropped to the floor. Zeb, recovering, moved in, saw the blood pooling from the center of the man's chest, and switched his attention to the doorway beyond. He moved up into the doorway and took a quick look beyond.

It was an L-shaped room. Zeb stood in the center of the long back of the L. To his right, the room ended. To his left, it continued several paces, then turned ninety degrees in the direction Zeb faced, toward the building's interior. He could see the doorway to the stairway foyer, and the shelves immediately before it that were being riddled by gunfire.

There was one shelf between him and the wall opposite. The wall itself was odd: newly plastered. Or perhaps newly constructed. But there were no gunmen in sight. He motioned Noriko forward, then crouched and moved in.

He maneuvered around a shelf loaded with buckets of sorted nuts, bolts, and other hardware, then stopped to lean against the new plaster wall. He felt dizzy, realized that it had been some time since he'd breathed, and took several belated breaths.

Over the near coast of Long Island, a sun—miniature, barely forty yards in diameter, but glowing, its surface curling with unimaginable heat—suddenly came into being, shining with supernatural cheer on the twilight coast below. It was already in motion, sailing westward in majestic flight, already arcing down toward its target, a white-and-green-checkered skyscraper across the street from the Monarch Building.

Below, pedestrians and drivers on either side of the river pointed. Some marveled at the sun's beauty. Others, knowing what it represented, felt dread, knowing that its descent meant death.

The autogun fire was coming in a more staccato fashion now, short breaks between bursts. During one of those breaks, Zeb saw Rudi Bergmonk stand up beyond the riddled shelf, fire twice from each of his two handguns, and then drop behind the shelf again. The autogun fire resumed.

Zeb felt Noriko move into position behind him. He moved up along the wall until he reached the corner, and peeked around it.

The gunfire was coming from a heavy wood door—from a chest-high slit in the door, fashioned perhaps for that very purpose. The door was now pocked with splintered craters from Rudi's return fire, but it did not seem to be seriously damaged; it could obviously keep its integrity through much more damage than it had sustained.

Zeb saw Doc rise and fire twice with his own handgun, then drop down.

Don't hit him where he's strongest. That was Zeb's fight-analysis voice. *Hit where he's soft. Hit what he's not protecting.* And that wasn't the door. Zeb looked up at the wall he was leaning on.

Plaster over brick? Or plaster over wood frame? The odd shape of the room suggested that this wall was added during renovation, not part of the original plan. It could well be light construction.

Zeb rose and backed away from the wall until his spine met the shelf behind him. If it were wood frame construction, where would the wooden braces be? One at the corner, surely; how far over would the next one be?

He hyperventilated for a few moments, during which Rudi popped up for another quick barrage and disappeared just as swiftly. He saw Noriko's eyes go wide as she divined what he was doing. She readied her pistol, drew her sword with her free hand, and moved next to him.

The pain is nothing. Ignore it. Fight through it. Zeb charged, closing his eyes, throwing an arm over his face just as he hit.

He felt the wall's surface give way, barely slowing him. He felt another impact, also trivial, and then a third on his right shoulder, a hard one. Collapsing plaster tripped him; he spun as he fell, opening his eyes, crashing onto his unhurt shoulder.

Ahead of him, a tall, willowy man stood beside the door, an autogun like Alastair's in both hands, eyes widening in surprise as he turned to look and aim at Zeb. Zeb swung his pistol around, squeezed off a shot, saw a bloody divot expelled from the man's leg above his knee. The man jerked, fired, his bullets going into the wall beside the doorway.

A shadow fell over Zeb from behind and he heard Noriko fire. Blood suddenly welled from the throat of the man with the autogun and he fell, looking mildly concerned.

Zeb rolled over to take in the rest of the room.

An upright cabinet that looked like it was made of aluminum, capped with an intricate knotwork of glass apparatus, stood against the wall behind the gunman. Further in were a desk and a table, a very long one. Behind the table stood a robed figure, slight of build, arms raised, high voice keening a chant that set Zeb's teeth on edge.

The table was capped by a framework of glass and metal. He'd seen one just like it, the top of the protective case over the scale model of Neckerdam at the museum.

Within the case, a tiny golden ball flew, dropping from just below the lid toward the barely-seen tips of model skyscrapers.

Over Neckerdam, the miniature sun's speed increased as it dipped toward its target.

The sun itself had no mind, no thoughts. Yet it felt sensations. A thing of temporary life, it felt something like desire as it homed in on the checkered thing of stone. It felt satisfaction. It felt the presence of powers, powers summoned to create it, powers anxious for its mission to be done so they could return to their rest.

It illuminated the stone canyons below and drew the eyes of the doomed.

Noriko leaped clean over Zeb and fired once more at the autogunner, making sure of him. Zeb scrambled to his feet, ignoring her, and charged the table.

He knew what the glowing ball was. The logical side of his mind tried to tell him it was nothing, a toy, but his gut knew differently and screamed at him to move. He swung the pistol at the padlock on one side of the table, smashed it free, heaved the glass-and-metal lid up with his other hand.

The berobed figure came at him around the table, a long knife in hand. Zeb didn't bother to look, just snapped a kick at the figure, felt his blow sink deep into his attacker's midsection. He heard his attacker gasp out breath and crash back into the wall.

The little sun was a handspan from the model of the checkered building. Atop the building was a curled piece of bronze metal, not apparently a part of the model. Zeb switched his gun to his left hand and swatted the sun as though it were a handball.

It burned at his palm. Sudden pain, far out of

proportion to the ball's size, made him cry out and stagger back. But the little sun flew up and out of the dio-
rama, hitting the plaster wall, burning its way into it.

Men and women in the streets of Neckerdam saw
the sun descend. Those near the Monarch and
Montgris buildings fled, some knowing that it was futile,
that death had them.

Then the sun reversed direction, took to the sky, flew
in an instant beyond the borders of Neckerdam, and
disappeared before it reached the horizon.

The figure in the robe rose. Noriko covered it with
her gun. As the robe's hood fell back, Zeb saw the
figure was Teleri Obeldon. She held her stomach and
side, obviously hurt by Zeb's kick, but there was more
than hurt on her face. There was blank, mindless fear.

She looked around as though trying to find a path
to escape. Zeb thought he heard voices, accusing
whispers in a language he could not recognize, coming from thin air around her.

"The gods' due," Noriko said. "She's done for."

Doc crowded through the hole Zeb had made in the
wall. He moved forward, wrapped his arms around
Teleri, and closed his right eye.

Staring only through his Good Eye, the eye that
saw traces of devisement and spirit-sign, Doc winced
from the brightness illuminating the room. Everything
shone with high-summer sunlight, every square finger-
measure of surface, so there were no shadows. It was
suddenly hard to gauge distance.

He could see Teleri, Zeb and Noriko, and other
things besides: wisps of glowing brightness, jointed like
arms, separating out into too-long fingers at the end.
They emerged from nothingness, from thin air. There

had to be a dozen of them, perhaps more—he couldn't see behind him. They were already present when he opened his Good Eye, but grew stronger, thicker, more numerous as he looked.

The nearest of them grabbed at Teleri. Doc lashed out with his fist, striking it. He felt no physical contact, just a jolt like electricity passing through his arm. But the glowing hand was flung away. It shook itself as a man would shake his hand after it had been shocked or stung.

"Her debt will not be paid today," Doc said. He spoke in High Cretanis, a language whose memory had mostly faded from the peoples of Western Europe, but the language by which devisements were most successfully cast and maintained. "Go away. I reject you. I evict you. I banish you."

All the arms shook and the whispering voices changed from words to laughter. Then the hands reached for Teleri again, three, four, five at once.

Doc lashed out at the nearest, hit it, flung it away. At the same moment, he shoved down on Teleri's shoulder, forcing her to collapse at his feet. That freed up his left arm, gave him room to strike. He swatted the second hand, across Teleri and into the way of the third; as he'd guessed, it rebounded from his chest, unable to harm him.

Unable for the moment. Teleri's spell had failed. Its success was to be the payment, the reward for the powers that had brought the tiny sun into being. With that payment denied, the hands were here to take her life. That being their only purpose, they could harm only her—until the mind behind them readjusted and decided to sweep Doc's life away.

So *many* hands. There should be only two. Wasn't this a solar deity? No sun-god he knew of chose to manifest so many hands at once.

He spun, kicking at hands reaching at Teleri from behind; his booted foot swept across both of them, knocking them aside. He continued the spin, his arms windmilling in a precise fashion he'd learned from Harris, one of the man's Oriental exercises, and he batted hand after hand away. With each contact Doc felt jolted, his arms growing numb, his legs growing weaker.

The voices changed in pitch, becoming annoyed, fretful. But there were too many of them. The arms moving closer, the hands striking faster. Doc picked up the pace of his own motions, striking, kicking, turning, remembering to compensate for his temporary right-side blindness; if he opened his right eye, full sight would return, but he would no longer see the arms.

There was an explosion of sound, the crackling of an electrical generator, starting up. The arms jerked as though electricity were flowing through them.

Teleri shrieked. Doc looked down, saw one of the hands grabbing her head, its fingers sinking deep into her skull. Teleri collapsed, flat on the floor, and was motionless. Then the generator noise changed pitch and all the arms faded to nothingness.

Doc opened his right eye. Gaby stood at an upright metal cabinet with glass apparatus on top. Gaby's hand was on a large knob. As Doc's attention fell on her, Gaby finished twisting the knob counterclockwise. The generator noise dropped to nothingness.

"Every time you moved," Gaby said, "as though you were reacting to something, the top of this thing was pulsing in time. I had a hunch."

"A good one," Doc said. He bent over Teleri.

She still breathed, but her breathing seemed strained. Doc reached for her left eye to open it, but both her eyes opened before he touched her.

She looked at him. "I can't feel my arms or legs," she said. Her voice, faint, was like that of a little girl.

"Let's see what we can do about that," Doc said. "Someone call for an ambulance. And call Alastair at Thown."

Teleri kept her attention on Doc. Her eyes were open a bit too wide, making her expression seem childlike, uncomprehending. "You shouldn't muddy the waters," she said. "Clean waters for health. You can't drink from muddy waters."

"What do you do with muddy waters?"

"Purify them."

"Purify them how?"

"I love you."

Doc shook his head. "Who taught you to purify the waters?"

"My father."

"Who is he?"

"I didn't want to kill you."

Doc was silent long moments, staring into Teleri's eyes. "I have to take you back to your father now, but I don't recall his address. What is it?"

"He's at—" Then she stopped for a moment and laughed. It was the laugh of a child at play, one who'd just realized she'd been tricked by a playmate and found it amusing. She continued to laugh, but tears welled from her eyes and rolled down her cheeks.

Then she closed her eyes and her head lolled as though she'd fallen instantly asleep.

Doc pressed fingers against the side of her neck, then checked her wrist for a pulse. He shook his head. He stared at her a moment longer, then rose to rejoin the associates. Harris took off his coat and laid it over Teleri.

"So that's it?" Zeb said. "She's dead, and magic did it, like they tried to do with Ish?"

Harris nodded. "Making bargains with gods is dangerous. I wish we could teach Doc that. Anyway, it's justice."

"It's not right. She ought to have been tried in court. Her sentence should have been decided on by . . . well, by something human."

"Zeb, remember," Harris said, "she's the one who dropped the bomb on the newspaper."

Doc spoke, his tone low, even pained. "Jurisprudence is a little different here. People don't presume that they have a greater right to extend justice than gods do." He sighed. "Very well. Let's get back to business."

The Novimagos Guard had come and sealed off the business, their investigators searching the office and storeroom, dealing with Teleri's hirelings—two slain, one merely unconscious. The guards brought with them the news of how the fireball falling toward the Montgris Building had vanished from the sky.

The searchers presented the associates with interesting items they found.

One was a small stuffed doll. It was dressed in hand-sewn khaki shorts and blouse, topped with a miniature safari hat and black human hair. A long pin protruded from its back. Doc, after studying it for some minutes with his Good Eye, spoke a few words over it and drew the pin from its back. Then he meticulously disassembled the thing.

Another was a set of gold-plated metal cases, some the size of shoeboxes, some the size of decks of cards, all with hinged lids. Doc tapped each a couple of times before opening them. They were gold-plated on the interiors as well. "Preservation boxes," he said. "Used by most devisers to keep substances from spoiling. These are all empty."

"It was the whole movie-voodoo thing that tipped

me off," Harris said, ignoring Doc's interruption. He
sat on a chair beside the long table in the little
room. "We knew they were using some sort of doll-
and-toenail-clippings mechanism to hurt Ixyail. Something they'd recreated from what they learned on the
grim world. And we assumed that they had a completely different new mechanism for this fireball
thing—until it occurred to me that it didn't have to
be different."

"The scrapings from the building plaques," Zeb said.
He sat with his back to the wall a couple of paces from
the body of the man Noriko had killed. His burned
right hand throbbed, though Noriko had carefully
wrapped it up in a bandage. He ignored the pain and
idly picked up Klapper bullet casings with his unhurt
hand. Hundreds of casings littered the floor. "That was
what was on top of the model of the building."

"Right. That's the hair and toenails stuff. The contagion element. And that's how I figured it out. So if
they were doing it that way, they needed the similarity element, a 'doll' of the Danaan Heights
Building . . . and a 'doll' of the other buildings they
threatened. So I realized we'd seen that doll. She'd
shown it to us."

Doc, studying the aluminum cabinet with the
chandelier-like glass cap, said, "But it can't be the
same table as the one in the museum."

"Right. I thought they had to be doing this from the
museum. I didn't figure out there was a second table
until I made a talk-box call to the craftsman who made
it, a fellow named Wenzel—Teleri mentioned his name
when we met her. Wenzel had two important things
to say: that he'd made two such tables, not one, and
that Teleri herself was the deviser who created those
cool overlays showing ley lines and underground
routes."

Zeb said, "Why'd she do it? Blow up buildings?"

"Well, that was what some of my calls were about." Harris looked chagrined. "We were moving so fast on our various investigations we didn't do all the homework we should have. I didn't, I mean. The key was Barrick Stelwright."

"The critic who left all that money to the museum."

"Right, Zeb. I just called some of the Foundation's friends who work at various newspapers and legal agencies and got some details about the disposition of Stelwright's estate. Where do you think the majority of it went?"

Zeb and the others shook their heads—all but Doc, who was studying the glass-topped cabinet with fixed and sober interest. Doc stepped into the device and looked at its ceiling.

"To the *Nationalreinigungspartei*, or Reinis, the National Purification Party—headquartered out of the city of Bardulfburg in Weseria, headed by King Aevar. Stelwright wrote columns for the Burian-language press, too, all of it very amusing support for the Reinis and their efforts at national purification."

"The Nazis," Zeb said.

"Their equivalent."

Doc leaned out of the cabinet. "Hair," he said.

Harris grinned. "Do you always start conversations that way?"

His employer sighed. "I need samples of everyone's hair. Right now."

"Right hair and now?"

"Harris."

With a pair of small scissors from the hardware shelves, they took small cuttings of each associate's hair. Doc carefully divided each cutting in two, tying it off and labeling it, arranging two complete sets of sample cuttings on two pieces of sandpaper.

Meanwhile, Doc spoke, his tone unusually subdued. "The little sun, and the larger one it summoned, was more than a destructive mechanism. It was symbolic of a sun-god or sun-goddess. I'm certain from the connection that Gaby saw detected between the actions of the arms and this box, and from residual energies remaining here, that this box is also oriented toward a solar god and utilizes his power."

Gaby asked, "What does it do?"

"I have a suspicion. That's what the hair is for."

A Novimagos Guardman appeared in the hole Zeb had made in the wall. He saluted in Doc's direction. "Sir, the hoodlum is awake."

Doc nodded absently. "Stand by with him. I'll have him brought in for questioning in a chime or less."

The guard left, and Doc continued, "It's probably significant that the *Nationalreinigungspartei*, and a lot of similar organizations scattered through both the Old and New Worlds, look to sun-gods as their patrons and mentors. As does the land of Wo."

Noriko nodded. "The godly ancestress of our royal clans *is* the sun."

Doc set one piece of sandpaper, with one small clipping of hair from each associate, inside the aluminum cabinet and shut the door. "I wonder how long I should run it . . ." He turned a sharp look on Harris. "The Sonneheim Games are dedicated to two sun-gods. Sonneheim *means* sun-home."

Harris nodded.

"I think we'll be joining the Novimagos team at the games, after all. Corporal, bring the prisoner in, would you?"

The guardsman brought in the man Doc had laid out. He was a well-muscled fellow, tall for one of the fair folk, dressed in an inexpensive red suit that was baggy in the shoulders, too broad for him. His hands

were manacled behind him. He was solemn and eyed
Doc and the others warily. He scowled at Rudi, who
shrugged.

"Your name?" Doc said.

The prisoner considered the question, then cleared
his throat and spat. The spittle landed at Doc's feet.

Doc considered that a long moment, then smiled.
It was, in fact, the cruelest and most distant expression Zeb had ever seen someone wear, and he suddenly
felt a measure of the fear common people were said
to have of the Daoine Sidhe. He shuddered involuntarily and saw Rudi doing the same.

Doc said, "You are guilty of conspiracy to commit
murder. At least thirty counts . . . depending on how
many dead are pulled from the ruins of the *Kingston
Guardian*. You'll die in the shock-chair . . . and I'll see
to it they keep the power flowing until your very soul
is burned away, so nothing of you even reaches the land
of Avlann. Guard, take him away."

The guardsman tugged at the prisoner's shoulder, but
the prisoner resisted him, his expression uneasy. "You
can't do that."

"You don't know me."

"I didn't kill anyone. I didn't know. *You can't do
this.*"

"Guard, get him out of my sight." Doc negligently
turned away.

The guard pulled more insistently. The prisoner was
halfway out the door in the wall when he cried, "I know
things you don't. I can help you." He resisted the
guardsman's pull.

Rudi grimaced. "You're a ruddy coward, Addy."

Doc sighed as if much put upon, then turned and
waved the guard away. "We'll see. If I hear one answer
I don't like, I put you on the railway to the shock-chair.
Name?"

"Adalbert Carter."

Doc frowned. "Were you once with Big Benno's gang?"

"Yes, sir."

"Why did you leave him?"

"One of my uncles in the Old Country recommended me to Goodlady Obeldon's employer. Benno didn't want me to leave him, but he got a talk-box call from the Old Country. Then he was only too happy to see me leave."

Doc considered that in silence. Zeb noticed that Harris's eyes had widened at that last statement. Obviously Big Benno was someone people didn't mess with . . . and yet someone in the Old Country had enough pull to force him to let go of a favored employee. Interesting.

Doc said, "So. Here is the question your afterlife hinges on. What do you think you know that will interest me?"

"She had orders this morning. Over the talk-box. To kill you."

Doc shrugged.

"She didn't want to. She cried. She was sweet on you."

Doc regarded him steadily, unemotionally. But Zeb saw the tightening of his shoulders. "Not relevant," he said.

"She said she already had gotten, and had sent on, what she needed from you, so the loss wasn't total. Her superiors were very pleased with the results."

"What did she mean by that?"

"I don't know. But you were her most important objective, and you had been accomplished—so she said. Killing you was just cleaning up. Her people watching the Monarch Building saw you go in and not come out, so she made her attack tonight."

The Sidhe Foundation members had driven out of the Monarch Building garage through Doc's sally-port, a tactic designed exactly to foil the sort of observers the man described. Doc said, "Who issued orders to her?"

"I don't know. They were always by talk-box. Voice only, no picture. I know that some of them were from overseas, because there was an overseas operator before the voice came on."

"Describe the voice."

"Cultured. Spoke Lower Cretanis as though he were very well-educated, but he had an accent. Burian."

"What kind of Burian?"

Carter shrugged. "Burian is Burian to me."

Doc dropped his gaze to consider that for a moment. Then he turned to the aluminum cabinet. "What does this do?"

"I don't know. She never used it when I was in the room."

"But you heard her use it?"

"Oh, yes. Daily. It made a terrible humming. It hurt her, too. Sometimes she'd come out of the room stooped, hardly able to walk, crying like she'd lost her only love. Took her a chime or more to recover."

"How long did she run it each day?"

The man stopped for a moment, calculating. "Fifteen or twenty ticks."

Doc heaved a sigh. "Very well. The Guards will take you away and you'll complete your confession to them. If I hear that you've cooperated fully—up to and beyond testifying against your fellows, when we find them—I'll take no steps to decide your fate. Find a good enough advocate and you might even come out of this alive."

At Doc's nod, the guardsman pulled the hoodlum out of the room and led him away.

They were silent a long moment. Then Zeb, his voice low, asked, "Could you do that, Doc?"

"Do what?"

"Destroy his soul. Keep him from going to heaven, or hell, or whatever it is you have around here."

Doc gave him a faint smile. "No. I wouldn't know a soul if it bit me, as Harris says. No art of the deviser has ever revealed one. But he doesn't know that. Let him think that I'm the cruel Daoine Sidhe with powers over life and death. I don't owe him the truth." He sobered. "But I need to find it myself. Let's see if my guess is correct."

He placed one of the pieces of sandpaper with hair samples on the floor of the aluminum cabinet, then closed and latched the door. There were a bare minimum of controls on the side of the machine—a knob that looked like it belonged on an egg-timer and a needle gauge under glass. Doc twisted the dial to the number 15.

As soon as he released it, pulsating light as bright as daylight shot through the glass apparatus atop the cabinet, and an ominous hum filled the room. Zeb felt his teeth vibrate, and the uncomfortable looks on the faces of the others suggested that they felt it as much as he did. His hand also began to throb with greater pain. Doc watched the proceedings with his own hand over his right eye.

A quarter of a minute later, the dial reached 0 and the humming ceased. Doc removed the sandpaper from the cabinet floor and compared it to the sandpaper with the second set of hair samples. The others closed around him.

Zeb whistled. The hair samples tagged with Doc's and Rudi's names were unaffected. Harris's and Gaby's were a noticeable shade lighter than their hair that had not gone through the process. Zeb's and Noriko's hair had not changed color . . . but little trails of smoke rose from them and the tips had gone to ash, crumbling away.

Harris asked, "What the hell is it, Doc?"

Doc pursed his lips. "Energy, power from a solar deity, was drawn to the device by that glass apparatus and focussed into the cabinet itself. In a sense, it bleached the hair."

"Just bleached it?" Harris shook his head. "Why wasn't the color of Noriko's and Zeb's hair changed?"

"Because it wasn't bleaching color. It was bleaching race, Harris. Suppressing racial elements that were at odds with light ancestry."

"Instant Aryan," Zeb said. "Just add water. I take it Noriko and I are just too far from the ideal."

Doc nodded. "Fifteen beats in that device would probably ignite either of you."

Harris asked, "Which solar deity?"

Doc rubbed tiredness from his eyes, then shook his head. "I couldn't tell. That's what is difficult. I could not recognize the characteristics of the deity, its signature. I couldn't even tell whether it was a persona or an archetype."

Zeb sighed. "Suppose you could clue in an outsider, Doc? Persona and archetype?"

"Well, it's a rather esoteric consideration," Doc said. "We don't know what the gods are, but we know some things about them. Such as the fact that gods that share similar traits seem to have odd ties to one another. Such as Astarte of the Middle East and Aphrodite of Panhellas. Both goddesses devoted to fertility and love.

"When you have a god with a name, who is associated with a people or a country," he continued, "devisers call that a *persona*. But you can also pray to a sort of amalgam god, the one who personifies the common traits but doesn't belong to a specific people, doesn't have a name or any stories associated with him. That's called the *archetype*. When you successfully structure devisements invoking the archetype, you tend to get a more profound effect. You also place yourself in greater danger if you make mistakes, when payment comes due.

"And that's what leaves me very confused. The devisement manifestations I saw a couple of chimes ago matched no solar persona I'm familiar with, nor either of the solar archetypes I've studied. It demonstrated many grasping arms, which is more characteristic of earth-gods and earth-monsters. I could feel neither a masculine nor feminine presence predominate, which is perhaps the oddest characteristic. Does this sound familiar to any of you?"

But the associates offered him only blank looks or head-shakes. Doc shrugged. "Harris, time?"

Harris looked at his wrist; he was one of the few people Zeb had seen who actually wore wristwatches, rather than carrying pocket watches, on the fair world. "Coming up on three bells. That's about nine o'clock, Zeb."

Doc raised his arms in a long stretch; Zeb heard the man pop and crack in several places. "Let's leave this hardware shoppe to the guardsmen," Doc said. "We'll sleep tonight and take to the air tomorrow. For Weseria and the Sonneheim Games."

Harris looked expectant. "On the *Frog Prince*?"

"No, one of the Valks, I think. Less distinctive, harder to track." Doc looked up at Zeb. "This will take us far from Neckerdam and could keep us there for weeks or more. I can't ask you to abandon your true life for that long."

"I think I need to come with you, Doc."

"I'm glad." Doc turned to Rudi. "Your part of this is done. You've earned the pittance I paid you."

Rudi shook his head. "Whoever it was led Albin astray from good, simple crime, whoever it was made me kill him, is where you're going. That's where *I'm* going. I'll go whether you take me or not."

"What about your brothers?"

"I don't know. I'll try to reach them tonight, but I've got no confidence I will—Albin was the details man, details like safe houses. I hope they'll just hole up so I won't have to worry about them through the rest of this." He shrugged. "That's why I have to be with you. If you run into 'em again, I'm out there in front to keep 'em out of trouble."

Chapter Twelve

The Weissfrau Valkyrie, Zeb decided, was a lot like the modern turboprops he'd flown in. It was smaller than standard passenger jets, far more subject to turbulence . . . and loud. Even when he shut his eyes and could no longer see the propellers through the small windows right and left, he could hear the engines—*feel* them, vibrating in his skin, in his bones.

He sighed and twisted so that he was lying half on his side in the reclining seat. It was a broad, comfortable seat, another sign that this was a private plane, not a commercial vehicle, and he was certain that he could sleep through this. If he could force himself to stop thinking about what happened in Neckerdam, he could make himself sleep . . .

Someone settled into the seat beside him, and he heard Ish ask, "Are you awake?"

He opened his eyes. "Reluctantly." He looked at her. She was, as usual, dressed in her safari chic, but was unusually pale, testimony to her recent collapse. Yet when the Sidhe Foundation had assembled for transportation out to the airfield, she'd joined them. Her tale of a miraculous cessation of pain coincided, timewise, with the moment Doc had removed the needle from the doll's back. She had ignored Alastair's protests that it was too soon for her to travel. A stubborn lady, Zeb decided.

"You like her." Ish's voice was decisive.

"Who?"

"You know who. Noriko."

"Sure."

"What do you intend to do about it?"

Zeb gave her his best none-of-your-business scowl, but she seemed undeterred by it. "Nothing. I intend to do nothing about it."

"Why?"

"Several reasons. The first one is she's put off by me."

"No. I think she was alarmed by your performance at the Fairwings plant. It doesn't mean she has closed the book on you."

"And second, once all this is done, I intend to return home. To the grim world. I mean, let's say she and I did get close. The fair world still isn't home to me; my life isn't here. And I couldn't exactly ask her to come back to the grim world with me; it's poison to her."

She gave him a disgusted look, one he suspected she'd practiced until she'd perfected it. "Logic like that has no place in considerations like these. If my father had been like you, I would never have been born."

"How so?"

"He was an explorer, a treasure hunter. He went everywhere in the world and brought back wealth to his family in Castilia. But then he came to the valley of the Hu'unal, my mother's people. They had little wealth, but they did have a treasure: my mother. So

he did as he always did, and took the treasure he found
back to his family."

"And?"

"And she almost died. The outer world, with its
liftships and talk-boxes and machines and noise, was
poison to her. So she went home, and he followed her."

"True love conquers all, et cetera, et cetera. Was he
ever happy there?"

"You are a cynic. But that is a fair question. My
mother said he was not happy, at first. He longed for
the life he had left behind. But the Hu'unal changed
him, and he changed the Hu'unal. He taught sanita-
tion and literature and the fighting arts of his home-
land. He taught the Hu'unal to send its smartest sons
and daughters into the outer world to learn about it,
so the people might join it some day. And he learned
that happiness was not found in gold and silver, nor
even in the smiles of worthless relatives who lived off
treasures brought back from distant places."

"That's a nice bedtime story, Ish. I think I'll sleep
now."

"So what awaits you in the grim world that will make
you happy when you return there? What is so bad
about the fair world that you have been unhappy all
the time you have been here?"

"I have now seen three unfortunate points in common between your world and mine: crooks, guns, and
matchmakers. Night-night." He closed his eyes and
settled again, trying to make himself more comfortable.
He heard Ish sigh in exasperation, then rise.

Leaving him alone. And even less likely to sleep than
before.

What *was* waiting for him in the grim world? He
had his business, a string of fighters he and his partner managed. He had his apartment. He had his family
in Atlanta. That brought a laugh, a derisive one. His

family would only accept him on his father's terms, terms that required him to acknowledge that his professional life so far was a waste of time, to acknowledge that he'd failed the family by refusing to join the family business. These were terms he was unwilling to meet.

What else? There was a succession of ex-girlfriends, all of whom he had disappointed in some vague and indefinable way, all of whom had broken off the relationships with conciliatory comments and best wishes. He had let each of them down somehow. Somehow he'd never quite understood.

What was it Karen had said, during their last dinner together? "You care so much," she'd said. "Maybe I just can't compete with that." But when he'd pressed her to clarify those words, she'd begged off, said she didn't know how. He'd gone home and, in frustration, had smashed half the furniture in his apartment— chairs, his dining table, one of his bookcases. He would have smashed the other half, too, if the police hadn't shown up and suggested that he'd better calm down. He felt his anger rise as he recalled the scene, his resentment at the way the officers apparently felt they had a right to interfere in his life, when he wasn't hurting anyone. Anyone but himself.

"Care so much." It occurred to him now, years after the breakup, that she couldn't have meant that he cared about her more than she did about him. She had to have meant that he cared about something else. Perhaps to the exclusion of caring about her? He shook his head. That didn't make sense.

He wasn't given to elaborate expressions of affection. That's not the way it was done in his family. He'd had to learn to compensate for the way he was raised. He kept birthdays and anniversaries on a calendar, with reminders two or three days ahead of each event so he'd have a present or a celebratory dinner ready on time. So other than these displays of affection, the affection genuine but the displays orchestrated carefully so they seemed spontaneous, what had Karen and the others been seeing? Been threatened by?

His anger. He tensed as his attention stopped circling around that answer and finally settled upon it.

He'd never been shy about showing when he was mad. But he'd never hit a girlfriend, never threatened to, never suggested they needed to fear him. And he was certain they didn't. He couldn't recall one hesitating to confront him, to tell him to go out and take a walk to calm down.

"Care so much." That had to be it, though. He felt things deeply, he blew up, his lovers could neither share in the emotion nor persuade him to get past it. It had to have been a wall between him and them, a wall none of them could ever put a hole in.

Someone knocked on his forehead.

"Hey." He turned and glared. It was Harris, slipping into the seat Ish had recently vacated. "What?"

"Just putting some information together." Harris sat beside him. "You interested in competing?"

"In those games?"

"That's right."

Exasperated, Zeb brought his seat back upright. "Hadn't thought about it. Isn't it way too late to be getting in on the competition? Isn't this like the Olympics?"

Harris shook his head. "Not really. The Sonneheim Games organizers basically recognize a specific set of nations. Those nations can send representative athletes to compete. Most of the team selections are announced in advance for reasons of publicity or whatever. But they don't have to be. Novimagos, the nation that Neckerdam belongs to, already has athletes there, but

Doc's in tight with the king and queen, so we're going to join its competitors and coaching staff. So we really ought to choose some events, other than the ones where Novimagos already has the maximum number allowed. Wouldn't do to be 'generic athletes.'"

"I guess not." Zeb rubbed his eyes. "Why are we going in as athletes? Is that going to fool anybody?"

"Nobody associated with the people we're looking for, no." Harris hesitated. "We're going in as athletes and coaches for a couple of reasons. First, because it will give us free run of the Sonneheim athletes' village. And second, because we'd like you to compete. You specifically."

Zeb looked at him. "Why me?"

"Because you'd be a lightning rod. This is different from the Olympics, even the Olympics of the Thirties, in a number of ways. None of the countries of the Dark Continent is a member of the Games. And you've doubtless noted that there are fewer African-type blacks in the fair New World than the grim New World. Lots fewer."

"I've noticed. You're saying I'd be one of the few black athletes to compete."

"If not the only one at these games."

"Meaning . . ." Zeb considered. "Meaning, considering the racist habits of the people we're looking for, I'd attract all the scumbags in a hundred-mile radius to root against me."

"Probably more like five hundred miles. You'd also attract a few people to root for you. In fact, if you could manage to win, at anything, it would do a lot to stand King Aevar's racial purification theories on their ear."

"Right." Then Zeb felt a chill. "Wrong. Count me out."

"What? Why?"

"You want me to be Jesse Owens."

"Something like that."

"Get a grip, Harris. Jesse Owens was one of my *heroes*. He went to the 1936 Olympics, won four gold medals—took gold in every event he entered. And he showed the whole world that the Nazis' idea of white racial superiority was so much crap."

"Right."

"Harris, Owens was a champion athlete. I'm a broken-down ex-fighter."

"I'm not broken-down and I'm not an ex-fighter, but you said the other day you could whip me. Which is it?"

"That was sheer cussedness talking."

"No, it wasn't." Harris leaned closer. "Zeb, if you're in the same kind of shape you were just a few months ago when we were still sparring, you're competitive with these people. Plus, your whole training regimen is based on modern methods and scientific knowledge. You're decades ahead of them in conditioning, in training efficiency. And, like me, you're one of the rare ones who knows something about both Eastern and Western fighting styles. You've studied boxing and *muay Thai* and escrima and God knows what."

"Mostly as a dilettante."

"But the big problem here is that you're just scared."

Zeb glared. "The hell I am."

"I know you're not scared of any beating. You're scared that you'll get out there and *not* win, and let down everyone who might be rooting for you, and that you won't change anyone's mind."

"Screw you."

"Thanks for the offer, Zeb, but I'm a married man."

Despite himself, Zeb snorted. "What are you going to compete in?"

"Nothing. To do what I need to for Doc, I can't lock

up that much of my schedule with events. I'll join one team and fail in the first round."

"Harris Greene throws his first fight."

"Something like that."

Zeb settled back and closed his eyes. The engine vibration cut through him, cut through the fear he'd denied feeling, the fear Harris had so easily identified.

When he'd fought in the real world—the grim world, he reminded himself—the people rooting for him had risked nothing more than pride in their regiment. Later, when he'd turned pro, they'd risked only a little money, a momentary disappointment. Here, more was at stake.

What had Harris said? Lightning rod. That's what they needed him for. It was more important to be a lightning rod than it was to win. And even if he didn't win, he wouldn't embarrass himself. He could do this.

He opened his eyes again. "Tell me about their fighting sports."

Harris looked thoughtful. "Well, their boxing looks kind of archaic compared to what you're used to; there's a lot of competition in the sport, but I figure you'll clean up anyway. There's also swordsmanship, a sort of rough-and-tumble fencing. There's Isperian fighting; you'd call it gladiatorial combat. With wooden weapons. Hardly anyone gets killed. There's wrestling. Sword of Wo—that's kind of like kenjutsu. Noriko plans to watch it. It's not normally at these games, but there's a sizeable contingent of Wo spectators and athletes visiting this time, so it's been put in to please them. And there's All-Out, the worst of them."

"Tell me about it."

Harris shuddered. "Nasty stuff. Two guys go into a ring and only one usually comes out conscious. They wrestle, they box, they break bones. It's an ancient Panhellene sport. Almost no rules to talk about."

"That's what I'll do, then."

"Whoa there, tiger. All-Out is likely to cause you some serious hurt."

"It seems to be the event best suited to my own style. And it won't be bad for what we're trying to accomplish to have me pounding the hell out of some of their Aryan supermen, right?"

"Right . . ." Harris sounded dubious.

Zeb gave him a smile, a hard one. "I'm likely to cause them more pain than they cause me. Sign me up, Harris." He settled back in his seat and closed his eyes.

The plane's course took it roughly north, to what would have been Nova Scotia on Earth but which the fair folk called Acadia. Zeb remembered that this was the region where Noriko held her soon-to-be-eliminated royal title. She remained in the cockpit all the while they were on the ground, not emerging to face her passengers.

Before, Zeb would have presumed it was aloofness on her part. Now, he supposed it was a wish not to face people while she was hurting. He stood, debating whether he should go forward to see how she was doing, but heard a snatch of conversation from the rear of the plane.

Doc was saying, " . . . knew it would affect her mind. She was aware that she was becoming less and less rational, and it terrified her. So why did she do it at that accelerated rate?"

Doc had to be talking about Teleri. Zeb, curious, headed back.

At the rear of the passenger compartment, chairs had been replaced by a circular table, bolted to the deck, with two semicircular benches around it serving as seating. Doc and Ish were there, poring over papers.

"Obviously, she wanted to be pure light," Ish said. "Grace, Zeb. Did you get some sleep?"

"After my stream of visitors finally went away, yes." Zeb sat beside her. "Who was going mad? Teleri?"

Doc gestured down at the papers. "Her journal and notes suggest that she'd been losing her grip on reality for some time. It's hard to tell, though, because these papers are rather difficult to decipher. Everywhere, she substituted vague references for names. For example, 'Fab' is probably the fabricator who built the bleaching cabinet, and he seems to have been important to her, but his identity and their relationship aren't evident." He shrugged. "Perhaps that's her father, whom she was so determined to protect."

"We know why she did it, even risking madness," Ish said. Her Castilian accent was almost gone again. "She wanted to be a pure light, like a Daoine Sidhe, and she wanted it for someone else. It's clear she wouldn't have risked it just for herself. So the question is not why, but who? Much as she was interested in you, Doc, it wasn't for your sake."

"How do you know that?" Zeb asked.

"All she needed to be was lighter—'better,' to her way of thinking—than any of her romantic rivals in order to be in a superior position. I was her only romantic rival, and she already was paler and weedier than I am. So it wasn't to compete with me."

"It had to be wrapped up in her desire to please her employers, then," Doc said.

Zeb shook his head. "More than just to please them. If she knew going mad was a possibility, she had to be even more frightened of the alternative. Which suggests that it was death. Maybe not just for her. Was the bleaching cabinet a production model, or a one-of-a-kind?"

Doc smiled. "A very good question. And the answer

is 'neither.' It was somewhere in between. Many of the parts appeared to come off a fabrication line—the main body of the cabinet, for instance. Others were hand-lathed or otherwise hand-tooled. This suggests a short production run, with the design incorporating standardized components for the sake of speed or simplicity."

"But it means there could be more than just a few of them out there," Zeb said. "Several dozen, maybe several hundred."

"Correct."

Ish frowned. "Not that I wanted her to, particularly, but she could have told Doc the truth, enlisted his protection."

"Yeah," Zeb said. "The fact that she didn't suggests that either she thought her employers were more powerful than Doc, or that it wasn't just her own death in question."

"We need," Doc said, "hard information about her family. But it appears that her identity was a fabrication. We can't find anyone with the Obeldon name who admits knowledge of her. We'll need to do some research." He turned toward the plane's bow. "Harris?"

Harris's head popped up from one of the forward seats. "Yes, boss?"

"What resources do we have on station in Weseria?"

"None. But the Novimagos crown apparently has a royal agent at the Games—he was actually just there to compete, but he's been put on duty and assigned to us. I made a talk-box call to ask him to get rooms for us, spending you into the poorhouse if necessary."

"Thank you. I look forward to poverty in Weseria."

"His name is Ruadan Crandunum. I don't know him."

"Nor do I, but I've heard of him. They say he's capable. What is he to compete in?"

"Officer."

"Thank you." Doc returned his attention to his papers.

Zeb said, "I wasn't aware that 'officer' was an athletic competition."

"One of the taxing ones," Doc said. "Three events in one. Riding, swordsmanship, and marksmanship, three classic benchmarks of the field officer."

"Ah."

"Did you choose an event?"

"All-Out."

Doc and Ish both looked at him. Neither spoke for a moment. Finally Doc said, "And until now I was wondering whether you were as insane as Harris."

"He'll have to catch up some before he gets to my level."

"Doc?"

Doc turned back toward Harris. "Yes?"

"One last thing, I just noticed in the newspaper: Prince Casnar is going to be there."

"Thank you." Doc noticed Zeb's curious look. "One of my half brothers, son of my father and Maeve, the Queen of Cretanis. He is the crown prince there. Always somewhat more fond of me than the rest of the family was, and another Daoine Sidhe who has some affection for the other tribes. Depending on his whim, he may be able to offer us some resources, too."

"So you're royalty, too?"

"I am an unrecognized bastard." Doc's neutral tone stripped the word of its usual negative connotations. "Royal blood doesn't always lead to royal acceptance."

Chapter Thirteen

From the air, Bardulfburg looked like a city that had grown up in the midst of a heavy forest, leaving the forest largely intact. Between stands of trees rose massive public buildings, all stone and columns and complex facades that reminded Zeb of aging city libraries. There were long banks of tenement housing, brick buildings that curved like serpents the distance of two or more city blocks. Monuments jutted into the sky, many of them statues atop high pedestals. A broad river and smaller streams cut across the scene, with arched stone bridges providing easy crossings. Bricktopped streets meandered across the city, conforming to no organizational plan Zeb could discern, crisscrossing at odd angles.

To the south, as the plane banked to descend toward the city's public airfield, Zeb could see the white circle of the Bardulfburg's coliseum, centerpiece, Harris had said, of the Sonneheim Games, surrounded by green playing fields and blockish structures that looked like antiquated college buildings. Then the plane dropped below the level of the trees surrounding the airfield and Zeb lost sight of it.

In moments they were on the ground and taxiing past hangars and other planes—mostly cargo craft, it appeared, and many of them Weissfrau Valkyries identical in form to Doc's plane. One hangar was set far back from the rest and far larger than the rest; its sliding front doors were open, and in the gloom beyond them, Zeb could see the gray curved nose of a zeppelin.

They came to rest within another hangar, its main door sliding shut behind them. Through a secondary door scaled to humans came a number of guardsmen, a dozen or so, who surrounded the plane. These men, fair of complexion and dressed in eye-hurting orange tunics and boots, glaring gold pants and gloves, carried rifles but did not seem overly intent. Zeb saw five of them out his port-side window and inferred an equal number to starboard.

"Time for bureaucracy and 'unavoidable delays,'" Doc said. He moved up to the forward port-sided door and began undogging it. "Harris, you have all the papers?"

"Yes, boss."

Zeb turned to look at Harris. "I don't exactly have papers here, do I? That's going to cause some trouble, isn't it?"

"You have papers." Harris waved a fistful of documentation at him. "Not even forged. A legal Novimagos passport. By the way, is it Zebediah or just Zeb?"

"Just Zeb."

"Hey, I got it right."

Harris was off the plane first and spent several minutes dealing with the officer in charge. Meanwhile, Doc's associates remained in the plane, stretching and readying themselves. Then Harris called the associates out.

The officer in charge directed them to a temporary table set up near the hangar entrance; there, lean, middle-aged men with the bearing of clerks disinterestedly went through their luggage while the soldiers performed a more alert examination of the airplane's cargo. Each associate was questioned by the chief officer, who spoke English, with a slight accent, on his purpose in visiting Weseria. The officer's tone was courteous when directed at Doc, Harris, and Rudi, barely civil when directed at the others.

Zeb found his attention drawn to the armband each of the soldiers wore on his upper left arm. It was black with a gold symbol on it. The symbol was a blocky, primitive eight-pointed star, formed by taking a square and then superimposing another square, turned at 45 degrees, atop it.

Gaby saw his interest. "It's the symbol of the National Purification Party, the Reinis," she whispered. "It's supposed to be a sun."

"Ah."

She lowered her voice still further. "The swastika was also a solar symbol. A pretty innocuous one until the Nazis adopted one form of it."

"This just gets better and better, doesn't it?"

The soldiers rejoined their commander, and one spoke briefly to him in what sounded to Zeb like German; the associates had referred to it as Burian. The commander gave Doc a minimal salute and said, "All is in order. Fair luck to you at the Games." Then he, his soldiers, and the customs agents departed, marching briskly out the hangar doors, the customs men carrying the folded table between them.

Harris heaved a sigh of relief. "I hate red tape."

Gaby gave him a smirk. "You love red tape. You get to show off how good you are at cutting through it.

What you hate is when the searchers get close to the hidden panel."

Zeb gave her his attention. "Hidden panel?"

"In the cargo compartment. Where we store the explosives, silly. And the extra sets of papers, extra guns, Alastair's bulletproof vest, that sort of thing."

"Of course."

The last soldier out through the door did not close it, and a moment later another man entered through it, walking briskly, a document in his hand. He looked, to Zeb's eye, like a gigantic leprechaun. Over six feet in height and burly, the man had bright red hair and was dressed in a suit and vest all in green; the illusion was complete down to a gnarled walking stick. He was clean-shaven and his expression suggested someone who had just come from a party or was looking for one. His features were handsome in a broad-faced, country-squire sort of way. "Doctor MaqqRee," he said, addressing Doc.

"I am," Doc said.

The leprechaun handed his document to Doc. "Lord Ruadan Crandunum, in the Crown's service, and now at yours. My papers. A pleasure to meet you at last."

"Not *you*," Harris said.

The others turned toward him—Alastair looking appalled at Harris's rudeness—except for Gaby, who was obviously having trouble suppressing a laugh.

Doc gave Harris a little frown. "You've met this man?"

"The first day Gaby came to the fair world," Harris said. "She and I went to a bar. He was there. I was right there with her, and he was hitting on her."

Ruadan's expression turned to one of surprise. "I have *never* hit a woman."

"It's an expression," Gaby said. She extended Ruadan her hand. "It means you were making the sort of offer no boyfriend likes to be on hand to witness."

Ruadan smiled at her. "He could have turned his back." He took her hand and bent to kiss it. He straightened and said, "I have, of course, followed your exploits in the press, Mrs. Greene."

"We're married now," Harris said. Then a look crossed his face, a realization of just how unnecessary that comment had been. "Which you know. Of course. Or else you wouldn't have called her Mrs. Greene. But we're married."

Ruadan gave him a nod that looked somehow both friendly and dismissive, as if Harris had said, "Of course we can't go swimming, we have no swimsuits." The oversized leprechaun turned back to Doc. "I have cars waiting and have secured rooms for you."

In two enormous cars, one an open-topped roadster and the other a hardtopped touring car, the Sidhe Foundation members and associates rolled through the city of Bardulfburg. They kept to the broad but winding main streets. Zeb found himself in the lead car with Doc, Gaby, Harris, and Ixyail, Ruadan driving, while Noriko drove Alastair, Rudi, and the majority of the group's baggage.

"Your quarters have a good view of the coliseum," Ruadan said. He had to half-shout to be heard over the noise of wind and traffic. "The former apartments of a Bardulfburg banker. He was largely forced out of business here because he was a dusky. There's a Weserian minister waiting to take over his apartments, which are choice, and he's scared off most of the parties who'd like to rent them. But the banker sold his lease to me, for your Foundation, just to spite the minister, so the minister won't be getting them for another couple of moons."

"Charitable of him," Doc said.

At street level, Zeb decided, the buildings of the city

were even more monumental than he'd guessed from the air. They rose, towering blocks of dressed stone and archaic-looking columns, like pagan temples—but the shine off the polished stones, the crisp lines of their steps and corners, demonstrated that much of this was new construction. A significant number of the cars on the street, most of them a gleaming green so dark as to be almost black, were also new. This was obviously a nation in the grip of prosperity.

Everywhere they drove he saw paintings on building walls. Many exalted the common worker—a laborer, smiling, wielding a shovel, or an assembly-line worker wiping sweat from his brow and smiling as he gazed off into the future. Others showed soldiers like the ones he'd seen and a different sort dressed all in black. Many featured athletes in various events, especially hurdles, javelin throw and horsemanship. Zeb thought the style of illustration to be primitive and cartoony, but it seemed a good match for the overblown architecture of this city.

The streets were decorated with banners, some run up on flagpoles, others hanging from angled poles projecting from building faces. About half were the gold-on-black Reini symbol; most of the rest showed a more elaborate design—a rearing, winged black bull squared off with an upright gold eagle in natural colors, a gold sword point-up between them, all on a white field.

Doc, in the front seat with Ruadan, noticed Zeb's attention. "That's the family crest of King Aevar's family, and, while a family member rules here, the national symbol of Weseria."

"Two sky-god symbols," Gaby said. "And the bull is an invocation to fertility, which you see a *lot* with these inbred European ruling families, starting centuries ago."

"Your understanding of fairworld heraldry is

improving," Doc told her. He turned back to Ruadan. "What else has been set up?"

"All the athletes also have quarters in the Sonneheim Athletes' Village," the leprechaun said. "Generally four to a cottage, a little cottage. They're not required to stay there, but most of the athletes aren't as lavishly funded as you lot, so the majority of athletes will be in their Village quarters. Those of you who register as athletes or coaches will have quarters there, too."

They turned onto a six-lane avenue thick with traffic. Unlike the other streets, where flags and banners were to be found once or twice a city block, here there were flagpoles every fifty yards or so, alternating between the Reini symbol and the ruling family's crest. "The Aevarstrasse," Ruadan said. "One of the king's big building projects these last few years. He wants visitors to Bardulfburg to come away impressed."

"It *is* impressive," Zeb said. "Where's he getting all the money for these civic improvements?"

"His father, the former king, was a bit of a puppet to a council of noble advisors," Ruadan said. "A very corrupt council. Three years ago, when the Reinis staged their coup and put Aevar on the throne, his first act was to disband the council, his second was to suppress the new coup they tried to stage, and his third was to seize all their properties. Since then he's been seizing properties right and left—especially from corrupt politicians and well-to-do duskies of the middle class—and he's been putting a lot of that revenue into improvements. And there have been occasional conquests of surrounding petty kingdoms. And a renewed spirit of patriotism and work ethic among the people. And a certain amount of cheating."

Doc raised a brow. "Cheating, how?"

"Defying the Burn Accord."

"Ah. Pity." Doc shook his head.

"Now you've lost me," Zeb said.

"It's an old agreement between nations," Doc said. "From a couple of centuries ago. The signatories agreed to form a board restricting the amount of coal, oil, and other such fuel sources they burned on an annual basis. Violators tend to suffer trade penalties when they violate it. But it's a standard trick among nations with poor economies to give themselves a bit of help by ignoring their Burn Accord restrictions."

"Not that Aevar would let you see it in Bardulfburg," Ruadan said. "No, this is his showplace city. No coal or oil burned here except by the trains. Otherwise there would be gray air here, too, like in many of Weseria's cities. And the Accord nations are taking their time about punishing him—they'd like to see Weseria become a strong trade nation again. Anyway, all those things Aevar has done have added up to the Bardulfburg you see."

The bank of imposing buildings continued along the right side of the Aevarstrasse, but ended to the left, giving way to a green lawn the width of a city block and a deep belt of forest beyond. In the distance, above the tops of the trees, rose the city's coliseum, styled, Zeb thought, in the fashion of the old Roman constructions, but shining white and new. Beyond it, half a mile or a mile in the distance to the west, rose a building just as magnificent—a gleaming white dome atop a circle of columns. Zeb couldn't even begin to estimate the size of the thing; at that distance, he couldn't make out any human-scale figures for comparison.

Ruadan saw his look. "The Temple of the Suns," he said. "Dedicated to the Games' godly patrons. It's another new building project. It will be dedicated tonight."

Ahead, where a statue of a horseman stood atop a ten-story-tall pedestal, Ruadan turned left onto another major street, which he called the Meinbertstrasse. Here, too, the right side of the street was lined with buildings, while the left alternated between forest and fields, many of which were lined or partitioned off into what had to be athletic fields. Eventually they had a clear view of the coliseum, with only fields and what had to be parking lots between, and it was there that Ruadan pulled over and parked, beside a round-cornered building of deep red bricks limned with fading green mortar.

Ruadan pointed up to a second-story balcony. "Your quarters," he said. "Good view, eh?"

The quarters were as appealing inside as out. They consisted of four large bedrooms, two ample common rooms, a library whose shelves stood empty, a decent-sized kitchen with a gas stove, and a single spacious bathroom with fixtures that were, to Zeb's eye, antiquated but charming, including a bathtub whose feet looked like reptilian claws. The single jarring note was the furniture, which looked well-used, with pieces largely not coordinated with one another—one bed was an aging four-poster, another a sled-style with scratches all over the headboard.

Ruadan shrugged, an unconcerned apology. "The owner took his possessions. I had a used-furniture dealer send over these furnishings. I'm afraid it was all I had time for."

"It's more than sufficient," Doc said. "Alastair, we'll need to set up temporary wards over all entrances, pipes, and ducts. Harris, find out who you need to offer some money to so we'll be notified if there have been any other last-minute changes in the occupation of this building. Ruadan, what's the schedule of events for the games?"

The leprechaun gestured to a table; on it was a stack of what looked like identical magazines, the covers of the same rough pulp as the interiors and decorated with a lean white-haired youth in running shorts, in the same artistic style as the illustrations Zeb had seen all over walls in the city.

"That's the official schedule, Lower Cretanis edition," Ruadan said. "The opening ceremonies were this morning at the coliseum, followed by early-round matches in some of the events, especially track and field, swimming and rowing. Tonight, in a little over a bell, actually, is the Parade of the Suns."

"Which is what, exactly?" Doc asked.

Ruadan smiled. "Oh, I shouldn't spoil it by describing it to you."

Shortly after nightfall, they joined the pedestrian traffic growing thicker on the street beneath their balcony and walked to the Aevarstrasse. There, the crowds gathered on either side of the street, packing in ever more densely to await the Parade of the Suns.

There were pockets where they did not press too close, such as around Zeb. He smiled, his amusement at the situation wavering between contempt for them and self-deprecation, as these white, white people rooted themselves in place so as not to be shoved into contact with him. They energetically kept their attention on the street so they would not have to acknowledge him. Zeb suspected that they didn't even notice that Noriko was a dusky with him around.

"Harris," Zeb said.

"Yeah?"

"In German, how do you say, 'You are wonderful, I would be happy to marry your daughter.'?"

"Here it's Burian, not German," Harris said. "And I don't speak it."

Doc smiled. "'*Sie sind wunderbar, ich würde gerne Ihre Tochter heiraten.*'"

"Thanks, Doc. You're a sport." Zeb practiced the phrase, just in case he actually felt like using it at some point.

Within a few moments, the space around Zeb was filled by celebrants who apparently did not mind his duskiness; some turned curious looks to him as he repeated the phrase Doc had taught him.

"Here they come," said Ruadan. He stared northward up the street.

Zeb followed suit. In the distance, he could see lights that swayed and bobbed as though they were being carried. The crowd quieted and Zeb could finally hear the sharp taps of distant military drums, the notes of trumpets. As yet they had not resolved themselves into music.

As the lights grew closer, Zeb saw that they were indeed being carried—they were, in fact, atop poles, shining fifteen or so feet above the street, brightly glowing balls that gave off sparks like the sparklers Zeb used to buy for the Fourth of July, but much larger; each ball had to be the size of a basketball at least. The men carrying them were dressed in black, bulky robes whose hoods concealed their faces, whose folds concealed their builds; their gloves were black as well. Even the poles the glowing balls rode atop were black, so the balls floated like miniature suns above the street. The sparks they gave off extinguished when they fell upon their bearers' robes; other sparks fell into the street and glowed awhile before perishing, and still more were spat out into the crowd, where onlookers patted or stamped them out.

Six of the pole handlers walked abreast, and there were six ranks of them, so 36 balls of fire floated along the Aevarstrasse. Zeb was reminded, and made uncomfortable by, the resemblance between these fiery decorations and the little ball he had swatted back in

Neckerdam. His burned hand throbbed, perhaps out of sympathy.

Behind the pole bearers came the marching band, a drum and bugle corps playing a military march that sounded, to Zeb's untrained ear, decidedly old-world. The members of the band wore the same uniform he'd seen earlier in the day, orange and gold with the gold-on-black armband of the Reinis.

A commotion, including raised voices and breaking glass, from further back in the crowd distracted Zeb and he turned away from the parade to look, as did several of the people around him. Several ranks back, two young men in dark suits faced a semicircle of soldiers in orange and gold. One of the men in suits held a bottle; its liquid contents looked black in the dim light. He shook it under the nose of one of the soldiers, shouting in Burian. His companion raised his fists into a boxing pose and suddenly all six soldiers drew truncheons and began to swing at the two men; Zeb could hear the sounds of the blows even over the crowd noise.

He stepped toward the fight, unsure whether he could reach it through the press of onlookers before him, but felt a hand grip him around the arm. He turned back; it was Doc who held him. Doc shook his head, his expression somber.

"What's that all about?" Zeb asked.

"I couldn't hear it all," Doc said. "The two men apparently wanted to cause some trouble, to throw bottles into the parade."

Zeb looked back at the altercation. It was done now; the soldiers were leaving, and the bent posture of two of them suggested they were dragging the unconscious forms of the troublemakers. "What was in the bottles?"

"Blood, I think. One of them shouted, 'This is the blood of those he's betrayed.'" Doc shrugged. "Support of the Reinis is not universal, Zeb. They're in charge . . . but not all the Burians accept King Aevar's placing of blame on duskies or foreign governments as he would like them to."

Zeb took several deep breaths to calm himself. Doc might be right; it might have done no good to get involved. But the sight of those soldiers swinging truncheons at two unarmed men lingered with him.

The noise of the crowd, a murmur of anticipation, rose as the musicians passed, and Zeb turned back to see. A moment later, the next attraction in the parade came into view.

It was a car, a massive black touring car, open-topped, that looked as though it could probably seat four wide-hipped men in both the front seat and the back.

A black pole, canted forward at about a 45-degree angle, rose from the floorboard of the rear seat; its tip wobbled fifteen feet above the street, five or six feet ahead of the hood, and from it was suspended a circle of gold. Zeb gave the circle a closer look and decided that it was fashioned like a laurel wreath, too large for any man's head, but with leaves all of shining gold.

There were only two people in the car. One was the driver in black leather livery and cap; he was at the wheel. The other was in the back seat, on the left side, sitting atop the seat. He was, other than Doc, the whitest man Zeb had ever seen, his skin in the streetlights almost glowing in its paleness, his hair white as fine paper. He had a mustache and full beard but did not look old; his skin seemed unlined and his motions, as he energetically waved toward the crowds on either side of the parade path, were those of a younger man.

His garments were much like the uniforms of his soldiers, but the portions that would have been orange ranged closer to brown, and the ones that would have been gold were a deeper, darker hue of that color; his military tunic featured a double row of buttons. As with his men, he wore the Reini sun on a black armband.

His car pulled a flatbed trailer. On it were two statues, one before the other, each nine or ten feet tall, rocking a bit with the trailer's motions despite the way they were roped into place; the trailer had small spotlights, strategically mounted at the corners, to illuminate them. The foremost statue was of a woman, hardy of build, more like a grimworld woman than the lean, sharp-featured females Zeb was growing accustomed to on the fair world; she wore a long tunic belted at the waist, pants, high boots, elbow-length gloves, and a tight-fitting hood with a pointed extension drooping from the back of her head, and carried some sort of long riding crop. She shone as though she were made of solid gold, though Zeb suspected, given her size, that the statue was simply covered with gold plate or gold leaf.

The male figure wore nothing but sandals and a plaited kilt. His features bore the lean aspect of the people of the fair world; his expression was hard and critical. He, too, was gold.

And then they were past. Next were ranks of soldiers clad in orange and gold.

"What's the deal with the statues?" Zeb asked. The crowd noise had risen, so he practically had to shout to make himself heard.

Ruadan raised his own voice. "The female is Sol. She is beloved of the northwestern branches of the Burian people."

"Think Scandinavia, Zeb," Gaby said.

"The male is Sollinvictus. Adopted by the southeastern Burians during ancient times, when they struggled against and traded with the Isperians."

"Germans and Romans, respectively," Gaby explained.

Ruadan's expression suggested that he thought Gaby's amendments were unnecessary. "They're both gods of the sun. Now, the individual athletes competing here win wreaths in gold, silver, and bronze for events. But whichever group of Burian athletes, northwestern or southeastern, wins the most medals, determines which statue wears that gold wreath for the next four years. At the last Sonneheim Games, Sol won; she's worn the wreath for four years, and she gets to ride in front in the parade, as you see."

"But the local boys back Sollinvictus," Zeb said.

"That's right. Anyway, they're going to be installed at the temple at tonight's dedication."

The crowd's cheering increased, and next came rank after rank of young men and women dressed, despite the chill air, in shorts and light tops of gold, each with the Weserian royal crest on the chest. Their marching was not as precise as that of the soldiers, but was credible. They smiled, obviously happy to be doing what they were doing, but glanced neither right nor left.

Athletes in lockstep. Zeb felt his stomach sour a little; he much preferred the unstructured athlete processions he was used to from the grimworld Olympics, seeing the competitors having a good time, waving to their fans. This was too political, too regimented. He wasn't comfortable with happy athletes in support of a government that might just be this world's Nazi regime. He glanced at Harris, who had actually competed in tae kwon do at two Olympics, but Harris, deep in conversation with Doc, gave no clue as to how he felt.

Behind the athletes came more ranks of soldiers, these in a different uniform—mostly black, boots and belts gleaming, little Reini suns gleaming gold on their shoulders. Zeb felt a chill. Except for the sun symbol and a few minor details, these could be German S.S.

"*Sonnenkrieger*," said Gaby. "Soldiers of the Sun. Weseria's elite shock troops."

"Why am I not surprised?" Zeb asked.

Finally, another six-by-six formation of robed men with sputtering miniature suns atop the poles they carried brought up the rear of the procession. Onlookers stepped into the street in their wake, following, some at the parade's brisk pace, others at a more sedate rate. Doc's group followed suit.

Zeb shook his head. "Let me see if I've got this straight, Doc. Sol and Sollinvictus are what you call personas. Put them together, or rather calculate which parts they and the other sun-gods have in common, and you get an archetype, something that doesn't really represent Burians or any other group and is a lot more powerful, potentially. Is that it?"

Doc nodded. "That's sort of simplified, but that's essentially it."

"So do these gods, the personas, actually dislike duskies?"

Doc shrugged. "The priests of these southeastern Burians say yes. Priests elsewhere say no."

"I take it that means the gods aren't talking."

"Only through their priests, Zeb."

"Typical."

Doc smiled. "You'd prefer it otherwise? You'd enjoy daily talk-box broadcasts from the gods?"

"Come to think of it, not really."

The crowd in the parade's wake grew thicker. Some portions of it split off from pursuit of the parade and streamed off down side streets. The parade continued southward, but once they were south of the coliseum, Ruadan led the associates westward.

Ahead, on this broad avenue, was the Temple of the Suns. Its face was illuminated by spotlights, and other such lights sent beckoning beams swinging through the sky.

As they neared it, Zeb finally got an idea of its size. The building was flanked on all four sides by sets of stone stairs that ran nearly the length of the city block; they rose to a height of thirty feet, so the temple itself was essentially built on an artificial hill. Though the hill was square, the temple itself was circular, bounded by white stone columns that were themselves forty feet in height, supporting a tremendous white dome of a roof.

Behind the curtain of columns was the wall of the temple, except on the eastern face; visitors arriving from the east could walk into a deep channel that led to the temple's heart. The interior was dark.

The crowd around the temple was already substantial, thickest on the east side, as Doc and the associates arrived; the associates were able to make themselves a place at street-side, up against wooden barricades erected and protected by soldiers of the Weserian army.

Within minutes, the parade, or what was left of it, arrived from the south—Zeb heard the distant music of the marching band, but a block or so away, most of the elements of the parade disengaged and marched away. Only the sun bearers to the front, a unit of Sonnenkrieger, the king's car and the flatbed with the statues, and the final sun bearers arrived to halt in front of the temple. The king quit his car with grace, waving to admirers in the crowd, and slowly walked, alone, up the steps. Meanwhile, Sonnenkrieger detached the ropes holding the sun statues upright and carefully lowered them. A detachment of twenty of the soldiers was in place to carry each of the statues up the steps.

Once the statues were moving, the sun bearers began to ascend the steps and the king's car and flatbed drove away.

At the top of the steps, the king came to a stop beside a microphone mounted atop a stand; the microphone was almost the diameter of a dinner plate. He tapped it a couple of times and looked reassured by the booming thumps that echoed across the crowd. He smiled and began speaking in Burian. His voice was rich, deeper than Zeb would have guessed for a man as lean as he was.

Doc translated. "'People of Weseria, and noble visitors from across the world, I, Aevar of House Losalbar, welcome you on this occasion of favorable auspices.'"

"Maybe," Harris said, "you could synopsize instead."

Doc gave him an admonishing look.

Harris shrugged. "Speeches age me at an unnatural rate."

"A shame they don't mature you at the same schedule," Doc said. He listened for a few moments. "'In choosing to build a single temple in honor of gods of different nations, the Weserian people affirm their ancient commitment to fostering cooperation and friendship between all the Burian nations.' I think you're right, Harris. I begin to feel my own life slipping away."

"See? See?"

Zeb shook his head, disbelieving. "I can't believe he's just standing out in the open like that. What if someone took a shot at him?"

"Odds are it would fail," Doc said. "He's a knowledgeable and powerful ruler. He doesn't have a court deviser on record, but he'll have invested in the services of one or more. He probably carries with him a number of blessings to turn the hands of enemies aimed at him. Such devisements wouldn't endure long once utilized . . . but it would be long enough for him to get to cover."

"Oh. A sort of magical bulletproof vest."

Doc sighed. "There you speak that word again." Then he looked startled and turned back to the king. "I don't believe it. He's already summing up."

The statues had by now reached the king and the Sonnenkrieger were carrying them the final few yards to the temple columns flanking the main entrance. As the king finished up his speech, the soldiers, with use of golden ropes, raised the two statues, that of Sol against the column on the north side, that of Sollinvictus against the column to the south, and began positioning them more precisely.

"Hereby dedicate this temple, honor of the gods, honor of the Games, honor of the Burian people, and so on, and so on. And so we ignite the Flame of the Suns, which will burn eternally in their honor and the honor of the people." Doc said. As he spoke the final word, the king stepped back, beaming, and the crowd erupted in a roar of applause. In the depths of the temple, a glow rose, then became a bright, flickering source of light.

The soldiers pulled the barricades aside so they guided, rather than impeded, the flow of traffic, and the crowd surged forward to ascend the steps. Doc stayed in place, and his associates grouped around him; the crowd flowed around them.

Ruadan gestured up at the main temple entrance. "Care to see? The murals on the main chamber's walls are lovely."

Doc shook his head. "Some other time, perhaps. We have other—"

"Noriko-chan!"

The voice came from the sidewalk behind them. Zeb

and the others turned to look, Noriko on tiptoe so she could see over the shoulders of Zeb and Harris.

Moving toward them, at an angle to the heavy pedestrian traffic, was a group of five men, all in nearly identical bronze-colored business suits. They looked, to Zeb's eye, Japanese, though on the thin and elfin side. With a quick apology, Noriko pressed forward between Zeb and Harris to meet them.

When they reached her, the foremost of them, a slight smile on his face, spoke, a quick spate of Japanese.

The speaker was slightly taller than the other four, his close-cut hair immaculate, his features aristocratic, the leanness of his face suggesting not weakness but the keenness of a blade.

"Please," Noriko said, "perhaps we could continue in Cretanis. I am among friends who do not speak the language of Wo." She wore an impenetrable smile and had pitched her voice higher than normal; that, and her cadence, suggested the speech of a young girl rather than a grown woman.

The speaker hesitated, then offered a gracious smile to Noriko's companions. "Of course," he said, his speech very little accented with his native language. "One reads so much of the Sidhe Foundation's superhuman exploits one forgets they cannot be masters of *all* languages and skills."

Noriko said, "Doctor Desmond MaqqRee, I present Hayato, prince of Sakura province."

Hayato did not react, but Zeb saw his four companions stiffen, two of them barely perceptibly; the posture of a third tightened noticeably and he paled. That one stared at Noriko, anger or hatred visible in his eyes, though his face remained expressionless. Hayato, for his part, merely offered Doc a nod, which Doc returned.

Hayato returned his attention to Noriko. "As I was saying, I am pleased beyond words to see you here, and I look forward immensely to your participation in the competition."

"I am afraid that I am not here to compete," she said.

"How disappointing, Noriko-chan," he said. His tone became a bit more flat. "One would think you would consider it your responsibility to represent your art even when living away from home. So nothing has changed? You have abandoned all your responsibilities, all your honor, forever?"

"Nothing has changed with you." Noriko's tone had become even more artificially sweet. "You still do not show enough intelligence to dispute bad decisions and support good ones."

One of Hayato's companions, the one opposite Zeb, reacted, drawing his hand back to slap Noriko. Zeb felt a familiar adrenaline rush, felt the sensation of unreality as time begin to dilate just a bit.

Zeb got his hand up, intercepting the blow with a hard block that had to have numbed the man to the bone, and stepped forward in a knee strike that caught the man in the left of his chest. Zeb thought he felt ribs crack. The man went down hard on the bricktop street.

Zeb dropped back, hands high, ready for retaliation, but the situation was already under control. The man on Hayato's other side, who had been opposite Harris, was now a step back, bent over, struggling to breathe, his face turning red. And Hayato stood taller than before, Rudi directly before him, one of Rudi's automatic pistols pressed up into his nose. The other two men of Wo were frozen in place, prevented from acting by the danger their leader faced. Ruadan, on the other side of Doc's party, had turned his back to the situation—acting as rear guard, Zeb supposed. There were noises of alarm from the pedestrians around them; a gap widened between the surrounding pedestrians and the standoff. But the soldiers who had manned the barricades were gone; no one moved to interfere.

"Don't be ridiculous," Hayato said, his attention on Doc rather than Rudi. "Your very actions suppose I support my companion's reaction. Instead, I must apologize on his behalf. His rudeness is inexcusable." He turned his head, moving his nostril off Rudi's barrel, to glare down at his fallen companion.

That man was coughing and couldn't seem to stop. And suddenly there was blood on his lips.

"Looks like I put a rib into his lung," Zeb said, affecting unconcern, trying not to show that he was working to slow his breathing. "You'd better get him to a doctor."

"Of course," Hayato said. He continued to ignore Rudi; he gestured at one of the companions behind to help the fallen man to his feet. "Noriko," he said, his voice gentle, "your parents would be very disappointed in you if they knew you were afraid to face me. Even with wooden swords." He offered her the most minimal nod, all he could manage without coming into contact with Rudi's gun again, and turned his back on them. He and his companions moved away into the crowd.

"Should I pop him, Doc?" Rudi asked, his tone low enough not to carry far.

"No," Doc said. He turned back to their original direction. "You have a fast draw and fine combat instincts, Rudi, but shooting foreign princes in the back is never a good idea."

Rudi returned his pistol to his shoulder holster. "I'd have shot him in the head, not the back. What do you take me for?" He fell in step with the others. "So, am I wrong, or was he being rude in spite of all his sweet tones?"

"Very rude," Harris said. "Condescending."

"I don't get it, though," Zeb said. "Noriko, you really hit him with a zinger, but I missed it. Not the thing about his decisions. Earlier than that."

"She presented Hayato to me, rather than the other way around," Doc said. "Implying that I am of higher rank. Since I'm an unrecognized prince and a bastard, she was suggesting that Hayato was lower than that in the social order. Very telling."

"I apologize," Noriko said. Her tone was subdued. "I used your situation, without asking first. It was inexcusable of me."

Doc offered her a reassuring smile. "Not at all. I was amused. It was quite deftly done. Feel free to do so again."

"You obviously knew this Hayato," Zeb said.

Noriko nodded. "He is a distant cousin. I trained in sword against him from when I was very young. He offered me no respect then and offers me none now. He wants to fight me again just to demonstrate that I am not his equal."

"Will you be fighting him, then?" Rudi asked.

Noriko shook her head. "It would not further our goals." But despite the common sense in her words, she sounded diminished somehow.

Chapter Fourteen

In the morning, Doc's associates separated into small groups to accomplish separate tasks.

Ruadan did not join them at all; the first riding portion of his Officer event was scheduled for today, and he would be spending most of the day at the riding ranges near Sonneheim Village.

Zeb and Harris had to report at competition headquarters, a building near the coliseum, to arrange for their participation in the All-Out. Gaby, though not apparently looking forward to it, decided to watch them in the first-round fight, and Noriko decided to accompany her.

Alastair, Rudi, Doc, and Ixyail chose to watch the coliseum's events while plotting out their own courses of action.

After a protracted and needlessly complicated sign-up procedure in one of the buildings near the coliseum—the whole affair made more difficult, Zeb could tell, by the Weserian officials' distaste at the thought of a dusky competing among them—Zeb and Harris had their Sonneheim Games identification papers and a schedule of times and places to be. On a hunch, Harris compared his typed schedule with Zeb's, then with another athlete competing in the All-Out, and discovered discrepancies between the schedules; if he and Zeb had followed the schedule as given to them, they would have shown up late to the first event and would have been disqualified. As it was, they barely had time to change into their shorts and tank tops, in the royal blue with gold stripes of Novimagos, and to trot over to the grassy field east of the coliseum before the start.

The grassy field was chalked off in ten-foot-by-ten-foot squares, a twenty-by-twenty grid yielding four hundred squares. The grass was still intact; Zeb guessed from its pristine state that this was the first event to be held on this field.

As they approached, they saw that event organizers, dressed in distinctive blood-red garments like sweat suits, were addressing the athletes through megaphones. Their words were in Burian, but most of the athletes appeared to understand; they spread out across the field, one athlete in the center of each square. It looked as though about half the squares would be filled. A crowd of onlookers, perhaps twice the number of athletes, was lined up along one edge of the field; Zeb couldn't spot Gaby there, but from the way Harris waved, it appeared that he'd found her.

Zeb and Harris handed their pertinent papers off to a referee in red, then obligingly took up position in adjacent squares on the western edge of the athletes. More athletes settled into squares around them. The instructions continued for some time.

"I think," Zeb said, "we'd have a better chance of succeeding if we knew what the hell they were saying."

"Blows to the balls are permitted," said a nearby athlete, "but biting them is not." He was just under Zeb's height, and strongly built, though with a noticeable potbelly. He had hair the color and apparent flexibility of recently-made copper wire and his skin was decorated with an abundance of freckles. He wore shorts and a short-sleeved knit shirt in green with red trim; on his shoulders were red emblems, silhouettes of gnarled, twisted men. "No biting anywhere. No eyegouging." His accent was unfamiliar to Zeb; it sounded part English, part French, part something else.

"Thanks," Harris said.

"You are welcome." The man moved over to shake hands with Harris and Zeb, though he stayed well within the confines of his square. He did not react visibly to Zeb's color. "Domitien Rath of Bolgia."

Zeb introduced himself and Harris.

Domitien continued his translation. "Referees will move among the athletes with hammers. When they see a violation of one of the rules, they will hit the athlete with the hammer. This tends to disqualify the athlete. Hitting a referee disqualifies the athlete. At a certain point, the whistle will blow. Look for the red flag waving. Run to the man next to the flag-waver. The first sixteen who reach him will get numbers. Actually, a few more than sixteen will get numbers, to allow for those who are disqualified but still conscious and those who die."

Zeb smiled. In a low voice, he told Harris, "This really sucks."

"Told you."

"What if a referee decides to disqualify me before I can besmirch one of his beloved local supermen?"

Harris shrugged. "Most of the refs are supposed to be above concerns like that. Priests of gods representing competitions, and all that. If we get one that isn't, well, improvise."

"Great." Zeb took a look at the competitors all around him. Many were very tall and strongly built by the standards of the fair world; he suspected that a large amount of the grimworld blood that was said to be mixed with fairworld blood was concentrated in these athletes. Most were thick-chested and well-muscled, though their musculatures were those of athletes, not body builders.

"A lot of 'em look like wrestlers," Harris said.

"Most of us are," Domitien said. "I am." He pointed to one unusually tall competitor, a bald man with a walrus mustache. "Champion of the national two years ago, and of other games in years past. One of two leading Weserian contenders. The champion of the last games died on the field, of course."

"Of course," Harris said.

Zeb shook his head, unhappy. "I hate grappling. Give me a punching contest any day."

"Almost time for the first whistle," Domitien said. "Grace and luck on you."

"And on you," Harris said.

The whistle blew. A roar of voices rose, shouts from the athletes meant to intimidate one another and shouts of appreciation from the crowd. Domitien advanced on Harris, all cheerfulness gone from his face, his stance low and arms spread wide.

No one came at Zeb from that direction. He turned. A pale man, huge, with white teeth surrounded by a thick brown beard and mustache, rushed at him with arms outstretched.

Zeb got an arm up and swept the arms aside; the man slammed into him, knocking him back, but Zeb kept his balance.

As Brown Beard came on again, Zeb dropped, keeping his weight balanced on his hands and one leg, and swept with the other leg, kicking his attacker's legs

out from under him. Brown Beard grunted as he hit
the grass and Zeb brought his sweeping leg back,
kicking him square in the nose. It was a hard blow and
rocked Brown Beard's head back, but the man simply
rolled backward and over his shoulder, coming up on
his feet, his nose streaming red.

Zeb was on his feet before his opponent. He
advanced, but a red-clad tackler in full flight hit Brown
Beard around the waist and carried him down.

Zeb spun—just in time for the bald competitor with
the walrus mustache to grab him in a bear hug, pinning his arms. Walrus Mustache grinned at him and
tightened his grip, squeezing Zeb's breath out.

Zeb brought his knee up, slamming it into Walrus
Mustache's side just below and up into his rib cage.
The *muay Thai* maneuver caught Walrus Mustache by
surprise, expelling his breath in a pained grunt, causing his eyes to widen. Zeb managed another knee-strike
to the same spot, then Walrus Mustache bent him over
backwards and fell on him.

Zeb used the impact to advantage, shoving upward
at the precise moment he hit the ground, and broke
his opponent's grip on him. This left Walrus Mustache
and his formidable weight still on top, but Zeb's arms
were free. He heaved his opponent's chest up, then let
go and swung his elbow into place, putting its point
right into the center of Walrus Mustache's chest as the
man's weight descended again.

Walrus Mustache coughed out a double lungful of
air and turned red. He began to stand, an impressive
demonstration of his durability, but he was slower now.
Zeb rolled him off and stood, backing away.

All over the field, men were already down. Some
were locked in painful-looking wrestling matches; a few
just lay still. There were also standing competitors,
some advancing on one another, others looking for new

opponents. Among the competitors wandered a handful of red-garbed referees carrying large wooden-headed mallets. As Zeb watched, one swung his mallet against the back of a competitor who was biting his pinned foe. The biter arched backward, then went limp.

Harris was on his feet; his right cheek was split, bleeding. Domitien was swaying on his feet a step away. Harris grabbed, fast and sure, and got his hand on Domitien's nose. Harris squeezed, said "Honk!"

There was a blur of motion and Walrus Mustache went away. Zeb tracked him for a moment, saw that a tremendously overweight competitor in red had tackled him. Zeb returned his attention to Harris. Domitien was now down, limp, and Harris was advancing on Zeb, mock menacingly. "We haven't sparred lately," Harris said.

Zeb snorted. "Try to make it look good." He brought his hands up in boxing posture and jabbed left-handed.

Harris caught the blow across crossed wrists, an x-block, and snapped a toe-kick at him. Zeb twisted and it merely grazed his hip. There was no real force behind it; had it caught him dead-on, it wouldn't have hurt much.

Right-handed, Zeb swept Harris's blocking arms up, then jabbed again with his left before Harris could get another block in position. The punch caught Harris in the upper left chest, but it, too, was a sparring shot, struck with only a fraction of Zeb's strength.

"Incoming," Harris said, "straight back."

Zeb spun and kicked out. His kick caught an onrushing competitor right in the gut. The man, a burly blond wearing eye-hurting purple and green, grunted and folded over. Zeb followed through with another spinning kick which caught the man in the jaw; Zeb heard a crack, felt the impact jar his leg, saw his attacker hit the ground hard and go limp.

Off to his left, Walrus Mustache was up again, now locked with and straining against his tackler. His opponent had to be the fairworld version of a sumo wrestler—Oriental, not as massive as a grimworld sumo wrestler but still heavy by local standards. The Oriental managed to overbear Walrus Mustache and throw him to the ground.

Harris grunted. Zeb turned to see him in the grip of a lean man with olive skin and dark hair; his attacker had grabbed him from behind, his arms under Harris's, and was struggling to get him into a full nelson, trying to get his hands locked behind Harris's neck.

Another competitor, a well-built blond man in the gold athletic uniform of Weseria, advanced on them. Zeb didn't know which of the three of them was his target, but he stepped around in front of Harris and the man who'd grabbed him.

The Weserian stopped short of Zeb and wiped his palms on his shorts. A few inches shorter than Zeb, he had handsome, rather bland features appropriate to many a 1930s movie star, and a build that reminded Zeb of champion decathletes—flat-stomached, muscular, well-proportioned, the ideal build, Zeb had always thought, to serve as a model for comic-book superheroes.

There was only a faint German taint to the man's speech. "You really should not be here." His tones were surprisingly kind.

"I have to be somewhere," Zeb said. "Might as well be kicking the hell out of you."

The Weserian smiled without humor and advanced in boxing stance. He struck first, a jab that turned into a grab as he seized Zeb's left, leading, wrist, then he stepped in for a body blow.

Zeb didn't try to break his grip. He yanked laterally, pulling the Weserian out of line so his punch merely grazed along the left side of Zeb's ribs, then twisted, bringing his forearm into the Weserian's face. The blow rocked his opponent's head back.

The Weserian took advantage of their close positions, kicking Zeb's legs out from beneath him, shoving and releasing him at the same moment. Zeb hit the ground shoulders first, a painful, jarring impact. But he slapped down with his arms, allowing him to keep his feet up in the air for a moment, and kicked. His heel caught the Weserian clean under the jaw and stood the man on tiptoe. The Weserian staggered back; Zeb rolled over backwards and up to his feet.

The Weserian advanced, fists up again, shaking his head. He was tough. Zeb smiled at him.

Then Zeb was hit from the side, slammed to the grass across a chalk line. He twisted to get his back to the ground.

The sumo wrestler lay atop him, thrashing around as he tried to get a grip on Zeb's arms.

A shadow fell across Zeb. One of the referees stood over him. The referee swung at him, his mallet head aimed squarely at Zeb's face.

The scene unfolded in slow motion, the mallet swinging, a long leg coming into frame and connecting with the referee's shoulder, the shock wave running across the referee's body like a ripple across the still water of a pond. The referee was slammed sideways, his mallet striking the ground a foot from Zeb's head, his body hitting the grass at a right angle to Zeb.

The kicker was Harris.

Zeb kept his left hand free of the sumo wrestler's grasp and struck the man, a knifehand blow to the throat. He sent the blow into the side of his neck, avoiding the trachea, but it still caught the wrestler off guard. For a moment, the wrestler lost interest in pinning Zeb. Zeb hit him with a forearm shot across

the nose, rocking his head still further, then heaved
and rolled out from under him.

Distantly, a whistle sounded. Harris said, "That's it!"
He looked around, pointed east, and ran that way.

Zeb got to his feet a little shakily and ran after him.
The referee still lay limp, and there were scores of men
lying inert or writhing in pain all over the gridded field.

Competitors were already reaching the referees
standing beside the man waving the red flag. As each
competitor reached the group, a referee handed him
something like a white coin.

Zeb reached the group a few steps behind Harris.
The referees offered him no trouble, only a coin—
which turned out to be a white wooden piece the size
of a poker chip, the number 8 painted on it in red.
Harris's said 7.

Within moments, the last of the coins, with the
number 24 on it, was handed out and a referee blew
two whistle blasts. Athletes who were still scrambling—
or limping, or crawling—toward the group now slowed
or stopped, panting.

Zeb looked around. Walrus Mustache was among
those holding coins. So were the blond Weserian and
the sumo wrestler. Domitien had been among the
athletes staggering toward the flag when the final
whistle blew; his face as bruised as though he'd decided
to compete in a knock-down-a-brick-wall-with-your-
head event, he stood outside the group of those who
had received coins, catching his breath, looking de-
jected. The brown-bearded competitor was still down
on the field, apparently unconscious.

Moments later, the referees took Harris's coin away,
disqualifying him for attacking a referee. He bore the
disqualification cheerfully. Two other competitors were
disqualified for biting infractions, and three others
collapsed unconscious within a couple of minutes of

the final whistle, disqualifying them. But no one came
for Zeb's coin—whatever the one referee had seen, or
pretended to have seen, that might have disqualified
him had not been observed by the others. So competitors receiving coins numbered as high as 22 received
entry into the second round, the round of 16.

"Fun, huh?" Harris said.

Zeb snorted. "Within certain retarded definitions of
the word 'fun,' sure."

"We need to look into the origin of the Kobolde who
attacked you at the Fairwings plant," Doc said. "I'd like
to do that myself, but I must suspect that I'll attract
more official attention than any of the rest of you.
Which leaves it to you, Alastair. Unless—Rudi, do you
speak the language?"

Rudi rolled left and rolled right, but couldn't get
particularly comfortable. The seats where they were
situated in Sonneheim Stadium were long stone
benches, and neither Rudi nor the Sidhe Foundation
associates had thought to bring any of the folded blan-
kets so many of the onlookers were sitting upon. "No.
Albin did, but he learned it late in life. None of the
rest of the Bergmonks do."

"A pity."

Rudi looked to the field, where teenaged boys and
girls were marching in slow, stately unison, each carrying the flag of a nation—a shorter version of the
Games' opening ceremonies, to be repeated each day.
"I have an idea."

Alastair shrugged. "Where did you get it? Buy it
from a street vendor?" He was dressed in a bulky
overcoat, just a little too warm for this stadium on this
sunny morning but suited to the concealment of guns
and knives enough for a gang of rowdies, yet his hands
were restless and his manner was tense. Rudi had seen

such behavior scores of times. Alastair didn't have his favorite weapon on him, and his hands still sought it.

Rudi snorted. "Don't be daft." Then he frowned. "Are there street vendors for ideas?"

"What's your idea?" Doc asked.

"You have to give them credit," Ixyail said. She was intent on the marching flag-bearers. "They certainly have a sense of style."

Rudi tried rolling his weight onto one buttock, but it didn't help. "I was thinking we ought to parade Teleri around."

Alastair gave him a look that suggested he'd just realized Rudi needed to be in a very special hospital ward. "Perhaps you've failed to notice that Teleri's dead."

"No, I noticed." Rudi gave up and resigned himself to having a sore rear end. "A few years ago, a bunch o' bad blades were kicked out of Big Benno's gang for being too crazy. Mad Dog Kolbjorn and his pals."

Doc nodded. "I remember."

"First thing they did was grab a banker's son for ransom. Killed him almost immediately, too, accidentally, wavin' a pistol around in his face." Rudi grimaced, not concealing his distaste at the thought of men so amateurish in the handling of their firearms and prisoners. "Remember what they did?"

"Kidnapped another boy," Doc said, "an urchin who looked like the banker's son. Let him be seen in their company all over Neckerdam so the banker would think his boy was still alive."

"Didn't do 'em much good," Rudi said. "Novimagos Guard found their nest and put a few hundred rounds into 'em. But . . ."

"But the idea's not a bad one." Doc frowned.

"Except," said Ish, "we don't have anyone who can be disguised as Teleri, even with all Harris's skills with his disguise box." Her Castilian accent had returned. "Gaby is too big. I am too short, and I cannot be made as flat as Teleri; my bosom refuses to be concealed."

Doc snorted.

"Quiet, you. And Noriko's the right height and build . . . but her features and skin are just too far from Teleri's."

"So we need to find a Teleri," Doc said. "It's a good idea, Rudi. A second lightning rod to attract trouble, and one more specific to our enemies than Zeb is." He considered. "I know where we can find her. Our double for Teleri."

"Ah, yeah?" Rudi looked down one row of seats, where an onlooker had stood and moved toward the aisle, leaving her blanket behind. One quick, deft grab and he could be sitting on that blanket . . . assuming that oh-so-moral Doc didn't object. "Where?"

"The jail."

"Forget I said anything," Rudi said. "We don't need to be going to any jail."

"It should be a novelty for you." Doc rose. "Your first visit to a jail without being under arrest. In fact, you'll be talking for us."

Rudi sighed. "Why did I ever open my mouth?"

"Doc!" The voice came from below them and left. Rudi had his hand on his gun butt even before he finished turning that direction, but he did not draw it from his pocket; the man trotting up toward them on the coliseum steps scarcely seemed a danger.

He was a light, as pale of skin as Doc but with hair that was honey-gold. Nearly as tall as Doc, but leaner of build, he was dressed in a dark red suit that could not have been more expensive or more awry: His coat was misbuttoned, the right side higher than the left, and his gold tie, which should have contrasted stylishly with his blood-red shirt, was pulled half loose; its end bounced around on his chest as he ran. His features were young and open, his expression delighted. Rudi noted scars on the man's face, faint ones the width of a finger on his left cheek and to the right of the point of his jaw.

Doc stood, and Rudi and the others followed suit. The newcomer, reaching them, threw himself at Doc in an embrace. "Doc! I did not know you would be here—who's this? Ixyail!" He released Doc and wrapped himself around Ish, who chuckled at his display.

Not releasing Ish, the newcomer extended a hand to Alastair, saying, "Doctor Kornbock, always a pleasure. And who's this?" He indicated Rudi. "A new associate?"

Doc wore a slight, indulgent smile. "Something like that. Cas, allow me to present Rudiger Bergmonk. Rudi, this is my brother Casnar, Prince of Dumnia, Crown Prince of Cretanis."

Rudi, concealing the distaste he felt at dealing with anyone so exalted, shook the prince's hand. "He can't be a prince. Where's his guard?" Indeed, Casnar had not been flanked by earnest-looking gunmen, nor was there any indication that he'd been trailed up the steps by protectors.

Casnar's smile became conspiratorial. "Available with the snap of my fingers but, thank gods, out of sight and mind until then."

Ish tugged Casnar so that the two of them sat. "Down, Prince, down. People behind us want to see." Rudi and the others did as well.

"Cas, are you competing in Sword?"

The prince nodded. "And putting myself on display here and there, appearing bare-chested to show off new muscles, wherever possible."

Doc snorted. "Whatever for?"

Casnar rolled his eyes. "Mother has decided it's time for me to be married and spawn. I suppose I agree. King Aevar is trying to foist his daughter Edris off on me." He gave a mock shudder. "Gods save me, she has all the heat and charm of a fillet of fish in an icebox." He turned his attention back to Ish. "What about it, Ixyail? Marry me."

She laughed. "A son of Maeve, marrying a dusky? Why, it would kill her."

Casnar's smile became positively wicked. "Another benefit. We'd be king and queen of Cretanis right away."

"Besides, I could never give up Doc."

Casnar looked at his half brother and frowned, considering. "Well . . . all right. You can keep him. We'll put him in a room down the hall."

"No."

"Then just come stay as an occasional mistress. I'll be sure to choose a wife who won't object."

She shook her head. "You have enough bastards scattered about Europe."

"One can never have enough, not when each one causes Mother to throw another fit . . . Say, Doc, are you competing?"

Doc shook his head. "Some of my associates are, though. I'm here to show them support."

"You liar. In a city teeming with Reinis and spies and crown princes, you're here just to cheer? Not a chance. You're up to something."

Doc rose. "Actually, I am. And I do have to be about it."

Alastair and Rudi rose. Casnar sighed and loosened his grip on Ish's waist so she could, too. The prince slumped where he sat, suddenly disconsolate. Then he brightened. "I'm having a party tonight."

Doc gave him an indulgent look. "Sort of like saying,

'The sun's coming up tomorrow morning, sometime around dawn.'"

"No, I mean a formal party. It's for the cold fish. Please, come, rescue me from tedium. Maybe you'll have a chance to shoot someone."

Rudi said, "I'm all for that, Doc."

Casnar's smile returned. "It's at the new Cretanis embassy on the Aevarstrasse. It starts at half past four bells. Please, Doc."

"If we can."

Doc's plan for finding a double for Teleri was based on the simple notion that they would let the authorities do the hard work of finding as close a match as possible.

At Bardulfburg's main police station, Rudi found an officer who spoke Cretanis and spent time telling him of the young woman he'd met at the parade last night. He'd fallen madly in love, he explained, but hadn't gotten her name before the trouble started. He didn't describe the trouble in any detail, he just made it sound like any crowd fight that might have occurred. But he did describe Teleri in great detail. The officer called the jailers and reported, "Yes, I think we have the one you speak of." He sent for papers on the girl and a receipt book. With money Doc had given him, Rudi paid her bail, then waited while she was brought up to the front, a young blond woman in a simple red skirt and blouse.

She received her possessions in silence, not betraying to the officers that she did not know Rudi. When all the paperwork was done, Rudi escorted her outside where Doc, Ish, and Alastair waited.

She did indeed look a lot like Teleri. She was a little shorter than Teleri, nor did she possess that woman's rare beauty, and a livid purple-yellow bruise stood out on her left cheekbone. But she had features that suggested sweetness of disposition and a mouth that looked as though it was deliberately fashioned to curl into a smile.

Not that she smiled now. She looked between Rudi and the associates with unconcealed nervousness, as though she would bolt but for Rudi's hand on her elbow.

Doc smiled and spoke a few words of Burian to her. Rudi could understand her reply, though it was heavy with a Burian accent: "Yes, I speak Cretanis."

"Excellent," Doc said. "I am Doctor Desmond MaqqRee of the Sidhe Foundation. These are my associates Ixyail del Valle and Alastair Kornbock; you've met Rudiger Bergmonk. And how are you called?"

"I am Swana," she said. "Swana Weiss."

"Swana, we have brought you from jail for a reason, but you owe us no more than a chime of your time. Once we've said a few words, you can choose to go about your business and we won't bother you again. If you stay, you might earn a considerable amount of money." Doc shrugged. "But we must know the truth. How do you feel about King Aevar and the Reinis?"

Rudi held his tongue. He couldn't read the paperwork on the girl, but he knew from conversation with the desk officer that Swana had been part of a protest last night. Like the blood-throwers they'd seen, she had been beaten and arrested by soldiers, in her case for shouting "Where are the seven?" at the king, a reference to some event Rudi didn't know about.

And despite himself, Rudi felt a little sympathy for the girl. She obviously didn't have any money, else she'd have arranged for bail earlier, nor could she have had any friends with money, for the same reason. It wasn't really fair of Doc to wave money under her nose like that. Then he frowned at his own stray thoughts.

Sympathy, Albin had always said, was a handle by which you could grab people and shake them down for money. It wasn't for the Bergmonk Boys.

Swana was not quick to answer. She looked between the four of them as if hoping she could see past their faces to the thoughts beyond. Then she gave up and shrugged. "I don't like them," she said. "I didn't like the old king either. But I am a loyal Weserian."

"We won't ask you to betray your nation," Doc said. "Not your principles or ideals. But we're looking for some people who've done very bad things. They've killed scores of people. And they may be favored, even protected, by the Reinis. We want your help to find them and stop them from doing more."

She drew a long, unhappy breath, and Rudi could see that she was thinking fast. She didn't share her thoughts. She just said, "Maybe. Tell me more."

Zeb, Harris, and Gaby were already back at the Foundation quarters for the evening when Doc and retinue arrived. Rudi came into the apartment first, a new suit bag slung over his shoulder. He offered them a disgusted look, and immediately headed off to the apartment's second common area, which had been converted into a bedroom for him, Alastair, and Zeb. He left the apartment door open behind him.

"This promises to be good," Harris said.

Doc, carrying two sacks with green-leafed vegetables protruding from the top, entered next. He looked between Harris and Gaby. "Did you two bring formal dress?"

"One outfit each," Harris said. "Standard Operating Apparel."

"Harris's outfit is wonderful," Gaby said. "It's a strapless formal in purple lamé with a big old bow on his butt."

Harris nodded. "Don't forget about the matching opera gloves. I love those."

Doc shook his head, a long-suffering look. "Get them ready. You're going to a party tonight." He headed into the kitchen.

Ish and another woman were in next. Ish carried a red cardboard suitcase and what looked like a makeup case made of wood. The other woman, a pretty blonde in green, carried a bag of groceries and a dog.

It was a mutt; it looked like the result of an impossible liaison between a bulldog and a Vietnamese potbellied pig.

"You've got to be kidding," Zeb said.

The blond woman set the dog down. It made an immediate beeline for Zeb and stood before his chair, wagging its stump of a tail, its mashed features suggesting a grin.

"This is Odilon," Ish said. "Odilon, that's Zeb."

Zeb stared unhappily at the creature. "It's what's for dinner, right?"

"No, it's Swana's friend, and you may not eat him."

"If he tries to hump my leg, all bets are off."

Swana clicked her tongue and Odilon trotted back to stand beside her. She looked suspiciously at Zeb. "Where you are from, do you eat dogs?"

"No, I'm actually partial to beef in orange sauce and General Tso's Chicken."

"Do you really sacrifice humans?"

Zeb gave her an incredulous look. "Where'd you hear that?"

"In school, my last year of school. They said the darkest duskies ran about with no clothes on, made human sacrifice, and wanted to, to degrade Burian women."

Zeb sighed. "Was this, oh, about the time the Reinis came to power?"

Swana considered. "Yes."

"And before then, is that what they told you in schools?"

"No."

"So what does that suggest to you? Take your time, but there's going to be a test on this material."

"I'm sorry." Swana shrugged. "I was just curious." She followed Doc into the kitchen. Ish smiled and headed to the hall leading to the bedrooms.

Zeb leaned back in his chair. "Sometimes I wonder if we oughtn't just firebomb the whole country."

"Hey, she asked, she didn't just assume it was true," Harris said. "Say, when all is done for the evening, you want to get some beer, run around naked, do a human sacrifice or two, and eat Swana's dog?"

Despite himself, Zeb grinned. "All right."

Chapter Fifteen

Noriko arrived a little later, saying nothing of the errand that had taken her from Gaby earlier in the day. Zeb thought about talking to her, seeing if she'd cheered up from her encounter with Hayato the other evening, but after only a bare few words of greeting she retired to the room she was now to share with Swana. She appeared not to notice that Doc, Harris and Rudi were standing by in full formal dress.

Doc wore a suit in an aquatic blue-green with gold tie and suspenders. The coat, double-breasted, with a double row of gold buttons, hung from the wooden coatrack beside the door. When he put it on, the ensemble would closely resemble a military officer's uniform of Novimagos. He sat reading Weserian news-papers and magazines, particularly their coverage of the Sonneheim Games.

Harris and Rudi were much more restrained in their dress; Harris wore a formal suit and vest in a dark blue, a suit color common on the grim world but which Zeb had seen few people wear here, and Rudi's suit was in a tan-yellow that seemed perfectly in keeping with fairworld costume. Zeb spent some time kidding Harris over his archaic broad lapels, but Harris's smiling, silent indifference to the jibes suggested he'd heard it all before.

Gaby and Ish emerged from dressing as Doc was consulting his pocket watch for the fifth time. The men stood. Harris whistled and said, "Little girl, you look good enough to eat."

Gaby offered a mocking smile and minimal curtsy. She was in a shimmering red gown with a slight train. Sleek and tight-fitting, it was sleeveless, with shoulder straps plunging into a daring bodice in front and offering a view of her back almost to her waist. She wore no jewelry but golden earrings and a single gold bracelet. Her hair was held in place by a decorative hairnet in the same red as the gown, and her lipstick was in a matching hue.

Ish's formal had a higher neckline but was equally form-fitting. It was all in black, and set off by white opera gloves and a simple string of pearls; her hair was piled high. The starkness of her gown made her seem paler than she actually was. Zeb wondered if that was a strategic move.

Doc pocketed his watch and bowed. His tone formal, he said, "We shall be the envy of all Weseria."

Ish offered him a smile. "Even if you are not, you must behave as though you are. Else I shall be *very* disappointed."

Doc straightened and turned to the others. "Very well. We're away. Zeb, if you, Alastair, or Noriko decides to go out for the evening, make sure that someone remains behind to guard Goodlady Weiss."

"Will do, Doc."

"Grace on you."

❖   ❖   ❖

The new Cretanis embassy was, Rudi decided, actually a storefront for nobles with too much money. It was a narrow three-story manor set back behind spike-topped walls. The building edifice was dressed stone, a speckled gray that was polished until it was smooth and reflective, popular only among builders who chose for their constructions to stand out in urban landscapes made up of more flamboyant colors, very modern; but the building corners were rounded, suggesting the mound-style building pattern so common in Old World construction. Rudi offered up a smile of contempt for the stylistic compromise. It seemed gutless, just the thing he'd expect of inbred, waif-thin royal lights of the Old Country.

Gates guarded by tall, lean lights who looked more like swordsmen than gunmen, for all that they had the bulges of pistols deforming the lines of their suits, admitted Doc's crew to a walkway of cream-colored flagstones, then stone stairs between granite columns. At the top of the columns, gargoyles leered down at the stream of well-dressed visitors passing between them.

The building's admitting chamber was long and narrow, decorated by tapestries extolling the virtues of armored, thin-faced noble warriors of Cretanis and their oversized horses. Finally, a set of double doors, opening and closing for each separate group of invitees, admitted them to the embassy's social chamber, a two-story ballroom already thick with besuited and begowned nobles and politicians.

Rudi didn't bother to hide his expression of disdain. All his life, reformers and guards had referred to his clan and others who lived outside the law as parasites living on the productive, deserving population. But he knew that *these* were the true parasites, clinging to royal titles bestowed in some cases before history began, clamped by ancient law and tradition to lands and properties they didn't deserve to profit from. How he could be here, pretending to be a *bodyguard* for one of them . . .

"Settle down," Harris whispered in his ear. "You're too cheerful."

"Just give me someone to shoot," Rudi said under his breath. "That's the only thing that can make this night worthwhile."

Harris suppressed a laugh. "There's free food."

"True. A point."

"And maybe someone will point a gun or swing a knife at one of us. Whoever that is, you can shoot."

"Oh, if only I were so lucky."

Doc bent to kiss the hand of the Queen of Bolgia and then exchanged a few words with her—how beautiful the city, how exuberant the people, how graceful the athletes, how boring the party, how soon before Casnar pulled one of his famous social gaffes and made the evening a memorable one? The queen was a tall woman, dressed in a leaf-green formal gown with an extended train and two small girls to carry it; her hair was black as a crow's feathers and her face unlined, for all she was the same age as Doc. She was of old stock, but a dark rather than a light. Smiling, Doc and Ish moved on.

Doc managed a glance behind. Harris and Gaby were now elsewhere in the party, socializing, joking, talking to the more drunken attendees, hoping to hear unguarded words. Rudi was also gone. Doc felt a little relief, there. Rudi was doing well, and had kept his mouth shut—except for those occasions when he raided the hors d'oeuvres trays carried by servants—but his surly manner had to make people nervous, even in his role as Doc's bodyguard.

There he was now, leaning against one of the white marble columns flanking the doorway, affecting disinterest in the proceedings. This was just as Doc had instructed him to do; Doc needed no bodyguard, but at this gathering needed an outsider who could take note of events in the room while he was too distracted by formalities to do so. Rudi, as experienced at casing banks as most folk were at going to film plays, would be that observer.

"Doc!"

Doc faced forward again, smiled, extended his hand. "Casnar."

His half brother, in contrast with his appearance at the coliseum, immaculate in a formal suit, shook his hand vigorously, then gestured toward the older man and younger woman beside him. "Your Majesty, Your Highness, allow me to present to you my brother, Doctor Desmond MaqqRee, and his companion, Ixyail del Valle. Doc, I present Aevar of House Losalbar, King of Weseria, leader of the *Nationalreinigungspartei*, and his daughter, Her Highness, Edris."

The king looked much as he had at the other night's parade, and was again wearing the uniformlike suit from that event; his smile fell on Doc like a moonbeam. His daughter was tall for a fairworld woman, statuesque in a manner that tended to draw admiring looks especially from Burians; her long hair, coiled in a style similar to Ish's, was a light brown with hints of blond throughout. Her gown, less daring than Ish's, was of an unusual cloth, a print showing leaves reaching the reds, oranges, yellows and browns of autumn. And despite Casnar's earlier words of her coldness, her features expressed intelligence and amusement.

Doc offered the king a formal bow, then bent to kiss the princess's proffered hand—glove, rather. He could see in his peripheral vision Ish managing a deep formal curtsy. He straightened. "I am honored," he said. "And delighted to meet you at last."

"As I am pleased finally to meet the leader of the famous Sidhe Foundation," the king said. There was no trace of a Burian accent in his speech; he appeared to have learned Cretanis from a native of that nation. "Are you enjoying the Games?"

"Certainly. Though I think I am enjoying Bardulfburg more. As an engineer, I am bedazzled by the range of styles and the skill of construction that have gone into the city's renovation." It was a ploy, merely an appeal to the vanity of the man who was known to be directly responsible for Weseria's civic programs, but it seemed to have its desired effect; Aevar's smile broadened.

"An engineer as well?" asked the king. "It seems there is little Doctor MaqqRee does not do. Are you also an architect?"

Doc nodded. "The Monarch Building in Neckerdam—the New World Neckerdam, I mean—is my design. Most of my designs are houses, though, fashioned for ease of maintenance and low cost in building. My engineering works consist mostly of bridges."

"Still, there is someone you must meet." The king looked about, among the partygoers, and raised his voice. "Ritter! Come here."

A balding blond head popped up from the crowd clustered around the buffet table, then began bobbing toward the king.

"Father, please," Edris said. "It's so unkind of you to inflict Daenn upon polite company." Her voice was the feminine equivalent of her father's—low, rich, with the accent of Cretanis. Given Casnar's description of her, it was also surprisingly warm.

Aevar gave her a little nod of concession. "True. But

I suspect Doctor MaqqRee has much experience escaping unwanted attention, and he can discuss architectural matters until his patience wears thin. Ah, here we are."

The balding head had reached them. It was atop a black Sonnenkrieger uniform with general's markings. The man was red-faced—from overheating, Doc suspected, rather than embarrassment—and his features were those of classic Old World nobility: lean, intelligent, an attitude of discipline rather than the more common dissipation. He held his cap under his arm and clicked his heels together as he came to attention before his king.

Aevar gestured to the newcomer. "Doctor MaqqRee, I present to you General Daenn Ritter, Master Planner of Bardulfburg, Chief Architect of Weseria and the Burian League. Ritter, this is Desmond MaqqRee—notorious in the press as Doc Sidhe."

"Grace on you," Ritter said. "Your work in encasing steel frameworks to limit ferrous poisoning is inspirational. It will be what you will be remembered for."

Doc offered him a mirthless smile. "You make it sound as though that will be soon."

"Oh, no." Ritter laughed. It sounded forced, or at least embarrassed. "I just meant that travelling the world, rooting out criminals, these are all good things—but buildings *endure*. Your true legacy will be that which you have made, and the constructions you have inspired. But please, tell me, why do you insist that your coating process be entirely chemical in nature, when devisement techniques are available?"

Doc suppressed a sigh. Edris had been right. It wasn't nice to inflict General Ritter on polite company.

It was a chime or more before they could pry themselves from the company of the king and his retinue.

Doc managed to catch Gaby's eye and nodded his head toward Rudi; he led Ish that way. Ish made an exasperated noise.

"What is it, dear heart?"

"He did not acknowledge me. Not once."

"Aevar?"

"Who else? His inelegant daughter did, but not the king." Ish brightened. "On the other hand, now that he has insulted me, I may begin to plot revenge."

Doc smiled. "Good thinking. But it begs the question, why did he not acknowledge you?"

"Because . . ." She frowned. "Because I am a dusky. But that is not obvious just from looking at me."

"Meaning?"

"Meaning he knows who I am, including my ancestry."

"And in spite of his political skills, he's not enough of a politician to ignore his dislike of your presence to avoid insulting you, and by association, me."

They reached Rudi's side; Harris and Gaby were there half a step before them. "Are we getting anything useful?" Doc asked.

" 'Gods forbid there should ever be another war between great nations,' " Harris said, affecting a Burian accent, " 'but if there is, it will be won by air superiority.' "

Doc frowned. "Who said that?"

"Head of Weseria's air force. Head of the combined Burian League's air force, now—League members are consolidating their armed forces 'to cut down administrative costs.' " Harris shrugged. "I took it to be a bad sign."

"It is a bad sign. We've learned that Weseria's hatred of duskies probably goes to the very top. And I just had an interesting talk with Bardulfburg's chief architect. I asked him if he visualizes the city's revisions in two dimensions or three. He said three."

The others looked at him blankly. Then comprehension dawned on Gaby's face. "He has a model of the city."

"That's right."

Harris waved that fact away. "Who cares? Our enemies, assuming they're associated with the Reinis and even the Crown, aren't going to bomb their own capital city."

"Smoke doesn't always mean fire, Harris, but you can always choke on it," Doc said.

Harris snorted. "You just made that up."

"No, no, it's an old saying."

"Sure it is. You start to lose an argument and you immediately invent a parable or something to shore up your argument, pretending you read it on a clay pot thousands of years old."

Doc sighed, then turned to Rudi. "You're the only one of us who's had the opportunity just to watch events unfold. What have you seen?"

Rudi shrugged. "Your brother's up to something."

Doc raised an eyebrow. "Half brother." He looked in Casnar's direction. The prince was bent over the hand of a noblewoman, kissing it repeatedly, with comical vigor, despite her protests and laughter. "What is he up to?"

Rudi shrugged. "I'm not sure. But he has three manners and accords one of the three to everyone he talks to. There's hail-fellow-well-met. That's for almost everyone, including some of the ladies. There's come-hither-darling, like he is with the honeydew right now."

"Both normal behavior for him. What's the third manner?"

" 'We need to speak in private.' He leans in close,

like they're planning a bank job. His face looks like he's whispering. Whoever he's talking to looks like he's whispering, too. Very serious, no humor to him."

"Show me who he speaks to this way."

Rudi began nodding toward various of the partygoers. "The fat one with the gray whiskers and the drunken walk. He's not drunk, by the way. The raven-haired woman, there, in the green formal with the gaggle of admirers all around her. That eamon in the old-fashioned coat and tie. That man by the window, the one who looks like he's posing for a cameo, 'Aren't I the melancholy young noble.'" Rudi's accent became authentically upper class and pretentious. "And a couple more I don't see at the moment."

"You're good with that accent change," Doc said.

"I do a lot of them." Rudi grinned. "Sometimes useful in my line of work."

"Mine, too." Doc looked among the people Rudi had indicated. "Daracy Arreclute, the League of Ardree's Minister of War. Dalphina, the Queen of Bolgia. Pheodor, the Foreign Minister of Odraia. And Eglantine, the young Crown Prince of Loria."

Harris looked uncertain and glanced at Gaby. "Geography's still not my strong suit."

"League of Ardree and Bolgia you know," Gaby said.

"Yeah. Approximately the U.S. and Belgium."

"Odraia is what we'd call western Poland, and Loria is portions of France."

"Thanks."

"Three Europeans and a New Worlder," Ish said. "I don't see any connection between them but the obvious, political alliances."

Doc shook his head, unhappy. "No, they stand out like a hammered thumb in this crowd. They are all representatives of nations that opposed the old Burian

Alliance in the World Crisis. Nations that have been calling attention to Weseria since the coup put Aevar on the throne. Cretanis, which Casnar represents, is another of them."

"What's Casnar doing, then?" Ish asked. "Planning another war with the Burians?"

"Possibly anticipating one," Doc said. "I have to find out."

"I'll hold him," Rudi said, "if you want to beat it out of him."

Doc offered a sour grin. "That would certainly cut the last of my fraying ties with my father's other children. No, I won't beat Casnar. I won't even ask him. If he'd wanted me to know, he would have told me already, meaning he's keeping this from me for a reason. No, I'll ask *him*." His pointed finger indicated the young, broody prince by the window, the one he'd called Eglantine.

"Why will he tell you?" asked Ish.

"Don't let anyone speak to me for the next few beats." Doc closed his eyes and let himself slip into the meditative state he needed for quick and simple devisement.

Almost instantly he could feel it, the hum of power surrounding him, sure sign that he was a finger's breadth from the place where the gods slept their shallow, uneasy sleep. He took that hum into himself and the sounds of the party around him faded.

He could no longer feel Ish's hand upon his arm. He could no longer feel his own hands, feet, arms, legs . . . Only the quickening pace of his heart reminded him that he still lived, that he still had a place on the mortal world.

Hear me, he thought, *O Trickster, O Thief, O Seducer In Other Men's Forms. Bless me with your virtuosity. Gift me with your limitless changeability.*

I pledge a trick, an awful trick, in your name, upon victims who will be shamed and reduced by it.

What that trick would be, he had no idea. Nor did he have a sense of how patient the Trickster would be in awaiting it. But these were the hazards of dealing with the gods.

He waited, reaching out for any glimmering of communication from the spirit he sought. Nor was it long in coming, a noise that resonated in his mind like a chuckle.

An acceptance.

Thanks to you, he thought, and distanced himself from that mind, from the hum of power. The sensations of his body, the noises of the party returned to him.

He kept his eyes closed. In his mind, he pictured Casnar as his half brother appeared at this party, splendidly attired in a very modern suit in the colors of Cretanis, red for the jacket, pants, and tie, green for the shirt, a wicked gleam in his eye.

Casnar's image floated before him in the darkness of imagination, staring at him, mouth turned as if he were curious about his sudden manifestation in this place.

Doc turned Casnar around and pulled him, donning him like a costume, adjusting him here and there so there would be no wrinkles, no unsightly flaps. *Only for Eglantine,* he told himself, and told the Casnar he wore. *Only for Eglantine.*

He opened his eyes. Eglantine was still there, silhouetted against the window by the brightness thrown up from the lights installed upon the grounds of the embassy. *Who's he posing for?* Doc wondered, his thoughts flavored by Casnar's likeness. *He's angling for somebody's pity. Ah, he seeks the sympathy of a woman.*

He forced himself to abandon that irrelevant train of thought, to keep himself from looking for the object of Eglantine's affection. He started forward, adjusting his pace to accommodate Casnar's build.

If he'd done it right, everyone present looking at him would see Doc as he was. Everyone but Eglantine. If he'd made a mistake, there were now two Casnars in the room for all to see, and that could cause problems.

But he reached Eglantine's side without incident. "Say, old Egg, you're not drinking too much, are you?" he asked, and was pleased to hear the words emerging in Casnar's whisper. "You should be clear-headed."

Eglantine smiled at him. "It's all for show," he said, his speech flavored by the accent of Loria. "Something you know quite a lot about."

"True," Doc said. "I assume you can prove it. You do recall what I told you."

Eglantine gave him a look of mock hurt. "Of course. Two nights from now, Ludana's temple, half-past four bells. Don't worry so much."

"I shouldn't. But I do." Doc gave him Casnar's hail-fellow-well-met clap on the arm. "Until then." He turned away.

When he was halfway back to his associates, he glanced back Eglantine's way. The prince was paying him no mind. In fact, the prince looked more melancholy than ever, and was already deep in conversation with a young woman Doc recognized as a well-known stage actress of Cretanis.

Doc let Casnar's semblance slip from him. He breathed a sigh of relief; the strain of such devisement was considerable, its cessation much like slipping a rucksack loaded with lead ingots from his shoulders.

But he'd taken only two more steps when the weakness hit him. His knees were suddenly wobbly, his head light as though he'd been awake for two days.

He almost cursed. Devisement also took a toll, sometimes sooner, sometimes later. This time it was almost immediate. He forced his legs to behave and continued walking, though every step required his total concentration.

His legs began to buckle again, but suddenly Ish was there, sliding in under his left arm, supporting him. An instant later Gaby slid in under his right arm.

"Smile," Ish whispered. "You're wrapped around the two most beautiful women in Bardulfburg."

Doc did smile. "Don't sell yourself short. In all of Europe, at least."

"Ooh, nicely done, Doc," Gaby said. "For that, I'll wait an extra day the next time I decide to ask for a raise."

"I think it's time to go," Doc said.

The two women got him turned around toward the door and started in that direction. His knees still felt as though they had no muscle to move them, but with Ish's and Gaby's support he was able to move normally, if a little drunkenly.

Behind, he heard Rudi talking to Harris in a whisper. "Did he just pop off a devisement? No preparation, no circle, props or toys?"

"That's right." Harris sounded a little mocking.

"No wonder he catches so many in the trade. Why, that's not fair."

They were only paces from the exit when the doors swung open, not to allow them out, but to admit another group—Prince Hayato and a retinue of three. Doc recognized the three as the men who had been with him at the Temple of the Suns, though the fourth, the man Zeb had kneed, was not with them.

"Doctor MaqqRee." Hayato approached and extended his hand. "It is good to see so diligent and studious a man enjoying himself."

Doc released his grip on Gaby to shake the prince's

hand. "I have perhaps been enjoying myself too much.
The wines being served are excellent." He returned his
arm to Gaby's shoulders.

"Is Noriko not with you? I was hoping to thank her
for this afternoon."

"No, I'm afraid she is not. To thank her?"

Hayato smiled. "For agreeing to compete in the
Sword of Wo, of course. I do hope she advances far
enough to face me."

"I'm certain she will."

Hayato offered a dismissive little nod, then he and
his retinue continued on into the party room.

Doc sighed. "Not good."

Ish gave him a worried look. "That she has chosen
to compete?"

"No—that she concealed it from us."

"Oh." She and Gaby set Doc into motion again. "I
will take care of it."

"*You* will?"

"Certainly. I am the daughter of a king and queen,
as noble as any in that room, and as experienced with
diplomacy."

Doc chuckled. "Your form of diplomacy, dear heart,
usually consists of a certain delicacy of motion when
squeezing the trigger."

She just smiled up at him.

Alone on the balcony of the room she shared with
Swana, Noriko heard the partygoers return. She heard
Swana leave the room to join them, clucking for her
absurd but well-behaved dog to accompany her. She
heard the sounds of the dog's nails clicking on the
hardwood floor as it scrambled to keep up.

Noriko heard the murmur of voices, Doc and the
others briefing those who hadn't attended the party on
the night's events.

She stayed where she was, leaning back in the stuffed chair she'd moved onto the balcony, watching the traffic move by on the street below, watching the pedestrians walk past. She was mere paces from them but, wrapped in darkness, she was invisible to them.

Invisible was best. Harris and the others sometimes made jokes about her imperturbability, her serenity in times of crisis, but she knew that if she were among them now, in the light, they would instantly recognize failure in her face and manner. She could not bear to be shamed that way.

In the other room, talk died down and doors shut. The associates were going to bed. But still Swana did not return.

Someone rapped at her door. Noriko ignored it. But after a second rap, she heard the door open and close. Moments later, Zeb joined her on the balcony.

He leaned against the rail, just a silhouette against a sky faintly lit by Bardulfburg's numberless street lights. "You all right?"

She suppressed a laugh. It would have sounded derisive. Zeb was even worse than Harris that way: He began conversations without preamble, without delicate maneuvering from a traditional form of greeting through intermediate conversational steps to the point where he wanted to arrive. No, he just dropped like a parachutist from an airwing straight onto his target.

"I am well," she said.

"That's good." He was silent for long moments, in which she hoped he would silently admit to conversational helplessness and go about his business, but it was not to be. "Doc bumped into Prince Hayato at the party, but unfortunately not hard enough to do him any permanent damage. Hayato said that you'd agreed to fight him in Sword of Wo."

Noriko closed her eyes. She *might* have been able

to keep the secret all through the Games. But, no, she'd been betrayed only hours after making her choice. She was to have no dignity after all. Perhaps the gods really did hate her. "Yes. But, please, do not tell me it was a stupid thing to do. I know that."

"That's not what I was going to say. But if you think it's stupid, why did you agree to do it?"

"I don't know." Her eyes burned as tears threatened to come. She took a deep breath, an effort to bring herself under control. She'd never cried before another person, not once, since coming to the West, not even when her husband Jean-Pierre had been murdered. She wasn't going to now. "Perhaps I am victim of a devisement. I don't care about beating him."

"But you do want to fight him?"

"Yes."

"So what's your goal, Noriko? In the best possible world, if you fought him and didn't beat him, what would you get out of it?"

"I don't know." Miserable, she shook her head.

"Well, it's just wrong for you to do this alone. Not advisable. I'm appointing myself as your trainer."

She opened her eyes to look at him. He was leaning over the rail now, watching the passing foot and vehicle traffic with the same disinterest she had recently felt. "What do you know of the art of the sword?"

His teeth gleamed in a too-brief smile. "What I know boils down to this: If you see a guy running at you with a sword, put two rounds into his chest to slow him down, then one into his brain to finish him off."

She tried to suppress a laugh, but sound emerged as an amused snort. "Good advice. But not for these Games."

"The thing is, Noriko, Hayato and his people are big on intimidation. We saw that the other night. They'll be working on you psychologically from the moment you show up. Hell, they already are. But they're not going to get anywhere doing that with me around. I've already caved in the rib cage of one of those stupid sons of bitches. They know I'll happily do the rest of them."

"True." Noriko couldn't fault Zeb's logic. That in itself was disquieting. This was *her* fight, against intruders from *her* past, and the prospect that it would even inconvenience any of the associates bothered her deeply.

But mingled with that worry was relief. She no longer had to keep this secret from her employer and her allies. "Thank you," she said.

"Nothing to it. Um, my first round is tomorrow morning. I've already checked the schedule—yours is tomorrow late afternoon. After my round, we can get together, do some warm-ups and practice, then go over and see what the Wo boys have to offer you."

"That would be good."

" 'Night, Noriko."

"Goodnight, Zeb."

Once he was gone, she settled into her chair, her shame and confusion exposed yet somehow already diminishing, and fell asleep there without meaning to.

Doc sat against the head of his bed watching Ixyail brush her hair. Such a simple little ceremony, he decided, but one he so enjoyed watching. He relaxed, letting the unnatural exhaustion that had afflicted him at the party fade away.

This room, he decided, smelled of age. Not of dirt, not of sweat—the rigorous cleanliness of the former resident and the building's owners would never allow for slovenliness. But the building was at least two centuries old. The interior walls smelled of paint layers thick, the oldest levels crumbling to dust. The hardwood floors smelled of polishes laid down generations ago and renewed since.

This was something Doc did not often experience in the New World. He missed it, the everyday odor of a place that had been occupied for longer than he had been alive, but it was one of the things he had had to abandon when he was exiled from Cretanis.

Ixyail glanced at him in the mirror and left off brushing her hair for a moment. "What are you thinking?"

He smiled. "Unromantic as it may sound, I was thinking that I wished you were back in Novimagos."

"That *is* unromantic. But sweet."

He rose and moved to lean over the little metal bin that had been placed in the room for refuse. He carefully positioned his head over it, then snapped his fingers.

A fine gray mist descended from the ends of his hair and flowed down into the bin. It was made up of a day's worth of dust, perspiration, and other foreign matter that had accumulated in the course of his activities. The devisement that drew it from him left his hair clean and renewed, the thick white curtain so many ladies had admired across the years.

Ish made an exasperated noise.

He straightened. "What's wrong?"

"What's wrong? That's wrong! The most useful devisement ever known to man, and I cannot learn it because I lack the Gift. It's torture to me every time you do it, sheer torture."

He smiled and rose. Moving up behind her, he took the brush from her hand and pulled it through her hair in long, slow strokes. She sighed and closed her eyes, relaxing into his ministrations. "I accept your apology," she said.

❖   ❖   ❖

Zeb dreamed of dogs.

First there was the big brute in Rospo's shop, sitting there still, eyeing him, and he was the only person in the shop. He tensed against its attack, but it didn't move.

He saw then that there was blood on the back of its neck, a lot of it, a stream of it to the floor.

The dog whimpered at him, long keening whines, but didn't raise its head from its paws. Zeb looked away.

When he looked back, the big dog and the blood were gone, replaced by Swana's dog Odilon in the same place and pose. But seeing his attention, Odilon rose, its stump of a tail wagging, and approached him cautiously.

Zeb knew that tragedy would soon overcome it, in the form of a speeding car or a pack of bigger animals, and he'd never see it again. That loss made him sad, and the sadness made him angry. He knew it was false. He knew he didn't really care about the dog, but the sadness did not fade. "Go away," he said.

The dog said, "Up with you, lad. Noses need breaking." Its voice was the same as Rudi's.

Zeb opened his eyes. Sunlight was beginning to stream in through the windows. Rudi was already up, sitting on the next bed over, tying his shoes.

"I liked you better when you were a dog," Zeb said.

Competitors in the All-Out's Round of 16 assembled at the same field where the preliminary round had taken place the previous day. In addition to the competitors, present were coaches, trainers, referees, and a far larger crowd than the day before; Zeb estimated that a couple of thousand people at least were ranged around the competition area.

"They're here for you," Harris said. "All-Out apparently doesn't get this much attention. But word spread like the flu that they had a dusky competing this time. Two duskies, actually, including you and the guy from Wo."

"So a lynch mob showed up," Zeb said. "Great." He continued with his warm-up exercises, bending so that his head nearly touched his knees, wrapping his arms around his legs, pulling in close to stretch leg muscles.

"Who you draw in the first round is a good test for whether the fix is in against you," Harris said, aping Zeb's exercise so their faces, upside-down, were at about the same altitude. "If it's just a fighter, there may be some fairness left in the world. If you find yourself set up against a succession of guys who are most likely to hurt you, even if they don't beat you, before you get to the upper rounds—"

"Then the fix is in," Zeb said. "I pretty much figured that out. You have any idea who the contenders are?"

"Local money is on Conrad Förster. They love him in Weseria. He's a colonel in the Sonnenkrieger in spite of his youth, participated in the coup that put Aevar on the throne—wiped out a group of royal guards to give his unit access to the king's chambers, was wounded and hovered near death, all that schmaltzy stuff. He's responsible for bringing men of Wo here on a regular basis to sort of help combine their wrestling arts with local boxing."

Zeb made a sour face. "Great, an innovator."

"Yeah, and he has won this competition in the national games before. Then there's Geert Tiwasson, a three-time winner, though they say he's a little past his prime. He's supposed to be huge and mean."

"Also local, I take it."

"Yep, though they say his father's family is originally from Ostmark—I think that's where Sweden is. Then there's Tanuki Kano, from Wo."

"The sumo wrestler?"

"Uh-huh."

"Yeah, I met him. He's going to be rough to take out."

The officials in red called the athletes forward, assembling before an elevated reviewing stand that had been put in place since yesterday's round. They divided the athletes into two groups. Zeb found himself in Group Two and was unsurprised by it. The members of Group One were each given small porcelain chits—white-glazed, some still faintly warm from having been fired earlier that morning—with their names impressed upon them. These they deposited, one by one, in a large black porcelain jar decorated in dull red geometric patterns.

One by one, the eight athletes of Group Two were called forward. Each groped around in the jar, grabbed one of the chits, and presented it to the judges.

Zeb was again unsurprised that he was the last of the Group Two athletes called forward. He took the last of the chits from the jar. The name on it was Tanuki Kano.

When he returned to Harris's side, he said, "The fix is in."

Chapter Sixteen

Two matches of the day's eight were scheduled before Zeb's. The field of play was a square made up of four of the previous day's squares, about twenty feet by twenty, right next to the reviewing stand. The red-clad judges stood upon the stand, and the athletes not involved in the current match, as well as their trainers, stood on the ground immediately before it. The crowd lined the other three sides of the competition square and stood many ranks deep.

The first bout was between a man who looked to Zeb like a potbellied Viking—blond-bearded, blue-eyed, with a cheerful manner but an intensity to the way he watched everything—and a paler but brown-haired man who had the most extraordinary build Zeb had seen yet on the fair world. His muscles were practically sculpted; he could have been a grimworld body builder. Yet his narrow face and long, thin nose were pure fairworld, and his features in general, which looked like they were crafted to laugh and laugh while bloodbaths were taking place before his eyes, were far from appealing.

The two men were made to stand three paces apart in the center of their square while one of the judges spoke to them in Burian. Then the judge lifted his hammer high and took two steps back, and the fight was on.

Both men crouched in wrestler's poses. The noise from the crowd rose and flashes of light erupted from the crowd as front-line photographers began snapping pictures.

The competitors moved toward one another, arms bent, hands open, then came together with a sound of collision like two sides of beef being swung into one another. The muscleman got his arms around the Viking's waist and toppled him, but the Viking's hands settled on his throat and began choking. The referee kept close, his mallet up over his shoulder in case he should need to hit someone.

"By the way," Harris said, "in these regular matches, being hit by that hammer doesn't mean you're disqualified. It just means you're doing something you're not supposed to. They keep hitting until you stop."

"So can you be disqualified?"

"Not at this stage, no. You can just surrender, pass out, or die." Harris offered a cheerless smile.

The muscleman got his hands under his opponent's and broke his grip. He rolled away, surprisingly fast in spite of his lack of breath, but the Viking scrambled after him. The Viking got his hands on the muscleman's right foot and twisted hard, attempting to break his ankle.

The muscleman shouted, a noise made hoarse and raspy by the fact he still hadn't caught his breath, and rolled in the direction of the Viking's twist. As he rolled over onto his back, he kicked, the blow smashing the Viking's nose flat. The crowd roared in appreciation. The Viking rocked back and the muscleman had enough time to get to his feet. Though still red-faced, he seemed much recovered.

They came together again, but as they grabbed, the Viking lowered his head and smashed it into the muscleman's face, knocking the fighter's head back and breaking his nose as well. Now both men had blood streaming from their faces. The Viking followed up, overbearing his opponent and sending him to the ground; the Viking fell atop him, scrambling for a grip, and managed to get his hands on the muscleman's left forearm, twisting it up behind his back.

The muscleman thrashed around with his feet and free arm, trying to maneuver his body to reduce the pressure on his arm, but the Viking held him in place and leaned harder and harder against the arm. He said something into the muscleman's ear.

"Telling him to surrender," Harris said. "You do that by tapping the ground three times."

Zeb offered him a grin that showed more confidence than he felt. "I don't need to know that, man."

The crowd grew more quiet, listening, it seemed, for the muscleman's answer, but the man just strained harder. So did the Viking.

Then the muscleman shook his head and reached out with his free hand, hammering the ground once—

His held arm broke at the elbow with a dull noise like a bunch of celery being snapped. The Viking's pressure bent it double so his hand lay atop his upper arm.

The muscleman shrieked, the noise audible even over the gasps and cheers from the crowd. The Viking was up and off him in a second, an expression of contrition on his face; he turned to the referee, hands outstretched as if pleading. The referee, unconcerned, waved his words away. More referees trotted down the step of the reviewing stand, carrying a stretcher.

Zeb felt his stomach lurch. He'd seen gunshot victims and other injuries, but the only ones that seemed to bother him were the ones that made the human body take a shape it was not meant to assume. The muscleman lay there, writhing, unable to keep his body still or keep himself quiet, while the Viking uneasily accepted the cheers of the crowd. The field referee pointed the mallet at him, acknowledging his victory.

"Oleg Stammgalf," Harris said. "He wasn't considered a contender coming into this."

The head referee, distinguished by the gold trim on his red referee's outfit, addressed the field in Burian and the crowd quieted a little.

"What's he saying?" Zeb asked. "Oh, never mind. Why did I pick a trainer who can't speak the language?"

Harris grinned. "'Cause I come cheap."

A fighter Zeb had engaged in the previous day's round, the large man with the walrus mustache, said, "He thanks the athletes for a clean match." His voice bore a heavy Burian accent. His attention was on the field—where the referees had transferred the muscleman to the stretcher and were now carrying him away—rather than on Zeb and Harris.

"That was a clean match?" Zeb asked.

The man nodded. "The referee did not have to punish any foul. No swinging of the hammer. The gods like that. No athlete died. The athletes like that. That is a clean match."

Zeb extended a hand. "Zeb Watson, representing Novimagos."

Walrus Mustache looked at him for the first time, expressionless, and shook his hand. "Geert Tiwasson. Of Weseria."

"Figures," Zeb said. "I expect I'll be fighting you in a later round."

Geert nodded and returned his attention to the field. "I look forward to it."

The second bout was between Colonel Förster, the handsome man Zeb had exchanged words with during the preliminary round, and Corcair Highknocker of Cretanis, a heavyset man with a bald head, a red beard, and red bristly hair on every other part of his body not covered by his athlete's outfit. Highknocker's outfit was not in the red and green of Cretanis, but all of purple; his love of the color, Zeb learned, was one of his well-known affectations.

This match was less spectacular than the previous one: The two competitors came together and wrestled around for a while, then Förster managed to maneuver himself into a superior position and choked Highknocker unconscious. Highknocker was carried from the field on a stretcher; Förster accepted the cheers of the crowd with quiet grace, then returned to the sideline.

"You're up next," Harris said.

Zeb nodded. "Got any advice?" He bounced up and down on the balls of his feet, loosening up, feeling the first waves of adrenaline and agitation roll across him.

"Not having seen Kano fight, that's kind of tough. First thing, if he's like the sumo guys of the grim world, he's going to be faster than you expect. Think of him as a modern NFL lineman."

"That's encouraging. Go on." Zeb stared down the sideline at his opponent, who was stretching in a low crouch. Kano seemed to be staring into the distance, paying no attention to anyone around him, though an older Oriental man of similar proportions, wearing a lime-green suit cut to his generous size, was at his side, speaking constantly in his ear.

"He outweighs you by about a hundred and fifty,

hundred and seventy pounds, so don't try to push him around. Leverage is something he knows about."

"I'm feeling better all the time. What else?"

Harris's voice took an exasperated tone. "What I'm telling you is that you have to dictate this fight and keep it centered in the things you know how to do and he doesn't. He knows pushing, grabbing, knocking down, pulling you down, a pretty mean slap. Oh, yeah, the sumo guys here do something that ours don't—a sort of stomp maneuver. It can break your leg at the ankle, and if he does it to you when you're down, he can break your arms or legs or cave in your rib cage. So don't let him do that."

"Don't let him kill me. At last I understand." Zeb gave Harris a smile. "Don't worry. I win or I lose. Except that I don't lose."

"Sort of a minimalist philosophy," Harris said, "but I like it."

"Tanuki Kano," called the head referee, "Zeb Watson."

Zeb moved out fast, arms raised to wave at the crowd as though anyone there might be rooting for him. He passed the field referee and turned back to wait for Kano. He wasn't smiling, nor had he yet put on his war-face; the expression he offered the crowd was one of deadly intensity. Some in the crowd responded not with boos, but there was also an increase in the volume of their conversation, and the first flash-bulbs began popping.

Once past the official, Zeb turned. Kano was close behind, expressionless, alert. He stopped just short of the official, facing Zeb.

Seeing him face-on for the first time this morning, Zeb was startled. Kano's shorts and shirt were white with red decorations, presumably the colors of Wo, and the decoration occupying most of the chest was a swastika. It wasn't the classic Nazi swastika—it was backwards, as if the image had been flipped, and with lines connecting the four ends of the design to the long lines, so the effect was that of a plus sign with triangles at each end. Still, it was recognizably a swastika, and he had to remind himself of Gaby's words of the other night—it had been a decorative symbol from ancient times, long before the Nazis got their hands on it.

He couldn't afford to be distracted by stray thoughts. He returned his attention to Kano's face, to his eyes, and projected a sense of invincibility and indomitable will. Kano returned his gaze with the implacability of a cow . . . or a boulder.

The referee spoke to them in Burian, doubtless the catalogue of rules and punishments, and at one point hefted his long-handled mallet significantly. Then he gestured for the two athletes to step back. When they did, he extended his mallet between them, then raised it, sign that the bout had begun.

Kano advanced, hands at shoulder level, with the relentlessness of a bowling ball set into motion.

Zeb waited until he was almost within grabbing distance. He held his left, guard, hand in place as a lure. Kano grabbed at it. Zeb pivoted, drawing his guard hand back, slapping Kano's hands out of line with his right, and launched a snapkick, slamming his foot into Kano's left knee.

The kick should have at least unbalanced the big man, but his left leg remained resolutely planted and apparently undamaged. Kano's cheek twitched, whether with momentary pain or amusement Zeb couldn't tell. With a deft move, Kano disengaged his right hand from Zeb's, caught Zeb's wrist and yanked; he got his left hand on Zeb's shoulder, preparatory to straightening Zeb's arm to apply leverage or break it at the elbow. Before Kano could finish the maneuver, Zeb dropped to his knees, under Kano's reaching hand. Using Kano's own grip on him for additional stability, he twisted, slamming his left palm into Kano's right knee from the side, a breaking technique.

The joint held, but Kano hissed and stumbled. Zeb took advantage of his momentary lack of balance. He twisted the wrist Kano held, breaking his grip but not breaking contact, and got his own hand locked on Kano's wrist. As he did so, he stood and twisted, getting a grip with his free hand on Kano's upper arm, locking his arm at the elbow. He drove with all his strength against this new lever and Kano fell, his face slamming into the grass.

Kano's legs thrashed around, kicking Zeb's out from under him. Zeb's back hit the ground, not too painfully, but in his peripheral vision he saw Kano already rolling over to grab at him. Zeb managed an awkward backwards somersault, getting his body out of the way of Kano's onrushing mass, and rolled up to his feet; though off-balance, he managed another snapkick, and this one caught Kano in the side of the face, rocking his head.

Zeb backed away. It went against his grain not to press an advantage, but he needed a moment to think. Kano was faster than he looked, as Harris had said, and at least as impervious to pain as Zeb was.

He became aware, momentarily, of the crowd noise. It had increased. There were still boos. Some in the crowd were shouting "Kano, Kano, Kano." Others, a smaller group, were shouting "Svart, Svart, Svart." Zeb suppressed a feeling of irritation.

Kano got to his feet, though Zeb was gratified to see that he was favoring his right leg. The blow to the knee had hurt him more than he had initially let on. That made his knee a vulnerable point. Kano advanced again, expressionless.

Zeb continued backing and allowed an expression of uncertainty to cross his face. Kano picked up speed. Zeb kept his attention on Kano's injured leg and, as the big man came almost within grabbing range, dropped—a controlled drop to his back, arms splayed for better stability—and drew up his own leg, chambering it. Kano adjusted, diving at him, but as his right leg planted for his final step, Zeb kicked with all his force at the joint. He felt the blow connect.

Then Kano landed on him. All the breath left Zeb's body. It felt as though his lungs left, too. But he forced himself to shove—Kano's armpit was directly above his face and Zeb got his hand in it, using it for purchase, and heaved. Kano rolled a little from the effort, not trying to hold on to him. Zeb wriggled free and felt a moment of elation. If Kano had not been hurt, he would have pinned Zeb.

Zeb got to his feet, trying, unsuccessfully, to suck in a breath. Kano was still lying there, curling around his leg, and Zeb could see that the leg was wrong— bent partly backwards as though the joint were reversed and slightly flexed.

Zeb managed to drag in a breath. It was not deep and not without pain, but it gave him the strength to move. He dropped to his knees beside Kano's legs and grabbed the foot of the injured leg, but didn't twist it. "Save yourself some pain, man."

Kano opened his eyes. His face was covered in sweat and finally was showing emotion, the pain of his injury too great for him to conceal, but he mastered himself, his features smoothing until only by the tightness of his features and pain in his eyes could his distress be discerned. He stared at Zeb a long moment, allowed himself an expression of dissatisfaction, and reached out to slap the ground three times.

Zeb stood. The crowd noise came to him again. A

portion of the audience was cheering, "Svart—Svart—Svart—" and "Novimagos! Novimagos!" He raised a hand, working the crowd a little, then shook the referee's hand when the man offered it to him.

Moments later, he sat on the sidelines with Harris. Harris worked on his back, massaging where it was stiffening from his impacts with the ground. "Pretty good, Zeb."

"Thanks." Zeb watched as two new competitors took the field, both of them tall, fair-haired men. "I thought German for 'black' was 'schwarz,' not 'svart.'"

"It is. 'Svart' isn't Burian. It's from the Scandinavian languages and it's used all over western Europe to mean 'dusky.' They were basically saying, 'Go, dusky.'"

"They could at least have used my name."

"Yeah. Well, I was chanting your name, but the rest of the crowd shouted me down. Maybe tomorrow they'll know who you are."

"Count on it."

"Or you could change your name to 'Svart.' First and last names. 'Svart Svart.' That way they'd always get it right."

Zeb ignored him.

"Anyway," Harris said, "we need to watch the rest of the All-Out matches, get some idea of what we can expect from your likely opponents, and then head over to the Sword venue."

"Sword?" Zeb shook his head. "No, I'm going to work with Noriko before her first match."

"You'll have time to do that. But first we go to watch the Sword competition for a while. This morning, I did a little makeup magic. We're going to debut our Teleri Obeldon there."

"Ah."

The Sword competition was scheduled for a new gymnasium on the Sonneheim Games grounds. When Zeb, Harris, Gaby, and Noriko arrived, the stands were already almost filled. The sidelines were theoretically restricted to athletes and other participants, which would have excluded Gaby, but no one challenged her when she stayed with the others; things here seemed relatively informal.

Zeb craned his neck to look back up into the stands. "Place is packed," he said. "There are more waiting to get in. There's a film crew here, for God's sake. Just amazing."

"Why is that amazing?" Noriko asked.

"It's a grimworld thing," Harris said. "Where we're from, sword competition is called fencing, and it just doesn't get a lot of respect or news coverage, even in the Olympic Games, which is our biggest competition."

"What does, then?" she asked.

Zeb and Harris looked at one another.

"Well, track and field," Zeb said.

"Women's gymnastics," Harris said. "Which is actually teen and preteen *girls'* gymnastics, come to think about it."

"And anything where our country is favored to win the gold," Gaby said. "Regardless of whether the public has any interest in the sport the rest of the time."

Harris nodded. "Nicely, cynically put, honey. Hey, there's Ruadan."

On the opposite side of the gymnasium, beyond the numberless lanes marked off by tape on the wooden floor, Ruadan was indeed standing. He wore the same swordsman's outfit the other competitors wore—neck to toe leathers in a light color, his being a pale yellow. He held an object that looked like a domino mask made of metal; the eye slits were narrow. He was only recognizable by his size, unusually large for competitors in this sport, and his bright red hair.

"Looks like the Sword part of the Officer competition is today," Zeb said. "Hey. Is that a Sonnenkrieger officer he's talking to?"

It was. Ruadan's partner in conversation was dressed in the sharp black uniform of Weseria's elite shock troops. The distance was too great for Zeb to make out the man's rank.

Harris offered up a grimace. "One more thing to check into. I'll add it to the list. Ah, there we go. Doc and Swana. Ish is a few rows behind them."

Zeb followed Harris's gaze. He didn't spot Doc until he found Ixyail, who was decked out once more in her safari-style outfit. Three rows below her, Doc, his complexion now ruddy, his hair black and short, wearing wire-rimmed glasses, was in a stylish green suit. Beside him, Teleri sat stiffly, watching the action on the gymnasium floor.

It was Swana, of course, but at this distance she was a perfect match for Teleri. Swana's hair had been cut to Teleri's style, its color adjusted to Teleri's; Swana wore glasses and green clothes nearly identical to those Teleri had worn at the museum. "Harris, you did a great job on her."

"Didn't I? Aren't I just magnificent?"

"In spite of your usual incompetence, I mean." Out of the corner of his eye, Zeb saw Harris grin at the jibe.

There was a pop from a loudspeaker, sudden enough to make many people in the crowd jump, and an announcer began speaking in Burian. He went on at length. Crowd noise rose, obscuring it, as the audience, obviously well-acquainted with the facts about the day's events, spoke more loudly to be heard over the announcer's voice.

After a pause, a new voice came over the system and began speaking in Cretanis. From what Zeb could gather over the crowd noise, this had to be a translation of the last announcer's words; this man welcomed visitors to early-round events in the Sword competition and the entirety of the Sword portion of the Officer competition. One blooding of a sword arm meant the competitor had to switch to his off hand or yield; two bloodings of torso, neck or head meant defeat.

"Wait a second," Zeb said. "Blooding? They're fighting with sharp blades?"

Noriko nodded. "Of course. You can often tell a swordsman. By the scars. Little ones, the width of a finger, means he fights with rapier. Broader ones means he fights with saber. Ruadan doesn't have any on his face, which says a lot for his ability to protect his upper body."

"Or to afford healing devisement to get rid of scars completely," Harris said.

"Great," Zeb said. "Harris, you said All-Out was the worst of the sports."

Harris shrugged. "More people die in All-Out. With Sword, there's a code of behavior, an assumption that all competitors are noble of spirit if not of birth. There's nothing like that with All-Out, where the competitors are supposed to be, well, more earthy."

"Earthy. What do you mean, like trailer trash?"

"'Of the people,' Zeb." Harris grinned. "You know, like Hercules. A great hero, but also a common guy. Everybody likes him."

Zeb shook his head and returned his attention to Doc and Swana. "So Ish is supposed to be guarding them?"

"No, she's not supposed to interact with them in any way." Harris began scanning the crowd in Doc's vicinity.

"She's just hovering because, well, it's Doc. No, Rudi is their guard. There he is. Two rows up from Doc and three to the left."

Zeb spotted him easily enough, though he didn't initially recognize him. Rudi was in a rumpled burnt orange suit; his features were aged, his hair gray, and he wore a thick beard and mustache the same color. He actually resembled Albin more than he resembled himself. "I bet he hates that outfit."

"Oh, he does. He likes to be stylish, at least in what Neckerdam gangsters call style. If we don't give him someone to shoot soon, he's probably going to kill me instead."

Soon enough, the Sword bouts got under way. They were, Zeb found, far more structured than All-Out. The crowd was allowed to cheer as the athletes were brought out to the lanes, but not once the fighting began. Four bouts ran at any given time, but the athletes who'd completed their bouts did not leave the field until the last of the four bouts was settled. Only then did all eight athletes receive the farewell cheers of the crowd.

Bouts didn't generally last long, either. Once the referee set the athletes into motion, action was generally not halted until a winner was declared, as the swordsmen themselves would step back to allow their opponents to switch their blades to their unhurt arms. And it generally did not take long for one swordsman in each pairing to pick up two injuries to his torso.

Women also fought, Zeb saw, though they did seem to have their own division and fought only against one another.

But he took in all these facts with only a portion of his attention; mostly, he was focussed on Doc and Swana in the stands, or, rather, on the people in the stands and aisles around them.

Not that any activity seemed to center around them. Zeb saw people pass in front of Doc and Swana at various times, moving to and from their assigned seating, and noticed one or two men attempt to strike up conversations with her. But she just smiled—Zeb saw that her expression looked a bit nervous, and wondered whether that was deliberate or accidental on her part— and shook her head to disengage from conversation. Doc glowered at such times, and the young men in question were comparatively quick to move about their business.

"Look, Casnar's up next," Gaby said.

Zeb turned his attention to the gymnasium floor. Prince Casnar, in the standard swordsman's suit but with a design, an eagle atop a mound of stones, on his back, was indeed taking up position at one end of a lane. A similarly-clad opponent, this one wearing an armband with three limbless trees in gold against a red background, faced him.

The two swordsmen saluted, holding their blades point upright before their faces and then extending them toward the sky, then dropped into fighting poses. Both men were right-handed, and their postures were right-side forward, right elbows tucked in close, left arms extended behind them for balance.

The opponent moved forward in a series of cautious half steps and offered an exploratory thrust, angling in high over the bell that protected Casnar's hand and arcing down to stab at his forearm, so fluid that Zeb was sure he saw the blade bend during its motion, but Casnar flicked his hand up, his blade and his bell collaborating to sweep the incoming blade out of line; his bell rang from the impact as he thrust, and suddenly his opponent was backing away, acknowledging by pointing, the small spot of redness now welling through his protective leathers. Casnar smiled.

"That's a surprise," Harris said.

"What, that Casnar acts like a party boy but knows how to stab people?"

"No. What Ruadan's doing."

Zeb turned his attention that way. Ruadan was still standing beside his Sonnenkrieger acquaintance, and was now pointing up into the stands. He kept glancing at the officer and speaking to him, as if asking questions, then looking back at the stands. Zeb followed Ruadan's gaze.

Zeb might have been wrong, but Ruadan looked as though he were pointing in the general vicinity of Doc and Swana. "This gets better and better," he said.

The crowd made a slight appreciative noise, indicating that one of the four matches below had ended. Zeb saw Casnar's opponent, now decorated by two bloody spots on his chest, walking forward, holding his sword by the blade so that the hilt and bell were extended forward. Casnar, at ease, tapped the hilt with his hand, and then the two men shook hands and stood together, watching the other bouts.

Not long after, Ruadan took leave of the officer he'd been speaking to in order to fight his first match. Unlike Casnar, who used rapier, Ruadan was announced as a sabreur. His first opponent was a swordsman of the kingdom of Loria, and the two fought in a style that was all edge—swords swung fast, directly at face and body and arm, blocked by the opponent's blade.

It looked to Zeb's inexperienced eye like the sort of swashbuckling he'd often seen in old movies on TV. The difference was that those actors had always moved at a pace that seemed sedate, while these swordsmen's attacks and defenses were fast, often mere streaks and blurs to the unaided eye. Nor did these athletes seem to be swinging at empty air or waiting for their opponent to be in the exact place needed to keep them perfectly safe.

Ruadan was blooded first, a slash that grazed his eye mask with a shriek of metal on metal and left a thin red line on his brow—a line that swiftly broadened and poured blood across Ruadan's cheek.

The referee quickly halted the bout. An assistant put a towel across Ruadan's shoulders and chest while another pinched the edges of the injury together and applied quick stitches without anaesthetic. Zeb saw Ruadan wince once, but the man offered no other reaction.

"By the rules of the sport," Noriko said, "they are not concerned with his blood loss. But if too much blood gets on his clothes, it becomes hard to register other injuries."

"Oh." Zeb shook his head. "In Sword of Wo, you *do* compete with wooden swords, right?"

"Yes." She offered a slight smile. "There, you can only break bones."

"Good. I'm relieved."

The referee blotted the wound, nodded to indicate that the bleeding was sufficiently slowed, and returned to his starting point at the center of the lane. The assistant whisked the bloody towel away and Ruadan took his starting pose. A moment later, the fight was on again. The other three bouts on the floor had ended while the stitches were being applied, so Ruadan's was the only one still going.

On the swordsmen's next approach, the two managed to lock blades near the hilts. As they disengaged, Ruadan brought his blade up and away in a draw-cut, slicing through two layers of leather, his opponent's glove cuff and sleeve. The opponent backed away, glanced at the cut, then pointed at it to acknowledge it as an injury. He transferred his saber to his left hand and action resumed. Now, though, he was at a decided disadvantage, and during the next two passes Ruadan

was able to draw blood both times, once in a slash that
took his opponent on the shoulder, once in another
draw-cut disengagement that brought his blade along
his opponent's rib cage.

The crowd applauded and the four lanes' worth of
competitors quit the floor.

Ruadan returned to the sidelines. A man in baggy
pants and top in Novimagos blue and gold was there
to await him and tend his injuries, but the
Sonnenkrieger officer was gone.

"Where's that son of a krieger?" Zeb asked.

"He left," Gaby said.

Zeb looked around. "Where's Harris?"

"Following that son of a krieger."

"Great." Zeb looked at Noriko. "I hate to miss what
Harris is up to, but it's probably time to get you set
up for your first round."

She nodded, her face giving nothing away, but reluc-
tance obvious in the stiffness of her motion.

The arrangements for the Sword of Wo event were
much like that of the Sword competition, except that
the event was set up in a large exercise room in a
school building several blocks from the coliseum
grounds. The crowd, seated in low-backed wooden
chairs doubtless scrounged from other rooms in the
school, was much smaller than that of the other event.
Zeb counted maybe fifty of them. All appeared to be
Burian lights and darks, many of them well-dressed and
sophisticated of manner, quite a few of them elderly.
Zeb got the impression from looking at them that he
was seeing a group gathered for a university lecture,
and realized that most probably weren't sports fans—
they were students and academicians curious about the
culture and people of Wo.

Which suggested—Zeb took a closer look around,

and was not surprised to see Colonel Förster in the audience. The man was in street clothes, but as radiantly blond as ever. Though he was seated in the most tightly-packed section of the audience, he was alone, not exchanging words with other spectators. Looking around, he spotted Zeb looking at him, but his gaze slid off Zeb as though he hadn't seen him.

None of the Sidhe Foundation members was here. Some were working on other assignments, of course. As for the rest—Noriko had said she didn't want an audience. Zeb hadn't had enough time to argue with her about that. Support from the audience, even just a portion of the audience, could make a difference to a competitor—did she just want to cede that advantage to her opponent? Did she want to lose?

"Noriko-chan!" Prince Hayato approached his cousin, hand outstretched, a smile of satisfaction on his face. He was dressed in the skirtlike pants and cumbersome jacket Zeb associated with kendo, though his outfit was painfully bright, the pants so white they almost glowed, the jacket in a bright red with the variant swastika of Wo reversed on the chest in white. "I am so pleased you have come. I feared you would regret your offer of the other night and choose not to compete."

She took his hand. "No, I am here."

Hayato waited a moment as if expecting her to elaborate. "Well. We have assembled you a full set of equipment. With Tanyu's injury, but the addition of you and a Shangan competitor named Chang Tian-yun, the one the Cretanis press calls Chang O'Shang, we have a field of seven. The referees have decided that I, as ranking noble, will have the bye this round." He gave her a very Western shrug. "Privileges of rank, I suppose. But it means the earliest I might face you is next round."

"Yes," she said.

Hayato again paused to allow her time to continue, but she did not. He turned to Zeb. "Though we could have a full field of eight if you chose to compete."

Zeb shook his head. "I barely know which end of a sword to hold. Thanks for the offer, though. No, I'm here for Noriko."

"Of course." It was impossible to tell from Hayato's tone which statement he was agreeing with—Zeb's support of Noriko or Zeb's incompetence with a blade. The prince gestured toward dark doors on the wall opposite the audience. "That is the changing room. You are the last to arrive, Noriko, so you will have privacy— though I imagine that your boy will ensure it. Your equipment is in the locker furthest left."

Zeb kept his face impassive. In his mind, though, he imagined throwing several hard blows and kicks into Hayato's midsection, just enough to rearrange his internal organs a bit.

"Thank you," Noriko said, but did not move.

Hayato offered her a minimal smile, then turned to walk toward the trio of judges standing in the center of the room.

"'Your boy.'" Zeb shook his head and willed his souring stomach to settle down. "Man, he does know which knife to twist. Would it upset you if I tore his head off and you didn't get to fight him?"

She gave him a little smile. "Remain focussed," she said.

"Like you, huh? That was actually pretty spectacular, Noriko. You fought your first round with him and sent him into retreat. In less than ten words, yet."

She walked with him to the door to the changing room. "I have been thinking about him. He is a master at making people feel bad in conversation. Then they do what he wishes and he relents so they feel better. But all his ploys, I realized, are ripostes. If you

do not take the first strike, if you do not respond to
his feints, he has nothing to work with."

"Good work. Is his swordplay the same way?"

"Unfortunately, no." She shrugged, suggesting that
this was just the way things were, and went into the
equipment room.

Zeb pulled the door shut behind her and turned to
wait. To keep the world full of her opponents at bay.

The drawing for opponents was performed much as
it had been with the All-Out, except that names were
handwritten on paper rather than impressed on porcelain chits. Noriko, whose borrowed armor was covered by what looked like a hastily-sewn surcoat in the
blue and gold of Novimagos, drew the name of Ikina
Toki. "I don't know him," she told Zeb.

They looked over the field of competitors, and there
was only one whom Noriko did not recognize, a big
Oriental man, unusually heavy among this crowd of
lithe sword competitors; he also appeared to be ten
or more years older than the next-oldest athlete
present. "Hey, I know that guy," Zeb said. "Tanuki
Kano's trainer. Terrible taste in suits."

"If he trains Kano, then he will be a former sumo
competitor," Noriko said. "Possibly trained in the sword
at little more than a hobby level. But much stronger
than I."

"And probably faster than he looks."

"You have finally learned that, have you?"

Zeb glanced at her, surprised. She was smiling at
him, her expression making it clear that she was teasing.

He grinned back. "Remain focussed."

In the first bout, two members of Hayato's retinue,
both in dark armor with white-swastika-on-red
armbands, were the competitors. When the Burian
judge lifted his badge of office—here, a live-steel saber

identical to the ones being used at the Sword competition—the men came together like cars colliding head-on. They shouted, they locked wooden blades and pushed, they jockeyed for position, they swung and blocked with their blades so fast that Zeb sometimes could not readily follow the motion.

Zeb decided that, at least superficially, the sport resembled the few kendo matches he'd seen on the grim world. The competitors fought in two-handed style, swords held before them, hands well spaced across the long hilts to give them maximum leverage. The style was all offense—no attacks ever just missed, they were intercepted by the opponent's blade.

In moments, the first bout was done, the taller of the two men catching the other's blade across his rigid mask. All action stopped instantly and the loser bowed. Then the referee came forward to interpose his sword between them. The two went on guard again.

"How many do they go to?" Zeb asked.

"Two kills," Noriko said.

Moments later, the winner of the first kill struck his opponent again. The crowd offered applause. Zeb and Noriko joined in. The athletes quit the floor.

"Noriko Nomura, Novimagos," the referee said. "Ikina Toki, Wo."

Noriko picked up her mask from the floor at her feet and put it on. She turned her back so Zeb could do the lacings there. Then he handed her the bokken, the wooden sword she'd been assigned. "Go get him, tiger."

She cocked her head. "Tiger?"

"It's an expression where I'm from."

"Ah. Be sure to use the same expression on Ish sometime." She offered him a little bow and took the floor. Ikina was already waiting on the far side of the referee.

Hayato drifted over to stand beside Zeb. "I don't think I've ever seen such a size mismatch in Sword of Wo," he said. "I expect Ikina will slaughter her."

"Because she's a woman?"

Hayato shook his head. "Because of the size. One presumes he can compete at some proficient level, else he'd not be here. His size and strength will be terribly difficult to overcome. In addition, she is, unfortunately, a trifle weak. Of spirit, I mean."

"She'll win."

"Because she's your friend?"

Zeb shook his head. He concentrated his attention on the competitors, who were receiving instructions from the referee. Both nodded and took a step back. The referee extended his saber between them. "Because she's a winner."

"Ah."

The referee raised his blade.

Ikina charged Noriko and snapped a blow at her, the blade of the wooden sword blurring with the speed of the attack. Noriko retreated and took the blow on her own blade, her backward motion robbing the blow of some of its force. Ikina continued his forward progress, shoving to hurl her back, and snapped another blow as their blades came clear. But she was raising her blade as he was drawing his back for the blow, and caught the top of his blade toward her hilt. She levered his bladepoint out of the way and brought her own edge across his mask. The sharp crack of the blow sounded like a small-caliber pistol shot.

Ikina bowed.

"I see what you mean," Hayato said. "She finds a way to win."

Zeb nodded. He estimated that the time from start to kill was about three seconds.

The competitors returned to the center of the floor

and the referee set them into motion again. Ikina began
with the same tactic—the correct tactic, Zeb estimated,
despite the first loss—but on his first blow, his bokken
broke across Noriko's. The blade clattered across the
floor toward Hayato; the prince put out a foot and
trapped it like a soccer player stopping a ball. Action
stopped while a referee brought Ikina another blade,
then resumed.

This kill was almost a replay of the last. Ikina used
his greater mass and strength to his advantage, driving Noriko before him, going in for the kill once he'd
put her off balance, but he didn't realize in time that
she was never sufficiently off balance for her defenses
to lower completely. The second time he shoved her
back, she managed to keep her blade in line, and
position his out of line; she twisted so that her hilt was
over her head, her blade point out ahead of her and
under his arm, and she yanked, a draw-cut that would
have cut through his armpit to the bone had the blade
been real.

He stopped and bowed. She returned the bow,
offered one to the judge and another to the prince,
then returned to Zeb's side. He began unlacing her
mask.

"I expected your skills to have diminished," Hayato
said. "And you have lost a little fluidity. Yet I think you
are better than before."

She drew the mask off. She was perspiring but
smiling. "I hope to have a chance to see you fight
before we meet. That you not have the advantage of
me."

The next fight was between a member of Hayato's
retinue and the man nicknamed Chang O'Shang. Chang
was tall for a fairworlder, especially for an oriental
fairworlder, almost as tall as Zeb. Only his neck,
well-muscled, and his head were bare; his armor was

dark and not adorned by any national symbol or colors. His hair was long and braided, though not in the Chinese queue Zeb knew from old photographs and movies.

The man of Wo was quick, possibly as quick as Noriko, but Chang was his equal there and his superior in strength and reach. The swordsman of Wo actually won the first kill, but Chang came back in the second and third bouts with harder, faster attacks that battered his opponent's defenses down and left him vulnerable to shots to head and shoulder.

"No matter who you draw tomorrow," Zeb said, "it's going to be interesting."

Chapter Seventeen

The restaurant was actually a beer garden, a place of long wooden tables whose antiquity was attested to by the way graffiti carved in them was covered by lacquer darkened by grime and worn smooth by friction from countless hands and arms.

On the walls were the coats of arms of dozens of kings of Weseria and smoke-darkened posters advertising various types of beer. There was no sign of the modern nation here, no acknowledgement of the Sonneheim Games, no Reini symbols.

Most unusual of all in the modern Bardulfburg, the place admitted duskies. Among the clientele were squat men and women the color of pecan shells who came barely up to Zeb's belt buckle; there were tall, fair-skinned lights; and there were men and women of every shape, hue and height in between.

Alastair and Gaby were already seated when Zeb and Noriko arrived, holding down a long table in the dimmest end of the room. Doc, Rudi, and Swana, all still in disguise, and Ish arrived minutes later, just as the waiters were bringing out the first orders of sausage and schnitzels. Harris was last to arrive.

Doc looked longingly at Gaby's plate of cutlets and spätzel. "We appear to have survived our first full day of trouble making. Now we need to assess the damage we've done. Gaby, would you like to go first?"

She shook her head. "Hell, no. You're the one with no food. You go first."

"Thus we demonstrate the respect I have earned from the Foundation associates . . ." With what looked like an effort, Doc dragged his attention from Gaby's plate. "The Teleri deception has paid off. Swana and I were followed when we left the Sword venue. Our shadows were not uniformed, of course, so we have no concrete knowledge of who they are. Still, it's encouraging that they're observant and numerous enough to have spotted her and interested enough to follow her. We had to go to some considerable effort to elude them and get here unseen, and we only lost them a couple of blocks from here." He glanced at Alastair, but the doctor, his mouth full of sausage, shook his head vigorously. Doc turned instead to Harris.

Harris cleared his throat. "You might not have seen, Doc, but our good friend Ruadan was among the competitors in Sword."

"I saw."

"And was spending a lot of his time on the sidelines talking to what looked like a good buddy in the Sonnenkrieger."

"That I did not see." Doc frowned.

"Anyway, at one point it looked as though Ruadan and his buddy were discussing our Teleri here, and the buddy took off. So I followed. He headed off to a talkbox booth and made a call. Since I don't speak Burian, I didn't get any of what he said. I didn't hear Teleri's name used."

Doc nodded. "Or mine, I hope."

"You were protected by the sheer brilliance of my makeup, Doc. Of course your name wasn't used."

"Of course. What then?"

"He returned to the door to the gym and waited. He was watching Swana, I'm pretty sure. He was there another twenty minutes or so, and then he was joined by six other guys in street clothes. All lights, young, really good posture. He pointed your section of the bleachers out to them and talked. I couldn't hear anything they said; I'd had to pull back down the corridor so as not to be conspicuous. Anyway, the guys filed into the gym by twos and merged with the crowd."

"And it was as we left the Sword event that Rudi noticed our first shadow," Doc said.

Rudi, finishing a glass of beer, nodded. He raised his glass to get the waiter's attention. "Two lights. Looked like military. Not too good at following."

Swana, obviously reluctant to speak up in this gathering, finally found her voice. "What will happen if they decide to do more than follow me? Do they not want to talk to this Teleri? Could they try to capture me?"

Rudi made a contemptuous noise. "They're no damned good at what they do. Sure, they'll try to grab you, but not tonight—we've already lost them once and will lose them again if they spot us on the way home."

"It's true." Doc's voice was reassuring. "And from now on, as it was this morning, you'll constantly be surrounded by more firepower than they're ever likely to bring to bear in a kidnapping attempt. Still, after we get back to the quarters tonight, I'll work with you on a set of answers you can give to officials if you're ever interrogated. These will be answers that will keep you safe long enough for us to find you and spirit you away."

They quieted as the waiter came over to refill Rudi's

glass and stayed that way moments longer as a woman, four feet tall and built like a Franklin stove, arrived with the food orders of the latecomers. Then Doc turned to Zeb.

"I've got nothing but glorious victory to report so far," Zeb said. "I wasted Tanuki Kano this morning in All-Out, and Noriko wiped out her opponent this afternoon in Sword of Wo. Oh, yeah, that guy Förster was at Sword of Wo. I don't know whether it's because of some conspiracy between the Reinis and Hayato's group or just because he's supposed to be curious about all sorts of fighting arts. Anyway, the opponent draw in the All-Out is fixed; I'm going to meet every badass on the field. I don't know whether the draw in the Sword of Wo is rigged."

"I do not believe it is," Noriko said. "That sort of thing is not among Hayato's many flaws of character."

Doc nodded. "Alastair? Can you now put off chewing for a moment?"

"Reluctantly." Alastair set his fork and knife down. "I found the tribe of Kobolde who tried to kill you at the Fairwings plant."

Doc's eyebrows rose. "You've done some travelling today, then."

"No. They're here in Bardulfburg. And they're very anxious to meet you. Not for a return engagement."

"Very well. Let's have the full story."

"Well, I estimated that the best way to find Kobolde would be to find Kobolde—meaning, I'd look for any that might be living in the big city and see if they could tell me anything about their country cousins. So I looked at the various newspapers and found one, distributed only in a few places, that is written for the dusky communities. I visited the newspaper itself and asked about Kobolde, and the editor told me they're pretty rare in Weseria—except for a performing troupe here in Bardulfburg. When I went to visit them, their responses—they're not proficient actors—made it clear that they were related to your captors."

Doc looked mildly amused. "I was held prisoner by a circus?"

Alastair nodded. "Oh, I'm not saying they're not a dangerous, violent group of madmen. They are. Very, very primitive deep-forest folk. But they also perform. Anyway, I went to talk to them. They were surprised to hear that I worked with you and tried to persuade me that you were using me—that you only tolerated me because I could help you get close to duskies and then destroy them."

"My master plan is at last revealed." Doc's voice was dry. Ish snorted, amused.

"I asked them why they thought this about you. It was partly because they see the way things are developing in the Burian lands, the way the lights in charge are taking more and more actions against the duskies, and since you're a light, you're obviously one of the enemy. It was also partly because they had a friend who helped explain such things to them, helped them get along in the world of the lights and darks." Alastair shifted, looking uncomfortable. "There was more to it than that. I got the impression that this 'friend' was also inciting them to acts of violence. Against the lights who are tightening the vise on them."

"That makes no sense," Ish said. "Someone leading the duskies in a guerilla war against the lights? No. We've assumed all along that the real Teleri and the people who kidnapped Doc were part of the Reini movement or at least shared their ideals. Now we have a third group, duskies waging a secret war against the lights?"

"It makes perfect sense," Gaby said. "If this 'third group' really is part of the Reinis or their friends . . . and they're inciting the duskies to acts of violence."

Alastair nodded. "That's what I told them. I said that their 'friend' had convinced them to murder the famous Doc Sidhe and was now probably working up plans to kill some of the high-ranking Reini leaders. That they'd be caught in the act and reprisals would be taken on behalf of an offended light and dark population against duskies. That got them thinking, though they're not admitting to anything. But they want to meet you, Doc. I also told them that Zeb was one of us. That impressed them. They want to meet him, too."

"So the All-Out is getting us some results," Doc said. "Well, let us meet them."

Ish shook her head, vehement. "They just want to finish killing you, Doc."

"Perhaps." Doc stared over the heads of the associates, past the dark wood panel of the walls, off into the unseen distance. "But we still need to meet these Kobolde. If we can convince them we're telling the truth, perhaps they can identify some of our enemies so we'll have a better idea of who specifically they are."

"I was going to take Alastair and Noriko and break into the Hall of Tomorrow, or whatever they call it in Burian," Harris said.

Doc frowned. "Explain that."

"It's an exhibit in one of the new buildings on the Coliseum grounds. I asked around and found out that's where the big model of Bardulfburg is. The one your friend General Ritter displays to show how the city looks now and is going to look in the future. I need Alastair's Good Eye and Noriko's skill with lockpicks."

"You'll have to do that tomorrow night." Doc gave Harris a conciliatory look.

"Then I'll go with you, Doc." Harris fixed his

employer with a stern look. "In case your bloodthirsty midgets decide to get violent."

"And I," Ish said.

"Me, too," Gaby said.

"Me," Noriko said.

Zeb just raised a hand to indicate he was in.

Doc turned his attention to Rudi and Swana. "Which leaves only the two of you."

"I want to get away from all this madness for the evening," Rudi said. "Eat a nice, slow meal. See a film play. Walk about a bit."

"That would be nice," Swana said.

Doc pulled at his beard. "Harris, can you get us all out of makeup?"

Harris patted himself down. From a pocket, he removed a small brown bottle half full of fluid. "Not with what's on me. I can probably get either you or Rudi out of your extra facial hair, but not both."

"Restore me to normal, then, and we'll leave to visit the Kobolde from here," Doc said. "When Rudi and Swana return to our quarters, they can get out of makeup themselves or wait for your return."

"He makes it sound so neat," Gaby said. "Here's what it really boils down to. Rudi and Swana can go home so that bad people can try to follow them around tomorrow. And the rest of us can go talk to the Kobolde so that they can try to kill and eat Doc, tonight."

"That would seem to sum it up," Doc said, and turned his attention to his plate.

The Kobold man—dressed, unlike those they'd seen at the Fairwings factory, in modern pants, shirt, and suspenders, but barefoot—met Doc and associates at the building's front door. He led them through the unlit antechamber into the main worship hall and gestured for them to sit on stone benches on one side; the benches had been pulled around so that, instead of facing forward down the hall, they faced the center of the room. Some twenty Kobolde, also in modern dress, were already seated on benches opposite; the building's hearth was between the two groups.

The hearth was, in traditional style, a stone circle with an upraised lip at the edge, holes sunken in the stone where metal posts could be set to suspend meat above the fire, but this hearth had never been used for cooking; it was free of ashes, its stone darkened by age but never by fire.

The building was Bardulfburg's temple to the goddess Ludana. Doc was familiar with this persona; under several variant names, such as Hludana and Hlodyn, she was goddess of the earth, of the spirits of the dead and the spirits of the newborn, for many of the Burian peoples. Interestingly, this was the place where Casnar's gathering was scheduled to take place tomorrow night. Doc supposed it was symbolically a rallying point for people opposed to the changes being implemented by the Reinis.

The temple was old, a massive thing whose interior and exterior walls were faced with irregular stone. The building had been recently fitted with electricity, but the light for this meeting was cast by candelabra, four floor-standing pieces each bearing nine candles grouped three by three. The light was dim, flickering shadows making the impassive faces of the Kobolde seem more alien and inhuman.

The Kobolde were taking every advantage—seating the Foundation members last to make them guests instead of hosts, placing them on hard benches while the Kobolde had appropriated flat bench pillows, keeping up a sinister facade.

Doc grinned. He hadn't anticipated the benches; that

was a nice touch. This tribe of fair folk might be rural, but they were obviously familiar with the politics of intertribal gatherings. Their other tactics, however, he had anticipated. "Alastair," he said.

Alastair stood and, carrying a cloth sack that looked fully packed, moved up to the hearth. On the hearth's lip, halfway between the two groups, he began placing items from the sack: loaves of bread, sausages, bottles of beer and wine. "We eat bread and we drink water," he said, a ritual phrase.

Alastair returned to sit. The two groups stared at one another again. But now, some of the Kobolde glanced from time to time at the food and drink—not out of hunger, but in slight confusion. *They* were supposed to be the hosts, but the newcomers had provided food. It blurred the lines of who was who. Suddenly a bit of their social advantage was gone.

In Burian, Doc asked, "Who speaks for you?" He heard Alastair murmuring translations to the other associates.

An older man, not the oldest of those present, but still possessing streaks of white in his black hair and beard, stood. "I am Valek," he said. "Prince of Glucksmännchenheim." His voice was deep and rough. It was not the voice of a leader who gave speeches or campaigned to win the affection of his people.

"I am Desmond, son of Prince-Consort Correus of Cretanis," Doc said, "Guard-General of Novimagos, Godsent of the Hu'unal. I thank you for being willing to meet with us." He did not stand; though it would have given him a psychological advantage, he did not need these people to be on the defensive for what was about to come. "Allow me to introduce my associates." He gave the names of Alastair, Ixyail, Harris, Gaby, Noriko, and Zeb, noting the interest of the Kobolde in the last one.

"In the interests of speed, and so that we may speak freely," Doc continued, "I make this public declaration before these witnesses present and before the gods: I formally abandon all rights to revenge against or redress from the people of Glucksmännchenheim for actions they have taken against me."

Some of the little men and women looked at one another, but none spoke before Valek did. "Why do we need to speak freely on this, or at all?" he asked.

"Because our mutual enemies have set us against one another." Doc composed his expression into one made up partly of sympathy, partly of a leader's acceptance of the inevitable. "Of the members of your people sent against me in Novimagos, twenty or more are dead. Some died in honorable combat against my associates. Most died because they were betrayed by their employers. Those men placed powerful explosives, magnacendiaries, in the building where I was held, so that all might die."

Valek looked dubious. "What proof do you have of this claim?"

"Only my pledge of faith, and logic. Alastair Kornbock has spoken to you already. He has guessed that your employers would be planning with you the killings of famous Burians, of highly-placed Reinis. Now I will go a step further. I will tell you who you are planning to kill."

Valek gestured for him to continue.

"General Rombaud Geisel, General Klas Schneemann, and Minister Datan Graumann."

Valek's expression did not change; he was much too experienced and canny a leader for that. But several of the other Kobolde showed surprise. For that many people to react, Doc surmised, the tribe must be very close indeed, with every member trusting every other . . . or else the murder plot must be well along toward completion, with all those involved having already received instructions.

"Why these names?" Valek asked.

"Since arriving in Weseria, I have been looking into the national politics and the politics of the Reinis," Doc said. "The politics that will ultimately doom you to flee the Burian lands. Even in their own ranks, the Reinis see members they consider weaklings, detriments to their plans whom they nonetheless cannot easily be rid of—these men have done too much for the party over the years.

"But if duskies were to assassinate these men, the people of Weseria would begin to cry out against the duskies, and the wrath of the Weserian government could descend upon the duskies. And the Reinis could promote the harder, crueler men they prefer into the positions made vacant by murder." Doc gestured, a palms-out motion suggesting reasonability, that there was no argument to be had with his logic.

Valek stared at him for long moments. Then he walked, a waddling motion, to the food Alastair had brought, selected a bottle of beer, and returned to his seat. "You are wrong," he said, and pried the cork from the bottle. "We are to kill Geisel and Graumann, but not Schneemann."

"But I was close," Doc said.

"Yes." Valek took a drink. The other Kobolde, evidently released by his action, began to move in twos and threes to select food and drink. Ixyail, familiar with the world of tribal politics and manners, hopped up to join them and selected a bottle of wine—it wouldn't do for the associates to ignore the food, as the Kobolde might suspect poison. Harris brought a small loaf of bread back for himself and Gaby.

"You are too wrong to be part of the plan," Valek said, "but too close for it to be just a guess. I will ask you to tell me more. But first I wish to speak with this man." He indicated Zeb.

Alastair moved to sit beside Zeb and spoke in his ear. Zeb spoke back and Alastair translated. "Ask whatever you like."

One of the Kobolde, obviously one who understood Cretanis, whispered in Valek's ear. Valek said, "These games are for lights and darks. Why are you here?"

Zeb shrugged. "If they were for lights and darks just because of where they were being held, I wouldn't care. But they're for more than that. They're to help the lights and darks think they're better than the duskies. That's not right. I'm here to prove that they can't point and say, 'We're better than they are.'"

Valek indicated Doc. "What if this man has tricked you? What if he is on their side?"

"He isn't. He's already risked his life to fight them. I was there. I was also there when the bombs went off and killed your people. Doc didn't plant them. Whoever hired your people planted them."

"Did you kill any of my people?"

Zeb hesitated a moment before answering. "Yes. I'm not sure how many. A couple at least."

"Why should we not kill you?"

"Because I'm going to do some real harm to the Reinis and the way they think. Maybe more than you can. Try to kill me, and you lose more people. Leave me alone, and you get to see me hammer in the faces of some of the local boys you don't like."

Valek considered that, then turned to his people and nodded. A half dozen of the Kobolde rose from their benches and approached Zeb.

Zeb stood. Doc could see that he was on guard, but not yet poised to repel an attack—the approach of these little folk was not quite threatening.

The nearest of the Kobolde dug around in a breast

pocket and brought out a scrap of paper and a fountain pen. These he extended to Zeb. He said a few words.

Alastair translated. "He'd like your signature. As a keepsake."

Rudi lingered over his meal long after Doc and his companions had left for the Kobolde errand. Swana, to his relief, did not seem inclined to rush him. Nor did she seem nervous two bells later, after they'd seen their film play—a mystery from the League of Ardree, in which a master detective deduced which of three impossible devisements had actually caused the murder—and begun their walk home, a roundabout route chosen by Rudi.

Had he not been in a city full of potential enemies, Rudi might have enjoyed the colorful foot and wheeled traffic, the Old World buildings, the presence of a pretty girl. As it was, though, he had to use the skills he'd sharpened looking for police and even rival gangs who might be shadowing him.

He took a zigzagging path back toward their quarters so that no one who remained behind them for more than a couple of blocks could be doing so accidentally. He kept his eye on storefronts across the street, trying to watch, in the reflections of larger windows, foot traffic behind him. He took note of passing cars in case one should show up more than once.

"So tell me, Swana, what do you do? When you're not being thrown into jail, that is."

"Last week, I was a store clerk. But they hired a new clerk who belonged to the *Nationalreinigungspartei*. Now I look for another job where they do not require you to be a Reini."

"Well, if it'll keep you working, why not join the party?"

"Because it's wrong. It's all about blame. They want to blame everything that has gone wrong in the Burian nations on foreign conspiracies and the duskies. But it was nothing more than bad rule that led to the last war, and now we just have new bad rule."

Rudi made a noncommittal noise. He didn't know much about the politics of the region and cared less. But he figured they looked less conspicuous talking than not talking.

Though it was probably too late to avoid being conspicuous. About fifty paces behind them was a lean, bland-featured eamon in a cheap, inconspicuous bright yellow suit. Rudi caught sight of him again when they turned at the next street corner. He hadn't been behind them for the last several blocks, but had been with them shortly after they left the beer garden—though at the time he'd been wearing a dark overcoat and a hat. Assuming, of course, that Rudi was remembering correctly and not just being suspicious, this meant they were probably being followed, and it was probably being done by two or more people trading off with one another.

Swana said, "If I may ask, why do you act and talk and dress like a gangster from the film plays?"

"I am a gangster, darlin'. Best shot for three kingdoms in any direction. But like you're a clerk without a store, I'm a gangster without a gang. For the moment, anyway."

"I thought that the Sidhe Foundation *caught* gangsters."

He managed a chuckle. "So did I." He sobered. "Listen, Swana, it's not going to do much good to keep it a secret from you, so I'll just tell you. We're being followed."

To her credit, she did not react, did not immediately look around for their shadow. When she answered, her voice was subdued. "Oh."

"And we need *not* to be followed if we're to get back to our rooms. Now, the problem is that the pumps you're wearing just aren't suited to running across traffic, jumping on the backs of passing motorbuses, that sort of thing."

She managed a faint smile, though to Rudi it looked nervous. "I suppose they're not."

"So what we're going to do is this. See that beer hall just up there? You're going to go in and I'm going to stay outside and look impatient. You find a coin talk-box and call our rooms. If any of the associates are back from this Kobolde thing, tell—oh, futter it all."

"What is it?"

"Well, Harris said our talk-box was probably being listened to by the authorities, Doc being a famous troublemaker and all." He walked in silence for a few paces and thought. "No, I have it. Find out if any of the grimworlders are there."

She frowned, puzzled. "Grimworlders? That's just a legend."

"Of course it is, darlin'. But the Foundation associates fall into two groups that call themselves grimworlders and fairworlders. It's a sort of code." Rudi spun the lie easily with part of his thoughts, while trying to remember as much as he could of the slang of the grim world from his brief trips there. "If there's a grimworlder there, have him come to the talk-box, and tell him this: It's Swana, and you've got a tail."

"I have a tail. Like a cat or like a dog?" She looked amused.

"It doesn't matter. You have a tail, and you want to shake it."

"Oh, please."

"No, you need to remember this. You want to shake your tail, and you can't shake your tail. Can they help you shake your tail?"

"This is no joke?"

"No joke. It's the private code of the grimworlders. They'll understand and they'll tell you what to do. You understand?"

"Perfectly. But why do you not make the call? Why do we not go in together?"

"If we go in together, they follow us in and keep us under observation, so they'll know we're making a call instead of getting a beer or going to the water closet or something. If I go in and you don't, they might choose to grab you right off the sidewalk—it's you they're following, not me - and Doc will have me dragged behind horses across the length of the New World, and I'll have to take it because I did something stupid enough to deserve it."

"Oh."

So he waited under the beer hall's awning, exchanging false nods and smiles with patrons entering and leaving the place, and made a show of impatiently checking his pocket watch a couple of times. He couldn't spot the man in the yellow suit, but a young woman pushing a perambulator had stopped to admire glassware in a shop two doors down when Swana had entered the beer hall and hadn't yet moved on.

Rudi frowned over that. He didn't like the idea of their opponents using female agents that way. Then it occurred to him that the Sidhe Foundation was doing the same thing, and he liked it even less.

Swana emerged from the beer hall. He took her arm and they continued. "Well?"

"Zeb was there. He and Noriko had just gotten back." She looked surprised. "You were telling the truth. He understood and told me what to tell you."

"Which is what?"

"We're to walk by where our 'convertible' usually is, and keep going, and there's going to be a 'mugging.'"

Rudi smiled. "Oh, he knows what sorts of words I'm likely to learn, doesn't he?"

Zeb sat in the driver's seat of the roadster, one of two vehicles Ruadan had left the Foundation. Its cloth top was up, keeping him in deep shadow. Zeb's knuckles would have been pale on the wheel, for he was gripping it with inappropriate pressure, even though the vehicle was not moving—it was parked on the street only a few dozen paces from the entryway to the building where the Foundation had its rooms.

His knuckles were not visibly pale because they were within thin black gloves, the sort Noriko wore to keep from touching iron. His merry-hat was pulled low over his brow and a dark green scarf was wrapped around his neck and lower face. In the darkness—which is where he expected to meet the man tailing Rudi and Swana—he'd be almost invisible. That would help when, with the twin automatics he carried in his overcoat pockets, he mugged the man.

The thought almost made him laugh. Honest, upstanding, tediously ethical Zeb Watson. This morning he was pretending to be a two-fisted Jesse Owens; tonight he was going to perform his first mugging. But the thought was only so amusing, and the coat and gloves and hat were making him sweat heavily, and Rudi and Swana still weren't here. He was getting irritable and wondered if all muggers were as impatient as he was. He was also hoping Doc or the others would get home soon. Zeb and Noriko had left the Kobolde meeting early to get rest for their matches tomorrow; now it looked as though that early departure had earned him no relaxation at all.

Further up the street before him, under a streetlight whose bulb she had ruined with a thrown rock, Noriko would be waiting a few steps into the alley. She would watch as Rudi and Swana passed, then as their pursuer passed, then as Zeb passed, waiting long enough to make sure that Zeb himself had not picked up a tail—and eliminating that tail if he had. This whole caravan of pursued and pursuers would continue on another few blocks, until they reached a spot where it was dark enough for Zeb to feel more comfortable. There, he'd draw his guns, demand the tail hand over his wallet, and keep him pinned there long enough for Rudi and Swana to double back and elude further pursuit.

Simple, it was simple. None of which kept his hands from shaking.

A gold-and-black taxicab pulled up in front of the Foundation's building and idled there. Zeb watched it in the rearview mirror, in case Rudi had gone crazy and taken a cab here, but no one emerged from it. It was waiting for passengers, not delivering them.

Zeb brought up the end of his scarf and dabbed the sweat from his upper face. He and Noriko had taken Swana's call, improvised their plan, told Swana what to say to Rudi, gotten dressed, gotten situated, all very quickly—perhaps too quickly. His time sense thrown off by their haste and his accelerated heart rate, Zeb did not know whether five minutes or fifteen had passed since he'd first gotten behind the wheel.

Then, in the mirror, he spotted them. They were at the back of a stream of foot traffic, walking slowly enough that the other pedestrians passed them at a steady rate, Rudi still artificially graybearded and the false Teleri looking unhappy beside him. Harris had said that her unhappiness was an act, designed to draw attention, designed to persuade those who knew Teleri that she might not be with her companions of her own free will.

Zeb breathed a sigh of relief even as his heart rate

accelerated further. Now this could end. It would only
be minutes. He put his hand on the door lever.

As Rudi and Swana passed the entrance into the
Foundation's building, two men stepped out of the
entryway behind them. Both were tall by fairworld
standards, dressed much as Zeb was except without
scarves.

One hefted something black, like a short club, and
brought it down on Rudi's head. The other brought up
a large cloth sack and brought it down over Swana from
above.

Zeb froze with his hand on the door handle. Rudi,
his eyes rolling up in his head, began to fall backward,
an action made slow by the sudden acceleration of
Zeb's senses. Swana's captor was cinching the cloth bag
tight around her waist; she struggled, a futile effort,
and cried out.

The door to the taxi was already opening and a man
emerging, and it was this last element that had caused
Zeb to freeze. This newcomer was coming out of the
rear door, meaning that there was at least one other
man still in the taxi. And if Rudi and Swana were being
followed on foot, that man was also still out there. Zeb
could spring out and charge, but, though five or six-
to-one odds might not deter him, the fact that any of
his opponents might have guns, and that Rudi and
Swana were in the possible line of fire, did.

Swana's captor picked her up by the waist and
hustled her into the taxi. Her legs kicked. The two
other men bent over Rudi, looking at his face, and then
moved so that one stood at his head, the other at his
feet.

Zeb swore, then started his car. He slipped forward,
half his attention on the action he was watching in the
side mirror, half on the dark building wall and unseen
alley ahead.

The kidnappers gave Zeb a few moments by putting Rudi in the trunk. First they put him down behind the taxi, then got the trunk open, then spent some time hoisting him in and doing something Zeb couldn't see, their actions hidden by the upraised trunk lid.

Zeb pulled to a halt beside the alley mouth. "Get in, get in!" he called, though he could not see Noriko. "It's blown, we're screwed."

A human-sized shadow detached itself from the blackness of the alley mouth and Noriko slipped into the back seat. Like him, she was dressed all in dark garments, in her case a silken pantsuit in black and a black scarf binding up her hair and throwing her features into deeper shadow. "What happened?"

The taxi raced past them, the growl of its engine made more distinctive by a mechanical clatter—bad lifters, Zeb thought. "They're in that car." He set his roadster into motion, pulling out behind the taxi.

"Drop back," Noriko said. She slid over the seat back to settle into the seat beside Zeb. "We don't need them to realize they're being followed. What happened?"

Zeb told her, meanwhile following her directions to fall farther back, to allow other vehicles to come between him and the taxi.

"Do you see their taillights?" she said. "One large single taillight on either side, oval instead of circular. Very distinctive, a late-model Alpenhaus. We don't see many of those in the League of Ardree. Plus the light on top is not glowing, indicating they have a fare. We've little chance of losing them, Zeb."

"Is there anything about vehicles you don't know?"

"I hope not."

In spite of Zeb's fears that they'd be stopped by Bardulfburg police just for being two duskies driving an expensive car, they were able to tail the taxi for a

considerable distance. Their path led them around to
the southeast, along back streets. These were narrow,
twisting roads built between long blocks of brick ten-
ements and were little trafficked by cars. Illumination
here was poor, streetlights being infrequent and often
burned out when they were present.

"They're trying to determine if they're being followed," Noriko said.

"That's not good. Because they are."

"Turn your lights off."

"I don't think so, Noriko. Too much foot traffic on
these streets." Indeed, residents of the district were
as common on the bricktop street as they were on the
sidewalks, moving aside only grudgingly as vehicles
passed.

"I will do it, then. Switch places."

"If we stop long enough to trade places, as often
as they're taking turns, we'll lose them."

"Don't stop, then. Just switch places."

"Are you—never mind." She *was* crazy, of course,
else she'd never be in this business. But she was right.

He waited until the street ahead was straight for a
while and clear of foot traffic. "Ready." Keeping one
hand on the steering wheel, he slid leftward on the
seat, into the middle.

Noriko brushed across him. Having to maneuver
around the steering wheel forced her to settle into his
lap; then she slid into the seat to his right, her legs
draped across his. She took the wheel and dragged her
legs across his, getting her feet into position beside the
pedals.

He slid into the passenger seat, suddenly made aware,
acutely aware, of her physical presence. *Focus, idiot,* he
told himself. *Now is not the time to be distracted.*

Noriko switched off the car's headlights and accelerated, trying to close the gap between vehicles. Zeb

grabbed the dashboard and wished that more of the damned cars of this world had seat belts. He couldn't see a thing on the road ahead beyond about thirty feet, and at the speed they were going couldn't have reacted to seeing something before hitting it. But Noriko seemed to have excellent night vision, and the fact that she swerved all over the road and occasionally tapped her horn to warn pedestrians ahead meant that she was seeing them in time to avoid them.

They took a half dozen more turns over the next half mile, during which time Zeb had to remind himself on several occasions to breathe, and then turned onto a major thoroughfare. Situating herself three cars behind the taxi, Noriko turned the headlights on again.

"Please, God, let them stay to the main roads from now on," Zeb said. His voice sounded weak. As they passed a streetlight, he caught sight of Noriko's face; her eyes were hidden by the scarf she wore, but she seemed to be smiling.

They made one more turn, leftward onto a street that was two lanes in each direction, and almost immediately passed entrances into what seemed to be a gravel-topped parking lot. Beyond it were long single-story buildings, people leaving taxis and other autos, many of them carrying luggage, to join lines leading to what looked like ticket windows.

Through the gaps between buildings, Zeb could see trains beyond—what looked to him like passenger cars, mostly. "Railyards," he said.

"We are in trouble," Noriko said.

Zeb returned his attention to the taxi. It had just turned right into a narrow bricktopped lane. It ran to what looked like a small guard station. There, guards dressed in the uniforms of Weserian soldiers flanked a barricade. One of the guards was already advancing to speak to the taxi's driver.

"We are so screwed," Zeb said.

"There is no place to park."

"Pull past that lane and slow down." Zeb clambered into the back seat and slid to the right-hand door, immediately behind Noriko. "I'll follow on foot. Follow when you can. I'll try to leave a sign for you."

"Chalk."

"Chalk?"

"Chalk." She reached over her shoulder, handing him a long piece of white chalk. Now dozens of yards past the turn the taxi had taken, she began to decelerate.

"Look for a peace sign."

"A what?"

"Uh, like an upside-down fork in a circle." He pocketed the chalk, then opened the door and jumped out.

The car was still doing nearly twenty miles an hour—he stumbled, nearly falling, then ran up to the sidewalk. People heading on foot toward the train station, luggage in hand, gave him a curious look. He dipped his hat so they couldn't see his eyes.

A fence—man-height, with spikes on top, of corroded green metal bars and with bushes equally tall planted behind it—ran the length of the sidewalk, all the way back to where the taxi had turned in, and forward as far as he could see. He cursed. It had to block public access to the entire rail yard, excepting only normal—guarded—entrances.

Well, by God, he was a Sonneheim Games athlete with something to do. He increased his running pace and jumped up, grabbing the rough bars, getting his foot on the horizontal bar about five feet up, and swung up and over the spikes. As he came down, he felt something yank at the back of his coat, heard and felt it tear—one of the coattails had to have caught on a spike. He rolled across the top of the bush, its thickness slowing his fall, and then dropped into empty air behind. But he landed on soft earth just on the other side of the bush. He came out of his crouch and sprinted into the darkness ahead of him.

Chapter Eighteen

Behind, Zeb heard a shout in Burian, some passenger doubtless raising a half-hearted alarm about this black-clad line-jumper.

Ahead, at right angles to his direction, were numerous train tracks, more than he could count, parallel lines of them, many of them with trains or at least a few train cars upon them—sidings, he assumed, places to store cars while they waited to be attached to trains. He paid them no mind. He kept his attention on the ground in front of him, which was rough, covered in ankle-high grass and dangerous with occasional pieces of broken concrete the size of footballs, and to the right, where the taxi, now clear of the little guard station, was now accelerating toward the rail yard. The narrow paved road it was on would lead it in a turn to the left, toward Zeb, then another turn right to take it between two of the long buildings, well away from the ones that seemed to be the civilian passengers' destinations.

The taxi veered along its path and slowed to a stop

between the two buildings as Zeb reached the pavement. He stood there, breathing heavily, not approaching closer for the moment—the space between buildings was illuminated, and the taxi's occupants would surely see him if he got too much closer. Remembering, he dug the chalk from his pocket and scrawled a peace sign on the pavement before him.

Four men piled out of the taxi. Three wore overcoats; one of them pulled Swana, still half covered by the cloth bag, with him, while the other two opened the trunk and looked in. But they did not drag Rudi out; after assuring themselves of something, probably just his continued presence, they shut the trunk again.

The fourth man wore a Sonnenkrieger officer's uniform. Even at the distance of forty yards or so Zeb recognized him, for his exceptional blondness, for his perfection of form.

Colonel Conrad Förster.

Förster took a cigarette from a case and lit it with a match, taking a casual look around as he did so. As his gaze swept across Zeb, he stopped, frozen in position, hand still cupped against the wind over the cigarette.

Zeb fought the urge to duck. Förster shouldn't be able to see him. Zeb was all in black and dark green, with bushes behind him so he couldn't be backlit. If Zeb ducked, Förster might detect the motion. So Zeb held perfectly still, though he slowly narrowed his eyes until they were mere slits.

Förster held his pose for several long moments, long enough for the men with him to act. Two dragged Swana around the corner of the building. The third got back in the car, in the driver's seat, and started it up, then drove it forward and around the corner to the left. In just these moments, Zeb had lost sight of both the people he was trying to protect.

Förster's gaze wavered, slipping off Zeb. He looked back and forth a little. Then he started and shook his hand to extinguish the match he still held. Irritably, he tossed the thing aside and turned to follow the men dragging Swana.

Keeping low, Zeb followed.

He reached the corner of the raised wooden platform beside which the taxi had been parked. This platform was empty of people, and the ticket windows of the building it was attached to were all closed.

From this vantage, he could see Förster, his men and his prisoner, all walking across tracks between them and a short train—one engine, one caboose, and five cars in between. None of the men looked back in his direction.

Zeb moved forward to look around the corner of the platform. This put him in clear sight of anyone looking in this direction, directly beneath an overhead light, but for the moment no one was looking at him. Two buildings down to his right, the place was thick with passengers boarding some sort of civilian train, but this portion of the yard seemed lightly populated at best. To his left, there was no sign of the taxi. Then he heard the car from behind him. He spun, still crouching, to see it turning back onto the narrow lane that had brought it here. It had circled the building and was now headed back toward the main street.

Zeb cursed. He couldn't follow both Swana and Rudi. Well, that was no choice. Swana was the innocent here.

On the pavement beside the platform, Zeb chalked another peace sign, this one with the three tines of the symbol pointing toward the train onto which Swana was now being dragged. He thought about adding to the symbol the many-digit number painted in white on the dark surface of the engine, and reluctantly made that

modification. Officials seeing the numbers might figure out what they meant, might realize that someone
was pointing out that train to the attention of others.
But if he didn't identify the train more precisely,
another train might be positioned onto a track between
the platform and Swana's train, and Noriko might be
misled.

Then Zeb moved out into the darkness, toward the
rear of the short train, his heart beating faster as he
waited for someone to note his presence, to call for
guards, to make this screwed-up situation even worse.

Whoever had dragged and carried Swana this far—
had kept her half upright as she stumbled and tripped
across rough ground and what felt like rail tracks, had
hauled her on his hip up narrow steps and scraped her
along hallway walls and across doors, had ignored her
demands for information—finally stopped. She assumed
she was on a train, from the familiar noises of the rail
yard and the narrow entry she'd been hauled through
after being carried up the steps. She heard something—
a door, she thought—slide open. Then she was shoved
through an entryway, her left shoulder scraping against
it, and was held upright.

Fingers fumbled at the rope around her waist and
loosened it. Her captors pulled the bag from her. She
was blinded in sudden light, but the comparatively fresh
air on her face was welcome. She breathed in its
coolness.

As her vision cleared, she saw that she was indeed
on a train, in one compartment of a sleeper car. It was
set up for daytime, its bench seats not yet converted
to beds, despite the fact that it was well after dark.
She turned to see two men in coats leaving the compartment, one man, a Sonnenkrieger colonel, remaining
with her.

He was fair, handsome, emotionless. He held a cigarette to his lips and inhaled as he looked at her, but he said nothing.

"Who are you?" she asked.

Slowly and deliberately, he expelled a lungful of smoke before answering. "I am Förster. Colonel Conrad Förster," he said.

"Why—" She heard the shrillness of her voice and realized that she must sound, and look, like what she was—a frightened woman hopelessly out of her depth. But that's not who she was supposed to be. Doc had been wrong, he hadn't been able to protect her, and now she was in their hands . . . but she knew, from the way things had changed since the Reinis came to power, that showing weakness before them would automatically make her a victim in their eyes. Showing strength wouldn't necessarily do her any good . . . but victims were to be victimized.

She took a deep breath and tried to bring her voice down into its normal range. "Do you know who I am?"

Finally, he smiled, a very slight smile, but at least it held no contempt. "No."

"Why did you pick me up in this manner?"

He shrugged. "I was told to pick you up. No manner was specified in my instructions."

She turned to the window. In it, she could make out her dim reflection. Her hair was a mess, strands having worked loose from the bun. Her lipstick had smeared and the pancake that had lightened her complexion ever so slightly, so that she might better resemble Teleri, was sweat-streaked. Though it was difficult to tell in the reflection, she imagined that she was still red from the heat of the sack. She made an exasperated noise and pulled the rest of her hair free of the bun, letting it fall loose around her shoulders. "You could have just asked. Do you have a brush?"

"I'm afraid not."

"A handkerchief?"

"Of course."

He handed her one. She used it to remove her lipstick. *There*, she decided. *More plain, less Teleri . . . but not so much a mess.*

She heard the door to the passageway slide open again. She turned to see another Sonnenkrieger officer, this one a general, enter. He was a tall man, blond and balding, his officer's cap held under his left arm. His expression, curiously, was not severe—his eyes were far more kind than Förster's.

He only looked at her for a moment before turning his attention to Förster and assuming a more serious expression. Förster saluted him and he returned the salute. "Any problems?" he asked.

"None, sir."

"Good. Dismissed."

Förster offered Swana a nod of minimal courtesy and left, shutting the door behind him.

The general turned to Swana. She returned his gaze—not defiantly, because that might incite him, should he be a cruel man despite his kindly manner, but expectantly.

"Teleri," he said.

She felt a sudden thrill and she cleared her throat to cover her emotion. He didn't know who she really was. Her disguise was intact for the moment. "Yes?"

"You don't know me?" His expression had gone from mere earnestness to actual vulnerability; he looked as though he were one wrong answer away from being hurt.

She searched his face, hoping that it would buy her a little time. She had only two answers available to her and either could be wrong. But if she said "Yes" and were challenged on it, she couldn't back it up. "I do not," she said, but tried to make her reply sound sad rather than accusative.

"Your father . . ." The man sat on one of the benches. He gestured for her to sit beside him, and she did. "Your father didn't ever show you cameos of me? He certainly showed me many of you."

"I . . . I . . ." It was time, she knew, to put everything on one roll of the dice. "I don't remember." She let tears flow, real tears brought on by the real terror she was feeling. "Since I've been in that monster's hands, he stares at me and I cannot remember, I don't know where I am most of the time, I can't recall my name some days, my mission is lost to me . . ." She closed her eyes and let the tears pour out, let her body shake with the magnitude of the terror she'd felt since being seized.

He took her about the shoulders and held her tightly. "Teleri . . . Teleri . . . May I call you by your true name?"

She felt herself split then, her physical presence, racked with sobs and shudders, somehow staying in place while her mind took a step sideways and evaluated her with an odd calmness. *Doc would be so pleased with me,* she thought. *If only I live long enough for him to hear about this.*

"I don't think I'd know it if I heard it." Her throat was tight, making her words emerge almost as a squeak.

"Adima," he said. "Adima, I am your fiancé, Daenn Ritter."

She forced her eyes open and turned to look at him. She knew there had to be wonder in her expression— her analytical self wanted her to appear wondering, but the emotion was real. If he were Teleri's fiancé, how could he not know she was not the real girl?

"I don't—I'm sorry," she said. "That memory is gone too. How can I not remember you?"

"We have never met. Our fathers arranged the marriage not long before you went to the New World. My father said you did not oppose it . . ."

"Of course not. Why would I? I would be proud . . ." She wiped away tears and tried to force her analytical self to the forefront. "You have saved me?"

"Yes. Your jailer is in custody, but he does not resemble the description of the man you have been accompanying. He is supposed to be taller, a light. We must know—"

"You are taking me to my father?"

"Yes, tonight. You will be with him within two bells. Can you tell me—"

Cut off his questions before you give him a wrong answer, she told herself, and burst into tears once more, yielding to the fear that gripped her. She let the volume of her cries grow until she could barely hear his words—now soothing, meaningless entreaties—above them.

Two bells. That might just be how long she had to live.

There was a guard on each of the train cars except the engine, coal tender and caboose. Zeb lingered in the darkness, well away from light shining from the windows of the passenger cars, and watched them. They wore the uniforms of regular Weserian soldiers and carried rifles slung over their shoulders.

These men were wide-awake and alert but relaxed; they were not anticipating trouble. Most turned at irregular intervals to survey a new direction. They often called out comments to one another, jokes by the sound of their tones and the response of the others.

One of them, the guard on the foremost passenger car, paced. He did not move from one end of the car to the other, just along a portion of its length, but the regularity of his motion was something Zeb could use.

Keeping low, moving in a crouch his back muscles were sure to complain about later, Zeb crossed the track well away from the caboose and slowly moved up parallel to the train at some distance from it. He kept to the darkness.

Opposite, he heard a shrill whistle from the passenger train at the station. Even at this distance, even with Swana's train between them, Zeb felt hammered by the noise. As it faded, he heard the cars' metal joints shriek as the engine strained to bring them into motion. Gradually the train came up to speed, the rhythm of its clattering wheels increasing. By the time Zeb was opposite the foremost car of Swana's train, the passenger train was gone in the distance.

Now, each time that foremost guard turned to pace toward the rear of the train, Zeb crept forward. Each time the guard turned toward the engine, Zeb froze in place, watching. Unfortunately, the rail yard was much quieter than it had been when the passenger train was in place, and Zeb's stomach lurched whenever gravel crunched under his foot.

But still the guard remained unaware of him, and he crept forward until he was beside the car, the corner of its roof blocking him from the guard's view. Ahead, beyond the coal tender, the engine hissed, like a gigantic cat unhappy about Zeb's arrival.

Zeb was also within the glow of light shining from the car's interior. Through the windows he could see that this car was divided into passenger compartments; the windows he was looking into opened straight into compartments, with doors and windows on the far side apparently opening onto a passageway. The nearest compartment seemed to be unoccupied, or else its occupants might be seated out of his line of sight, but one compartment back he could see Sonnenkrieger soldiers seated, talking, laughing.

Just ahead, a man shouted in Burian and Zeb froze. Footsteps clattered across the top of the nearest car, and Zeb could hear more from the other cars. But when he turned to look, no one was staring at him. In fact, the footsteps were receding, not approaching, and then Zeb could hear boots ringing on metal ladders. The soldiers were descending.

This engine's whistle blew. It was like being hit by a ten-foot wave. The noise cut through Zeb's clothes and skin, awoke the pain of his bruises, struck at his ears like hammers; he cupped his ears with his hands and winced away from the sound.

Then, as the whistle faded, the engine offered up a mighty *chuff-chuff* noise; its wheels turned and it began to move forward.

Dammit, Noriko, where are you? Zeb grabbed the nearest handrail on the car. He stepped up onto the platform and the train slowly began to carry him forward into the darkness.

As the train got under way and began to bear Swana toward her death, Ritter held her with tenderness, saying soothing words as she cried.

Gradually she let her sobs subside. She relaxed into his embrace, leaving her eyes shut, feigning exhaustion.

"It will be well," Ritter said for the tenth or thousandth time. "Your father will be able to free your mind from that monster's embrace. You will be well again."

She nodded, like a child too sleepy to speak.

"Are you tired? Would you like to sleep until we are there?"

She nodded again.

"Here." Carefully, he slid out from beneath her and

lowered her so that she lay the length of the padded seat. She heard him rummaging in the rack above the seat, and then he gently lifted her head to slide a pillow beneath it. "I will be two compartments down if you need me."

The lights dimmed, Swana heard the door open and close, and she was alone.

She stood, her hand on the wall behind her against the rocking of the car, and tried to force herself to think clearly.

She moved to peer through the glass in the compartment door, and could see no people in the incomplete view of the companionway the window afforded her. She'd have to poke her head out into the companionway to see its full length, and she might be spotted.

And even if she weren't, what then? She'd have to get to the end of the car, into the vestibule, and then . . .

Jump. There was no other feasible solution. If she hid on the train, they'd find her. So she had to get off. If she wanted to do that before the train's next stop, she'd have to jump.

And she'd have to do so as soon as she had the opportunity. If she waited until the train slowed to a safer speed, they might walk in on her. Stop her.

Well, if she was going to jump, she might as well do it from right here, rather than venture into the passageway and risk discovery. She moved to the window, unlatched it at the top, and lowered the glass. She was instantly battered by wind. The door behind her rattled. That would alert Ritter or others soon. She had to go fast.

She stepped up onto the seat opposite the one on which she and Ritter had used and leaned out through the window. Tree branches whipped by, close, with a suddenness that terrified her. She could dimly see the boles of the trees mere paces from the dirt and gravel that lined the tracks, and though she was no expert in such matters, she guessed that the train's speed had to be at least a hundred destads per bell, maybe half again that rate. There was no way she could survive a fall at that speed.

No, maybe she could. Maybe she would fall on soft grass instead of unforgiving dirt and gravel. Maybe the gods would smile on her.

Besides, interrogation at the Reinis' hands had to mean death. Didn't it?

Or, once she told them everything about the Foundation and its plans to trick them, might the Reinis let her go? She could claim that Doc had forced her. She could invent some story of blackmail . . .

She stood there, indecision freezing her, her new thoughts about sacrificing Doc and the others filling her with shame, and something struck her on the shoulder.

She shrieked and looked back, but no one stood behind her. She looked up.

A man's head protruded over the edge of the roof. He held the edge with both hands. His features were masked by a hat clamped low on his brow and a dark green scarf wrapped many times around his mouth and nose. Only his eyes and the black flesh of his upper face showed. The scarf over his mouth flexed as his jaw moved, as if he were saying something—

Black flesh? She gaped at him. "Zeb?"

Finally she could hear his words, if dimly, over the roar of wind across them. "Don't jump . . . too fast . . ."

"Are you here to rescue me?"

He nodded. He released his grip with one hand and pulled the scarf away from his mouth, then braced himself again. Desperation in his eyes told her how difficult it was for him to hold that perch, how close he was to being slung free with every lurch of the car.

Now he shouted, and the increased volume and the fact that she could see his lips allowed Swana to understand him. "We'll get you out of here! I'm sorry. This never should have happened."

"Will we jump?"

"Maybe. That's one way to do it." His voice, even distorted by volume, sounded uncertain.

"How else?"

"Listen. If we escape now, you'll be safe and Doc will send you wherever you want to go. But if you let them take you where they're going—"

"No!"

"If you let them take you there, we can see where that is, see more of who's giving the orders. That'll help us figure out who to stop. *Then* we'll grab you back."

"Are you sure—are you certain you can save me if we go that far?"

He took a moment to answer, and when she saw his eyes soften into sympathy she knew the answer. "No," he shouted. "I can't be sure. But you can be sure of this. I won't just let you go. I'll come after you and I'll either get you out of there or die myself. I promise. But it's your call, Swana. You decide you want me to take you off this train now, that's what we'll do."

She looked at him, at his earnest face, so dark, so alien in comparison with all the people she'd ever met, and yet in spite of his alienness she knew he was telling the truth.

She also knew shame at what she'd been thinking just moments ago, and knew that she couldn't bear for him to think as badly of her as she was thinking of herself right now.

"They're taking me to see Teleri's father," she said. "General Ritter is here. I know of him. He is chief architect of the Reinis. He's also Teleri's fiancé but they have never met and he thinks I am her. I'd better get back."

He nodded.

She pulled away from the cruel, invasive sympathy still evident on his face. She raised the window and latched it.

Then she lay down again where Ritter had last seen her. Her face twisted with her effort not to cry once again.

On hands and knees, Zeb made his way forward to the front of the roof of the car. Once he was seated there, staring forward into the night, the thick smoke and occasional sparks and cinders billowing forth from the engine's smokestack washed across him again. He rearranged the scarf across his face—protection from the smoke and sparks, protection from night air that had grown surprisingly cold.

He'd been lucky in several ways, as lucky as a man sitting on top of a train full of enemies could count himself. He'd managed to board the train just after the guards atop the cars had been ordered down. In his creeping around atop the thing, he had managed not to get thrown off, had managed to lean out far enough to peer into the various compartments of the lead car and see the many Sonnenkrieger and regular soldiers there and, most importantly, had managed to find Swana. Had he not seen her in the first sleeper car, he would have had to make the dangerous transition to each car in turn and repeat the process there.

He might be lucky in another way, too. Noriko had never caught up to him, but a car was following this train. He'd spotted it minutes after the train had left Bardulfburg, headed southeast. Then, the car was two headlights on the road paralleling the tracks some distance to the right. It had just been a car at the time, but he'd seen the same headlights return again and again—though roads led it away, it always seemed to find a new lane in the train's wake. *Let it be Noriko*, he told himself.

Whenever the train blasted through a town or village, Zeb flattened himself on the roof, presenting no silhouette for onlookers to see. The rest of the time he sat up, hands gripping the nearest air vent, his merry-hat clamped firmly down on his forehead. He was growing more and more fond of that hat and its tenacity.

And, oddly, it occurred to him that there was something very liberating about his current situation. True, he was a black man in a country governed by white racists, he was sitting on a gigantic egg carton full of men who'd be happy to shoot him. But for just this moment, they didn't know he was here. He rode atop them, cloaked in the night, his training and the pistols in his pockets and the promise he'd made to Swana making him more dangerous than any of them, and he felt freer and more alive than at any time in the last dozen years. A laugh bubbled up out of him, and had any of the soldiers aboard the train heard it, they would have been chilled by the mad humor in it.

Swana woke, jarred from her sleep by the shrill noise the train made as it braked, jarred further by the fact that she had actually fallen asleep. She would have liked to spend more of her last few chimes of life awake . . .

No. She couldn't think like that. Zeb would save her. Or she would save herself.

"How do you feel?"

Startled, she jerked upright. Ritter was seated opposite her, concern in his eyes.

She rubbed her eyes, to give herself a moment to

think, and then turned an artificially calm expression toward him. "Better," she said. "I am so ashamed of my panic. You probably think me a complete fool."

He shook his head. "No, of course not. You proved your courage when you volunteered for this assignment. Proved it again when you sent the package home. Anyone would be unsettled by what you've gone through. Myself included."

She managed a small smile for him. "Would you cry?"

"No. It would do harm to my career. But it will do none to yours."

"Are we there?" Swana had no idea where "there" was, but it seemed to be the thing to ask.

"Just pulling in to Goldmacher."

"What a relief." She wondered what she would say when she met Teleri's father. She wondered whom she ought to be. It would probably do her no good to appear as frightened as she was, no harm to pretend to be a hardened adventurer like the Sidhe Foundation agents.

It occurred to her that, though she wasn't Teleri Obeldon, she *was* actually a spy. For this one brief moment she was what she had seen on the screen in film plays. The thought made another smile cross her lips.

The train shuddered to a halt and they both stood. "Welcome home," Ritter said.

As the train came into the village station, Zeb flattened himself and slid over to the left side of the car, so as not to be seen by anyone standing at the station. He leaned well out over the edge so he could see into Teleri's compartment.

And he bit back a curse. She and Ritter were on their feet; the Sonnenkrieger general was dragging a briefcase from an overhead rack. As Zeb watched, they moved out of sight into the passageway. They were leaving.

And Zeb heard orders being barked in Burian, followed by the sound of booted men moving at a trot, boots and hands making ringing noises against the ladders on the ends of the train cars.

Zeb rolled to sit upright at the edge of the roof, giving himself a moment to get his balance and position right, and then pushed off. He dropped right past the window Swana had tried to jump from and hit the gravel beneath it. He landed in a crouch, the impact jarring his legs and the places in his back still sore from the morning's fight, and rolled off into the darkness beyond the car.

By the time he came upright, a soldier was climbing up onto the roof of his car by the ladder at the front, but that man's posture and casual motions, even in silhouette, suggested that he hadn't seen anything wrong. Zeb stood, his legs a little shaky, and then moved as fast as he dared through the grass, paralleling the train.

His timing, though accidental, was perfect. As he came around the engine, several yards ahead of it in the darkness, he saw Swana, Ritter and two Sonnenkrieger soldiers descending from the train's first passenger car. Swana seemed oddly poised, in control, considering her state when he'd last seen her.

Ritter led her forward to the end of the station and down the steps there, where an automobile waited, idling. It was a massive thing, black, with little Reini sun-flags flying from posts at the front corners; the driver's compartment was separate from that of the passengers and open to the sky. Ritter held the door open for Swana while she stepped up on the running board and into the passenger compartment, but then he placed his briefcase in beside her and shut the door. He waited outside and consulted a pocket watch.

Zeb continued circling around and moved in toward the car, approaching its right rear. At the very least, he needed to see and memorize the numbers of its plates, but he'd prefer to get on or in it, perhaps in the trunk.

As Zeb reached the rear bumper, on the far side of the automobile, Ritter straightened, looking irritable, as another Sonnenkrieger officer approached from the direction of the train. This man was younger, apologetic of expression, also carrying a briefcase. They exchanged a few words in Burian, Ritter's words harsh, the new man's words conciliatory. The new man opened the door for Ritter, then followed the older officer into the car.

Zeb heard gears grind in the car. He swore to himself. There wasn't much to hold onto on the rear of the car—the bumper didn't offer the sort of purchase he needed. But at the front end of the right-side running board, where it rose up to become the beautifully curved housing for the front wheel, a niche held a spare tire. Zeb scrambled forward on hands and knees, got one hand on that tire and was just lowering his weight onto the running board when the car pulled forward.

Zeb rolled sideways, half off the running board. Wrist strength kept him from falling clean off. He lay on his back on the narrow ledge, his right leg supported, his left leg swinging off and threatening to rotate the rest of him off as well. But he kicked down and his left heel made hard contact with the ground, just enough to allow him to swing back up atop the running board. He lay there on his right side, both hands now gripping the tire, and prayed that the vehicle make no hard turns to the left.

He held on as the car made bumpy progress along a winding dirt and gravel road, mostly going uphill. Occasional glances over his shoulder told him the lane was lined with trees.

Then the car made an abrupt left turn and slung him off the running board. His grip on the tire failed. He hit the ground hard enough to knock the wind out of him and he rolled, uncontrolled, several yards.

Then the ground dropped out from under him.

Chapter Nineteen

Zeb had just enough time to feel a metallic thrill of fear, then his back hit solid ground—a surface that was slightly yielding, not stony. The impact sent slivers of pain through the sore muscles in his back, but he knew he'd fallen only a couple of yards. He wasn't injured.

He lay there a moment, dragging in a couple of pained breaths, then sat up.

He was in a ditch. The road beside it turned leftward, and the car's taillights were still readily visible. The vehicle had pulled to a halt and a pair of Sonnenkrieger guards had advanced, one of them speaking to the driver.

Zeb stared at what was beyond the guards. He sighed. It wasn't worth cursing. Just another obstacle. One he'd have to get past fast.

The guard talking to the driver saluted and straightened. The car moved forward, across the narrow wooden bridge, through the gateway, into the castle beyond.

❖   ❖   ❖

Ritter dismissed the man he'd introduced as Major Tryg, then conducted Swana from the car through the manor house doorway carved with wooden reliefs showing tall, long-haired women gardening or playing on a riverbank. Beyond the door was a small anteroom, and beyond that a hallway lined by standing suits of armor and tapestries showing long-dead warriors on a boar hunt in dark forest. There was dust in the air but none to be seen on the armor or the floors. "Surely your memories are returning to you now," Ritter said.

Swana considered her answer. "Not so much memories," she said, "but I feel happy here, for no reason I can remember." She was pleased with the lie. It sounded convincing to her.

"A good sign, a good sign." He led her down the hall, through a door to the left, up the flight of wooden stairs beyond it. A hall on the second floor brought them to a room that had to be a laboratory or workroom of the manor's owner. It was filled with tables, each one covered with books, papers, stones carved into primitive manlike shapes. On the walls were hung maps of the Burian lands and the world. Among them was a map showing what the ancients thought the outlines of the world to be. Also on the walls, curiously, were bows and quivers full of arrows.

Swana offered Ritter a smile she didn't feel. "Messy as ever."

"Some things never change." He took a pile of books and a winter coat from a low stuffed chair and deposited them, with complete disregard for the papers and goods already there, on a table. "Please. Sit. I'll fetch your father."

"Thank you." She sat.

As soon as he was gone and the door closed behind him, she jumped up again. Maybe, in this moment of their inattentiveness, she could escape. Or perhaps she could find out something that would be of value to the Foundation members. But which? She didn't have much time.

Glass doors opened onto a small curved balcony. She opened them and stepped out. The balcony overlooked the small cobblestone courtyard at the heart of the castle. Ritter's car was still parked before the manor doors, the driver leaning against it, lighting a cigarette. He glanced up and saw her, gave her a friendly wave. She waved back.

There were ground-level doors leading up into the wall towers, the bigger opening leading through the wall and to freedom beyond . . .

And a shadow. It walked like a man across the cobblestones, a black silhouette like the god of death. Its head was flanked by two black bars protruding from its shoulders. Silently, it headed straight for the driver. But it stopped for a moment, looking up at her.

She felt a thrill of fear. Zeb, it had to be Zeb, and the bars had to be rifles on his back. But how could he have gotten into the castle, past the guards, without alerting anyone? Perhaps it was the spirit of Death after all.

It turned its attention from her and began its slow movement toward the driver again. Released from its spell of fear, Swana turned away and moved quickly back into the room.

No, she couldn't think that way. It had to be Zeb. And if he was there, risking his life for her, she had to make his risk worth something.

With frantic speed, she moved from table to table, looking at everything, trying to sort the important from the irrelevant.

From one table lit by a desk lamp she took a handful of handwritten papers on which the words for god and sun appeared often. These went under the waistband of her skirt.

One table was covered with odd objects. Black rubber egg-shaped balls. Stuffed toy bears. Puppets—some of Sonnenkrieger, some of peasant men and women—the size of a hand but not connected to controlling strings. Each one was in a small wooden box without a lid, and also in each box was a sort of paperweight—a gold arrowhead encased in glass. The paperweights were of a curious shape, with four indentations along one edge. She took a puppet of a handsome Sonnenkrieger, superior to many of the others for the quality of its making, the extraordinary skill that had gone into the painting of its face; she slid that into one garter under her skirt and picked up the corresponding paperweight. The ridges now made sense; her fingers slid into them, giving her a secure hold on the smooth glass. She nested the paperweight between her breasts, pushing it further down in her brassiere.

On another table she found more papers, these bearing wax seals, one of them bearing Aevar's signature; she folded them and tucked them into the other garter.

And she fancied she heard a faint cry, a dull impact, from below the balcony.

The next sound could not have been the product of imagination. Male voices outside the door grew in volume, one of them bearing the distinct accent of the lower class of the Burian northlands: " . . . feed her first, I think, you idiot."

Ritter's voice suggested that he didn't take the insult seriously. "Well, of course. I meant, after."

Swana hurried back to the chair Ritter had cleaned for her. She sat and composed herself even as the door handle lowered.

The door slammed open, propelled by a heavy, red-faced man. He looked young enough, but his expansive stomach and gold-rimmed glasses suggested that he was of middle years. He wore dark green pants and a yellow shirt with the sleeves rolled up in cuffs at his elbows, and his smile was bright enough to add illumination to the room.

"Adima," he said, his voice booming, "welcome . . ." Then his voice trailed off and his smile faded.

He turned to Ritter. "What sort of joke is this?"

Ritter frowned at him. "Joke?"

"This is not Adima."

Ritter looked at her, disbelief on his face.

Swana hardened herself for what was to come and gave him a little nod, apologetic but not conciliatory. "It's true," she said. "But you were very sweet, General. Adima is a very lucky girl." *Or would be*, she thought, *if she weren't dead*.

The other man's face reddened further. He advanced on Swana, head lowered, like a wrestler moving in on an opponent. "Where is she?"

"Where you won't find her if you treat me badly."

The man grabbed her upper arms. She jumped at the contact but did not look away from him. "You have *no idea* of how badly we could treat you," he shouted. "Where is she?"

Ritter moved up so his face was just over the shoulder of the other man. From Swana's position, it looked as though the other man had just sprouted a second head. "Ordinarily I might object to a lady being treated this way," Ritter's head said. His voice was oddly reasonable. "But you have made me look ridiculous. I do not appreciate it. So I may permit Doctor—this man to do exactly as he wishes to you."

"That would be foolish." It was taking every bit of her concentration to keep Swana from flinching away from their threats, their experienced intensity, but she was managing. For the moment.

Then she smelled it. A stray breeze entered through the balcony doors she'd opened, bringing with it the odor of soot. Of char.

There was a thump from the balcony, heels hitting stone, and suddenly he was there—a silhouette, the spirit of Death, black from head to toe except for his eyes, a pistol in each hand. The bars were gone from its back. "Move away from her," the specter said in the language of Cretanis.

They hesitated. The older man glanced at Swana, and in that moment, she knew his thoughts. He would grab her, haul her up as a shield before Zeb could fire—

She shoved him. Suddenly off balance, he staggered back a step, bumping into Ritter. His moment gone, he glared at her and raised his hands. Ritter raised his as well.

Zeb glanced at her. "Come here. Don't get between me and them." She could tell his voice was deeper, harsher than she'd heard it before. He was obviously trying to disguise it. He couldn't disguise his strange New World accent, though.

She rose. As she did, Ritter grabbed the edge of the nearest table, toppled it forward, began to dive behind it—

The older man lunged for Swana—

Zeb fired. Swana heard and, in the confined space of the room, even felt the force of the explosion from the gun. The older man folded, whether hit in the stomach or some place further down Swana could not tell.

Ritter's table crashed down, Ritter behind it. Swana could barely hear the sound of its impact. Ritter's hand came up over the lip, his own pistol in it. He began firing in Zeb's direction, not exposing his face to return fire.

Zeb opened up, firing from each gun in turn, his shots blowing holes in the tabletop, sending splinters in all directions.

Zeb stepped to the side as Swana reached him, continued pouring fire into Ritter's table, and shouted to be heard: "Over the rail!"

She moved out onto the balcony and stepped out of line of the opening so Ritter's return fire would not hit her. She heard bullets whistle by less than a pace to her right.

Below the balcony, the car that had brought her here waited, idling. Around the courtyard, from doors to other buildings and the tower entrances, men were emerging—some in incomplete Sonnenkrieger uniforms, one with a bib still around his neck and the cooked wing of a bird still in his hand.

There was just no time to be afraid. Swana kicked off her shoes, sat on the rail, swung her legs over it, and jumped.

The impact with the car's roof was hard and she fell to her knees, sending sharp pain through her kneecaps. Then she slid off the roof to the front right, dropping into the driver's seat.

Another impact rocked the car and Zeb dropped into the passenger side of the compartment. The slides of both his pistols were locked back, showing the front few fingerspans of the barrels they normally hid. Men were running toward the car. "Go, go," he said.

She put the vehicle in gear and aimed it for the way out. A soldier stood before her, waving his arms, then thought the better of it and dove out of the way as she drove through the space where he'd stood. A moment later they were rattling across the wooden bridge and on the road beyond. Swana took her glasses,

with lenses that were flat and corrected no problems
with vision, and threw them out the window. She'd
never need them again. She'd never be Teleri again.

"Where are the guards who were there?" she asked.
Shorter than the car's last driver, and now lacking heels
to increase her height, she had to sit forward in the
seat to manage the pedals.

"In the moat." Zeb pocketed the pistols and leaned
forward to fumble around in the darkness of the floorboards.

"Drowned?"

"Moat's dry." He straightened. There was now a rifle
in his hands. In the faint light the moon gave him when
tree branches were not overhead, he looked at the
action, checked the bolt.

"Where did you get that?"

"From the guards in the moat." Zeb looked over his
shoulder. Swana checked the rearview mirror. There
were no lights following them.

"The guards," Zeb continued, "were there to stop
and challenge cars. They weren't really thinking in
terms of someone arriving on foot. I got as close as I
could, and then I got lucky. It was just a matter of time,
really. One of them lit a cigarette for the other one.
When the match flared, I knew they'd be night-blind
for a second. I rushed them. Managed to take them
out before they got a shot off."

"They're going to call the village, the train station,"
Swana said.

"Yep. Is that where you're going?"

"It's the only place I know how to reach. I paid
attention to the road as we were driving to the castle."

"Good for you. That's the right answer. They'll have
set up something to stop us, but with any luck we
haven't given them enough time to set up much."

❖   ❖   ❖

The road led them through another few turns, then the trees fell away to either side and Zeb and Swana could see the village before them. Zeb hadn't seen it from an upright position before; it was small, a little valley town, a concentration of buildings graduating into a scattering of farmhouses. He saw the small train station, a cluster of hemispherical one- and-two-story brick buildings well-lit by streetlights that had to be the center of the community, and the one road leading through it all and out the other side.

On the near edge of the village, a mere few hundred yards away, a dotted line of lights crossed the road.

Zeb swore.

"What is it?"

"Roadblock. They've pulled up a bunch of cars side by side to block the road. We're looking at their headlights."

"What do we do?"

"Head toward 'em at full speed. Maybe we'll see some way to get through when we're closer. If we don't, we turn around and head back the way we came. Maybe we can ditch the car and get away on foot."

Swana did as she was told, accelerating on the straightaway toward the cars, searching for some way past. But it looked as though the roadblock spanned not just the road but the shoulders and open space beside the shoulders, all the way to trees on either side. She could see no way through, though now she could see silhouettes of men behind and around the cars. Probably soldiers, she thought, and could not keep from shuddering at the thought of their rifles.

She was a few ticks of the clock from having to spin around and head back. She heard Zeb say, "Okay, turn—"

Then one of the roadblock cars pulled back and

away from the line, opening a gap. There were flashes of light and loud snapping sounds from its vicinity— gunshots, she thought. It pulled back and aside enough to make a clear path through the roadblock.

Zeb pointed. "Go, go, go!"

She floored the accelerator, leaning forward and rocking as though it would help her go faster. The roadblock's headlights were closer and brighter, and as she reached the gap she realized that she couldn't really see it, could only estimate its size by the hole left in the row of headlights—maybe it was too small, maybe she'd hit a car on one side or the other—and then she was through, looking at a few village streetlights and open country beyond.

"It's Noriko," Zeb said.

"What?"

"In the car that pulled back."

"Are you sure?"

"No. But I'm sure that it's the same type of car as our roadster. And it's the only thing that makes sense."

In the rear-view mirror, Swana saw that the road-ster was accelerating behind them, gaining quickly on them, and that the roadblock was breaking up, its cars turning in their wake. "They're coming."

"It's okay. I've reloaded."

The roadster pulled up alongside them. Swana saw its driver, visible only as a woman in a dark outfit with flaring sleeves, wave. Then the roadster pulled out ahead of them and took the lead.

"I hope that means she knows the way back to Bardulfburg," Zeb said.

Rudi was first aware only of a sensation. It rose and ebbed like the tide, yet it somehow was not soothing. Then he discovered the sensation was pain, a slow throbbing in his head; at the peak of each wave, it hurt so much that he could not hear, could not think, could not keep himself from groaning aloud.

He was moving, held between two men. They gripped him by his elbows; his hands were tied behind him. There was cloth over his eyes so he could see nothing more than a little light.

They sat him in a chair and whisked his blindfold away. Though waves of pain still regularly made it difficult for him to see, he could make out his surroundings—a smallish room with irregular stone walls, a naked light bulb in a socket hanging from the ceiling, high narrow windows toward the ceiling. They had been painted black. Rudi did not see but inferred a set of wooden stairs leading upward; this had to be a basement.

The two men who'd dragged him here still flanked him. They were tall lights in sharp-looking overcoats. A third man, also a light and very fair-haired, sat in a chair opposite him. This man was dressed in workingman's clothes, rust-brown pants and vest with a light short-sleeved shirt, but his build and haircut suggested he was military.

There was a little table beside the man. On it were Rudi's automatics.

The man offered what looked like the weary smile of a bureaucrat faced with the day's fortieth little problem, then spoke to him. The words were Burian. Despite the pain, Rudi attempted to look interested, cocked his head, nodded occasionally, and waited for this discourse to end, which it did on what sounded like a question. Then he said, "Sorry, eamon, I don't speak Burian."

The man lost his smile for just a moment, then it returned. "My apologies," he said. His speech was heavy with the Burian accent. "I was not aware of your deficiency. You are obviously alert enough. We have questions for you."

"Who is 'we'?" Rudi asked.

The man to his left slapped the side of his head. Ordinarily it would have done little more than sting. But with the pain Rudi was already experiencing, the blow was like being hit by a hammer. His head swam, his vision closed down for a moment and he sagged in his chair.

He was able to keep his jaw shut, able to keep from crying out, just barely. He wouldn't give them the satisfaction.

His questioner continued as though he hadn't spoken. "Your name and home?"

"Vorti Conna, of Lackderry." These were the false details Doc had insisted he come up with. He was glad he'd committed them to memory. Even now, with his head ringing, he could recite them with a measure of confidence.

"Where are your identity papers?"

"Me wallet and passport are in me breast pocket."

The man to his right looked at the questioner and shook his head.

"I'm afraid they are not," the questioner said. "Now, where might they be?"

"I was hit over the head," Rudi said. "Maybe the robber has them."

The questioner sighed. "Who is the young lady you were with, and how do you know her?"

"Her name's Teleri Obeldon." Rudi shrugged and took the opportunity to flex against his bonds a little. They felt like tough cord, well tied. He doubted he'd be able to break them, nor could he exert himself fully against them with three men watching. "I think she's me boss's woman. He hired me in Beldon to watch her, to keep her from runnin'." Rudi remembered Doc had said this would be part of the story they'd concoct, a story that would lead investigators to people and places Doc would specify. But they hadn't had time to do it last night on account of Casnar's party and Doc's exhaustion; they were supposed to get those details in place tonight. Now it was too late.

"Who is your employer?"

"His name's Duncan Blackletter." There, that ought to confuse them. The Bergmonk Boys had worked for Blackletter in the past. Rudi knew him well enough to convince people that he had spent time in his company.

For once, his questioner seemed taken aback. "Describe this Duncan Blackletter."

"Tall old man. A light, probably the lightest light I ever saw, you included. Skinny. Tough and mean as leather boiled in poison, but he's always solicitous of his people. Asks how you're doing, if you've had enough breakfast, that sort of thing."

"You have failed to mention that he's dead."

Rudi managed a toothy smile, his first of the interview. "You know, when he hired me, he said that a lot of people thought he was dead. I took it as a joke."

For a moment, the questioner looked a trifle more disturbed, then his expression returned to cheerful curiosity. "Where are you staying?"

"We just arrived this morning. We haven't been able to find rooms. That's what Goodsir Blackletter is doing now—looking for rooms for us."

"How were you to find one another?"

"We were supposed to meet at a beer garden." Rudi gave them the address of the place from which Swana had made her talk-box call. "At half-past three bells." Rudi didn't know what the clock was now, but it had to be that time or later, depending on how long he'd been unconscious.

His questioner looked over Rudi's head, then nodded to the man to Rudi's left. That man took off at a dead run, and Rudi heard, with a measure of satisfaction, the man's footsteps pounding up a wooden staircase.

"Goodsir Conna," the questioner said, "I fear I do not like your answers."

"They're the only answers I have." Rudi tried to sound reasonable.

"Look at it from my, ah . . ."

"Perspective."

"Perspective. Thank you. When I ask many questions and I get many answers, and yet they all lead to phantoms—no papers, no address, no knowledge—do you know what I think?"

That your subject's lying as though it were all the rage. Rudi had been questioned too many times by local authorities to think he'd fooled the man; he'd merely played a single round of the questioning game. But he said, "No, what?"

"That there is deception at work." The questioner stood and took the place of the man who had just left. "I don't wish you to deceive us. I wish you to be helpful, informative. In fact, I wish to improve you. And that is just what I am going to do now." He seized Rudi's arm; the other man grabbed his other arm and they hauled him to his feet. "In just a few moments you will feel like a new and better man. And I suspect you will be more cooperative."

They swung him around to face the rear wall. There were the stairs up, there was the clock on the wall . . . and, to the right of the clock, there was another of those mechanisms like the one they'd found in the business that had been Teleri's base of operations. It had the same cylindrical base, the same array of glass tubing on the top of the case.

Rudi felt his mouth go dry. He forced a smile anyway. "What's this? A talk-box? Do I get to make a call?"

"Not exactly," his questioner said. The two men moved him toward the case.

❖   ❖   ❖

The pursuing cars gained on Zeb and Swana. When he heard the first crack of a rifle, he said, "Keep down. It's time." He stood, bracing himself against the partition between driver's and passengers' compartments, and aimed his rifle back at the pursuing vehicles.

The jolting and swaying of their motion kept throwing his aim off, but in a brief few seconds when the road was steady, he centered his aim on the left front windshield of the car immediately behind and fired off a shot. He saw no reaction from the vehicle and cursed to himself. *Right side, dummy, right side is where the driver is.*

The driver of that vehicle fired back, apparently holding a handgun out his window. The bullet came nowhere close. Someone in the next car back also opened up with a firearm—two, three, four shots, from a rifle by the sound of them. Zeb heard something hammer dully into the back of his car.

He switched his aim to the driver's side of the closest pursuer and began squeezing off shots whenever he felt he had a chance. He fired his fifth shot before he saw any reaction: That vehicle suddenly veered, then went straight off the road and smashed into some sort of standing stone the height of a man, knocking it over. The car continued rolling, then came to a halt against a dark mound Zeb assumed to be a haystack.

Gunmen in the next car in line continued to fire. Zeb heard more thumps against the rear of his car, then heard the rear window shatter.

Zeb worked the bolt on his rifle, ejecting the fifth shell, and discovered it was empty. He dropped beside Swana and groped around in the floorboards for the second of three rifles he'd taken from guards at the castle. "One down," he told Swana. "Five or so to go."

"Do you have five more rifles?"

"Don't be snide." Second rifle in hand, he stood once more.

The closest pursuer had moved up. Its front bumper was less than a yard from Swana's rear bumper, and the vehicle was sidling up to pass Swana on the right.

"Don't let him come alongside!" Zeb shouted. Swana glanced in her rearview mirror and swung the wheel to the right, too sharp an angle. Zeb was thrown off balance; he fell against the top of the left-side door and hung there, half his body suspended over roadway, teetering toward a fatal fall . . .

Which also gave him the opportunity to see the next car, which was coming up fast on the left side.

He felt something seize his left ankle and yank it down to the seat. His feet found purchase but he didn't straighten or push off from the window; he stayed leaning out over empty space and took a shot at the car on that side. There was a tinkling of glass and its left headlight went out. He swore, adjusted, and fired as fast as he could work the bolt action. He thought it was on his third shot that the car began to swerve, but he kept firing until he was sure, until that car sideslipped to bang against the car to its right, then slid leftward and went off the road into a low stone fence.

Two down. Zeb dropped again and began fumbling for the third and last rifle. It was more difficult; Swana was swerving all over the road, doubtless trying to keep the other cars from passing. "Thanks for the grab."

"It was nothing."

"Has anyone ever told you that you're brave *and* smart?"

"No."

"Well, they should. You are." Rifle in hand, he stood. He saw the taillights of Noriko's car, still leading them by fifty yards or so, and he turned.

The next car back was still right on their tail, jockeying to pass, but no one in it was firing. Perhaps its driver had no guns. The next two back had no such limitations; they fired almost continuously, and both the partition glass and the windshield between Swana and Zeb blew out. She ducked; he swore.

He returned fire against the nearest of the cars shooting at him, but he went through his entire five-round clip without seeing any reaction from the driver. Aggravated, he hurled the useless weapon at the nearest pursuer.

The whirling rifle smashed in through the driver's-side windshield. The vehicle veered right, then rolled, its distinct automotive lines becoming somehow blurred and confusing as it flipped, side-top-side-bottom. Zeb saw pieces fly loose—a door, small broken bits, a larger mass that might have been a man.

The other three cars parted and managed to get around the disintegrating thing without suffering further damage themselves. Zeb shook his head over their driving skill—one more thing he did not need to have going against him—and drew the automatics from his pockets.

They were the weapon he'd first taken from Noriko's trunk back in Neckerdam and another just like it that he'd picked up as he and Noriko were formulating their plan to divert Rudi's and Swana's shadow. They were heavy things that fit his hands admirably, and he'd just reloaded them. Each carried seven shots in its clip and another in its chamber.

The next two cars came on side by side. They hung back for a few moments, so close to one another that passengers could easily have stepped from running board to running board. Then they parted, accelerating—and their passengers, at least three in each vehicle, opened fire on Zeb's car. A sound like golfball-sized hail hammered against the car's rear panel; more glass shattered throughout the vehicle; Swana's rearview mirror exploded and she cried out.

Zeb ducked for cover, keeping his head low. "You all right?"

"Yes." But the steering wheel was shuddering and she was having to use all her strength to keep it under control. "I think—I think a tire is hit. I can't keep up the speed . . ."

Zeb growled something inarticulate. He could see, back through the passenger compartment, that one of the pursuers was coming alongside on the driver's side. He glanced back out his own window to see the second pursuer coming up on his side. They were timing their approach, coming up together, and still firing continuously into the passenger compartment. Only the fact that the passenger and driver compartments of this car were separate, and built of good sturdy metal, had kept him and Swana from catching rounds in the back so far.

"Veer right," Zeb said. "Force him off the road." Then he prepared to stand, to lean out left, to exchange fire with the passengers of the car there until he took a bullet in this cross fire.

"I can't," Swana said. "She's—"

Noriko's roadster slowed into view, dropping into position on Swana's side, its deceleration so rapid that the pursuit car on that side smashed into its rear. Zeb saw Noriko turn the wheel to lean the roadster into the side of Zeb's car. Then Noriko stood, one hand on the wheel, and turned to face backwards. She raised her own handgun and fired into the windshield of the pursuit car, shooting as fast as she could get the weapon back in line after each shot.

Zeb let out a wild cry of jubilation. He leaned out his window and fired, almost point-blank, into the driver's window of the car pulling alongside. He saw a handgun raising to aim at him, saw the driver drop it, saw the driver's body and head jerk as Zeb's sustained fire poured into them. There was someone in the seat beside the driver, a muzzle blast from that man, an impact against Zeb's door, and then Zeb switched his aim to that enemy.

That car drifted to the left, onto the shoulder of the road and beyond.

Zeb saw the telephone pole ahead of it a split second before it hit. Then the car was gone, vanished into the distance behind them like it had been swept from the scene by a vengeful god.

Zeb looked back. The car that had just hit the pole burst into flame. The fire illuminated the car Noriko had fired into; it had crashed nose-first into another low stone fence. The headlights of the final car were still there, steady in pursuit, gaining.

Zeb's car was still slowing. He glanced over. Swana was struggling less with the wheel. Noriko was still alongside.

Zeb pocketed his automatics. He grabbed the side of the steering wheel. "Get into the roadster. Now."

"What, jump?"

"Jump."

"I can't!"

"Have you forgotten that you're brave and smart? A brave girl wouldn't be afraid of jumping. And a smart one would figure out that she'll get killed if she stays in this rolling wreck."

She glared at him, then slid against the window. Zeb slid more into place behind the wheel. He felt Swana stand, felt her legs against his shoulder as she reached over to the roadster and grabbed at it—then one of her legs rose past his face, clipping his nose and the brim of his hat, and she was gone.

He stood on the brake and Noriko's roadster shot on ahead. With the last of his vehicle's momentum he slewed around leftward, putting the car across two lanes. He killed the engine and hopped out to stand on the driver's side running board. He drew his pistols and aimed them across the roof at the oncoming car.

Muzzle flares erupted from its passenger side. He returned fire into the driver's-side windshield, emptying both pistols, hearing thumps and slams strike his own vehicle.

The oncoming car veered left and then right, as though the driver were indecisive about whether to pass Zeb on the right or the left. Then the car leveled off and steered straight at Zeb, and he realized the driver was probably already dead.

Zeb dove clear, hit the pavement with a bone-jarring thump, heard the shrieking collision as tons of metal met violently.

Then he was up on his feet, turning to face the wreckage, which was still sliding. He noticed absently that his left-hand gun had its slide locked back. It was empty. He pocketed it. He had no idea how many rounds he had left.

He moved up to the wreckage as it came to a stop. It was a roadster. There were two men in the front seat. Both wore Sonnenkrieger uniforms. The driver was covered in blood, his chest pinned to the seat by the steering wheel.

The other man was hunched forward over the dashboard, unmoving, blood all over the side of his face. Zeb thought he had to be dead, too, but as Zeb came close his eyes opened.

His lips moved. Zeb couldn't understand the words. "Speak Cretanis," Zeb said.

"Who . . . are you?"

I'm a black man with guns and I despise your whole political party and everything it's trying to do. But Zeb simplified the thought for the injured man. "I'm your worst nightmare," he said.

Then he took off after Noriko's car, which was parked about fifty yards up on the side of the road. He wanted to run, but the best he could manage was a hobbling trot. Still, he didn't feel too bad about the way things had ended here.

Chapter Twenty

They put Rudi in the cabinet. He made more jokes as he pretended not to know what it was.

His questioner said no more. He only smiled. Then he closed the door, and Rudi could only see a little of him, the amount revealed by the small panel of glass in the door.

Rudi flexed against his bonds. They held, cutting into his wrists.

Then there was a buzzing, the same buzzing he'd heard in Teleri's base of operations in Novimagos, and it cut into him worse.

It wasn't bad at first, just a slight burning sensation. A mild sunburn that affected him from head to toe. He had to shut his eyes against it.

Then it began to go deeper. He could feel it sinking through his skin, into his muscles, into his eyeballs, as though he'd decided to take a bath in horse liniment.

It hurt to breathe. He could feel the burning in his throat, in his lungs. He grunted with each breath; it took an effort to keep each grunt from turning into a cry.

Then the burning went deeper. He felt his bones burn. He felt his skin catch on fire, though he could not bear to open his eyes to see—he knew they'd catch on fire, too. Now he couldn't keep himself from crying out, couldn't keep himself from giving them that satisfaction.

Fire erupted in his elbows, in his knees, in his fingers and toes. His legs gave way and he fell to the floor of the cabinet.

And then the buzzing noise ended.

But the pain didn't stop. He lay there, feeling the burn suffuse his body, unable to move, unable to think.

He heard the cabinet door open and felt fresher air on his face. It hurt, like a burn suddenly rubbed down with ice.

"Believe it or not," his questioner said, "that was good for you."

"Futter you," Rudi said. His voice emerged as no more than a whisper, but he was pleased that he could still form words.

Hands seized his arms, crushing the burning sensation deep into his tissues, and carried him out of the cylinder, slamming him down into his chair once more.

"Let us begin again," his questioner said. "If I do not like your answers, I will give you more of what is good for you. Thirty ticks next time. And if I must do it once more, sixty ticks. Do you understand?"

Rudi forced himself to open his eyes. The man's face was only fingerspans from his own. If Rudi had his full strength, he could have kicked the man hard enough to deny him further children. But he doubted he even had strength enough to spit. "Futter. You. Do *you* understand?"

"Pity." Then the man frowned. He reached up to brush fingers across Rudi's beard and mustache.

Where he touched them, they crumbled and fell away. The questioner made a little hissing noise and ran a finger through Rudi's hair, which also crumbled. "Makeup and wig," he said. "Made of duskies' hair, like so many. They fell apart before you did, but in much the same way you will. Now I have many *more* questions." He turned to return to his seat.

The window on the wall above him shattered in. Both the Burian men turned to look.

But there was the crack of a firearm and the light bulb above their heads exploded in a rain of glass fragments.

In the sudden darkness, Rudi heard heels hit the floor, heard cries in Burian. One of those sets of cries choked off. Another continued for a moment, then there was the sound of an impact and they became shrill cries. There was another impact and they ceased completely.

The door at the top of the stairs opened, throwing a little light across the room. There were still two men standing in the room, but both wore hats and wool coats—Rudi recognized Harris and Doc under the brims of the hats.

A man in common dress moved into the doorway at the top of the stairs. He held a rifle at the ready.

From the window that had smashed in came a noise, a horrible roaring that Rudi knew well—an autogun. The doorway and banister around the man disintegrated into wood splinters. The man retreated.

Doc bent over Rudi. "Can you walk?"

"No."

Doc picked him up by the shoulders, as easily as if Rudi weighed no more than a baby, and carried him to the wall. His grip caused the burning in Rudi's shoulders and arms to grow—he was shocked to see that no flames burst from his upper torso.

Doc handed Rudi up. Hands, Alastair's, came down to grab his collar and shoulder. Rudi forced himself to ignore the pain and said, "Me guns . . ."

"Got 'em," Harris said.

Alastair dragged Rudi out through the shattered window. Rudi found himself on a sidewalk under nighttime stars. Ish stood nearby, also in dark clothes, her shotgun in her hands. She had it aimed at the nearest doorway. As Rudi watched, the door opened and a man in civilian clothes stepped out. Ish fired; the doorjamb above the man's head fragmented. The man retreated, slamming the door shut. "We haven't much time," Ish said.

Alastair grunted under Rudi's weight as he carried him to the car waiting at the curb. It was, Rudi saw, the sedan Ruadan had acquired for them. "We're fine," Alastair said. He pushed Rudi into the rear seat and hauled him upright.

Gaby was behind the wheel, her attention on the window. "Beer hall," Rudi told her, though it was an effort to speak. "I'll give you an extra lib if you get me there in half a chime."

"Very funny," she said.

A moment later, Harris, Doc, Alastair and Ish slid into the car and Gaby set the vehicle into motion. Rudi held his breath for the first city block, as he did during any getaway. But there were no sirens, no more gunshots. He sagged and exhaustion took him.

They assembled in the main room, several tired people, some of them injured, some of them recently under a likely sentence of death.

Zeb took the easy chair near the doors to the balcony. He had discarded his hat and coat but could not

escape the smell of soot and burn that permeated them:
That smell was on everything he'd had with him
tonight, including his skin. He kept his handguns close
to him; all the associates, equally rattled, were doing
the same.

Rudi was on the large couch, laid out with a pillow under his head, Alastair seated on an adjacent
hassock, examining him. Rudi looked like hell, facial
muscles occasionally twitching, powdery remnants of
a false beard still spirit-gummed to his face, their dark
ashes in marked contrast to his hair now that his wig
had been removed. Rudi held a beer bottle and took
swigs from it when not answering Alastair's questions.

Harris and Gaby were on the other couch in a
snuggling pose that made them look like any young,
respectable couple—if one ignored the revolvers he'd
placed on the end table beside him, the rifle propped
up against the end of the couch near her.

Swana, the only one present without firearms at
hand, had another stuffed chair. She was barefoot and
held her dog in her lap, even when Odilon wanted to
hop down.

Doc and Ish, poring over the items Swana had given
them, had the table, the butt of Ish's shotgun serving
them as a paperweight.

"How did you find me?" Rudi said.

Doc and Ish exchanged a look. "That was simple,"
Doc said. "You were carrying something I'd given you.
I'd meant it to end up in the hands of the people
extorting money from Neckerdam."

Rudi took another drink from his bottle. "Albin, you
mean."

"Yes, Albin. It was a deviser's trick, very subtle.
Warmed by a body, it sent out a signal like an Aether
talk-box. And I, as the deviser who made it, could
follow that signal."

Rudi frowned, thinking, then his expression cleared. "That coin, the one you gave me . . ."

Doc nodded. "That's correct."

Rudi dug around in his pants pocket, the effort obviously painful to him, and pulled out the paint-streaked silver lib. "It was lucky after all."

Doc smiled. "So, we got back to our quarters probably not long after Zeb and Noriko left. Noriko called us from the train station and said you and Swana had been taken onto a train. But when I detected the coin's emanations, when I began to follow it, they led me far from the train station. We assumed you'd been separated." Doc looked regretful. "We had to concentrate our available resources on rescuing you, Rudi, and hoped Zeb and Noriko could serve for you, Swana."

"They did," Swana said. She was agitated, often looking at the apartment's main door as though she expected men to come bursting through it at any moment. "Do you think they will know it was you?"

"No. I felt for the wards when we returned, before we entered the building. They were intact; no one had been in. Words on talk-boxes travel much faster than cars; they could have had forces here long before we returned. So they don't know, though they may suspect." Doc frowned and turned to Noriko. "Speaking of which, how did you make it back all the way to Bardulfburg? There had to have been more road-blocks."

She shook her head. "When I first got to the village where the train had stopped, Goldmacher, I made note of where the talk-box lines were. After Zeb had dealt with the last pursuit car, we shot the line out. We took back roads back to Bardulfburg anyway, just in case they had an aether talk-box at the village or the castle, but it doesn't appear they did."

Doc nodded. "Another piece of evidence. The lack of an aether talk-box is significant." He glanced at Zeb, doubtless reviewing the man's explanation of what had happened and looking for points in it that still made no sense. "Noriko, what were you doing in the road-block?"

Noriko smiled. Zeb thought he detected some mischief in the expression. "The train was stopped, Zeb and Swana were gone, so I looked at the map to see if I could guess where they'd been taken . . . and suddenly Sonnenkrieger were everywhere. I knew it had to be because of Zeb. They commandeered my car to be part of the blockade. The soldier didn't even give me a good look. I got in back and he spoke to me, issuing orders, but I don't speak Burian so I ignored him. Then, when Zeb's car came at us, I hit him with my gun butt." She shrugged. "I pushed him out of the car and you know the rest."

"Yes. Good work." Doc turned to Swana. "Goodlady Weiss, allow me to extend you my most profound apologies. We erred badly in estimating how much time it would take them to try to 'rescue' Teleri. The mistake was mine, and based on long experience with the amount of time it takes bureaucracies, even military bureaucracies, to act." He gestured at the papers before him. "Based on several things—these documents, the locations where you and Rudi were taken, and the decisive action of the Sonnenkrieger—I've come to the conclusion that what we're up against is not an official program of the government. It seems instead to be a conspiracy, a faction of the government, something like that. I'm not certain.

"But that's not relevant for the moment. I don't know whether your true identity is compromised, but we should act as though it is. We should get you out of Bardulfburg, out of the Weserian lands altogether.

Tell me where you'd like to go and what you'd like to do. We'll accomplish it."

Swana's eyes grew wide. "Truly? Anything?"

"Almost anything. You're not even limited to anything within reason. Anything just on the wrong side of the border of reason will also do."

"Oh, my."

"Think it over—"

"I don't have to." She straightened. "I want—could I—I want to go to university. I can't afford to."

Doc smiled. "You can afford to now."

"And I have—I am being greedy, but this is not just for me." Swana looked flustered, unhappy at suddenly being the child clamoring for more presents, unable to keep herself from doing so.

"Go ahead."

"I have friends, they were students here in Bardulfburg. Seven of them. When the Reinis took over and Aevar deposed his father, my friends protested in a street rally. The black-shirts, what the Sonnenkrieger were before they were official, took them away. My friends never went to trial, no one knows what happened to them."

Doc considered, silent for a moment. "That may be beyond the scope of what we can accomplish during this trip to Weseria. But the Foundation will investigate."

"Thank you."

"And we'll get you out of Bardulfburg now."

"I can wait. Who will you spare to take me out of the country? I will not have any of you be hurt or captured because one of you had to be my bodyguard for another day or two." Her gaze fell on Rudi and she shuddered. He gave her a broad, drunken smile and raised his bottle to her. She continued, "We can find out much sooner whether the authorities know I impersonated Teleri—will they not be watching my apartment? If they are not, I can go home. I'll return to my own clothes and no one will be the wiser."

Doc mulled that over. "We'll consider that." He returned his attention to the papers and items Swana had appropriated. "Much of this is experiment notations, a deviser's notations. This deviser evidently works in a variety of disciplines but has a most undisciplined mind.

"One of the experiments is to be a breeding program. They are assembling female volunteers for the first phase."

Zeb grimaced. "Eugenics. Great."

"In another, he appears to be working with priests to learn the workings of the mind of a god, a persona. He does not name the god. He writes here, 'The god does not tolerate the dark, or the dark things. Night is hateful to him; he dispels it. Those of low flesh are hateful to him; he consumes them, while those he loves are warmed by his radiance.'"

"That doesn't sound like observations," Gaby said. "More like a prayer."

"Indeed." Doc leaned back in his chair. He looked disturbed. "Also, it's the first instance I've run across in which a god is said to express a racial preference. Tribal and national preferences are not uncommon, established in ancient times by agreements between god and tribe—but racial preferences?" He shook his head.

From the bottom of the stack of paper, he selected one item and drew it forth. It was a colorful document, calligraphy in many hues on parchment, recently much folded so Swana could carry it. "This, however, gives us concrete information. It's a document drawn up and signed by King Aevar, appointing a Doctor Trandil Niskin as his personal deviser."

Harris smiled. "The court magician. His very own Merlin."

"Lest you think me a sloppy investigator," Doc continued, "this was something I looked into before we boarded the airwing for Weseria. Aevar does not publicly acknowledge a personal deviser. Officially, he has no 'court magician.' This has been a secret appointment.

"So let us add up the numbers." Doc set the document down and began counting off on his fingers. "Atypical speed of response on the part of our enemies. Rudi taken not to any official army or Sonnenkrieger building but to what can be most charitably described as a hideout—and one with one of the bleaching devices in it. A secret appointment of a multidisciplinary deviser probing the mind of a god of the sun . . . and instituting a breeding experiment. Ties between the deviser and the Sonnenkrieger including use of personnel—Sonnenkrieger as guards for Niskin's castle—and the arranged engagement of a Sonnenkrieger general to the deviser's daughter. What we have here is a program or set of programs that Aevar either doesn't know about or can't afford to have laid at his door if discovered. We may also have aspirations of rule on the part of the deviser— the marriage plan seems possibly dynastic."

"This is good," Harris said. "People keeping secrets may want to kill us to keep them, but it may mean they can't dedicate a whole nation's resources to stopping us."

Alastair left off his examination of Rudi and began packing things away in his bag. "One other thing, perhaps very minor."

"Yes?" Doc said.

"The name of the village where the castle is."

Doc frowned. "Goldmacher. Yes."

Zeb said, "The word sounds like it would translate pretty directly to English. Gold-maker?"

Doc nodded, still thoughtful.

"Is that some sort of craftsman?" Zeb asked. "A goldsmith?"

"No." Doc picked up the paperweight Swana had brought back. "It is literally one who makes gold. From lead. An alchemist. Alchemy is a transformative act few have ever successfully accomplished."

Alastair said, "The fact that it's the village's name suggests that devisement arts have been practiced there for a long time."

"And now this," Doc said, as though he hadn't heard Alastair. He covered his right eye to look at it with his other. "Ah. The missing piece of one of our older puzzles." He held it over the puppet Swana had brought back and said, "*Bitte.*"

As if it had been resting all along, waiting for this opportunity, the puppet sprang to its feet and stood, swaying. It looked up at Doc, its pose so characteristic of someone awaiting orders that several of the associates laughed.

Not Zeb. As soon as the puppet moved, his right palm itched, then burned as though someone had applied a match to it. "Son of a bitch!" He jumped up, too, furiously rubbing at the spot of the pain. It did not subside, but the surprise of the pain faded and he realized it did not hurt enough to injure him—just to surprise him.

He looked up to see all the associates' eyes on him. He smiled weakly. "Sorry."

"That is the hand you hit the little sun with," Noriko said.

"Yeah."

Doc, frowning, set the paperweight down. The puppet collapsed, its invisible strings cut.

Zeb looked at his palm. "The burning's stopped."

Doc picked it up again. The puppet sprang to its feet. "And now?"

"Burning again." Zeb closed his hand into a fist. The pressure seemed to help ease the sensation.

"Interesting." Doc looked at the puppet. It nodded and began walking across the tabletop, its motion cartoony and exaggerated. "Now?"

"The same." Zeb took his seat again, watching the puppet in fascination. "Man, when I was a boy, I'd have given anything for one of those."

"Right now," Doc said, "I'd give much to have what you have."

Zeb looked at his palm. He recalled the night of the Parade of the Suns, when his hand had throbbed as the suns on the poles came near. "It's not just the puppet, is it? It's solar magic. Solar devisement."

Doc nodded. "I suspect so. That little sun you deflected might have been the fingertip of the god whose name we seek. You may have been blessed."

"By a god who wants to burn me like toast."

Doc smiled. "We take our blessings where we can get them. Very well. It's late. We have investigations and competitions to see to in the morning, so it's off to bed. We should be more diligent tonight, though. Alastair, can you take first watch?"

Alastair smiled. From beside Rudi's couch he picked up his autogun. "Happy to," he said.

Someone shook Zeb. He opened his eyes, took in unfamiliar surroundings, and was momentarily confused. *What am I doing here?* Then he remembered why he was on the couch where Rudi had been doctored a few hours before.

Noriko left off shaking him. She was seated on the edge of the couch, leaning over him. "What are you doing here?"

Zeb looked at the doors to the balcony. A little light was trying to force its way around the edges of their curtains. He yawned and stretched. "Rudi was in a little pain still. Making noises as he slept. I couldn't get to sleep. So I came out here." He grinned up at her.

"You don't seem too put out."

"I'm not. I'm doing great, actually. In spite of having about twice as many bruises as I have muscles."

"Why?"

He considered. "It's kind of hard to explain." *No, it's not, you're just out of the habit of explaining anything. To anyone.* "I don't know. I may be reading things wrong. Putting too much weight in the things people say, the way they're saying them."

She shook her head, not understanding.

"Last night, when Doc finished his debriefing, as I was heading off to take my bath, it was all back-clapping, good-work-Zeb, that sort of thing."

"Which you deserved."

"But it was more than that. There was just a sort of ease to it all. Like it was family. Like I belonged." He took a deep breath. "It's been a long, long time since I belonged to anything."

"I know what you mean."

"I imagine you do."

"I woke you because you were talking in your sleep. Laughing and saying, 'Get off, get off.'"

The memory came back to Zeb. "Oh, man. I was dreaming."

"About what?"

"Rospo's dog. You know, the one who was killed. He was alive again and playing with me."

It was still too dark to see Noriko's features, but he could tell from the way she cocked her head that she was puzzled. "But you hate dogs."

"No." He sighed. "No, I love 'em."

"But every time I see you with them, you keep your distance."

"Yeah."

He was quiet for a long moment. She said, "Perhaps this is one of those times when the correct answer is, 'Go to hell'?"

"No, certainly not. It's just something I haven't talked about. Ever, I guess." He pulled himself up to lean back against the sofa's high arm. "I used to have dogs all the time. Growing up in Atlanta. My dad started a little trucking company that got bigger and bigger, so we had a nice house, big property, lots of room for dogs and brothers and sisters.

"When I was in high school, I had two dogs. Hogan was pure Alsatian—looked a lot like the dogs you see with the soldiers around here. Goober was a mutt with a lot of Doberman pinscher in him—big and black. Dumb and noisy as a hubcap full of ball bearings. Anyway . . ." He felt his throat constrict. He cleared it, trying to force the sensation away.

"Anyway, the day after I graduated high school, my dad comes to me to tell me my college plans. He was always like that, making plans for everyone regardless of what they wanted. He'd submitted applications to schools in my name, gotten an acceptance from one he liked. I was going to go off to college, be the first male in the family to get a degree—Mom had hers, but my dad wanted the boys to do it, too. He told me I was going to get it in economics.

"Problem was, I was sick of his bossiness, which was the only way he ever dealt with anyone. I also had no interest in economics. I told him I'd pick my own school if I decided to go at all . . ." Zeb shook his head over that one. "We went around and around on it. A shouting match that went on all day long. The rest of the family stayed clear of us. He was never able to make me give in. That was the first argument with him I ever won. I went out with some friends that night, and when I got back home, my suitcase was on the front porch, packed."

"He made you leave home? What did you do?"

"Went into the army. And found out that what I suspected from high school was true, that I had a real knack for fighting. So anyway, on my first leave I went home . . ." The constriction in his throat became a knot, and he had to swallow to get any air past it. When he spoke again, despite his best efforts, his voice was hoarse. "My dad wasn't there. Mom was. And when I couldn't find Hogan and Goober, she told me my dad had had them put down."

" 'Put down'?"

"Euthanized. Put to sleep." Seeing from her posture that she still didn't understand, he sighed. "He had them taken to an animal doctor and killed. Mercifully, painlessly. But unnecessarily. They'd been whimpering outside my door every day ever since I went away. I guess he thought he was doing them a favor—it's what he told Mom, anyway." Zeb stared off into the distance of time, remembering the kitchen table where they'd sat when his mother told him. Remembering her face, ageless and beautiful, her expression aware that she had failed once again to stand up to her husband when it mattered. "That was the last time I was ever in that house."

"Did you ever see your father again?"

"At his funeral. Just a year after I got out of the Army. He'd had a stroke. Burned out like a light bulb. My brother Pete runs the family business now, and he and my sisters all have college degrees. They don't talk to me. I mean, they talk, but they don't say anything. I'm just a guy who used to belong to the family. Like an ex-friend. Mom talks to me, but we have so little in common, it's like we're speaking different languages, and the guy translating for us doesn't have any interest in the conversation."

She was silent for a long moment. Then: "So you knew."

"Knew what?"

"What it was like for me to be an exile from my family."

"Yeah. But not from your country. That I don't know anything about."

"It's the same, only nothing is familiar, and you are always on edge. . . . Why do you dream of Rospo's dog?"

"I don't know. Maybe because we got it killed, like I got my dogs killed. Less directly. But if we hadn't been investigating, Albin Bergmonk wouldn't have been trying to cover up, and that dog would be alive."

"You will make yourself crazy, accepting the blame for every tragedy."

"Then I'll just stick to dog tragedies. Kind of limits the field."

Her shoulders moved, another laugh suppressed. "Thank you."

"For what?"

"For telling me."

"You're welcome. It's kind of good to have it out of me. Like a tumor taken out. And I forgot to say, thank *you*."

"For what?"

"For finding us last night. For not letting us die. Which we would have if you hadn't busted open the roadblock, if you hadn't zoomed in at the last second to foul up their attack on us."

"Oh. That is my job."

"There was nothing personal to it?"

"I . . . The desperation I felt was very personal."

He took her by the shoulders but she was already

leaning into him. They kissed, lips exploring, then tongues, and Zeb felt something like electricity jolt through him. "I've got an idea," he said.

She chuckled. "I know what your idea is."

"Let's take the day off."

"There's something important going on today. Perhaps you've heard of it. The Sonneheim Games. Competition. Action."

"I'm ready for action right now. Besides, the All-Out is one of the little competitions. Barely anyone shows up to see it."

"I'm going to go. Before you convince me." Her tone was amused, but go she did.

"You have got to be kidding," Zeb said.

He, Noriko, and Harris had had to be redirected by the sole judge now standing on the field where the All-Out had been held on previous days. In halting Cretanis, the man explained that the event had been moved this morning. "Ball-Field Number One," he said over and over.

Now they looked at Ball-Field Number One, where the fair world's equivalent of soccer would be played in the afternoon.

The stands were packed, and more thousands of observers waited at ground level at either end of the field.

The royal flag of Weseria flew from an observation platform at the center of one of the stands. Under the platform's canopy were seated King Aevar and several men in military uniforms. Reporters held up boxy cameras as Zeb neared and fired them off; the mass clicking sounded like a field of insects suddenly roused. Some shouted questions at Zeb, but he couldn't even make out the English words in the confusion of voices; he merely smiled and waved.

One old man, his skin so white and his hair so pale a gray that he looked like a black-and-white photograph whose clothes had incongruously been colorized bright green, stepped out in the lane between lines of onlookers and threw something at Zeb. Zeb swatted at it, flicking it down to the ground; it was nearly flattened by his blow. He looked at his object; a tomato, overripe. He smiled at the old man as he passed. "Thanks," he said.

The Sidhe Foundation associates walked, as directed by soldiers directing foot traffic, to the sidelines where the athletes were assembling.

Zeb saw Kobolde on the opposite side of the field, three of them that had worked their way up to the front of the crowd; had any been further back, he would not have been able to spot them among the taller members of the audience. He waved at those he saw. "What the hell happened with this crowd?" he asked.

"You did, buddy." Harris flashed him a smile; he looked smug. "Yesterday it was you against Kano, dusky versus dusky, and nobody cared. Today you're going to be beating up on some white boys."

"Don't remind me." Zeb held his head between his hands, miming dismay. "Two matches today, and me without enough sleep. This is going to suck."

Noriko said, "You grimworlders use that phrase a lot."

In the drawing of this round's opponents, Zeb found that he belonged to the half of the field that stood aside while the other half filed up to the pot and drew white chits.

Three fighters took chits from the pot and the names of their opponents were called. Then Oleg Stammgalf, the Viking who'd broken his opponent's arm the

previous day, drew the last chit and Zeb Watson's name
was called. The crowd cheered more loudly for that
announcement than for any of the others.

"Good, this is good," Zeb said.

"Good, how?" Harris said. "He's tough."

"I've got his number." Zeb gave his companions a
smile. "More importantly, I was drawn fourth, so my
match is last. I'm going to get a few minutes' more
sleep." He sat down, then stretched out on the ground
behind the ranks of athletes and trainers. The ground
was hard, the crowd noise was high and the sun was
already slanting into his eyes, but he knew he'd be able
to find some more rest.

Harris leaned over him. "Zeb, are you crazy?"

"I work with you, don't I? That's answer enough.
Wake me when the third bout starts." Zeb closed his
eyes.

He napped only a few minutes, during which some
part of him was still awake, listening to the shouts of
the audience, the sounds of impacts and pain from the
field. But when Harris prodded him with his toe, Zeb
awoke feeling better. His gamble had left him more
alert rather than more groggy.

He rose and went through his stretching exercises
with more than even his usual diligence. He ignored
the sights and sounds of the third match as it pro-
gressed; instead, he thought about his bout to come.
He mentally reviewed the previous day's fight
between Oleg Stammgalf and his muscleman opponent, repeating again and again Stammgalf's actions
as he closed with the other man. Harris and Noriko,
sensing Zeb's desire for distance, did not interrupt
him.

Eventually it came, the three pained thumps and
audience cheer signifying the end of the third bout.

A minute later, the main referee called, "Oleg Stammgalf, Dhenhavn. Zeb Watson, Novimagos."

As with the previous morning, Zeb moved quickly out onto the field, moving past the referee and turning to wait, as though being the first in place gave him the home-field advantage. Stammgalf, a broad smile on his face, took his time getting into position, as if his lack of interest were only appropriate in this situation.

They faced each other as the referee made his recitations in Burian, but then the referee did something he hadn't before: He gestured with his mallet to the king's viewing box. Stammgalf turned in that direction and executed a graceful bow. Zeb followed suit only a moment behind, and, seeing Stammgalf holding the bow, did so as well.

Up on the viewing stand, King Aevar was chatting with his companions; he noticed the competitors' actions and waved toward them. Stammgalf and Zeb straightened; the referee extended his mallet between them and raised it. The bout was on.

Zeb trotted backwards and assumed his boxing pose, but with his right leg further back than usual. He gestured with his fists, a "come and get it" motion. A few members of the crowd laughed, but whether it was in response to Zeb's sudden retreat or his gesture he couldn't tell. Others began chanting Stammgalf's name. Zeb heard someone in the crowd cry out, "Svart, svart, svart," but that was drowned out by a woman's voice—he recognized it as Gaby's—shouting, "Watson! Watson!"

Stammgalf shrugged and dropped down into his wrestler's crouch, arms wide to grab, then moved forward, his motion fast and sure.

As the man came within range, Zeb pivoted on his left foot, his plant foot, and snapped out as fast and hard a side kick as he had ever launched. He saw

Stammgalf's body language change, a sudden shift in the man's rhythm as he tried to twist out of the way. Zeb saw his leg chamber and then snap out in a perfect, pure line. He saw Stammgalf's expression change, become startled.

Then he felt and heard the impact as his heel connected with Stammgalf's jaw.

To the crowd, it had to have sounded like a single huge crack, but Zeb felt each component of it—the clack of Stammgalf's jaw snapping shut, the beginning of a grinding as it skewed out of position, the second, more subdued crack as his jaw broke.

Zeb brought his kicking leg down and back, still in balance, as Stammgalf tottered backwards and fell.

Stammgalf raised his head, his jaw at an odd angle, and tried to come upright. Then he lowered his head and his eyes closed.

The crowd went silent, even Gaby. The referee moved up to stand over the fallen fighter and extended his mallet above him. He began counting in Burian. He reached ten without Stammgalf ever stirring.

Zeb turned to bow again to Aevar. The king was sitting forward on his chair, his expression perplexed; he gave a little flick of his hand. Zeb straightened, raised a hand to the audience, and returned to the sidelines.

In the stands, Gaby started her chant again, and a few people around her picked it up. It rose in volume, though only a fraction of the onlookers joined in. Others booed.

"Sweet," Harris said. "But you're not going to be able to surprise anyone else that way."

"I know it, man." Zeb shrugged. "But I'm still tired from last night, I have another match to fight this afternoon, and I needed to win one without getting beat up."

A few feet down the sideline, Geert Tiwasson turned his walrus mustache toward them. "The way things have been," he said, "you will probably draw me next. And that will not work with me. I have been kicked by a horse. Kick me if you wish. Then I will break you into small pieces."

Zeb sighed. "And uphold the glorious destiny of the lights' superiority to the duskies. Thanks, I've heard this speech."

Geert offered him a smile. There was no humor in it. "You do not understand. I do not care about your skin. I do not care about the words of men who speak of such things. They are little men. I am great. I suspect you are great. But I am greater, and that is why I will beat you. That, and because I will regain the title. That is my only reason to be here."

Zeb gave him a long look. "Fair enough," he said.

Doc and Ish found Ruadan emerging from the Sonneheim Village stables, his garments—the familiar officer's uniform of Novimagos—drenched with perspiration. To Doc, he stank of human and equine sweat. Ruadan drew up upon seeing them, then bent, with a courtier's grace, over Ish's hand.

"How did you do?" Ish asked.

Ruadan shrugged. "Thirteenth today. But I was very strong in Sword. I am third overall. I have a decent chance to take the gold wreath. And how are your, ah, activities?"

"Exactly what we wanted to talk to you about," Doc said. "Walk with us."

Ruadan agreeably fell in with them and accompanied them. Doc was distracted by the layout of the Village itself: It was a collection of round wooden huts and moundlike larger buildings of brick, set along graded, beaten-earth tracks, all amply shaded by trees.

It was all heavily landscaped with well-cut grass, deep flower beds, and meandering creeks with wooden bridges over them wherever they intersected the trails. Everywhere, athletes moved, some in the shorts and light tops of track events, others in the baggier garments often used in training, always in bright national colors or with national armbands. Doc noted that Ruadan's attention was often drawn to the female athletes.

"How did you get into the Village?" Ruadan asked. "Admission is supposed to be limited to athletes and other participants."

Doc smiled. "How would you do it?"

"A bribe."

"That's how we did it. But I'm surprised that this would be your approach. Wouldn't you save yourself some money by asking a favor of your Sonnenkrieger contacts?"

Ruadan considered, then shook his head. "My actions would be much more likely to go into a file if I do that. I dislike having my movements listed in a file."

"Ah. Well, perhaps you could tell us about your involvement with the Sonnenkrieger."

"I don't think so." Ruadan looked amused. "That's a matter of royal security."

"As a general, though on detached duty, in the Novimagos Guard, I'm going to have to make that an order, Ruadan."

The other man laughed outright. "How amusing. But I'm going to have to decline, Desmond."

Doc stopped and stepped off the trail. Ruadan and Ish followed suit. "Well, that complicates matters," Doc said. "But trains leave Bardulfburg every bell. If you have any sense, you'll be on the next one."

Ruadan shot Doc a curious look. "Why would I?"

"Because I intend to speak to King Aevar today

and inform him that it was you who took a shot at him."

"Someone shot at Aevar?"

Doc shook his head. "Someone will. And will miss. And the rifle will be found in your quarters. I don't know whether it will be your true quarters or your quarters here in the Village; I can decide that later."

Ruadan's voice lowered, became grim. "Why would you do this?"

Doc shrugged. "Because I cannot trust you, and you won't address questions whose answers might allow me to. So I'll just get rid of you, and later apologize to the Crown of Novimagos for inconveniencing them."

Ruadan glowered. He was silent for a long moment. "And I'd begun to think that you were unfairly tarred with the brush of the Daoine Sidhe reputation," Ruadan said. "Very well. I do have Sonnenkrieger contacts. What of it?"

"What are they to you?"

"Mostly I sell them state secrets of Novimagos."

"That's not very nice."

"It's my job. Executed by the order of and with the permission of Bregon and Gwaeddan, your king and queen and mine." Ruadan shrugged. "Officially, I'm a minor lord of Novimagos, with the ear of the Crown owing to my alleged charm and wit. And impoverished. Unofficially, I'm in the Guard, my rank matching yours. I am known as a man who trades information back and forth, secrets for money, secrets for secrets, between numerous governments. But the flow of information benefits Novimagos more than any other party I deal with. I am a loyal son of the Crown." His voice took on a bitter edge. "And I do not need for some immigrant Cretanis bastard to question that loyalty."

Doc let the comment slide. "Perhaps not. How can you prove your assertion?"

"Send a message to the Crown. Use any return address you choose. The message should be this: 'What wine does Crandunum most enjoy?' You'll have an answer back within the bell. It will come from a sender you do not know, and will not refer to me by name. But in language couched in the terms of business, the sender will describe my tactics, and you will know that the Crown knows of my actions."

"Very well. Yesterday, at the Sword event, you were pointing out someone in the crowd to a Sonnenkrieger general."

Ruadan frowned as if remembering. "No, he was pointing her out to me."

"You were the one pointing."

"Yes. He—Tryg—said, 'Look, Ruadan, there. The stands opposite, third row, that woman. Do you recognize her?' Or some such. There were many women there in the stands, including," he nodded to Ish, "our own fair Ixyail, whom I did not mention to him. While I was trying to find out which one he was referring to, I may have pointed. I don't recall."

"Who was he pointing at?"

"A light, young, wearing spectacles. I didn't know her, though I know who she is now."

"Who?"

"Her true name is given as 'not known,' but she is listed as 'also hight Teleri Obeldon, also hight Adima Niskin.' This morning, the Sonnenkrieger issued orders for her to be found and brought in. They are offering a reward. My Sonnenkrieger contacts of whom you are so suspicious showed me her picture, in case I should see her." He frowned. "There were two warrants issued."

"The other one?"

"Very strange. He is listed only under a *nom de guerre*, *Alpdruck*. A big man wearing dark clothing and carrying automatic pistols. He may or may not be in the woman's company."

"Ah." Doc gave no hint that he knew what Ruadan was talking about, but was certain that Zeb would be pleased. "Interesting. That does seem to answer my questions. Thank you."

Ruadan glared instead of offering a "you're welcome." He cleared his throat. "Are you done with blackmail for the day?"

"I believe so."

"Don't ask for any more favors, Desmond." He turned to walk back toward the stables. But a few steps down the trail, he turned again, all seriousness. "No, I'll do you one favor for free. If you're looking for a weakness in your organization, for the source of your mistrust, look to your gangster friend."

"Bergmonk?" Doc said. "Specifically why?"

"It shouldn't surprise you that I've looked in on you and yours from time to time while you've been here. Your friend Rudi has been seen in coin talk-box booths not far from your quarters, dropping a lot of coins in to make his calls."

"Interesting," Doc said.

"If you ask him about it, be sure to threaten his career, too. It's only fair." Ruadan turned and left, his pace brisk.

"I don't trust him," Ish said. "A man cannot pretend to be loyal only to money and not have that way of thinking become real. At least partly real."

"Perhaps. But even if he is a problem, he is probably not our immediate problem."

At the nearest coin-operated talk-box, Doc dialed the number of the Foundation's quarters. Though Rudi was supposed to be there, resting from the treatment he'd received last night, no one answered.

Chapter Twenty-One

Zeb and Noriko entered the building where the Sword of Wo was held; the door guard, a Weserian regular army man who appeared as though he'd been a boy only last week, looked at their Sonneheim Games identity papers and passed them through with a disinterested nod. Zeb was grateful to see that there were no unexpectedly large crowds here; the building was as lightly trafficked as it had been the previous day.

"You've been quiet," Noriko said. "Ever since we left the All-Out."

"I've been—it's been sort of—ah, hell. I've just been mad. Because of what Geert Tiwasson said."

"About crushing you?"

"No, about *why* he was going to crush me. I'd just sort of assumed, Swana's example to the contrary, that everybody with a Burian name was buying in to the Reinis' light-is-right racist dogma." He added, his tone grudging, "Which has me making basically the same mistake they're making."

She smiled at him. "Maybe your mind is out of

training. Harris's certainly was when he first came to the fair world."

"Yeah, but in his case it's a lifelong condition."

They entered the Sword of Wo chamber, where competitors and audience were already gathering. Zeb looked for but did not see Colonel Förster among the attendees.

In the draw for this semifinal round, Chang O'Shang drew Harada Sen and Noriko drew Prince Hayato. "This is good," Noriko said as she rejoined Zeb. "The distraction he poses me will end today, whether or not I win."

"You seem pretty happy."

"I will accomplish my goal with him today."

"You'll beat him."

"I told you, I do not care about that, Zeb." She flashed him a smile, calm and confident. "But I realized what I did care about with him. You helped me do that."

"And what was it?"

The referee called Prince Hayato's name and Noriko's. She shrugged. "I'll tell you later. Help me into my helmet."

Noriko and Hayato endured the words of the referee, waited for his signal to begin, and came at one another with the blindingly fast blows and curious shouts unique to the Sword of Wo.

Unlike the fight between Noriko and Ikina, this was no mismatch of size against grace. The two were almost identical in speed, Hayato perhaps a bit stronger, Noriko perhaps a little more precise. Circling, but demonstrating little wasted motion, they struck, blocked, counterstruck, retreated. Their exchanges became punctuated by short moments in which the two stood back out of sword's reach and caught up on their

breath. Then they came together and Hayato was able
to batter Noriko's block down. He struck her in the
side of the neck before she could counter the move.

She bowed. They resumed their start positions and
began again. Again, their exchanges grew long and the
breaks they took to catch their breath became more
numerous. Yet this time, Noriko took advantage of
increased sloppiness in Hayato's technique—she took
his last blow as she was backing away, was able to
maneuver his edge and point just slightly out of line,
and stepped forward to hit him in the center of his
chest with her point.

He froze, looking at the wooden swordtip against
his armor, then took a step back and bowed. Zeb
discovered that he was holding his breath; he released
it slowly.

Noriko and Hayato returned to their start positions
a trifle more slowly than before, trying to squeeze out
every last moment of rest they could, and then came
together in their final exchange.

Hayato came out strong, battering at Noriko's
defenses, his speed only slightly diminished by the
tiredness he had to be feeling. Noriko's circle of
defense withdrew—she had to block incoming blows
more and more closely to her body as her strength
ebbed. Her counterstrikes were fast and sure, not as
strong as at the match's start but sufficient to count
as kills had they landed, but Hayato's defense was
strong and not failing.

Hayato raised his guard high to catch one of her
blows near the tip of her blade but at the round hilt-
guard of his own weapon. He snapped his blade down
and caught Noriko on the shoulder, a hard impact, a
kill.

She stopped and bowed. He bowed in turn. The
audience applauded. Hayato and Noriko exchanged a

few words, then turned to the sidelines and quit the
field, both of them moving toward Hayato's trainer and
away from Zeb. They were still talking. Zeb frowned,
but stayed where he was. This was obviously a private
matter between the cousins.

Eventually, as Harada Sen and Chang O'Shang were
taking the field, Noriko rejoined Zeb. He helped her
off with her helmet. She was smiling.

"You're happy." He set the helmet down at her feet.

"Yes."

"Can I ask why?"

She turned to watch Harada and Chang receiving
the referee's instructions. She nibbled at her lower lip,
a very Western gesture for her. "It's hard to explain.
Do you know what he said to me afterwards?"

"No."

"He asked me to return to Wo and rejoin the foreign office."

"As a spy."

"Yes, of course."

"And this made you happy?"

"Zeb, he *asked*. He did not order me. He did not
try to blackmail me with the regard of my relatives and
my dead parents. He just asked. I said no, of course."

"Uh, I still don't get it."

"Zeb, respect is a good and proper thing. I had some
for him, but before today he had none for me. You
showed me that having too much respect for an opponent was like handing him an extra blade. I defeated
Hayato yesterday when I talked to him, when I did not
rise to his baiting, when I made him feel like a fool
for playing irrelevant word games. I defeated him again
today when I fought him well, fought him to a standstill
at times, and never became the weak thing he has
always thought I was." She shrugged. "Just now, for the
first time in years, he offered me respect. Just the

ordinary respect grown family members should offer, nothing more." Her smile broadened. "Naturally, I did not let him suspect that this meant anything special to me."

"Naturally."

The referee raised his sword from between Harada and Chang. Noriko and Zeb left off talking to watch.

The shadows were already growing when the All-Out competitors convened for the semifinal matches. Again, the event was set up at Ball-Field Number One. The crowds were bigger, the press corps had swollen, and Aevar's viewing box was even more heavily populated; the king's daughter Edris was there, as was Prince Casnar.

This time regular army men lined the lanes the athletes arrived through, and Zeb received no impromptu gifts of rotten fruit. Also, an airship—Zeb learned that they were called liftships here rather than zeppelins—floated overhead, westerly winds threatening to move it from its position above the field, its engines engaging every so often to keep it more or less stationary.

Colonel Conrad Förster drew Hathu Aremeer, a competitor of the nation of Donarau, one of the southern members of the Burian Alliance. He was a light, shorter than any of the other competitors, burned red from recent exposure to the sun, his long brown hair streaked with blond, his broad, unhandsome face reminding Zeb of a number of Army boxing opponents he'd had unhappy experiences with.

That left Zeb only the name of Geert Tiwasson to draw. He handed his chit to the referee and rejoined Harris and Noriko. "So I'm the only non-Burian left in the competition?"

Harris nodded, his attention on the stands, as he

tried, as he always did, to pick Gaby out from the audience. "If you'd been awake for the last match you'd have realized that."

"Keep prodding, Greene. So, you've seen one more match with Tiwasson than I have. Anything new to report?"

"Yeah. He doesn't really show it, under all that muscle, but he *is* an old jock. You keep him at bay for forty, fifty minutes, you're sure to wear him down."

Zeb offered him a sour smile. "You're a big help."

"There she is." Harris waved until he appeared to have caught Gaby's attention, then turned back to Zeb. "Yeah, there's this. With every round except the first one, he's set up in anticipation of the type of fight his opponent offered in the previous round. He studies his opponents very closely, good for him, but I suspect that he commits himself to their repeating their strategies."

"Sort of like what I did with Stammgalf."

"Sort of."

"Guess it's time to shake things up, then." Zeb turned to Noriko. "Any advice, champ?"

She flashed him a quick smile, then pointed up at Aevar. "Him. He has told the press that you should not be competing, that you kicked Stammgalf like a horse because you're more animal than man. I think you should remember that every pain you inflict on Tiwasson, Aevar will feel."

"Good point."

But Förster's match with Aremeer was first, and Zeb was again able to see the skills that had brought the Sonnenkrieger to the final rounds of the All-Out.

Though Aremeer was a cunning wrestler and a tough boxer, Förster's bag of tricks was far deeper. When Aremeer grabbed him and bore him down, Förster demonstrated phenomenal grip strength in digging his hand into Aremeer's side under his rib cage and causing

enough pain to break the hold. When both were standing again and Aremeer grabbed for him once more,
Förster caught his incoming forearm, twisting it down
and back, throwing Aremeer to the ground in a credible
jiu-jitsu maneuver; Zeb heard Aremeer's breath leave
him with the impact. When Aremeer, in a surprising
display of agility, brought his legs up from ground level
to wrap around Förster's waist, the colonel struck him
a hard boxing blow to the balls.

And that fight was essentially over from that point.
Aremeer rolled away, tried to keep his distance to give
himself a moment to recover, but he couldn't quite
manage to straighten himself out of a fetal position.
As he was rolling, Förster kicked him once in the side
of the head and Aremeer went limp.

The crowd roared its appreciation. Förster bowed
to his king, then raised a hand and gravely accepted
the appreciation of the audience. Then, coming to the
sidelines, he pointed to Geert Tiwasson, a challenger's
gesture, a wordless "You're next."

"Wrong opponent, asshole," Zeb said under his
breath.

Stretcher bearers took the still-unconscious Aremeer
from the field, and the referee called, "Geert Tiwasson,
Weseria. Zeb Watson, Novimagos."

Zeb started out fast onto the field, his usual tactic,
and felt his foot snag something. He pitched forward,
seeing in his peripheral vision Tiwasson behind him,
tripping him. Then he hit the grass, his hands and
forearms taking most of the shock of impact. He heard
Harris say, "You son of a bitch," and a laugh from
Tiwasson. The big Weserian walked past Zeb, taking
the field before him, saying as he passed, "Must be
careful, this field is tricky." Zeb barely heard it over
the roar of laughter from the audience.

Zeb felt a wash of anger. He tried to keep it from

his face. One step into the match and he'd already lost points to the big Weserian. The crowd's laughter continued as he rose and followed Tiwasson to the center of the field. Tiwasson waited for him on the other side of the referee, a broad smile under his walrus mustache.

Zeb rose, schooling his face into an emotionless mask, and took his position. He didn't listen to the referee, just kept his intent stare on Tiwasson until the mallet was lifted out of the way between them.

Tiwasson brought his hands up and took a boxing pose. He waited. Zeb mirrored his pose, moved forward, threw a left-hand jab, a feint. Tiwasson's block was slow, unsure, though his return strike was fast enough. Zeb threw a combination, left-right-left, alternating between Tiwasson's face and midsection, and managed to plant a pretty solid hook in the man's ribs; Tiwasson lost his smile in a grimace of pain and backed away a step.

All right, Zeb thought. *We have a measure of your speed. Let's go to work.* He stepped forward, took Tiwasson's hook on the X-block of his crossed forearms, and moved in just a trifle too close for the man's next punch to have any power, then snapped his leg up to plant a knee in Tiwasson's ribs.

He hit hard, much harder than his hook of a moment ago, but this time his opponent didn't grimace. Tiwasson snapped his left arm down to trap Zeb's leg. He pulled, unbalancing Zeb just a little, forcing him to hop once to keep his balance. Tiwasson slapped Zeb, nothing more than a stinging blow, but it put the man in a position to hammer his forearm across Zeb's face on the way back.

Zeb's vision jerked as though he'd momentarily become unconnected to the world. When he could see again, his vision was tinged with red and Tiwasson's fist was coming at his face. He managed to get an arm up, partially deflecting the blow, but it still grazed along his jaw, snapping his head sideways. He saw the crowd in the stands, a monochromatic field of red onlookers, mouths open to shout, though he could not hear their voices.

Zeb let his support leg buckle, but Tiwasson, rather than allow himself to be dragged over, dropped him. Tiwasson followed through instantly with a kick toward Zeb's groin. Zeb twisted, took it high on his thigh instead, and pain exploded through his leg.

I'm losing, he thought, and knew resentment that the crowd was so happy about it.

His straying gaze fell on Noriko on the sideline. Her expression held sympathy for his pain, and something else besides. He'd seen it before, when she'd looked at him right after the fight with the Kobolde. It was a recognition of the alien place where his mind was right now.

A shadow fell over him. Not Tiwasson—the referee. Zeb's leg was already chambering to kick the man away, but something, just the memory of his fleeting glimpse of Noriko, held his attack in check. *Why? Why not get rid of him?*

Then comprehension returned. His vision went back to normal. His hearing came back to him, and Zeb could hear the roar from the audience, even the faint "Watson—Watson—Watson" from one section of the stands.

"*Drei,*" the referee said. Three. He was counting Zeb out.

Zeb put his arms on the ground and shoved, rolling over sideways and up to his feet. The crowd's roar increased. Tiwasson stood on the other side of the referee, his expression graduating from simple amusement to a grudging recognition that this wasn't over yet.

He's been outthinking me. Thinking two and three steps ahead, Zeb told himself. *Not any more.*

The referee got out of the way. Zeb moved forward. When just within Tiwasson's striking range, he stopped and planted his feet. *He's smart. Just let him glimpse a weakness and he'll target it.*

Tiwasson glimpsed it, Zeb's apparent immobility. He threw a hook that came in toward Zeb's side but was just there to mask his real attack, a kick at Zeb's lead leg. Zeb felt the kick coming rather than seeing it. He brought his left leg forward in a stop-kick that connected with Tiwasson's shin with a sharp crack. Tiwasson grunted.

Tiwasson's right hand was still out of position. Zeb swept his left out of the way, an effort because of Tiwasson's strength, then stepped in close and turned so he was just in front of the big man and facing the same way. He put his elbow into Tiwasson's chest, trying for the solar plexus.

He missed that vulnerable spot but still connected hard, his blow jolting through Tiwasson's torso. Then he spun again, sweeping with his leg, and took Tiwasson's legs out from under him. The big man hit the grass with a grunt, flat on his back.

He'll kick, Zeb thought, and twisted to get his hands into position.

Tiwasson kicked with his unhurt left leg. As the leg rose, Zeb caught his kneecap and pushed with one hand, grabbed his ankle and yanked with the other, avoiding the kick and hyperflexing the big man's leg.

The leg didn't break—Tiwasson was too strong, too big. But his face twisted in pain as the hyperextension hurt.

Zeb let go. He couldn't do more damage to the leg without allowing Tiwasson time to come up with a countermove. He threw a left-foot kick, little more than an insult blow, into Tiwasson's side and used the maneuver to push off from him. Tiwasson was already rolling up to his feet.

The big man didn't look as steady as he had before, though.

Zeb came on again, hands up in boxing position. As he came within range, Tiwasson threw his right hook again. Zeb blocked it, the impact jarring his fist and wrist, and swept his other hand to the side to catch Tiwasson's left jab.

Which left Zeb in close but Tiwasson's midsection exposed.

Zeb brought his foot up, planted it against the big man's stomach, and pushed, a *muay Thai* maneuver designed to separate opponents; as Tiwasson stepped back, the big man's injured legs betrayed him, caused him to stagger. Zeb spun into a kick, snapping out before Tiwasson was in view again, trusting his fighting experience, and his foot took the big man in the jaw.

The kick was as good as the one he'd thrown against Stammgalf, but Tiwasson had been right; he was stronger than the fighter from Dhenhavn. Tiwasson's head was snapped to the side by the impact; he turned that direction, mostly away from Zeb, and staggered forward, clearly off-balance, but he did not fall.

Zeb felt his head becoming light, felt his own balance becoming unsure. *Tiring. Need to catch my breath.* But he didn't; he couldn't afford to abandon this advantage. He charged forward, readied himself for Tiwasson's backward kick but there was none, and threw a hard blow into Tiwasson's back at kidney level.

Tiwasson grunted and spun, flailing at Zeb. Zeb went under the blow by the simple expedient of dropping into splits. As Tiwasson finished the spin, facing him,

Zeb braced himself against the ground with one fist and brought the other up into Tiwasson's balls.

Tiwasson's grunt of pain was echoed by the crowd. The big man staggered forward, an involuntary motion rather than attack, and tripped over Zeb. He came down on his knees and threw up.

Zeb came up to his feet and took a breath. He wondered how long it had been since he'd had a deep one. He could feel pain in his thigh from Tiwasson's kick, taste blood from his nose. He stood over Tiwasson, ready to plant another blow in his back, and asked, "Are we done here, man?"

Tiwasson hesitated, stomach rippling as it threatened to send him into another round of vomiting. He didn't look at Zeb, but he nodded . . . and reached out to tap the ground three times.

A roar rose from the crowd. Some of it was made up of outrage. Some of it was appreciation for the fight the audience had just witnessed. Zeb didn't care. For the moment, he was done.

He turned to offer Aevar a bow. The king's platform was full to capacity with onlookers, and Casnar and Edris were still in attendance, but the king wasn't there. Edris, sitting in her father's chair, gave Zeb a little smile and a shooing gesture.

Walking off the field, Zeb pointed to Conrad Förster and mouthed the words, "You're next."

Chapter Twenty-Two

"It's been pretty much smashed flat," Alastair said. "Keep your head tilted back."

Zeb did as he was told; he stared at the pastel green color of the ceiling in the associates' main room. "Guess my career as a beauty contestant is over."

"Oh, no." The doctor sounded amused. "I keep the associates in good tune. I'll pull it back into shape now, brace it up with some filling, and, most importantly, put a few words in the right ears." He pointed up, his expression significant, in a gesture that Zeb had found was consistent between the grim world and the fair— a reference to the Powers That Be. "By morning it'll be ready for Förster to smash flat."

"Thanks." Zeb turned his attention to the others. Gaby and Harris were getting dressed—or something; Zeb decided not to speculate—but the rest were gathered in the main room. "Doc, what did you say they were calling me?"

"*Der Alpdruck.*"

"Which means?"

"The nightmare."

"Oh, right." Zeb smiled. "That's what I told the last guy."

"Well, you made quite an impression. And managed to keep secret the fact that you're a dusky. Nothing in what Ruadan said suggested they were looking for a dusky."

Ish shot a quick look at Rudi, who was stretched out on the couch where he'd been attended the night before. She returned her attention to Doc quickly enough that Zeb doubted anyone else had seen her sudden change of focus.

Harris and Gaby, dressed in street clothes, arms around one another's waists, emerged from the hall and sat on the other couch beside Noriko.

"Now," Doc said, "while you athletes have been occupied today, the rest of us have been about some useful errands, as well. Alastair?"

"Trandil Niskin," the doctor said. "Our friend in Goldmacher. He's actually *from* Goldmacher. His official genealogy only goes back a couple of generations, to an orphan woman whose own child did not have a father listed, but circumstances suggest that the old lord of the manor was the father, which suggests Trandil may have grown up believing he was owed that particular castle, birthright, and so on.

"This Trandil worked his way through school. Graduated from the University of Bardulfburg in Scholars' Year Fourteen Oh One—that's thirty-four years ago, Zeb. He took degrees in theology and biology—"

"Interesting match," Zeb said.

"Then, later, added additional degrees in devisement theory and anthropology. I can't imagine a mind strange enough to embrace all those studies with equal facility. Anyway, guess who was going to school there at the same time he was."

"Aevar," Gaby said.

"Good guess, but only half right. Aevar, and Barrick Stelwright."

"Our museum patron from Neckerdam," Doc said.

Alastair nodded. "After graduation, Stelwright returns to the League of Ardree and begins his career as a reviewer and essayist, Aevar joins the Weserian army—as a lieutenant, naturally, he's the sort of nobleman who's willing to start all the way at the bottom—and Trandil gets married and takes a job in Weseria's Ministry of Health, mostly writing books and pamphlets on things like hygiene, immunization, care for baby, that sort of thing. On the side, he gets involved with one of a bunch of little organizations that want to 'cleanse' the Burian lands, get rid of foreign influences, make it the flagship nation of lights all over the world."

"Where are you getting all this information?" Zeb asked.

Alastair grinned at him. "Well, I started with official histories of the Reinis published by the Weserian government. Then I did some digging around over at the university, and finally I spent some time in the catacombs of a local—and failing, I might add—newspaper that caters to duskies. The same one that helped me find the Kobolde."

"Catacombs? You were wandering around in tunnels with bodies and stuff?"

Harris shook his head. "Not literally catacombs, Zeb. That's what they call the newspaper archives. The morgue."

"Oh, right."

"So," Alastair continued. "The nations of the Burian Alliance get into border clashes with surrounding nations, get really full of themselves, start sinking shipping of nations supporting their enemies, and all of a sudden we're in the midst of the World Crisis, which some of us remember with far too much clarity."

Doc nodded, no humor in his face. "It was after it was done and the Burian Alliance broken that the Reinis truly emerged as a political party. The national governments were too busy coping with reparations, worldwide economic depression, and that sort of thing to pay them much attention."

"Back up, Doc," Alastair said. "One thing those of us in the New World tend to miss is the Burian outlook on the World Crisis. It wasn't just their worst wartime loss as a culture. They also talk about 'the withering.' Are you familiar with it?"

Doc shook his head.

"Basically, the loss of most of a generation of lights, all killed during the war. For example, at the start of the World Crisis, there were two hundred sixty-eight known Daoine Sidhe in the Burian lands and Cretanis. At war's end, there were fewer than twenty, including you, the royal family of Cretanis, and Duncan Blackletter."

Doc frowned. "The Burians kept track of this sort of thing?"

"Oh, yes. They have an abiding interest in noble genealogy. Every noble, from petty lord to king, feels obliged to trace his ancestry back to a god, you know. So there were just a few Daoine Sidhe at war's end, and over the next few years, most of them die of one cause or another. Nothing suspicious; many of them are old, and all of them, like you, are basically insane."

Zeb saw Gaby shift in her seat, looking uncomfortable. Zeb had heard Noriko say that Gaby and Harris were chiefly responsible for the death of Duncan Blackletter earlier this year. Even Doc suddenly looked more grim.

"Most of them had children before they died, of

course," Alastair said. "But those children weren't
Daoine Sidhe. Most were crosses with other pure lights,
but not Daoine Sidhe. So how many Daoine Sidhe do
you suppose the Burians know of now?"

Doc's frown deepened. "How many?"

"Six. You, Queen Maeve of Cretanis, and her two
sons and two daughters by your father." Alastair gave
Doc a cynical smile. "You're the object of mixed feelings over here. One of the last known Daoine Sidhe.
But you, uh, commingle with a dusky."

"Proficiently," Ish said, deadpan.

Doc grinned. "Thank you, dear."

"By the end of the World Crisis," Alastair continued, "Aevar had risen to the rank of general in his
father's army, acquitted himself very well. Niskin was
a field doctor. Stelwright was a foreign correspondent,
reporting on the war for newspapers all across the
League of Ardree. At the time, he was criticized for
a lack of patriotism in his reporting, but in years since
he's been praised for his unbiased analysis of events
of the time."

Zeb snorted. "Unbiased. He probably just didn't
want to say anything bad about his Burian buddies."

"In hindsight, that may have been exactly the case.
After the war, the *Nationalreinigungspartei* is formed
in Weseria and spreads to surrounding nations; Aevar,
who is out of the army and acting more independently,
and Niskin are both early joiners, and Aevar becomes
front man for the party organizers. He later purges
them once he's assumed true control."

"Purges as in kills?" Doc asked.

"No, he just drives them out of the party." Alastair
shrugged. "Some die later when they form new splinter
groups and then have violent clashes with the Reinis
and the government. This whole process is extremely
violent. Riots, rallies in which political opponents are

beaten, that sort of thing. Niskin publishes a paper on the dangers of breeding with darks and duskies—it can lead not just to a debased race, but to insanity, you know."

"I'll be careful," Doc said.

"The full version of the paper, which was published just in one limited edition, proposes a national plan for improvement of the race. Incentives for lights breeding with lights. Increased tax burdens for dark and dusky families—the bigger the family, the higher, proportionately, their taxes go. The Reinis embrace the idea; the government reacts rather badly, and Niskin vanishes from the face of the world."

"Kidnapped?" Zeb asked.

Alastair shook his head. "I think not. I suspect that he and his family—which includes a school-age daughter named Adima by this time—went underground, doing work for the Reinis. They don't show up again on the record until three years ago, when the Reinis seized control of Weseria. At that time, Doctor Trandil Niskin is ceded the castle and territory of Goldmacher—and that *is* the last we hear of him."

"But we know that he has developed, or is about to develop, his bleaching cabinet," Doc said. "And, in all likelihood, the devisement that destroyed the Danaan Heights Building is his. And the long-distance puppetry."

"And," Rudi said, "he had to have been working with Duncan Blackletter. Sending us Bergmonks to the grim world to find things."

Doc nodded. "He has been busy. What is his plan, then?"

Alastair spread his hands, palms up, suggesting that he was out of information. "Unknown."

Ish looked unhappy. "You are the plan, Doc. Everything they did in Neckerdam was in relation to you.

Sending the Bergmonks to the grim world to find you. Kidnapping you. Then, when you escaped death at their hands, setting things up so you'd fail to stop the destruction of building after building and be humiliated."

"That makes no sense," Doc said. "That first morning, when I was done doing honors in my father's name, they could just have used a rifle instead of a dart-rifle. I'd be dead. Much simpler. The Reinis are devoted to that sort of efficiency. Why did they not kill me then?"

"I don't know." Ish turned to Rudi. "Is there anything you've failed to tell us about all this?"

"Wait a tick," Rudi said. "I'll ask me brother Albin." He returned her stare, emotionless.

"So I take it we'll be visiting Goldmacher tonight," Zeb said.

Doc shook his head. "No. I expect they will have increased security there, or that Niskin will have moved his operations. We need more information before we stage another assault on Goldmacher. Tonight we'll be visiting Casnar's gathering. At the Temple of Ludana."

"Right, right."

"Are you up for it?"

"Let's see." Zeb counted off on his fingers. "In the last day, I've jumped off trains and cars—"

"And a balcony," Noriko said.

"And a balcony. I've been shot at, punched, kicked, slammed into the ground, overheated, dehydrated . . ." Zeb counted up his fingers and smiled. "Sure, I'm up for it."

Doc turned to Rudi. "And you?"

"I think I'm still a bit worn down," Rudi said. "If you think it's life-or-death that I be there, of course, I'll come. Otherwise, I'll get me some more rest."

"We'll be fine," Doc said. "Get all the sleep you

need. All right. So it will be me, Zeb, Ish, and Gaby at the Temple of Ludana. Harris, Noriko, and Alastair at the Hall of Tomorrow. Rudi here. Do we have everything we need?"

"I hate to be a pest," Zeb said. "But I did like the anonymity my coat and such gave me last night, but they stink so bad of coal smoke now—"

"Not a problem," Harris said. "That's the sort of detail I tend to all day long. I had your hat cleaned and the rest burned—too many leads for the local police if I got them cleaned, too. I bought replacements. At different stores, of course. And got you a present. All in the name of your scaring the hell out of those you don't bother to beat up."

"Thanks." Zeb gave him a grin. "You've actually gotten kind of efficient in your old age."

"Keep it up, Army. I'll show you old age."

"I'm not sure I get it," Zeb said.

He sat alone in the back seat of the Foundation's sedan; Doc and Gaby were in the front seat. They were parked on a side street within clear view of the front and right side of the Temple of Ludana, with its curious mixture of straight, fluted columns and walls of irregular stone. Small fixed spotlights at ground level kept the front of the building bathed in light, but they kept their attention on the side wall, where shadows had moved at irregular intervals for the last half hour.

"There's nothing to get," Gaby said. "All that movement is Casnar's guests sneaking in a side door."

"Not that. First Doc says Ish is going to be with us. Then he drops her off a block from our quarters. What's that all about?"

Gaby gave Doc a look, too, as though she were curious but just hadn't bothered to ask.

Doc considered, then shrugged. "She's watching

Rudi. He's been seen going to talk-boxes and making calls when he's supposed to be doing other things."

Zeb felt his stomach tighten. "Do you think he's given us up?"

"Not to the Reinis, no." Doc shook his head; the motion was emphatic. "We'd all have been dead by now. But I don't know what he's up to, and I feel it would be a good thing to find out." He drew out a pocket watch and consulted it. "Still a chime before the appointed bell. We need to get in there if we're to find out what my brother's up to. Gaby, you'll come in with me. Zeb, if I could prevail on you to stay outside as a watchman?"

"Sure. Final question. Something I meant to ask about when we were here last night."

"Go ahead."

Zeb pointed at the front of the temple, then at other buildings along the street. "The temple's the only building with main doors facing this way. With all the other buildings, I'm seeing ass end. Is there a reason?"

"Tradition," Doc said, and got out. "These are old buildings. Most old buildings in Europe face east to greet the rising sun. Ludana's provinces include death, so she faces westward, toward the setting sun—toward lands of the dead."

"I'm sorry I asked."

"No, she's a beneficial goddess. The death she concerns herself with is the one that holds the promise of rebirth."

"Oh, cool. I'll go for that death instead of one of her competitors' inferior deaths."

Doc gave him an admonishing look, then he and Gaby left the car. They hurried toward the temple, circling around to find an entryway at the building's rear.

Zeb, trusting the spot they'd chosen to park—well

away from any streetlights—to help keep him concealed, moved into the deep shadow of the adjacent building and put on his disguise of the other night.

Harris had been right; the overcoat he'd bought for Zeb was far superior to the other one. Not only was it of a better make, but it was reversible, medium green on one side and black on the other.

And in one pocket Zeb found Harris's gift. It was a knit ski cap, also in black, but Harris had apparently had it modified. The openings for eyes and mouth were now covered by a sheer black material, something like the stuff ladies' stockings were made of here. When he put the thing on and looked in the car's side mirror, he saw only a creepy black outline. He decided to dispense with the scarf; this was disguise enough.

He grinned to himself. That feeling of liberation was still there; the anonymity the disguise and the darkness afforded him charged him up once more. He clamped his hat on his head.

Keeping to the shadows, his hands in his pockets on his pistols, he moved toward the temple, circling around toward the left side of the building and the deep, dark alley there between it and the next building over.

Ish, wearing drab green street clothes that made her as anonymous as any woman in Bardulfburg, her hair now pinned up under a blond wig, waited at her sidewalk table, a book open before her, her attention on the front of the Foundation's apartment building half a block down.

She'd only been there a few minutes, but had to school herself against impatience. *Whyever did Doc choose me to wait and watch?* she asked herself. *He knows I hate waiting.* But she knew the answer. No one else he might have left here would be as likely to get the job done. To follow the man if he left. She added an item from her own agenda: to kill him if he had turned traitor.

A moment later she saw him, Rudi, his bulky overcoat making him more anonymous, emerging from the building's main doors. He looked up and down the street, then crossed.

Now that he was on the same side of the street as she, it was harder for her to see him. She rose, but he had turned and was moving toward her at a brisk pace. She sat again. A few moments later, he passed, giving her no sign he'd noticed her. She rose to follow.

It was best for her not to be truly herself now. He might feel her eyes on the back of his neck. No, she should be half herself, half the other one. That would help her if she had to kill him. She let Rudi get thirty and forty paces ahead, and did not look at him as she followed—she concentrated on the sidewalk at his feet, on the storefronts to his right.

He stopped at a coin talk-box and stepped into the booth. She did not slow her pace; she walked up to the booth, heard muted bell-like ringing as he deposited a single coin into the device, and she continued on past. Had he seen her duck into a storefront or falter as his gaze fell upon her, he would probably go suspicious; this way, she had a chance to remain unseen for a few moments longer.

A few paces further, she reached an alley mouth and turned into it. In moments, she shucked her overcoat, wig and hat. Above her were bronze bars over a painted window; above that was a stone ledge, lighter in color than the building's brick. She leaped up onto the window sill, not bothering to grab the bars for balance, then instantly leaped again, scrambling up onto the ledge. The same arrangement was in effect above, another window, another ledge, and in moments she stood on the ledge two stories above the street.

The ledge was a double handspan wide, ample room for someone with her gifts. She turned the corner and headed back toward Rudi's booth, moving as fast as a normal person moves on a sidewalk.

She was in plain sight on this ledge, but above the tops of the streetlights, and no one down on the sidewalk was looking up. That, and the fact that the wig and coat she'd discarded were the only light-colored things she'd been wearing, made it less likely she'd be seen.

She walked the length of this building on the ledge. The next building, the one Rudi's talk-box booth stood before, had no such ledge, but there was a series of balconies half a story down. She dropped noiselessly to the nearest balcony, between its owner's potted plants, then moved from balcony to balcony, taking the rails and gaps between them like hurdles.

That put her immediately above Rudi's booth. It had glass on three sides, looking out on the street and down the sidewalk in both directions, but none facing the building. She could not wait until the sidewalks were clear of traffic, so she swung over the balcony rail, dropped to grab the bottom edge of the balcony, and swung to land behind the booth, a single fluid motion. She came down in a crouch, quiet, and looked both ways along the sidewalk. People approaching from her left had not noticed her. A blond man approaching from the right was looking at her, blinking in some surprise; she offered him a conspiratorial smile, put her finger to her lips to shush him, and jerked her thumb at the booth. *Let him read into that whatever he wishes*, she thought.

Apparently he did. He grinned at her and kept on going.

She leaned up against the booth and listened.

"No, not until we're sure," she heard Rudi saying. "Better for me to stay here and keep gatherin' facts. I've done all right so far. Huh?" He was silent for a long moment. "No, he's a dead man, I promise you. I'll pull the trigger on him myself." Another silence. "I understand. I'll talk to you then." He hung up.

When he stepped out of the booth, Ish moved up behind him and put the barrel of her snub-nosed revolver into his back. "Grace on you, Rudi."

He jerked in surprise. "Ish." He hazarded her a look over his shoulder. "Ah, you look very different with your hair all up like that."

"Walk," she said. "Back this way. Keep your hands where I can see them." She got him steered back toward the alley. She was cold inside, cold with what she knew she had to do to him, colder still that someone had dared to betray Doc.

"You don't sound like yourself, Ish."

"Why did you do this, Rudi? Did they offer you money?"

"Money?" He sounded scornful. "It's a matter of revenge, Ish. Surely you understand revenge."

"Oh, I do."

"Why aren't we going back to the rooms?"

"I left my coat back here. In an alley."

"Ah, of course."

In silence, they passed several pedestrians headed the other way. None apparently saw the gun, almost invisible in the darkness, in Ish's hand.

As they neared the alley, they came upon a pedestrian, a lean, dark-haired man walking with his hands in his overcoat pockets. Rudi stopped. "Ish," he said, "allow me to introduce you to Innis, my gunman friend."

The man stopped as well, looking confused.

Time dilated for Ish. She saw the man's hand begin to emerge from his pocket. Another tick of the clock and his gun would come into view, then he could turn it on her. She shifted her aim to cover him.

Rudi's elbow took her on the side of the jaw. The world snapped sideways and her vision became skewed. Oddly, there was no pain, just a feeling of detachment.

Her view of the world continued to slide sideways as she fell. The man's hand emerging, empty, from its pocket. Rudi's fist rising with majestic slowness toward the man's jaw.

Then all was darkness.

In the alley beside the Temple of Ludana, Zeb stared up at a single ray of light.

The alley was otherwise as black as tar paper. But ten or twelve feet above the ground, the shutter over a window was slightly askew and a thin shaft of light slanted from it to the concrete alley floor.

Zeb wouldn't have guessed there were shutters up there had this one not been misaligned. Now, looking at the way the shutter itself seemed to be tilted rather than just slightly open, he decided that it had been damaged. *Worth taking a look*, he decided.

The window was above a sort of wooden box with a slanted lid. The lid wouldn't open; by touch, Zeb found a padlock keeping it shut. He put some pressure on the lid and gauged, from the way it did not give, that it would hold his weight. He scrambled up on it. From the highest point of the lid, against the building wall, he could easily reach the bottom of the shutter.

When he tugged it, it swung open, but sagged on its bottom hinge; the top hinge was, in the new light spilling from the window, revealed as broken. The other half of the shutter opened normally. The window beyond was open. Zeb got a good grip on the lip of the window and pulled himself up to look within.

He found himself looking through a row of gray stone columns at a long, stone-floored room beyond. It was the chamber he and the associates had met the Kobolde in the previous night. Now the candelabra were gone; dim light came from electrical bulbs out of sight beyond the columns, where the ceiling was higher. It had only seemed bright by comparison with the blackness of the alley. The stone benches where they'd sat last night had been moved, arranged like pews in a church, and more brought in behind them to seat a congregation before the hearthstone.

There were no people. There was nothing at all suspicious to see. But from here Zeb could see the marks, as though from a crowbar, on the hard wood on both halves of the shutter, beside the broken interior latch.

Zeb grabbed the top of the unbroken shutter half. With much pulling and grunting, he managed to squeeze himself feet first through the window and dropped to the floor beyond. The sound of his leather heels on the stone floor seemed as loud as a pistol shot, but no one came to investigate.

From here, he could see the high ceiling beyond the colonnade, the three chandelier-style light fixtures, one of which was lit with only four of its twelve bulbs glowing.

Zeb heard distant murmuring, voices in some other chamber, one beyond any of the several doors he counted leading from this room.

He moved out into the chamber to take a look around. If someone had broken in, why into this chamber? Windows and doors had to have led into smaller, less conspicuous parts of the temple. But nothing, other than the window, seemed out of place.

No, that wasn't quite right. His attention fell on a white mark on the circular hearthstone. A portion of the stone had been chipped away; the damage was cleaner, whiter than the rock surrounding it. Zeb felt a moment of unease, but decided this couldn't be too bad; it wasn't the building's dedicatory plaque, after all.

There was a sound, the faintest tap of leather on stone, behind him. Zeb spun, drawing his right-hand automatic from his pocket.

Against the far wall, where the greatest number of doors were arrayed, stood a man. He was taller than Zeb, very fair, with white hair well on its retreat toward complete disappearance. His features were long and pointed, his nose and chin especially so; his fingers, coming up and spreading as he reflexively raised his hands, were unnaturally long, with pointed nails at their tips. He wore a formal suit in an eye-hurting red, with tie and waistcoat in green, and pince-nez glasses. His eyes were wide open with surprise, his expression frightened but somehow comical. His mouth worked but no words came out.

"Speak Cretanis?" Zeb asked.

The man found his voice. "Yes. Cretanis, Burian, Lorian, Isperian, Castilian . . ." His accent seemed like a halfway point between British and German.

"Never mind that. Who are you?"

"I am the high priest of Ludana." The man shrugged. He did not sound as though he were puffed up with his own importance.

"Put your hands down. I'm not going to shoot you." Zeb lowered his gun, but kept it in hand.

"Ah. Thank you. May I go?"

"Not yet. Back there. There's a gathering of princes and such?"

The man hesitated, then nodded. "You are here to, ah, confront them?"

"No, I'm just looking at your damage. Your busted shutter, and this."

"Yes." The man moved uncertainly toward Zeb. He looked down at the damaged stone and grimaced. "It apparently happened last night. Unnecessary knockerism, that."

"Knockerism?"

"Damage for no purpose? Is the word no longer used?"

"Oh, yeah. Knockerism. Why would they damage a hearthstone?"

"I suspect the damage is symbolic. The hearthstone *is* the heart of the house." When Zeb didn't reply, he continued, "In ancient times, it would be the first stone laid in a new home, and cooking would be done on it."

Zeb felt the unease return, stronger than ever. "So this would be the stone most identified with the house."

"Of course."

"Uh, does this temple have a dedicatory plaque?"

Finally, the man smiled; his amusement was obviously at Zeb's ignorance. "Too old a building for that, I'm afraid. Plaques like that are a modern conceit."

"Shit. Where are the princes?"

The man hesitated.

"I'm not going to hurt them, you damned fool. Where are they?"

The man gestured at the largest door on the wall to his left.

Zeb headed that way. "Other than them, is there anyone else in this building?"

"A few subordinate priests, temple workers—"

"Get them out now. This place is going to blow up." Zeb threw the door open, revealing darkened hallway beyond.

"A bomb?" The man's voice emerged as a squeak.

"Worse."

✧   ✧   ✧

Rudi ascended the steps of the Temple of the Suns. He was still swearing to himself—swearing because he'd been caught out by Ixyail and had to abandon his role with the associates, swearing harder because he'd been forced to strike a woman. But at the top of the steps, he was able to wrest himself away from unhappy thoughts for a moment; he paused to admire the building's soaring columns, the massiveness of the dome. Then he passed between the statues of Sol and Sollinvictus, and the Weserian army guards who stood beside them, and headed into the main temple chamber, the long room that was always open to the elements.

It was, he saw, fairly crowded. A huge fire, the so-called Eternal Flame, blazed toward the rear of this chamber, at the exact heart of the temple; the fire itself was a circle some six paces across and rose to the height of a man. It was surrounded by visitors to the temple who stood about in admiration—far enough back not to be scorched by the heat.

Rudi's lip twisted. *As though it weren't a simple gas flame,* he thought.

On the long walls of the main chamber were murals done in the same style as most of the rest of the art he'd seen in Bardulfburg. The one on the north wall showed the goddess Sol in her glowing chariot, closely pursued by a flying wolf; the beast's mouth was open and slavering in anticipation of a meal. The one on the south wall showed Sollinvictus, also in a shining chariot; he held a bow in his hand and trained it on some unlucky target far below.

Other visitors to the temple walked the length of the murals or stepped back to try to take in their immensity. Some bumped into the people circling the central flame. An aether crew was set up against the

wall beneath Sollinvictus' chariot, just where the god
would shoot if he released his bowstring, the announcer
talking into a microphone in Burian in the cultured
tones of a broadcaster.

Rudi looked over the two pieces of art. Just like
everything new in this city, he decided, the murals
slanted their message to the Weserian outlook on
things. They represented the two sun-gods in equal
dimensions, and thus the builders could say they dealt
equally with both. But the paintings made an invincible champion of the favorite local god, while making a victim of his northern counterpart. Legend said
that Sol would someday be dragged down and
destroyed by her pursuer, true . . . but the only reason
to display this story above all others was to enhance
Sollinvictus' superiority.

Rudi turned his attention back to the crowd. *He said
he'd be here.* But his contact was nowhere to be seen.

His contact had been right, though. Something was
up. The place was busier even than a newly-dedicated
civic monstrosity ought to be. He saw priests, distinctive
in the red-and-orange robes of their office, hurrying
about. Odd that so many of them had the lean, hard
look of military men. He saw a fair amount of traffic
in and out of the inconspicuous brown doors that lined
the main chamber; men in suits and street dress
entered and emerged at a rate that suggested they were
banks of offices rather than temple precincts.

He saw the man who'd tortured him. The light who
had promised to improve him was walking more or less
his way from the temple's main entrance, angling
toward the door beneath the forward hooves of
Sollinvictus' chariot horses. He wore a nice suit, an
incongruous black but with a festive gold waistcoat
beneath, and seemed intent on his mission; he did not
notice Rudi.

Of course, Rudi thought, *I'm not in disguise now.*
He turned to follow the man and tapped the butt of
the automatic under his left arm. *It wouldn't be too
hard just to get up beside him and put seven shots into
his gut. Getting out past the guards might be tricky,
though.*

"*Hear me.*"

The words echoed through the chamber, loud and
sudden enough to make Rudi stagger. He fell to one
knee and clapped his hands over his ears against the
volume. All around him, all across the chamber, people
were shouting, running—there seemed to be no consistent direction to their flight—or doing as Rudi was
and protecting their ears.

"*I am Volksonne.*"

The voice, that of a male, seemed to come from
everywhere. Oddly, the words were in Cretanis, but
Rudi thought he could hear words in the same voice,
words he didn't understand, echoing faintly beneath
them. Rudi caught sight of something strange happening in the vicinity of the Eternal Flame and turned that
way.

The flame was rising, condensing in its upper
reaches, becoming approximately human in shape.

"*I am the god of the people. I am the god of the
pure, of the clean, of the rightful. I claim this house
as my own.*"

The flames settled into a shape, that of a man ten
paces in height. His skin and garments—modern trousers and a shirt with the sleeves rolled up to the elbow,
they could have been the everyday clothes of a working
man or the casual attire of a member of the noble
class—were at times red, orange, or gold, seemingly
made up of fire. His face was handsome, with the
directness of a soldier and the perfection of a star of
film plays.

He was still surrounded by the circle of gas flame. The people who had stood about it were backing away, some of them having fallen and now scuttling away on their elbows. But the fiery thing who called himself Volksonne did not lower his gaze to study them; he stared off into the distant east, beyond the limits of the temple.

In the space between the god-thing's words, Rudi heard the aether announcer's voice, speaking faster, the pitch of his words rising with his alarm.

"I will lead the people of the Burian lands to new greatness," Volksonne said. Rudi noticed that his lips barely moved, and everyone on the floor listened with the same raptness, as though all understood his words. *"I will shower blessings on the faithful, disaster on our enemies. I will cast light to dispel the darkness. Go now. Leave this house. Be witness to the destruction of evil."* He gestured to the main entryway. *"Go."*

Some of the witnesses were already going, already halfway to the outside. Others scrambled in their wake. Rudi was hit by several of the fleeing visitors, men and women too rattled to notice or care about people in their way. He rose and followed, but kept as much attention as he could on the fiery circle.

Volksonne stood there, but was no longer pointing due east. His arm was rising into the sky. As he gestured, he became less distinct, with flares bursting everywhere from his skin. Then, with a roar of flame, his now-indistinct body collapsed back into the circle of fire.

Rudi made it outside the temple building. The crowd had stopped there, no longer fleeing, nor heading down the steps as he'd expected them to.

He followed their gaze.

Up in the eastern sky, a new sun shone. It roared

to the west, toward them, then over and past the Temple of the Suns, arcing toward the ground.

Harris emerged from General Ritter's private office onto the walkway that overlooked the main chamber of the Hall of Tomorrow. The chamber featured displays along its walls, pictures in the same style that decorated much of Bardulfburg, but these showed happy blond people in faux futuristic clothes flying along with jetpacks and picnic baskets, acting as foremen in factories worked by robots that looked like water heaters, returning from work to homes with architectural styling that made them look like Roman villas.

Displays were scattered around the chamber. Some were model kitchens with appliances that had to look futuristic from an early 20th-century perspective. Others showed sleek automobiles that looked like flattened train engines painted in bright colors. On one table was a mockup of an automated book reader— a book lay open under a green light and a voice emerged from the associated speaker, reading the text in Burian.

Then there was the model of Bardulfburg. It was longer and wider than the corresponding model of Neckerdam, but on the same scale. Much of the model was in naturalistic colors, showing buildings and grasslands in their proper hues, but many of the models were slightly brighter than the buildings they represented.

Noriko, her revolver in hand, standing guard, turned to look up at Harris. "Have you found anything?"

Harris shook his head. "The office is a front. There's next to no paperwork in the file cabinets. No blueprints or anything. Ritter has to do his real work somewhere else. That and the fact that there are no guards on this place, and the locks were simple enough for you to do in your sleep—"

Noriko smiled.

"—suggest to me that the government has no real worry about this place. Alastair, what've you got?"

Alastair looked at him, but did not take his hand away from his normal eye. "Watch this. *Übermorgen*."

Color welled up from the lower portions of the model. There was more of it than with the Neckerdam model, and it rose higher, in many places taking the shape of new, gigantic buildings superimposed over what looked like older neighborhoods.

"It will fade in a few moments," Alastair said, "but you can do that all day long. The activation word is on plaques at both ends of the table."

"Another toy," Harris said. "But is it *the* model?"

Alastair shook his head. "It doesn't have the additional devisements laid on it that Teleri's second one did. It does have some written annotations on it that I can only see with my Good Eye. All the buildings erected since Aevar came to power are brighter in color to stand out, and they all have dates of dedication on them in that special writing." The swell of colors faded back into the table's depths, and Alastair picked up the model of the Temple of the Suns, holding it forth for Harris. "See?"

"No Good Eye, Alastair, remember? Two bad ones."

Alastair began to fit the model back into place, then leaned over it and peered at the base left on the model. "Who in the world is Volksonne?"

"Big guy from Nyrax," Harris said. "I went to school with his daughter, took her out a couple of times." At Alastair's confused look, he relented. "I'm kidding you. Never heard of him. Noriko?"

She shook her head, her attention still on the doors.

"The name sounds like that of a sun-god," Alastair

continued. "In Burian, it would be 'People's Sun' or 'Nation's Sun,' more or less. But Volksonne isn't one of the typical names or epithets of the god of the sun, like Invictus is." He gestured. "The writing's here on the base."

"We have a problem," Noriko said. She was no longer staring at the door. Her attention was on the chamber's high windows.

Outside, it had just turned from nighttime to day. The sun was overhead . . . but setting with unnatural speed.

Zeb raced down the hallway, which had numerous doors to either side, some of them closed, others open into small offices. He slowed, listening, and heard the murmur again, this time louder, from ahead. He could make out words, a woman's voice speaking in Cretanis: " . . . turn to the question of Burian rearmament. Since the ascendancy of the Reini party, we've seen a strengthening of military forces, including increased enlistment in armies throughout the Burian League, and—significantly—funding for those armies . . ."

He turned the final corner as he reached it and saw before him a double door, partly open . . . flanked by Doc and Gaby, half concealed within the shadows of the poorly-lit corridor.

They looked at him, surprised. "What's happening?" Doc asked, his voice a whisper.

Zeb took a deep breath to settle his nerves and slid to the left, out of line of sight of the doorway. Beyond, he caught a glimpse of a large round table; at the far end, behind a lectern, stood a tall woman, young except for her commanding bearing, with hair as dark as the night outside.

Zeb pitched his voice to match Doc's. "They're going to—"

Then it hit him, a sudden burning sensation in his right palm. It caused him to drop his automatic; it clattered against the stone floor. He stared for a moment at his palm and knew what the sudden pain represented.

He bent to retrieve the gun. "No time to talk," he said, and stuffed the pistol in his pocket. Then he charged through the door into the room.

He heard cries of consternation from the people seated around the table. He ignored them, leaping up between two seated attendees and skidding to the table's center. "Shut up and listen," he said, pitching his voice deep—not just to disguise it, but because it was the voice of command he'd developed for the Army, for the ring. "A missile is about to hit this building. It's going to blow up and you're going to die. Get out now."

There was no immediate reaction, just a rise in the hubbub of voices. Someone said, "Put up your hands."

Zeb turned. One of the men rising to his feet had a gun in his hands, a small pistol, and was aiming at him. "Don't be a moron," he said. *"Run or die."* He suited action to words and ran back the way he'd come, leaping off the table, charging through the door. The man with the gun did not fire at him.

Gaby was at the first intersection. He reached her and turned toward the main hall, the only way he was sure of that led to the outside. She fell in step beside him. He could hear leather shoes clattering up the hall behind him. His hand burned worse than ever. "Where's Doc?"

"Gone after his brother." There was pure agitation in Gaby's voice. "Casnar made some opening comments, then handed the meeting off to the Queen of Bolgia while he went in search of a water closet."

"Great." Zeb crashed through the door into the

temple's main hall. The big doors at the far end, leading to the antechamber and then to the street outside, were open. A man and a woman in workers' clothes, leaving by that exit, turned to look at Zeb. Then turned away and ran faster.

Zeb and Gaby got to the street moments after the workers. They turned to glance at the onrushing brightness of the descending sun. It seemed huge, large enough to engulf the entire temple and portions of buildings to either side, and Zeb fancied he could feel its heat already. Fear gave him greater speed; he raced back toward where Doc had left their car, Gaby showing no difficulty in keeping up with him.

The sun came to earth. Zeb heard the sound, an enormous *crump* that was the building's upper story being instantly consumed.

Then there was the blast, heated air roaring out to engulf him, to hammer him forward . . .

Zeb came to with his head ringing. He tasted blood and his nose felt as though it had been pounded flat again.

He lay facedown on the street, and in his peripheral vision he could see flames flickering in the distance. When he tried to roll over, an irregular surface above him prevented his action.

Dazed, he looked around. There was a wheel beside his head to the left. He was under a car. Beyond, in the distance, the flattened Temple of Ludana burned, as did the near edges of buildings to its left and behind; flames roared up into the night sky. Men and women, mere silhouettes, arrived on foot to stand just beyond the point where the heat would do them harm. Zeb heard distant sirens becoming louder.

He couldn't have been out for very long. There was no sign of Gaby, but he didn't remember making it all the way back to the car, and someone had to have shoved him beneath it. He elbow-crawled out from under the vehicle on the sidewalk side and stood, automatically dusting himself off. His hand no longer burned, though the bruises he'd picked up in the last two days' worth of fighting, especially the one on his thigh, twinged in protest.

A car, its headlights dark, roared past him. As it came close, he glimpsed the nearest occupant, the man on the passenger side, through the window. Reflections of the nearby fire in windows all around gave Zeb a little light to go by, and he recognized the man. Casnar, a thin smile on his face. Then the car was past and down the block; only when it reached the next intersection and turned did its headlights come on.

Still feeling unsteady, and very conspicuous here despite his dark clothing, Zeb climbed into the back seat of the sedan.

Moments later, two of the distant silhouettes grew larger as they approached; they resolved themselves into Gaby and Doc. Gaby ducked to peer under the car as she got near and Zeb waved at her from the back seat. "Zeb! Are you all right?" She got into the driver's seat; Doc got in on the passenger side.

"I feel like I've been through a garlic press one square inch at a time," Zeb said. "I can barely walk. But I'm functional. Did you put me under the car?"

"I had to drag you a few yards and then shove you for a while. You're heavy."

"You're strong."

Doc stared, apparently emotionless, at the raging fire. "Your timing was close to perfect, Zeb. Minimal loss of life."

"Minimal? I was hoping for none." Zeb sighed. "Who died?"

"My brother. I couldn't find him."

"No, he got out. I saw him driving away."

Doc's head whipped around. He stared at Zeb. "Say you're not joking."

"No, he drove off. I'm sure of it. He was with someone—somebody else was driving."

"Drove off." Doc repeated the words as though they were in a language he'd never heard before. "He hadn't had time to look around, to assure himself—did he look as though he were being compelled?"

"No. In fact . . ." Zeb's stomach sank as the implications of what he'd seen sank in. "In fact, he was smiling just a little bit."

Doc turned to face forward. His motion was slow. He expelled a long breath.

They watched the building burn. A fire truck arrived, scattering the people in its way as it set itself up next to the nearest hydrant. More cars passed their sedan. "That was Dalphina," Gaby said as one roared by. "She was at the back of the room. She would have been one of the last ones to get out."

"So they might all have survived," Doc said. "Good." There was no emotion to his tone.

Gaby gave him a close look. "Doc. Back to our quarters?"

"Yes."

"No." That was Ish, leaning in through the window opposite Zeb; she appeared so suddenly and silently that he jumped, startled. She opened the door and climbed in; despite the darkness, Zeb thought he caught a glimpse of a stain or bruise on her jaw. "It's not safe there."

"Explain," Doc said.

She leaned away from him, taken aback by what she apparently read in his face. "I caught Rudi calling someone on the talk-box. A local call, one coin. He was talking about killing someone—you, I expect. I confronted him, but . . ." She made a noise of disgust. "I've always suspected that if you have someone covered and a new problem appears, the thing to do is first shoot the one you're covering. Now I know it's true." She gave Doc a look of apology. "He got away. I'm sorry, Doc."

Something finally penetrated his shell of emotionlessness, a flicker of concern, and his face transformed, became human again. "Are you all right?"

"I won't be chewing through rawhide bonds anytime soon," she said. "But I am well."

He smiled at her words, at some memory they shared. "Very well. Harris and the others will, if I know them, be coming here. We'll wait. Zeb and I are terribly conspicuous. If I could prevail on you two ladies to linger closer to the fire, direct our other associates back to the car if they arrive, learn what you can . . ."

"We're on it," Gaby said, and exited. Ish leaned forward to kiss Doc, then followed.

In the comparative silence that followed, Zeb said, "Your brother was in on it, wasn't he?"

"Half brother. And it appears so." Doc leaned into the seat, but the action didn't look like relaxing; it was a slow collapse. "It explains a lot. Such as how they knew to capture me at the temple where I'd be honoring my father. Such as how they knew Ixyail is a dusky."

"What are you going to do?"

Staring forward, not meeting Zeb's gaze, Doc shook his head. "I wish I knew."

Chapter Twenty-Three

Half an hour later by Zeb's reckoning, Gaby returned to the car with Harris. Two more fire engines had arrived in the meantime, and there was a steady stream of pedestrian traffic from the surrounding area toward the fire. The late arrivals, intent on the spectacle before them, paid no attention to the occupants of the car. Gaby and Harris climbed into the front seat. "It's gotten stranger," Harris said.

Doc, resting with his head back against the seat, nodded but didn't open his eyes. "Tell me."

"Alastair's up there with Ish and Noriko. He's been listening to news on the radio in someone's front window. Here's the short form: The god Volksonne called for the deaths of enemies of the Burian people, and his fireball dropped on the Temple of Ludana, killing a lot of treacherous foreign dignitaries like the Queen of Bolgia. It's being described as the most extraordinary mandate of the gods in a thousand years." Harris looked uncomfortable. "Prince Casnar is calling for a board of inquiry, priests, devisers, that sort of thing, to take a look at this manifestation and make sure that it's really divine. He was talking about you joining the board."

Doc offered a cynical smile. "He would. Let us start again. Who or what is Volksonne?"

"A sun-god. Apparently manifested himself at the Temple of the Suns tonight, which suggested that he's kicking out Sol and Sollinvictus. People saw a man made of fire at the temple and heard his words."

"Dalphina of Bolgia is being described as dead? Despite the fact that we saw her driving away from here?"

"Yep. And a bunch of the others you pointed out at the party the other night. All described as dead, killed by the god."

"And Casnar has been quoted, but made no mention of the fact that he was among those 'enemies of the people' when the fireball showed up."

"Correct."

Doc opened his eyes. "I must accept my dear brother's invitation to be part of his board of inquiry. I think I'll get started tonight. Go get Alastair and Ish. We're visiting the Temple of the Suns."

They parked both cars two blocks from the temple, at the point the brilliance of the spotlights illuminating it had begun to fade. There was a steady stream of foot traffic up the street toward the gigantic building, curious pedestrians drawn by the talk-box news reports even at this late hour, and the Foundation members could see the tiny specks of distant people climbing and descending the temple's white stairs.

"I'm going to make a big, public entrance," Doc said. "I want most of you in there first. Ixyail, are you with me?"

She shook her head, making a face. "Doc Sidhe is

not accompanied by women with big purpling bruises on their chins."

"No matter how beautiful."

She smiled. "No matter how beautiful. I'll stuff myself into that horrible blond wig again and be anonymous."

"Very well. You know what you have to do, if you get a chance." He looked at the others. "All of you."

They nodded, looking grave.

Doc turned to Zeb. "You'll have a hard time getting through the main door unnoticed, no matter what. Would you like to wait outside?"

"That never seems to work." Zeb stuffed his mask and gloves into his pockets, then struggled out of his overcoat. "Care for the next All-Out champion to accompany you?"

"That should prove to be diverting," Doc said. "And your prescience when it comes to solar devisement might be helpful."

"Admit it, Zeb," Harris said. "Just days ago, you never would have thought you'd be grateful to a burning sensation."

Zeb scowled at him, then turned his coat inside-out and struggled back into it.

Doc and Zeb waited until all the others left the sedan and a couple of minutes longer, then exited and followed them.

A crowd lingered in the street below the temple, men and women watching the building and talking among themselves, but Zeb could see no barricades barring their way; there was, in fact, a steady stream of people moving up and down the stairs, unimpeded by guards.

"Looks like some folk aren't too anxious to meet the god face-to-face," Zeb said.

Doc smiled. "For that matter, neither am I."

They moved through the press of the crowd. Moments later they passed between the columns and got their first close-up look at the temple. Zeb glanced between the circle of fire, the murals decorating the walls, and the groups of people standing by. "Lots of press," he said. "Lots of Sonnenkrieger."

"And plenty of the curious." Doc gestured toward the fire. "Look, there's Casnar. With the mislabeled cold fish."

When they approached the prince of Cretanis, his face lit up. He left the side of Edris and rushed forward to embrace Doc. "I'm so glad word reached you," he said. "I've been calling your quarters. No one was there."

"We went to visit the Temple of Ludana," Doc said.

Casnar's expression changed, became a mask of regret. "Gods, how awful. All those noble leaders dead."

"How did word come that the crowned heads of Europe were packed into that place?" Doc asked.

Casnar shrugged. "Valets, manservants to whom they'd entrusted the news of their rendezvous. My valet heard before I did." He turned to Zeb. "Goodsir Watson. I've had the pleasure of seeing you fight."

"And will again, I hope." Zeb shook his hand.

Edris, moving at a more stately rate, reached them. "Doctor MaqqRee. And it is Goodsir Watson, is it not? What do you make of it all?" Her gesture took in the entire temple interior, and she offered a mischievous smile. "Not the architecture or the ghastly art, I mean."

"Let's find out." Doc put his hand over his right eye and walked about. Zeb noticed two others in the chamber, one a small blond woman in a white formal gown, the other a very overweight man in a suit, incongruously accompanied by a servant who kept an umbrella positioned over his head, doing the same.

Doc was back moments later. He smoothed hair down on the back of his neck. To Zeb, he looked rattled. "There are definitely residual traces of godly devisement hereabouts," he said. "Solar in character, of course."

Casnar nodded. "Could it have been Sol or Sollinvictus?"

"I won't know until I've had an opportunity to examine sacred relics of those two faiths."

Edris said, "At last, something I can do. I'll arrange to have some brought here."

Casnar smiled. "I take it this means you're joining my little investigative panel."

Doc gave him a smile. "Did you imagine I wouldn't?"

Casnar and Edris moved off to speak to the man under the umbrella. Zeb said, "She does a good job of pretending not to share the Reinis' tastes."

Doc shrugged. "Alastair's researches say that her mother was Lorian, and she was raised for some years and educated in Loria, where the Reini attitudes are much less common. She may, in fact, *not* share them. What does your hand tell you?"

"About Edris? Just kidding." Zeb glanced at his palm. "I've had a steady itch since we got here. Very minor, though. Like some big solar devisement engine is just idling. Nearby, not exactly here."

"Let's take a walk about, then. To see if you can pin it down more precisely."

They did. They traded slight nods with Gaby and Harris, who affected to be fascinated with the mural of Sollinvictus, and with Alastair and Ish, who hovered near one of the broadcasting crews, listening to the live aether broadcast.

"It's strongest here, near the flame," Zeb said. He

moved close enough to the fire to be uncomfortably warm. He slowly stretched, raising his hands as high as he could, then brought them down again. Then, just as deliberately, he knelt and put his palms to the floor. "It's underneath," he said.

Doc frowned. "Godly, and yet not godly."

Zeb stood. "What do you mean?"

"Godly manifestations tend to fix on places that are suited to them. A mountaintop, a cave, and so on. From the aether broadcast Alastair described, it seemed that Volksonne manifested here, in the fire. So the hearth itself should be the center of his appearance, and strongest in his personal emanations. Not the basement." He offered up a sigh. "I hate basements. I've seen so much wickedness initiated in basements."

"Okay. Let's assume it's a human thing in addition to a godly thing and the bad people are down there. How do we get to them?" Zeb took a look around the big chamber; he saw at least thirty doors on the long walls. "We can't just throw open doors until we find the one we want. Someone would notice."

"Astute of you."

Zeb frowned. "Hey, you have a basement."

Doc turned an innocent expression toward him. "That's true. I'd forgotten. I must be one of them."

"Not what I meant. What if they have what you have? A tunnel out?"

"My sally-port." Doc frowned. "They'd be fools not to. Let's find it."

They circulated among the crowd, Doc picking out his associates by eye contact, nodding toward the exit to indicate that it was time to leave.

Once they were gone, Rudi straightened, his head emerging from the collar of his overcoat like a turtle's emerging from its shell. "There's a relief," he

said. He glanced up to where, on the mural immediately above, the foremost hoof of Sollinvictus'
chariot horse was poised to come down on him, then
returned his attention to his companions. "Let's be
about it, then."

Doc saw Zeb's hand twitch. "Here, stop here," Zeb
said.

They were all packed once more into the sedan.
Now a block west of the temple, they could see the
spotlights moving slowly across the sky, though the
temple itself was hidden by the bulk of a government
building in the way.

Noriko pulled the car over and parked it on the left
side of the street, directly in front of an old building
that, with the blocks of brown brick and gray concrete
on its face, with its large windows but conventional
design, looked very academic. Its doors were illuminated by an overhead light, but there were lights
behind none of the windows.

They heard the roar of a car engine. Noriko shut
off her lights. Ahead, out of what looked like an alley
to their left, a dark car emerged. It turned away from
them and its taillights receded.

Zeb glanced at his palm. "It's gone now."

"Was it in the car?"

"I don't think so, Doc. It flared up suddenly, then
stopped just as suddenly. Not like fading with distance."

Doc opened his door. "Alastair, Zeb, with me. Everyone else wait here."

The three of them moved up to the alley mouth and
peered in. It was a dark alley, short, with brick walls
to either side, but it appeared to open up onto some
sort of courtyard. Doc saw shadows that looked like
piles of stone. The piles were faintly illuminated on
the left side; there had to be a bulb lit.

Doc moved forward and waved the others on. Around the next corner, he got a much better view.

It was a courtyard. It had once been paved with flagstones in alternating colors, but now some of those stones were gone, leaving little pits behind, and other stones had been replaced by poured concrete.

Arrayed throughout the courtyard were statues and other examples of monumental decoration. Doc saw figures of noblemen, tombstones, Khemish-style pylons; there was a frieze showing gods of Panhellas at a dinner, but instead of being securely fixed to a building's summit it leaned against a brick wall. And, though some of the pieces were perfectly fine, others showed a lack of a grasp of anatomy, or, especially, composition.

Around the alley corner to the left, just a few paces in, was one spot of pavestone illuminated by an overhead bulb. Beneath it was an upright wooden chair and on it an old man. His head was bald, his features unlined, his clothing nondescript green; he wore spectacles. He held a book in his lap, but looked up as Doc peered around the corner. "Good evening, young man," he said in Burian.

Doc stepped out in plain sight. He gave the old man a smile and approached. "My apologies," he said, "for intruding. But I've become lost."

"It happens." The old man gestured back toward the street. "One block down in that direction is the Temple of the Suns. You can find your way to anywhere in Bardulfburg from there."

"True." Doc gestured at the artwork. "If I may ask, what is all this?"

"Student art." The man looked regretful. "That which the students didn't take away with them. This used to be the Bardulfburg Academy of the Arts. Now it's a warehouse, and I am its night guardsman."

"Not too dangerous a post, I hope."

The man laughed. "I spend my nights reading and keeping people from parking here. Sadly, I also spend my nights shooing away people I would otherwise like to hold conversations with. I hope you understand."

"Of course." Doc looked at the nearest section of wall. Then he punched the old man in the stomach.

The old man folded up over the blow, wheezing out the last of his breath. Doc moved behind him, grabbed him around the neck, and choked him to unconsciousness.

"My, my." That was Alastair, stepping out into the courtyard. "Remind me never to have a polite conversation with you."

"Come here and take a look at this."

Zeb and Alastair joined him. He pointed out a portion of the brick wall—one specific brick. The mortar above it was deeper than elsewhere, and the top of the brick featured an odd set of ridges, four grooves. Alastair frowned at it. "That's familiar."

"I get it," Zeb said. *"Bitte."*

"Correct," Doc said. "Alastair, get the others." From his pocket, he brought out a torch and snapped it on. In the brighter light, he took a closer look at the pavestones.

Dark patches on their edges, signs of tires having passed over them, led to a section of wall between two upright statues. The statues were twice the height of a man, artistically crude, with broad faces showing only slight indentations for eyes and a slight rise for a nose, with only suggestions of features elsewhere on their bodies. Doc found they were not actually standing before the wall; they were inset in it, with surrounding brick quite new, but painted to be a match for the rest of the wall.

The associates arrived. Doc waved Alastair toward

the switch on the wall and the rest to take cover behind the pile of artless statuary. Then he frowned. "Where's Zeb?"

A voice just beside him said, "Right here."

Despite himself, Doc jumped. Against the wall beyond the second statue, Zeb, now in his dark outfit, was no more than a silhouette. "That's a good scare."

"I owed you one."

"Stay there." Doc moved to the opposite side of the first statue, then nodded to Alastair.

The doctor gripped the misshapen brick and said, "*Bitte.*"

There was a faint rumbling. The left arm of Doc's statue and the right arm of Zeb's rose, swinging open a section of wall between them. Light spilled out into the courtyard. Doc and Zeb swung around the corners.

Beyond was a concrete tunnel leading down at a slight angle. It was lit by a succession of overhead light fixtures. To the right, on Zeb's side, was a booth. It looked like a checkpoint booth, but there was no glass in the windows. Within, a Sonnenkrieger soldier was grabbing at a talk-box with one hand, unholstering a pistol with the other, his expression alarmed . . .

Zeb stepped up and hit him once in the gut, followed through with a blow to his gun hand and, as the man bent forward in pain, to the side of his head. The soldier crashed to the floor of his booth. Zeb leaned in and hung up the talk-box handset.

"Everybody in," Doc said. "Bring the other guard."

The tunnel led them down and in a broad rightward curve, then back to the east. They heard the outer door grate down into place not long after they were out of sight of it. Harris sweated and swore under the weight of the outdoor guard, while Zeb and Alastair carried the soldier.

Once the tunnel was pointed eastward, they came across a heavy door in the side. Noriko took several moments to pick the lock and peered within. "Stairs, unlit," she said. "Going up. I think it's part of the school."

They stashed the guards there, binding and gagging them, and continued. Alastair looked more comfortable with his autogun in his hands, and Noriko had her long, scabbarded sword tucked through the scarf that served her as a belt.

The tunnel went arrow-straight for a block to the east—"Typical Burian engineering efficiency," Doc said—and then rose into what appeared to be a broader open area. The associates ascended that final ramp quietly, cautiously, Doc and Zeb in front.

They reached the opening and peered about. This was a garage; in it were a gold and black Alpenhaus taxi, two open-topped Sonnenkrieger staff cars in gleaming black, and an inconspicuous red sedan. One corner of the chamber was set off by light construction as an unroofed office; a door led into it, and a double door was set in the opposite wall. There were no people to see.

Beyond the double door was a corridor, dimly lit as if now were not the normal hours of occupation. The corridor went some distance right and left, and another corridor led straight ahead; at its end, they could see a poorly-lit stairwell leading up.

Doc sighed. "All right. Ixyail and I will take the left, Zeb and Noriko right. Harris, Gaby, Alastair, take the stairs ahead. Everyone, make your way upward; I hope we can find access into the temple proper rather than having to work our way back down again.

"Our priorities are finding out whatever we can, especially about the fireballs and how they might be stopped, and getting out alive to make some productive use of this information.

"And we have to do so quickly. The absence of those guards will be discovered soon enough.

"Go."

Noriko, quieter, took the lead. She left her sword in its sheath but kept one hand on its hilt and the other further back on the sheath, steadying and controlling it as she moved. Zeb stayed a few paces back, one pistol in hand, looking backward almost as often as forward.

The corridor they explored smelled of fresh paint and was lined with doors, all on the left, east, side. Most were not locked. Alternately, Noriko and Zeb eased them open to take a peek in. A storeroom whose shelves held cleansing agents, mops and buckets. Bathrooms that looked and smelled as though they'd never been used. A cage-style door that was made to slide open showed them the interior of an unlit freight elevator.

At the end of the hall was a set of double doors, and they were locked. Noriko knelt before them and brought out her picks. Zeb kept guard behind her.

She took a while. "Good lock," she whispered. "Ah, I've got it." She pocketed her things and got her hand on her hilt again before pushing the door open a fraction to peer within. "Come look." She opened it wider.

Zeb joined her. The chamber beyond was large. There was no one in it. It was something of a mess, in contrast with the Burians' usual neatness. He saw shelves with tools scattered on them, tables with mechanical parts in a state of partial assembly, a line of aluminum cabinets, a set of wooden shelves with curious glass appliances on them—

Zeb took a second look at that and at the cabinets. "This is where they put the bleaching cabinets together," he said. He followed her in. While she relocked the door, he took a look at the doors on the left-hand wall.

One led to a private office. It was unlit, but in the faint illumination spilling in from the main chamber, it seemed very messy. There was something familiar about the sloppiness, and then Zeb had it—the only other place he had recently seen such disorganization had been the laboratory of Dr. Niskin. He looked at the effects on the office desk and found what he was looking for: a framed cameo showing Teleri Obeldon, younger than he'd last seen her, with a woman who looked like a slightly older Teleri, both seated, smiling, on a wooden bench on a porch. The next door led to another long, dark chamber, this one featuring huge iron bucketlike apparati and, beneath them, devices that resembled huge stoves—stoves lacking grills or burners suited for cooking food. "Manufacturing," he said.

The last door in line led to a set of stairs leading only upward. By contrast with the room, it was brightly lit, and was not industrial in the least; the steps were wood, the railings of good craftsmanship. "Looks like we go up from here," he told Noriko.

The corridor Doc and Ish took had no side doors, just a right-hand turn forty paces from the garage. Doc peeked around the corner and saw only a set of double metal doors another five paces down. He signaled Ish forward and she joined him at the door.

He pressed an ear to it, then shook his head. Ish put her nose to where the doors met—they were so closely fitted that it could not be described as a gap—and sniffed, then lowered her head all the way to floor level, her nostrils flaring.

She straightened. She showed two fingers, then indicated an altitude near the top of Doc's head, then offered a Novimagos hand-to-chest salute.

Doc well knew her private code: two men, on guard.

Which was odd. They were guarding the door on its exit side rather than its entrance?

Above the door, in the wall, was a niche, two handspans wide by a handspan tall, with a couple of wires trailing from it. It looked to be a spot where the builders intended to add a sign or perhaps a viewer. It was in keeping with the unfinished appearance of this place, Doc decided. He removed his coat, dropping it in the corner, then put two hands beside his face as though he were suggesting sleep. Ish nodded.

Doc reached up to grab the niche and pulled himself up. Straining slightly, he brought his body parallel to the floor, holding it above the tops of the doors.

Ish lay down, assumed a fetching pose of unconscious helplessness, and gave out a bark of pain. She closed her eyes.

There was a moment of silence, then murmurs from the other side of the door. It opened outward, swinging beneath Doc's body. He couldn't quite see the man who stood there, but heard him speaking in Burian: "A woman!"

Another man, nearby: "They didn't say anything about a woman."

The first man moved out into Doc's sight: a Sonnenkrieger soldier, his rifle in both hands, approaching Ish, curious but alert.

Doc waited until the man stood almost over Ish. He swung down and dropped.

Just inside the door was another soldier. The man's eyes widened and he took a step back, trying to bring his own rifle to bear. "Delwin—"

Delwin was already moving, turning to aim. Ish kicked out, sweeping his legs out from under him. Doc lunged at the other soldier, sweeping the rifle barrel aside, and put a fist into the man's gut.

Doc wasn't a full-time student of hand-to-hand combat the way Harris and Zeb were. On the other hand, he'd had much longer than they to develop his skills. The soldier's left fist came up; Doc caught it with his right, got his left hand around the soldier's jaw, and drove his head into the wall. The soldier's eyes fluttered, but he still struggled; it took Doc two more fast impacts of head on wall to put him down.

He turned. Ish was up, the other soldier's rifle in her hands, butt toward the man, who was slumped on the floor. There was blood on the butt.

Doc turned the other way, down the hallway their intrusion had revealed. It was dimly lit, with metal double doors at intervals on the left, north, wall. Though it was difficult to make out, he thought the corridor turned to the right at the far end.

There were no more guards in immediate sight. Doc hoisted his soldier over his shoulder and moved easily to pick up Ish's by his collar. He carried both men through the double doors. Ish closed the doors behind him, then preceded him up the corridor.

Harris led the way up the stairs, Gaby a few paces back, Alastair and his autogun bringing up the rear.

It was a curious stairwell; there were no doors at the landings. He would have expected it to give him access to each level of what he assumed was a basement complex.

Eventually it ended in a small round room. Its walls were concrete, recently painted in gold. Three doors, heavy metal things, led from it. If Harris still had his sense of direction and hadn't miscounted the number of flights of stairs, one door led approximately north, the opposite one south, and the third to the east. He shrugged at Alastair.

The doctor covered his left eye and took a look about, then pointed at the eastern door.

Harris tried it. The handle twisted easily and he pulled the door open an inch.

Beyond was a circular chamber, perhaps ten paces across and ten or more high. Its curving walls seemed to be stone or concrete, and stairs inset in the walls, both to his right and his left, rose to a balcony level eight paces up. The balcony rails were of rounded metal, a style Harris associated with schools of his younger years, but were of a bronze color.

Doors led off the balcony level, three of them, each with frosted windows. The center window, across from the door by which they'd entered, was lit, and Harris could see the silhouette of a man standing before it. The two doors flanking it were dark.

Alastair whispered, "The place is alive with solar devisement. Godly solar devisement. The god was here not long ago."

"Comforting," Harris said. "What say we behave like complete idiots and ransack the place before he gets back?"

Alastair shrugged. "Suits me."

The fact that they had still run into no guards, heard no sounds of trouble, bothered Zeb. But when he exited the stairwell into the treasure room, he momentarily lost his qualms.

It wasn't really a treasure room. There were no chests full of gems or coins, no decoratively-arrayed displays of jewels. But there were some things Zeb would have traded a lot of wealth, if he had any, to find.

There was a model of Bardulfburg, for instance, with a newly-painted blast crater installed where the Temple of Ludana had once been.

There was a chart, a 3-D diagram of the Temple of the Suns and its basement levels.

Zeb spent some time looking at it. The diagram showed that the temple surrounding the main open chamber was divided mostly into offices. The uppermost basement level—which, because the temple itself was elevated, was actually at ground level, bordered by all those flights of steps—was temple warehouse, except for odd circular chambers immediately beneath the temple-level Eternal Flame; one circular chamber ran down into the ground twenty feet or so, if Zeb calculated the scale correctly, and was adjacent to another that was thirty or forty feet high. There was no access to these chambers from the uppermost basement level, just from lower levels.

Below ground level, portions of the basement complex on the north side looked like more storehouses, others like a hospital ward, others like an emergency shelter. Portions on the south side looked like private offices and warehouse again.

Stairs led from an office floor above the emergency shelter to the main temple level, and from a corridor in front of the larger circular chamber to a small room in the midst of offices at the main level. Only these two staircases provided access to the surface. No elevators led from the main or first basement levels to the underground levels, though there appeared to be one servicing lower floors on the emergency shelter side of the complex.

Zeb was able to find the tunnel and the garage, then trace his path to the bleaching cabinet assembly chamber and the room he was in now. He memorized what he could of the complex's layout.

Also in this room was an impressive chest of drawers. It stood taller than a man, with each drawer being only a handspan wide and tall. Zeb pulled one drawer open. Its contents were small pieces of stone and metal shavings, most the size of a thumbnail, each with a string attaching a paper tag to it. On each tag was written a street address.

He took a deep breath. Unless he missed his guess, every one of these pieces of rock had been chipped from a hearthstone or incised from a dedicatory plaque. Many of the drawers were empty; this was obviously a collection project that was far from complete.

A door led into a private office. It was larger than Niskin's, furnished with drafting tables and an impressive map case. He found Noriko going through the drawers of the map case; they seemed filled mostly with blueprints. "General Ritter's office, I expect," she said.

He nodded. "We ought to get Alastair or Doc in here to decipher the Burian tags on that map of the temple."

"Let us go, then."

He took a final look at the temple diagram. If Harris, Gaby and Alastair had taken their stairwell all the way to the top, it would have led them to the bottom of that curious circular chamber. From the office they were in, a trip down a corridor past rooms whose labels he could not decipher would bring them to the same chamber.

In the circular chamber, Harris and Gaby crept up the stairs to the left, Alastair those to the right. The guard outside the illuminated door remained motionless, apparently unaware of their presence.

When they reached the balcony level, Gaby, with Harris covering her, eased open the left-hand door and peered in. It was dark; she snapped her torch on and waved it around.

At the room's center was a raised dais, circular. Around the walls were arrayed a series of devices pointed toward the dais; to Gaby, they looked like machine guns whose barrels were made of glass. The walls of the chamber added to its mad-science appearance; she saw bank after bank of machinery and large switches that put her in mind of Frankenstein movies.

This, too, was a tall room. In fact, a metal ladder led up one wall to a platform just below the ceiling. There seemed to be bars and levers up there.

Against the wall to the right was a huge screen— not impressive by the large-screen TV standards of the grim world, but she'd never seen a screen this large in the fair world. Cautious, she moved in.

Harris followed. "Looks like the kind of talk-box the Leader of the True Race would use to address his people," he said, keeping his voice low.

She touched the screen, closed her eyes, felt beyond its surface. "It's not really a talk-box. I can't get to the communications grid or the aether, either one, from it."

"That's weird. Is anything hooked up to monitor it?"

"Not that I can feel."

"Turn it on, then."

With the slightest of mental exertions, she did. There was a snapping noise from the screen, then a white dot appeared at its center. A moment later, words swam into focus.

Harris sighed. "I am sick to death of Burian. Let's go back home where everybody uses Cretanis to threaten the world so you can understand them."

"Hush. I'll get Alastair."

She stepped back out the door. Down the curved balcony, Alastair, too, was exiting the room he'd chosen to search. He gave her an all-clear signal; she waved him over.

A moment later, he began translating. "'I am Volksonne, la la la. God of the people, god of the mostly hygienic, god of the better-than-everyone-else.'"

"I suspect," Gaby said, "that you're taking liberties with the translation."

"Never. I'm very circumspect about my translations."

Harris said, "This is just the speech from earlier tonight."

Alastair read on ahead. "No, it's not. 'I return once more to cast purifying fire on the naughty, and this time I smite the fewmethead who would lead the Burian people into ruin.'"

Gaby gave him an arch look. "What?"

"'The fury of my you-can't-get-better-anywhere anger now descends on the house of Aevar...'" Alastair whistled. "This is a death sentence for the king."

Gaby touched the screen again and it went dark. "That probably answers the question as to whether this whole Volksonne thing is Aevar's plan."

"Great," Harris said. "So he's completely, utterly innocent of the other stuff. We can relax—he's just the pocket Hitler we've always assumed he was."

"Cynic." She moved to the door. "I think it's time for *me* to cause some trouble."

Harris took a prospective look up the ladder. "What do you plan to do, honey?"

"Make a phone call or two."

"There's a talk-box in the office I was just in," Alastair said. "I don't recommend you go through the building switchboard, though."

She gave him a confident smile. "You're talking to the goddess of the talk-box."

"I apologize most humbly, Great One."

Doc reached the nearest set of doors. The first one he opened led to a large room, a warehouse in miniature, its shelves loaded with cardboard boxes and wooden crates.

He carried the unconscious soldiers in. Ixyail closed

the door, then bound and gagged the prisoners as Doc looked at the labels stenciled on the crates. "Canned food. Medical supplies." He reached a portion of shelves where there were no crates, just pieces of paper. He studied one. "This shelf is for baby formula."

"You're joking."

"No, I'm not. They're to lay in supplies in the middle of next year." He moved on. "Baby food here."

Ish rose from gagging the first soldier. "I thought this was a place of conspiracy. They should have ammunition. Listening devices. Tools of torture." She bent over the second man.

"Here we have boxes of books. Burian-language literature." Doc frowned again. "Primers and other children's books as well. Chalk. Erasers."

"It's a school, then."

"I hope the answer is that simple."

There were four rooms along this hallway, all store-houses. The first had been nearly full, the next two were partly stocked, and the last was echoingly empty. At the far end of the hall were a staircase to the right and a freight elevator to the left; both led only upward. They silently took the stairs up to the next floor.

Here they found a similar hall, but it was well-lit, with occasional viewing-style windows on the walls and in some doors on either side. From his angle, Doc couldn't see much beyond the windows—a suggestion of darkened chambers, large ones.

The first room they looked at, on the right, which would be the north wall, was small, with cold metal doors that opened onto metal-sided interiors—refrigerated pantries, not turned on, empty. Next on the right was an industrial-sized kitchen, dark, never used; an observation window allowed Doc to peer into it without entering.

Back across the hall, the next chamber down from

the warehouse also featured an observation window. Within, the far wall of the long room was lined with tables, and on them, talk-boxes—triples, it appeared, with screens for viewing. They were all dark. Beneath each was a row of switches. Doc entered as Ish kept guard at the door. He turned on one of the sets; after a moment, its view swam into focus. The view was dark, hard for him to make out details, but it seemed to be an overhead look at a plain bedroom, furnished and very tidy, completely impersonal.

He flipped one of the switches beneath the set. The view changed to another dark scene, some sort of lounge with many sofas and comfortable chairs. The next scene was that of a dimly-lit dining room. No, it wasn't as personal as a dining room, more of a cafeteria, with long white tables with benches permanently attached.

"They have set things up," Doc said, "so that a whole community, including babies, might live here under constant observation."

"Why?"

"I don't know. And I don't intend to leave without finding out."

The next room down featured a second observation window, this one on its interior wall, facing southward. Through the window they could see a dim chamber, a huge one whose ceiling seemed to be on a level with this room's but whose floor was much lower. A few lights burned dimly out there, illuminating the tops of curtainlike partitions. There was also a door on the east wall. Doc moved into the room, tried the door, found it unlocked. He gave Ish a nod and opened it.

It opened out onto a metal catwalk, just a spare metallic grid with rails. It hung from the ceiling by metal supports, as did metal rigs that looked like scaffolding at the same level as the catwalk; light fixtures, only a few of them lit, hung from the scaffolding undersides.

The floor had to be eight or ten paces down. The chamber itself was huge, divided by hanging gold curtains into separate areas. One area had long tables and numerous chairs placed around them. Another featured several sofas and stuffed chairs. A third held the cafeteria tables Doc had seen in the talk-box screen. It all seemed very antiseptic.

"With the lights below the catwalk," Doc said, "whoever is down there couldn't see people up here. An ideal arrangement for what looks like a prison that is meant to be somewhat comfortable." He led Ish out further along the catwalk. "Now we just need to find out who is supposed to live here."

Harris clambered up onto the platform above the dais and looked around.

It was an odd little chamber. Stairs in the center led up to the low ceiling, in the middle of which was a hatch. To Harris it looked like a submarine's hatch, complete with a wheellike closing mechanism. He climbed up to the top stair, which forced him to stand bent over beneath the hatch, and carefully turned the wheel. It was new, well-machined, and well-oiled; it turned with a minimum of noise until the bars it moved were drawn in to the center of the mechanism.

He took out his revolver. There was no telling what might be beyond, or whether he might be noticed the moment he opened the hatch. Then, slowly, he straightened.

The hatch resisted his effort. He shoved harder at it, and the thing yielded—weight alone appeared to have been working against him.

The first thing he was aware of was brightness and heat—hot air rolled across him and he began sweating.

The thin line of sight the hatch afforded him showed only flame, as though he were emerging a few feet from a fireplace. He heard no noise but a quiet roaring.

He raised the hatch higher. There was flame all around and the heat grew worse, but still there were no cries of alarm.

He maneuvered the hatch high enough to allow him to peer up. It looked as though the hatch were capped by a slab of stone larger than the hatch itself. He could now see the tops of the flames on all sides of him. Above them to either side he could see the flickering forms of giant horses, painted in a cartoony style on tall walls . . .

He eased the hatch shut. He moved to the ladder opening and leaned over it. "Alastair!"

The doctor, examining one of the glass-barreled machine guns, looked up. "What?"

"This hatch opens into the middle of the temple's Eternal Flame."

"You stay there. I'll get steaks. We can grill them."

"No, no, you putz. Go tell Gaby about this. And then figure out some way to distract the people around the flame."

Immediately a ringing arose, like the world's loudest alarm clock, or a school class alarm stuck in the on position. It came from a metal disk high on the wall, but seemed to come from all around them.

Harris clamped his hands over his ears and glared down at Alastair. "That's actually sooner than I wanted."

Alastair's hands were over his ears, too. "What?"

Doc and Ish crouched on the catwalk above what looked like a curtained-off lecture area. Rows of padded chairs were arrayed before a table and a lectern. "Guess what," Doc said.

"You want to read those."

"Let's find the way down."

"*Halt!*"

Ahead a dozen paces, where their catwalk crossed another one at right angles, stood a Sonnenkrieger soldier. He must have moved up very quietly, and the darkness of his uniform had concealed his approach; now he held a rifle on them. At this range, it would have been difficult for him to miss.

"The usual," Doc said. He stood, arms up, a showy display of surrender—then twisted aside.

Ish's handgun boomed. He fancied he felt the wind of the bullet's passage just behind his back.

The soldier jerked and looked surprised. His uniform concealed the location of his injury, but Doc estimated from his reaction that he'd taken the shot to his chest. Ish fired twice more, and the soldier slumped against the catwalk rail. His rifle fell into the main chamber and made a loud crack as the wooden stock hit the floor.

There were shouts—distant, but probably from within the chamber. A moment later Doc saw heads bobbing as men ran toward them along the catwalk, and he heard the ringing of their boots against the metal.

Doc glanced at Ish. She was in her dark clothes, her wig discarded. The men probably hadn't seen her yet. "Get those papers, find out what you can," he said. "I'm going to draw them off."

"Kiss me."

He did. He waited while Ish kicked off her shoes and leaped over the rail to the nearest scaffolding supporting light fixtures; it swayed as she landed. Then she was moving at almost a sprint into the darkness.

Doc fired twice in the general direction of the oncoming soldiers, aiming into the ceiling, then turned and ran back the way he'd come as noisily as he could manage.

An alarm sounded, a loud, persistent ringing . . .

Chapter Twenty-Four

Above, at the top level of the Temple of the Suns, the alarm was a more muted ringing, but it still stirred the crowd. Visitors to the temple raised their voices, a volume increase brought on by anxiety and curiosity.

Edris gave Casnar a look. The Cretanis prince was frowning, his head cocked at a listening angle.

"That is an alarm, isn't it?" she asked.

"Yes, but—do you hear that? A sort of pounding?"

She listened. She did hear an irregular clanking. "That is odd."

A Sonnenkrieger colonel emerged from a door beneath Sol's chariot. "Your attention, please. Everyone please leave the temple precincts for the moment. Please remain calm, you are in no danger."

"What is the problem, Colonel?" Edris asked.

The officer bowed and gave her a reassuring smile. "Your Highness. Forgive me. I did not know you were in attendance." He moved closer so that others of the crowd, some now beginning to move toward the chamber entrance, could not hear. "It seems that a dusky,

451

probably an anarchist, has found his way into the temple warehouses in the basement. We suspect he is armed. Probably trying to visit revenge on the priests of this temple for the destruction of his temple tonight, in the irrational way of duskies." He shrugged, a that's-the-way-they-are gesture. "Until we have him captured, we'd prefer for civilians to remain outside."

"Well, I will be a civilian for the moment," Edris said. She turned to catch the attention of her body-guard, who hovered a few paces away, and began moving toward the exit. "Coming, Casnar?"

"I'll be along in a moment. I have a question about security for the colonel."

Alastair peeked out the door of the chamber with the dais. As he looked, he saw the central door, the guarded door, swing in. A Sonnenkrieger private stepped in and took a look around. Alastair froze, his hand on his trigger.

The soldier's look was only cursory. He stepped back out and shut the door, his motion suggesting he was unconcerned.

Alastair shut his own door, then called up, "Harris! It's getting uncomfortable down here!"

Harris didn't answer. Alastair just heard more pounding and clanking from his direction.

Ish maneuvered along the scaffolding almost as though it were level ground until she was two curtained-off sections away from the lecture area. Below was some sort of lounge, unoccupied, decorated by a sofa, two chairs, an icebox and some counter space. To her left, she could see men, Sonnenkrieger, racing by on the catwalk where she and Doc had stood moments ago.

She holstered her pistol, made sure that her shotgun

hung securely from its cord on her back, and bent to grip the metal railing she was standing on.

Immediately her fingers tingled. She gave a hiss of irritation. *Unsheathed steel*, she thought. Her stockings had protected her feet, but she didn't have time to bring out her gloves yet.

She swung free, dangling beneath the poisonous metal framework, and hung over empty space, then dropped onto the sofa. As she hit, the impact driving her down into a crouch, she rolled forward off the furniture, hit the floor, and rolled up to her feet. The shotgun made too much noise clattering across the floor, but she felt no sudden pains or twinges—it was as successful a drop from that height as she could have hoped for.

She turned toward the lecture area, but her thoughts were on Doc, not papers.

Finally Harris descended the ladder. "Thanks for aging me a dozen years," Alastair said.

"You're welcome. Ready to go?"

Alastair growled at him.

They left the dais chamber, unnecessarily silent considering the alarm bells still ringing. Gaby must have been keeping watch at her own doorway; she moved out to join them. Moments later, they exited the lower door. The little chamber beyond was still empty.

"Right, left, or down?" Harris asked.

Alastair tried one door. "Locked. Not left."

Harris tried the other. "Same here. Looks like we go—"

His door swung open. A man-shaped silhouette filled the doorway—

Harris swung by reflex, a blow that should have caught the intruder in the balls and incapacitated him, but the silhouette blocked it with a palm and skidded half a step back. "Harris! Cool it."

"Zeb!" Then Harris caught sight of the shadow behind this shadow. "Noriko."

In a few words, they told one another what they'd found. Harris said, "I really, really need to see the city model. Right now."

"I'll show you, man."

Doc made it back into the corridor and raced back toward the exit to the garage and tunnel. He heard the pursuing soldiers reaching the turn behind him as he got to the intersection.

Forward, out, or up? he asked himself. Out was no choice; his friends were still in the complex. Up, the most central option, appealed to him. He turned up the corridor toward the stairs Harris, Gaby and Alastair had ascended not long before.

Ish took up the papers from the table. Above, footsteps were still clanking along the catwalk, but she was in deep shadow and no cries suggested that anyone had heard her.

It was too dark to read the papers. They'd probably be in Burian anyway. She stuffed them beneath her waistband and looked around. The exit from this place would probably be against the wall. She decided to bet on the wall beneath the rooms she and Doc had been exploring.

She took two steps. Then hands emerged from the curtain, grabbed her about the face and shoulders, and dragged her through.

At the top of the stairs, Doc found three doors. Quickly, he checked the knobs on each. Two locked, one unlocked. Lacking Noriko's skill with lockpicks, not having time to set up an appropriate devisement, and with booted feet pounding up the stairs behind him, he had no choice. He went through the center door.

And found himself in a circular, tall chamber with a balcony far above—a balcony lined by Sonnenkrieger who put him in the sights of their rifles almost as soon as he entered.

Among them were General Ritter, Colonel Förster, and a potbellied man Doc did not know but recognized from his description.

Doc forced himself to take on a pleasant expression. "Doctor Niskin, I presume?"

The potbellied man peered down at him. He did not seem jovial. "Doctor MaqqRee. Fortunate for me that you did not find this chamber before now. You might have caused me some trouble."

The door behind Doc slammed open. He didn't have to turn; he heard the Sonnenkrieger swarming in.

General Ritter said, "We're under control here, Tryg. Assign some men to guard that door. Send the rest out to find MaqqRee's confederates."

A man behind Doc asked, "Shall I bring them to you?"

"Just kill them."

The soldiers behind Doc filed back out again.

Ritter continued, "And, Förster, see what you can do about this noise. I think the situation is more or less under control."

Förster clicked his heels and entered an office along the right side of the balcony. Moments later, the alarm chopped off.

"You've had some distant contact with Tryg before," Ritter said. "He is a most persuasive man. I'm going to make him minister of propaganda, I think. He's managed to persuade an entire Kobolde tribe of your evil, Doctor MaqqRee, and has arranged for them to prune the Reini party of some of its weak branches. When things settle down a bit, of course."

Doc didn't bother to reply.

Niskin looked at Doc. His expression was grave and, oddly, Doc thought he saw some vulnerability in it. "I must ask you," he said, "and rely on your reputation for honesty, and the fact that you really have nothing to gain by lying to me. What has become of my daughter?"

Doc sighed inwardly. "She is dead."

Niskin rocked back. He might have fallen had he not been holding onto the balcony railing. But he nodded as though this were the answer he expected. "At whose hands?"

"In a sense, at yours. It was Volksonne who killed her."

"You lie."

"She cast that fireball devisement three times in Neckerdam, but only two landed. What do you suppose that means?"

Niskin just stared at him. It was a moment before Doc realized he wasn't seeing him—the man was just staring into the distance of time. Tears began to run down his cheeks.

"Doctor." That was Ritter. He looked apologetic. "I am sorry, Doctor, but this man's intervention could cause us considerable trouble. We need to move up the schedule."

Niskin nodded but did not speak.

"Förster," Ritter continued, "prepare yourself. We'll do the next one immediately."

Förster emerged from the office and clicked his heels. "I must point out that the temple has been cleared. There is no audience. No newsmen."

Ritter made an exasperated noise. "Well, we'll just have to put him out in the street, then. No, on the temple roof—we'll know no one is standing there. Prepare yourself."

Förster saluted, hand straight up as if gesturing to the sun, and moved around to the left-hand door.

Ritter said, "Come up, Doctor MaqqRee. I'm sure you will find this interesting."

"Done," Harris said.

The door by which they'd entered the city-model chamber opened and Noriko slipped in. "Soldiers coming," she said.

"Everybody out," Harris said. "Down staircase."

The door to the down staircase opened and Gaby slipped in. "Soldiers coming," she said.

"Ish," said her captor. "Miss me, darlin'?"

"Rudi!" She struggled, but could not break his grip. She managed to draw her pistol, but before she could bring it into line, another hand, not Rudi's, caught it and wrenched it from her grasp.

She looked up. Three other silhouettes besides Rudi's hovered over her. The man who'd taken her gun said, "That's not nice."

Rudi sounded hurt. "Why do you keep trying to kill me?"

"For betraying Doc."

"You're daft. I never betrayed Doc. I accepted money from him."

"You admitted to it. For revenge, you said."

"Not revenge on Doc!"

"You know," said the other man who'd spoken, "soldiers might hear and come at any time. The alarms have stopped."

"So they have," Rudi said. He released Ish. "Let's keep our voices down. Stand up, darlin'. We're all in the same fix. Oh. Let me introduce you to me brothers. Ixyail, this is Egon, Jorg, and Otmar."

She looked at them, surprised. "The Bergmonk Boys?"

"We're famous," said one, and giggled.

"I brought them here on my own coin," Rudi said. "To do what your lover might be too squeamish to."

"Doc said you didn't know where their safe house was—"

"I told him a wee lie about that." Rudi didn't sound contrite. "We got in upstairs through a door I saw one of me kidnappers come out through. Ottie's clever about such things, and about pockets too. But when we got down to the level above, soldiers spotted us and began chasing us. We ran down here—and the futtering staircase we came down on rose up behind us. So we've been hiding."

"No way out," said the one who'd giggled. "Unless you know of one."

Ish took a look around, though her view was mostly blocked by curtains. "No," she said. "Except for eight paces straight up." She rose. "Where's the staircase you came down by?"

They all pointed back the way Ish and Doc had come from, except the one who'd giggled, who pointed ninety degrees to the right.

Ish handed Rudi the packet of papers and her shotgun. "Hold on to these."

"What are the papers?"

"They're for Doc. You really plan no vengeance against him?"

"On my honor."

"Go to where the stairs come down." She began unbuttoning her blouse.

"Uhhh . . . if you don't mind, I'd prefer to stay. You might even move to where the light is better."

Ish glared. "You'd better leave."

In the dais chamber, Förster stripped down to his boxer shorts. Dr. Niskin handed him plain garments—

common trousers and shirt, their color a close match for his skin tone—and Förster put them on.

"Let me see if I have worked out all the details," Doc said.

Niskin gestured for him to continue. Then the doctor threw a switch on the side of the large-screen talk-box against the wall. Its picture, lines and lines of text, began to swim into view.

"You start with puppets that move without strings," Doc said. He cast surreptitious looks at the three Sonnenkrieger who had joined them in the dais chamber, but they were keeping him under close, alert surveillance. "And at some point it occurs to you, or someone, that you might create an even grander puppet. A puppet indistinguishable from a god."

Ritter smiled. "That was my notion, actually. An idea that was just too compelling to put into the hands of a man like Aevar; he'd either be too pious to implement it or would use it mostly for his own benefit." He shrugged. "But even for a deviser of Niskin's skills, there were many, many obstacles to overcome."

"Such as the fact that godly devisements are untainted by mortality, and any sufficiently educated deviser could see past the deception."

"Correct," Ritter said. "So Doctor Niskin began doing research among devisers who thought outside conventional lines. Which led him to your old friend, the Changeling."

"I don't understand—what techniques, exactly, did the Changeling bring you? And why did he work with you?"

Niskin ignored the entire exchange. He moved from switchbox to switchbox on the wall, making sure electrical connections were secure.

Ritter said, "He told us how his mentor, Duncan Blackletter, had already created something living that was untainted by mortal devisement. He took some of us to spy upon a big man named Joseph. Blackletter had made him out of clay. The Changeling called the man a golem and said that Blackletter had learned portions of the art of fabricating him on the grim world." He smiled. "What a challenge it must have seemed to him to convince us that the grim world really existed. Eventually he took some of us there. That convinced us. We met Blackletter. We came to terms. Blackletter would rule Donarau, to the south. King Duncan. A genuine achievement for a career criminal such as himself. He would have fabricated his own god to support his regime, I suppose." The general shrugged. "I cannot say we were disappointed when he died before claiming all we owed him. And we owe him much. We owe him Volksonne."

"Volksonne is more than a puppet," Niskin said. He still didn't turn to meet Doc's gaze. "He lives. He lives in that large chamber. He is awake only when we wake him, and he thinks little more than we allow him to think, but he has godly life."

Förster moved to stand atop the dais. "And I grant him form. I direct his motions." He held up an object in his left hand. It was one of the gold arrowhead paperweights. "See here, the greatest weapon in the world. It fits in the pocket, but it commands a god."

"So it's you, Ritter, and Niskin and Förster here. And some handpicked Sonnenkrieger and temple personnel, I suppose," Doc said. "Who else? Casnar, of course. And Edris."

"Casnar, yes," Ritter said. "Edris, no. Casnar will marry Edris when her father dies, assuming he can persuade her, which he probably can, and thus will rule Weseria as well as Cretanis, someday. I will be leader of the Burian League."

"And when will Aevar die? I assume you have that planned."

"Plans change." Ritter's expression suggested that this was a minor inconvenience. "He would have died on the last day of the Games, his palace destroyed as he dressed for the closing ceremonies. But, because of you, we need to get details settled sooner. Ready, Doctor?"

Niskin nodded. In succession, he threw the switches all along the wall, except for the last; with each switch, three of the glass machine-gun barrels illuminated and poured light onto Colonel Förster.

"Improvise a bit," Ritter said to Förster. "Don't name him. Since he might be listening to broadcasts even now, we can't give him even a few ticks of advance warning."

"And give me half a chime," Niskin said. "I need to get to the model chamber." He shot Ritter an accusing glance. "This change in plans hasn't given me much time."

Förster, glowing gold as though lit from within, nodded, and looked down to a spot, a red letter X, just beneath the talk-box screen. Niskin threw the last switch. "Hear me, my people," Förster said.

Where Edris and her bodyguard waited in the tight-packed crowd, there were gasps as the glow appeared. Edris looked up to the top of the temple.

Atop the dome stood the burning man the press had spoken of. He looked down upon them, his expression benign. "*Hear me, my people,*" he said, and the word rolled across the crowd and echoed from the buildings behind.

"*I am Volksonne, god of the people. I am the god of the pure, of the clean, of the rightful.*"

Edris realized that she heard some of the words in Burian, others in Lorian, both languages she had spoken since childhood. It took her a mere moment to determine that she could attune herself to hear only one set of words, as though she were dialing between broadcasts on a talk-box set.

The crowd quieted, though Volksonne's words could be heard above the loudest noise they were likely to make.

"I return to cast cleansing fire on those who would keep the Burians from their true greatness. Now I destroy one who has not kept faith with his gods or his people, one who would tempt the Burians into ruin. I send my fury against this smiling traitor. Congregate, and in less than one chime's time you will bear witness to justice."

With those words, the flaming man dissipated, and sparks rained down across the temple dome from where he had stood.

Edris shook her head, dispelling the wonder of the moment. She turned to her bodyguard. "We need to find a talk-box. So I can tell Father."

"No need, Highness," the man said. He nodded up the street.

In the distance, where the crowd thinned, many large cars in Reini black were pulling to a halt. Weserian army soldiers spilled out of the second and subsequent cars. And even at this distance, Edris recognized her father emerging from the first vehicle.

Alone, naked, Ish lowered herself into a crouch.

She did not concentrate—rather, she freed her mind, letting her perceptions move where they would.

As always, when unfettered, those thoughts moved to *her*. To her other self.

She smiled, feeling her other self embrace her. Though they had never met in the flesh, she almost felt the glossy fur move beneath her hands as they touched.

Then they traded places.

She opened her eyes. There it was before her, the curtained-off chamber filled with sofas and chairs. But now the colors were all different, muted. Every little movement of the curtains, blown in the light breezes from the air vents far above, attracted her eye. Dust motes she could not have seen a moment ago drew her attention.

The sofas looked comfortable. They were hers if she wanted them.

She looked up. Beyond the lights, she knew, were metal branches that would take her where she needed to go.

She leaped, and her scrabbling claws caught metal.

Zeb and Alastair held the door leading to the hall to Volksonne's chamber. Alastair, kneeling, leaned out, firing a burst. As he withdrew, Zeb, standing, leaned out and fired three shots at the distant silhouettes, then jerked back. Return fire hammered into the doorjamb beside him, and just over his head the wall opened in a pencil-sized hole as a rifle slug penetrated. "I don't know," Zeb shouted. "Lots. Eight or ten or more."

Harris, at the door to the stairs down, shouted, "At least that many down this way."

"Well, pick a direction and let's go, man. The numbers are just going to get worse if we wait."

Alastair shouted, "Stickbomb!" And a green object, like an elongated tin can on the end of a wooden handle, clattered into the room, fetching up against a chair.

Zeb felt his insides seize up. He'd never seen a fairworld grenade, but Alastair's word left no doubt as to what this was. He stepped forward, exposing himself

to fire, and grabbed the thing, then heaved it back out
the door. Alastair slammed the door shut as Zeb fell
back. Bullets struck the door.

A moment later, an impact from outside hammered
the door, blew it off its hinges, knocking Alastair off
his feet. Zeb moved up and fired another four shots
down the hall. The slide of his pistol locked back.
Alastair, looking groggy, got into position.

Suddenly there were no more rifle shots from that
direction, but Zeb didn't kid himself that the
Sonnenkrieger down there were quitting the combat—
he heard one of them shouting, loud tones of protest
and anger. Zeb ejected his spent clip, snapped another
one into place. "What's he saying, man?"

"No stickbombs," Alastair said. "They have to take
this room intact."

"But not us, I take it."

"Correct."

Ish found the metal stairway down. It emerged from
a door against the wall near where she and Doc had
entered the catwalk, just a few paces down from the
catwalk; earlier, she'd mistaken it for one of the lighting
fixtures.

The first pace or two of it was metal platform, and
there was a man there, a Sonnenkrieger soldier with
his rifle at the ready. He was staring down into the
darkness.

She didn't want to go on those stairs. She'd been
walking on metal since she reached the light fixtures
and all four of her feet burned from the contact.

She looked at the stairway. The length of stairs was
parallel to the ground; each individual stair was angled,
at the moment, like a mountain peak, pointing straight
up. Machines did not interest her now, but it looked
as though she had only to walk out on those stairs and

her weight would cause the other end to lower, turning the whole affair into a true set of stairs, one she understood. That was good.

She crept closer. She was at right angles to the soldier, within his peripheral vision, but she was black within blackness, and moving atop the light-bearing scaffolding, not on the catwalks. He did not see.

At last he did, when she leaped. He turned, swinging his rifle into line, his eyes widening in surprise. Then she hit him, overbalanced him, carrying him over the rail. He yelled as he fell, and she leaped free, her claws digging into his flesh for purchase.

She crashed down atop the stairway and looked around, assuring herself that no one had seen her clumsy landing. She heard the soldier's impact on the floor below, heard his cry end.

The far end of the stairs began to lower—slowly, too slowly. Grudging the continued contact with the metal, Ish moved out further along the metal rig, and the far end descended more quickly.

The end of the stairs crashed down not three paces from the Bergmonk Boys. Rudi took a step back, his eyes widening.

Near the end of the thing was the biggest black cat he'd ever seen—a panther or jaguar, he supposed, as big as a human. It eyed him as though he were its next meal. He raised Ish's shotgun.

The cat turned and began trotting up the stairs, looking back at him once over its shoulder.

He turned back to his brothers. Even in the dim light, they looked uncertain. "What are you waiting for?" he asked. "Never seen a housecat before? Let's go." He started up the stairs.

❖   ❖   ❖

Ritter took a rifle from one of the soldiers. Dr. Niskin led Doc and the two other Sonnenkrieger to the bottom of the tall chamber. Niskin and the soldiers left by way of the door there; Ritter didn't offer Doc the same courtesy.

Ritter told the last soldier, "Wait outside. Don't let anyone enter. Don't worry about noise. There's going to be some." The man saluted and left.

Which left Doc under Ritter's sights, and only Förster as witness. Förster stood outside the door to the dais chamber, lounging against the doorjamb. He lit himself a cigarette.

"You know," said Ritter, "I fully intended to love her."

"Adima Niskin?" Doc asked.

"Yes. And though you didn't kill her yourself, you were responsible for her death. You interfered with a most complicated devisement, and she died because of it."

"If you're working up a rationale for killing me," Doc said, "trust me, I've heard more compelling ones."

"No, not for killing you. But I think your involvement determines *how* I should kill you."

There were words exchanged outside the balcony-level door. Ritter did not look away from Doc, but grimaced at the distraction. "I think the god himself—"

The voices outside grew louder. Exasperated, Ritter shouted, "Very well, let him in!"

The door opened and Casnar entered. He looked among the three men present and his face fell.

"Just in time for the execution," Doc said.

"Damn it all, Doc." Casnar leaned over the rail to look at him. "You could have stayed out of it. You could have survived."

"How kind of you to think of me. If I may ask, if

you didn't want me dead, why did you help them kidnap me?"

Casnar sighed. "We needed your seed."

Doc paused, appalled and amused at the same time, and barked out a laugh. "You what?"

"For one of many breeding programs Weseria is instituting. This one is quite special. The devisers say they can implant a woman with your seed and the child will have only your traits, none of the mother's. The laboratory for that program, the quarters for the women are all here. They take up nearly half of this complex." Casnar brightened. "Tomorrow that program will begin. In twenty years, Doc, Weseria will have an honor guard of pureblood Daoine Sidhe in Reini uniforms. The race will survive."

"Even if you were part of the plan to murder its father."

"I tried to protect you," Casnar protested. "I arranged for you to be taken, then released. All we needed was your seed. Once you were released in Neckerdam, you could have gone back—"

Ritter interrupted him, his face apologetic. "I fear you're a bit behind the times. When Albin Bergmonk reported failure on the grim world, I assumed MaqqRee's associates would be interfering, so I changed those orders. Adima was ordered to kill him. I thought it best."

Casnar glared at the general. "Then you're responsible for all this mess. All this wasted time."

"I will apologize at length when it is all done."

"Let him go, Ritter. He can't prove anything now. In just a little while, Aevar will be dead and you'll have everything you want. You can afford to be a little magnanimous."

Doc smiled. "I continue to be impressed by your filial devotion, Cas."

Ritter shook his head. "No. I'm sorry. No."

Casnar took one last, long look down at his half brother. "I'm sorry, Doc."

"I'd be far more impressed with that if you'd throw yourself at Ritter and let him shoot you. I'd be sure of your sincerity then."

Casnar shook his head. He turned to leave.

"My best to your mother," Doc said.

When Casnar was gone, Ritter asked, "Where was I?"

"How you're going to kill me."

"Yes, that's right." Ritter brightened. "I'm not. Nor is Förster. Volksonne will kill you."

Ish ran on ahead, leaving the Bergmonk Boys far behind her. They no longer concerned her. Nor did the gunshots she heard, the sound of a full-scale battle, from ahead. Only Doc did.

She caught his scent and followed it back to the garage intersection. She growled—she could not tell if the trail she was following was that of his entering or leaving.

Then she caught his scent going down the corridor toward the stairs. That had to be new. She followed.

It took her only moments to race up the stairs to the last landing, to hear and smell men above her. She turned the last corner and crept up a few steps.

Three men. She could smell them, could smell the oil and metal of their guns. She hated guns. She could leap on the men and kill them all . . . if they didn't have guns.

She waited and tried to think. Thought did not come easy to her. It shouldn't be this hard, even when she was this self. Her other self would know what to do. But she didn't want to change again, not so soon.

❖   ❖   ❖

Harris felt something burn him, like a glowing fire-place poker dragged across his upper leg. He swore and backed away from the doorway. He looked down. Blood was welling from his leg, but it looked and felt like a deep graze or gouge, not a direct hit. Noriko leaned in to take his place, fired several shots with her revolver down the stairwell. "Alastair!" Harris yelled. "Maybe a devisement?"

"You want me to heal them? Other devisements are a little outside my line," the doctor shouted back. He fired a short burst down the hallway he guarded.

A familiar chattering began from the stairwell down. Harris swore loud enough to be heard over it. "Now they've got an autogun down there."

Above the roar of the firearm came voices—cries of pain and surprise, cries for mercy. A moment later, there were no more gunshots from that direction.

Harris peeked around the doorjamb. One landing down, the Sonnenkrieger who had been firing upon the associates now lay dead or dying.

A redbearded head poked around the rail at the turn of the stairs. "Don't shoot."

Harris was speechless for a moment. "Jorg?"

Rudi's head peeked out beside his brother's. "We heard shootin'."

"Are you on our side?"

"Don't be stupid. Of course we are."

Harris turned a grin to the others in the room and waved them forward. "We're out of here. Go, go, go."

They reached the intersection beside the garage, Harris, Gaby, Zeb, and Noriko. It was clear. Harris lined up to cover the hallway Doc and Ish had origi-nally taken while Zeb aimed up the corridor toward the stairs. "All clear," Zeb said.

Behind them, Alastair came on at a run, and the Bergmonk Boys followed him. "They're not coming on," Alastair said. "They've taken up position in the model room. Guarding it."

"That's not good," Harris said. "That means they might be planning to use it. This place is going to be a real mess in the very near future. Where's Doc?"

Zeb shouted, "Freeze!" Then he raised his sights. "Ish! Harris, give me your jacket."

Walking down the staircase, her steps uncertain, came Ixyail. She was naked. Zeb and Harris ran up to her. Harris moved to cover her with his jacket, then took her chin in his hand. "Ish, are you all right? Can you understand me?"

"I . . . I . . ."

"Where's Doc? Do you know where Doc is?"

She pointed up. "At the top. Soldiers. I can't . . . I can't . . ." Her eyes fluttered.

Harris caught her as she fell. He grimaced. "Looks like iron poisoning. I've seen this before." He and Zeb returned to the others. Alastair and the Bergmonk Boys had joined them.

Harris turned to Gaby. "Get her out of here."

"Wrong."

Harris turned to Zeb, but the man in black just shook his head. "You're the one with the leg wound— you need to get out of here."

Harris turned to Rudi.

"Futter you. I'm not done here yet."

"Harris," Gaby said, "order the evacuation if you want, but you're coming with us."

"I'll go up and get Doc," Zeb said. "Rudi and I."

"And I," Noriko said.

Rudi said, "Jorg, take Ish. You boys, go out through the garage with Harris and these ladies, and kill anyone who tries to stop them."

"Right," said Otmar, and giggled. "What about you?"
"I'll be along."

"This should be interesting," Ritter said.

Förster smiled and raised the glass paperweight. "*Bitte*," he said.

This time, Doc did not have to use his Good Eye to see the wisps of light appear. First they were odd and innocuous, like pipe cleaners made of neon. Then they lengthened, swelled, combined, forming a human silhouette. In moments, they took on more and more solidity, swelling out into a man seven or eight paces in height. He glowed only faintly, perhaps reduced in glory because he was not standing in flames. He stood on the floor opposite Doc, his head just at the level of the balcony where Förster and Ritter waited.

Volksonne had features like Förster's, a little more perfect, showing no expression. Förster gestured, and Volksonne turned his eyes toward Doc.

He reached for Doc. Doc spun out of the way of the grasping hand. He kicked at the back of the hand, felt his foot connect, saw the blow jar the god's arm. Then he felt pain as the sole of his shoe ignited. As he stepped back on that foot, the flame was smothered.

Whatever Volksonne was, god or puppet, Doc couldn't beat him into submission. Ritter and his rifle guarded the upper door out, Sonnenkrieger guarded the lower. That meant Doc's only likely chance for survival lay with devisement—and the god wasn't likely to give him even the few moments he needed to cast one successfully.

Volksonne turned after him, his movements fast and sure, and grabbed again. Doc threw himself forward into a somersault that carried him under the outstretched hand and between Volksonne's legs. He felt heat radiate from the god. He heard Ritter and Förster laugh.

Casnar emerged from the door directly beneath Sollinvictus' chariot wheel and froze at what he saw.

King Aevar, Princess Edris, and two full squads of Weserian Army infantry were advancing toward the Eternal Flame. The king's face was set and even paler than it usually was. Edris, hurrying to keep up with him, was speaking to him.

This was a disaster. Now Aevar would not be at the palace when the fireball descended to consume it. Casnar gulped and stepped forward to greet the king, but a temple priest in red-and-orange robes was there first. "Your Majesty."

The king drew to a halt before him. "Turn off the Eternal Flame," he said.

"I, uh, I . . ." The priest was completely dumbfounded. A moment later, he found his voice again. "But, Majesty, I can't. If we do that, it won't be Eternal."

"Captain."

The army officer present drew his pistol and put the barrel to the priest's forehead.

Suddenly sickly of appearance, the priest turned to shout across the chamber to another in the same temple uniform. "Turn down the Eternal Flame to inspection levels, open east facing." That priest ran to a side door.

Casnar moved toward the soldiers and royals, circling around so that they would not be between him and the way out. None had noticed him except Edris' bodyguard, who noticed everything.

The captain kept the pistol to the priest's head, and Aevar maintained his expression of barely-contained fury for long, silent moments. Then the Eternal Flame began to lower. First the height of a man, it slowly shrank to less than two handspans high . . . and finally half of the flame, the eastern half circle, vanished. The western half remained diminished but still ablaze.

"Majesty, will this suffice?" asked the priest. He was begging. "It is the best I can do without violating temple oaths to the gods."

"It will do," Aevar said. "Now open the hatch in the center."

Casnar felt himself grow cold. The king knew too much. Aevar might survive the destruction of his palace, but one way or another, he would have to die tonight. Casnar thought through a dizzying number of options, of stories, of excuses—it was his strength.

There was supposed to be a mad dusky loose in the Temple. If Casnar could get the king to the levels below, and that's where the man obviously wanted to go, they could simply shoot him and find a dusky to blame. It didn't have the cachet of the king being wiped out by the god—wait a moment, the public wouldn't have to know that he died here, they'd assume he died in his palace. But that left the regular-army soldiers and Edris as complications . . .

The priest said, "I don't know what you mean, Majesty. I know of no hatch . . ."

Casnar was briefly diverted. The official priesthood here knew that there were Sonnenkrieger offices below, but didn't know how extensive, nor did they know about all the special Sonnenkrieger projects taking place. This priest was telling the truth. Casnar leaned in to see if the king would have him killed for it.

The king moved out onto the temple's hearthstone. Its surface was irregular, with several cracks marring it. Three of them crossed one another in a triangle close to the stone's center. It was this feature, which disguised the hatch the builders had engineered, that had caused this particular stone to be chosen. The king moved unerringly to stand beside the triangle and gestured at it. "Captain, have your men break through this."

Casnar's gaze fell on a discoloration just outside the triangle. It looked as though small pieces of rock had been broken away. The breaks were white, very fresh, and Casnar felt another jolt of fear go through him.

Doc, or one of his associates, had to have been there. And had known enough to take a sample from the hearthstone. That meant this temple was doomed.

Several soldiers moved out onto the hearthstone and began attacking the triangle with their gun butts. Casnar moved up beside the king's daughter. "Edris, may I have a word with you?"

She gave him a smile. "Of course."

"By the street, please. This is a matter of some delicacy." Perhaps he should ask her tonight, now, to marry him.

"Later, please, Cas. My father needs me."

"Edris—"

"Tell me here or it will have to wait."

He sighed and gave her a smile. "It can wait. By your leave." He turned and headed out.

Well, perhaps it was for the best anyway. He would still be king of Cretanis.

Chapter Twenty-Five

Noriko, most silent of them, ascended the stairs well in advance of Zeb and Rudi. When she peeked around the final turn of the stairwell, she could see three Sonnenkrieger on duty at the upper landing. One had his back to her, leaning against the rail that overlooked this flight of steps; Noriko could only see the heads and shoulders of the other two, who were partway across the chamber, facing the first man.

In moments, they'd hear Zeb and Rudi pounding up the stairs behind her. There would be a gunfight. Whoever was beyond the doors these men guarded would hear.

She drew her sword. Keeping as low to the floor as she could, she moved around the turn. The men were distracted; she was in dark clothes. She had a chance . . . Leaning so she was almost at the same angle as the stairs, she moved up, one step, two, three, four . . .

As more of the chamber came into view, she could see there were no more than the three men she'd seen.

They talked among themselves. The man with his back
to her and one of the men opposite held rifles at the
ready. The third, an officer, had a pistol holstered.

She heard, faintly, the footfalls of her companions
behind her. In a moment, the Sonnenkrieger would
hear, too. She gathered her feet under her and charged.

The soldiers' eyes were still widening when she
reached the landing and swung her sword back. Her
blow, thrown against the man at the rail, cut entirely
through his right forearm. He shrieked; his severed arm
and the rifle hit the concrete floor.

Noriko spun. Her blade took the other rifleman in
the neck. It seemed to pass through him harmlessly,
but she felt the blade bite and knew better.

The officer threw himself at her, bore her backwards.
She twisted, trying to free herself, and broke his grip,
but he still drove her ahead of him. She was periph-
erally aware of the second rifleman falling, his head
detaching, falling separately. Then she hit the metal rail
beside the first man she'd cut. She felt ribs on her right
side give way from the impact and suddenly she had
no breath. Her vision began to contract almost instantly.

The officer shoved, straightening, pushing her further over the rail. She could not bring her sword to
bear. He was grabbing for his pistol. She let go of the
sword hilt, wrapped a leg around his waist, and got her
hands on his pistol hand, struggling to keep it from
the gun butt.

Then the officer was torn from her. He staggered
a couple of steps back. A night-black silhouette, Zeb,
stood beside him. The officer tried again to draw his
pistol, but the silhouette shoved him, then spun into
one of the beautiful side kicks she had seen Harris execute so many times. Zeb's foot caught the man
in the gut and threw him back into the wall. He
staggered there, momentarily unable to move, and

Zeb moved forward to hammer him with blows of the fist.

Meanwhile, Rudi reached the landing. He spared a glance for Noriko, for Zeb and the officer, then he swung the pistol in his hand against the temple of the one-armed rifleman, who still stood, his face paling in shock. The rifleman and the officer went down at the same moment.

Noriko smiled and slid down to sit on the concrete.

Zeb leaned over her. "Noriko—oh, Je-zus. Are you all right?"

"I will be fine," she said. It was a lie, and one she couldn't quite conceal, as her voice was weak, but she couldn't have him waiting for her. She drew her pistol out. "I will guard your back. Find Doc."

He hesitated, then straightened. He held his right hand before him and swung around as though he were consulting some sort of gauge. He turned to face the central door. "Ready?"

Rudi pulled out his second automatic. "Ready."

Zeb reached up and swatted the light bulb overhead, shattering it, plunging the landing into blackness.

Ritter moved beside Förster and poked his head into the dais chamber. Yes, there was a definite pounding noise coming from the hatch overhead.

Förster seemed to have things in hand here. Doc, avoiding a kick from Volksonne, was rolling to his feet in the center of the chamber. Förster no longer needed Ritter and his rifle; Doc would never be able to reach the balcony.

Ritter moved to the main doorway and stepped out. "Go to the Flame," he told the Sonnenkrieger on guard there. "Someone is trying to batter his way through. Bring him here. If at all possible, keep it inconspicuous."

The lieutenant in charge saluted and led his men away at a trot.

A combination attack finally got through Doc's guard—Doc ducked one hand but Volksonne caught him with the other. The blow threw him against the concrete wall, searing his left shoulder. He rebounded from the concrete and fell, stunned or unconscious.

Förster contemplated him. He brought Volksonne upright and made the god stand still, though he could feel that Volksonne wanted to finish this fight, wanted to take his due. Förster would wait until Ritter returned. It was only correct that Ritter get to see Doc's last moments.

"Förster."

The voice echoed through the chamber, mocking, seeming to come from everywhere at once.

Förster looked around. Some trick of Doc's? It couldn't be. The man was barely conscious at best.

Then Förster saw the speaker.

The man stood at the balcony level, a mere six or seven paces away, around to Förster's right. He wore black from hat to shoes, making him a silhouette, so he could have entered from below and crept up the stairs while Volksonne chased his prey around on the other side of the chamber—but that meant the guards . . .

The darkness of the man's clothes didn't conceal the fact that he held a pistol in his left hand and had it aimed at Förster.

"*Alpdruck*," Förster said.

"Drop the glass thing," the silhouette said, in Cretanis.

"This?" Förster held it up before it. It required only a slight mental adjustment to think through it, to make Volksonne detect the silhouette's presence. He sent the god into motion, commanding it to reach toward the silhouette. Then Förster tossed the control mechanism forward. "Catch."

Alpdruck shouldn't have been able to do it. Volksonne's motion was too fast. Yet Alpdruck threw himself backwards and the hand missed him, slamming into the wall beside him. The control mechanism clattered to the floor at his feet.

Förster threw himself forward, clean over Volksonne's arm, and crashed into Alpdruck. They went down hard together. Förster struck out blindly at the man's gun hand, connected, heard the pistol go clattering off into the darkness. He raised his hand for a *coup de grace*.

Alpdruck's knee came up, connecting with his side, knocking him over. Had he not been in the condition he was, Förster knew that his ribs would probably have caved in under the blow. As it was, his breath was nearly driven from him. He felt his opponent roll away from him, heard the man rise.

Just across the rail, Volksonne looked between the two men and then down at his original target, Doc.

Doc slapped the flames licking at his shoulder until they subsided. He rose, ignoring the pain he felt.

A pale figure raced past Doc, to the stairs on his right. Doc shook his head and focussed. "Rudi—"

The gunman just said, "Present for you." Barely looking in Doc's direction, he tossed something.

Doc caught it. It was one of Rudi's automatics.

He turned. Volksonne stood mere paces away, staring dispassionately down at him. Doc saw Förster on the balcony just beyond the god, squared off in fighting stance against—no one. No, there was someone there. Zeb, barely visible in the glow Volksonne cast.

Volksonne turned back toward Zeb and Förster. He reached up toward them.

❖   ❖   ❖

Zeb saw Förster spring to his feet as nimbly as though he hadn't just suffered one of Zeb's best knee strikes. The colonel ignored the god-thing standing mere paces away. He was smiling again, the invincible smile he'd offered in the preliminary round of the All-Out. "Whoever you are," Förster said, "you really should not be here."

"I have to be somewhere," Zeb said. "Might as well be kicking the hell out of you."

Förster's eyes widened. "Watson." He brought up his hands and advanced in a boxing stance. Then he stopped and looked at the glowing figure reaching toward them.

Volksonne grabbed—not for Zeb, not for Förster, but for something on the balcony behind Förster. It seized the object, picked it up, the object ridiculously tiny in its giant hand.

The paperweight.

On Volksonne's fingertip, the glass of the paperweight began to glow. It deformed, flowed. Drops fell away to sizzle against the floor. A moment later, all that was left was the arrowhead that had once been its center. Volksonne pinched it between thumb and forefinger and glowing gold began to drip down after the glass.

Volksonne changed, his form flowing as freely as the glass and gold had.

His skin faded, became transparent, leaving behind only a latticework of glowing golden light, a framework suggesting a complete body. It twisted, malformed, until it was not human in proportion; its arms and legs became thick and short, its torso long, its head round and disproportionately large.

And everywhere from the latticework protruded spindly lesser arms, thirty or more, their hands grasping, clutching.

Zeb heard whispers now, the voices of dozens of unseen mouths, their incomprehensible words filling the chamber. Coldness blew through him as though his insides had a vent to the outside air.

The center door on the balcony level crashed open. General Ritter entered, his rifle raised . . . but his expression of anger vanished, replaced by one of wide-eyed shock, as he saw Volksonne.

"Take a good look at your work, Ritter," Doc said.

Ritter turned and ran.

Rudi swore. He reached the balcony level just in time to see Ritter disappearing through the door. He scrambled after the man, rounded the doorway, and aimed. "Stop right there!"

Ritter skidded to a stop, glanced back at Rudi, and raised his hands.

Rudi ran after him.

The new Volksonne turned away from Zeb and Förster. It moved unsteadily, as though it were unused to walking, as though those thick legs bore a tremendous weight. It faced Doc.

Doc took a deep breath. So often he'd been lauded for the speed and ingenuity of his improvised devisements. On occasion, he had to wager his life on their success.

Such as now.

He knelt, relaxing into the flow of his meditative state.

He heard and felt a footstep. Volksonne, coming closer. He shook away the stray thought, the unwanted awareness of the god-thing's proximity. And as he descended into the state he wished, he sought a mind, a name.

Skoll, he thought. *Fleet of foot and ferocious of*

jaw. Surely you cannot sleep with your enemies so active.

Distantly, he felt another footstep.

Why chase across the sky when your prey is here? Come to me. Invest me with your rage, your power. I will give you form. I will put the throat of the sun between your jaws.

Another footstep.

With Skoll, there was no laughter. There were no words. But a new sensation cut through Doc's body. It was hunger, a need so aching and pure it drove all thought from Doc's mind.

He opened his eyes. Volksonne stood above him, reaching for him with one great arm, all the lesser arms on it at full extension toward him, grasping.

Doc felt his body all around him, extending in all directions from the little bit of flesh that was his mortal form. He bared his teeth and leaped for Volksonne's throat.

Zeb saw the sun-thing advance upon Doc, saw Doc look up. And then there was something around the man, shadows and fog. Only when it moved did he recognize its outline—that of a giant wolf, crouching, Doc's form lost somewhere within it.

The smoke-wolf sprang upon Volksonne, carrying the sun-god backwards. Volksonne fell, the impact shaking the chamber, the wolf atop it. Doc, still kneeling, was visible behind the two gigantic things. The wolf's growl vibrated throughout the chamber, making the metal rails sing, causing the floor beneath Zeb's feet to rattle.

Förster advanced and Zeb wrenched his attention away from Volksonne. Förster, seemingly uninterested in the spectacle of combat between the sun-god and wolf-god, led off with a combination, left-right-left, fast and sure. Zeb backed away, blocking the first shot and putting himself out of range of the next two, gauging his opponent's attack.

Zeb's hand burned. His right palm was in more pain than it had been at any previous solar event. He couldn't hold a gun in it. He could barely keep it in a fist. His second pistol was still in his right-hand pocket, but the way his hand was misbehaving, he couldn't possibly get it out before Förster would be all over him.

He parried Förster's next jab and put his toe into the man's kneecap. Förster grunted but did not falter; he closed before Zeb regained his footing and put two blows into Zeb's ribs.

Zeb leaned into, not away from, his opponent, brought his forearm across Förster's face, felt the man's nose go flat under his blow. Förster staggered back. Zeb put a weak right into his stomach, followed through with a beauty of a left hook to his right side. He avoided striking at Förster's head— the surest way to crush his own knuckles and fingers was to pound them into a bony target like a man's jaw—but was rewarded anyway with the sight of Förster backing away.

Förster recovered almost instantly, dropped back into his stance. "I will win," the colonel said. "I'm fighting not just for myself. My cause lends me strength."

"It lends you cliches, anyway. Besides, I've got something you don't."

"Which is?"

"I can really take a beating." Zeb moved in, parried part of Förster's wicked hook, and threw his own combination, left-right-left, side-gut-side. His right-hand punch landed harder this time. He ignored his own pain, fighting through it, fighting *with* it.

✧   ✧   ✧

There was no one else in sight in this hall. Mindful of the doors that lined it, Rudi ran up to Ritter and stood a mere pace away. "It was you, wasn't it?"

Ritter looked around, but seemed to find no rescue at hand. His expression was pained. "I, what?"

"You who convinced Albin to come along on this plan of yours. You're going to kill Aevar, so it wasn't him. Albin would never have thrown in with a mere colonel or with your mad deviser. So it was you."

"It was I." Ritter grimaced. "And now it appears that I am your prisoner. Unless you'd like to be very rich."

"How rich?"

"How rich is the king of an industrial nation? In a few moons, Weseria will seize Donarau. You can rule it. Not as a puppet king, as a true ruler."

Rudi grinned. "You know how Albin died?"

Ritter shook his head.

"Pretty much the same way you're going to."

"I have surrendered. I am defenseless."

"You've mistaken me for one of the good eamons." Rudi aimed at Ritter's eye and pulled the trigger.

Doc tore at Volksonne's throat. He felt its greater arms wrap around him, squeezing, crushing, burning. He howled his pain, scrabbling at it with his paws—then remembered.

This was the sun beneath him. He was destined to win. He had pursued it across the skies since before man walked the world. He was destined to kill it, no matter the cost. He surged forward again, clamped his teeth on its throat, and tore.

Substance that was not flesh came away under his teeth. Doc swallowed, bit again. He felt his back compressing, his fur and skin burning, but now his jaws were growing out of proportion with the rest of his body. He bit again and again, swallowing more and more of his foe's godly form.

And suddenly the pain diminished. Volksonne was thrashing about, not gripping him mercilessly, not burning him. Doc lunged for a flailing arm, one of the greater ones. He grasped it, tore it away, swallowed.

Förster felt his strength flagging. He knew a sudden moment of fear. He'd hit Zeb Watson again and again, but the black man in blacker clothing just wouldn't go down.

He backed away, past the opening in the rail that led to the stairs, and then threw himself forward as Watson reached that spot. He felt Watson's fist connect with his ribs, his increasingly-vulnerable ribs, but shoved and saw Watson flail as he went over sideways and back.

Then Watson's hand caught him by the collar and Förster, too, fell that way.

He hit the stairs hard, cracking his kneecap and suddenly tasting blood, and his own consolation was the knowledge that Watson must have hit harder. He rolled across more steps, then the ground dropped out from under him.

He tried to twist in midair, tried to rotate to land well. He hit back-first and pain jolted through his entire body, particularly where Watson's blows had weakened him.

But Förster was Sonnenkrieger and Watson was merely a dusky. The colonel forced himself to rise. He turned.

Paces away, the smoke-wolf stood astride the spasming body of Volksonne, growling, eating.

But immediately in front of Förster, Watson was already up, already on guard again. "Weren't you listening, stupid?" His voice sounded pained.

Watson lashed out, his trademark combination. Förster got his hands up. But the attack was a feint; Watson faded back and came around with a side kick that took Förster in the gut. Förster slammed back into the concrete wall, the little bit of his breath remaining now leaving him.

Watson stepped in, brought his left knee up into Förster's vulnerable side. Förster felt ribs crack. He unloaded a hook into his enemy, connected with his shoulder, but the blow had no strength to it.

Watson swarmed over him, and Förster could no longer keep up with the blows, with the bewildering complexity of the combinations. He felt impacts against his gut, sides, knees, face. Curiously, the blows seemed less and less painful. Yet he could not defend against them.

There was a final blow. Somehow Watson had slammed the entire floor into Förster's body.

Watson knelt beside him. Increasingly detached, Förster knew that, with the alleged humor with which most New Worlders seemed to be afflicted, Watson would now begin to count him out.

But Watson didn't count. He leaned in close and whispered, *"Sie sind wunderbar, ich würde gerne Ihre Tochter heiraten."*

The last bit of Volksonne disappeared down Doc's throat. He shook his head and looked for more to eat.

Before him were two morsels wrapped up in cloth. He sniffed. They were made of raw meat and blood. He lunged. The one in black cloth jumped away. Doc seized one in flesh-colored cloth, shook it briefly until he heard its spine snap, and gulped it down. He turned to the one in black again.

It spoke, its voice dim and distant: "Je-zus, Doc, turn it off!" But the words meant nothing.

He bared his teeth and advanced on it. It backed away. It smelled delicious.

Then there was another voice, far louder, shouting right in his ear: "Wake up, you daft eamon!"

Startled, Doc opened his second set of eyes. Before him, he caught a glimpse of the giant smoke thing shaped like a wolf; then it faded to nothingness, revealing Zeb beyond it.

Doc turned his head. Rudi stood beside him, eyes wide. "Thank you," Doc said.

"Think nothin' of it. Time to go."

Doc stood. As his hearing cleared, a new noise came to him, a clanking from high in the dais chamber, voices speaking in Burian: "Almost there, Majesty."

Zeb held up his right hand and swore. "Doc, it got worse just before Volksonne disappeared. Fireball time."

"The palace—"

"Worse than that. It's coming *here*. Harris rigged it." Zeb turned toward the lower exit. "Time to run."

But Doc ran the other way, up the stairs and into the dais chamber, with Rudi at his heels.

Zeb swept Noriko up and ran down the stairs, his rate of speed dangerous, his jarring gait sending waves of pain through her.

"Fireball?" she asked, when her breath would allow her.

"Yep." He hit the first landing, skidded into a turn, continued down.

"Thank you."

"For what?"

"Coming back for me."

"Had to."

"You had to? Why?"

He rounded another turn. "I'm your guardian spirit. You were waiting for me, weren't you?"

"Yes." She tightened her grip on him. "You'll bring me harmony?"

"Count on it, Noriko." He rounded another turn.

"Stand back, Majesty," the colonel in charge of this unit waved Aevar back. "We have to make sure it is secure—"

White arms emerged from the hole his soldiers had battered open, followed by a torso, and Doc emerged. The soldiers surrounding the spot backed away, bringing their rifles into line.

Aevar glared. "Doctor MaqqRee. You're going to explain—"

Doc flashed him an unfriendly smile. "This is my explanation: Run. Or die."

"You don't speak to me—"

Doc reached back into the hole and pulled. The hole sprouted Rudi Bergmonk as though it were part of a magical gangster garden. Doc set Rudi onto his feet.

"Fireball's coming," Rudi said. "You're about to be the crispiest king in Europe."

Aevar looked Doc in the face and decided that the man wasn't joking. "Evacuate," he told his officer.

They ran.

Dr. Trandil Niskin watched as the tiny glowing ball appeared above the model of Bardulfburg. He staggered, released by the completion of the devisement from the awesome drain it made against his strength.

When he'd done this in the past, he'd known the pleasure, a sense of accomplishment perhaps no other man could know.

This time there was no elation, just a sense of duty.

His daughter was gone. The last person in the world who had loved him. He would now have riches, titles, fame. He would serve his leader well—but, as the only one living who knew how to summon the sacred suns, the only man who could maintain the machinery that summoned Volksonne, he would be indispensable and would dictate the terms by which he spent the rest of his life.

But one thing he could not dictate. Adima was gone. He'd feared it when lines of communication to her in Neckerdam broke off. Now he knew. Bitter tears rolled down his cheeks. He did not care whether the Sonnenkrieger guarding the two doors into this bullet-pocked office saw them.

Curiously, the little sun did not begin to arc toward the model of the Royal Palace and the little chip of white stone lying atop that building. Its course took it further south and west, toward . . .

He swallowed the lump that had suddenly appeared in his throat. "Oh, please, no."

The Sonnenkrieger officer looked at him. "What is it?"

Niskin glanced at him, then looked back at the model.

There was no mistake. The ball was dropping straight for the Temple of the Suns.

He could disrupt the devisement, of course. Interpose his flesh between the miniature sun and its target. But the god would demand its due of him. He would die.

He would die either way.

But Desmond MaqqRee, the man responsible for his daughter's death, was here in the temple.

What did it matter that the entirety of Ritter's plan would die? At least Adima would be avenged.

Niskin returned his attention to the officer. "Nothing is wrong," he said. "Here, come take a look. You will find this interesting."

❖   ❖   ❖

Some of the soldiers tripped descending the stairs outside the temple. Their fellows hauled them to their feet. Others shouted for the crowd to move back.

The crowd didn't have to be told. A sun was high in the sky, roaring down toward them. People ran in all directions, even up the stairs toward the temple; the soldiers kept them from reaching their objective.

Doc, Rudi and the royals were across the street and crouching behind cars when the sun of Volksonne came to earth for the last time. It struck dead center in the temple dome and burned its way through as though the stone roof were paper. The temple's walls blew out, hurling columns before them, and chunks of column bounced down the temple steps. The explosion hurled burning debris out across the city for blocks in all directions.

Doc had no trouble descending into his meditative state. *Hear me, O Trickster. Here is the gift I promised you, a loathsome trick, done by my command, done in your honor. I pray it brings you laughter.* He opened his eyes again.

The roar of the blast was done. Flaming cinders still fell among the crowd, but Aevar rose, unconcerned by the danger they posed. Assuring himself first that his daughter was unhurt, he turned to his officer. "Bring in the fire guard," he said. Then he turned to Doc. "As I was saying, you're going to explain this."

Doc gave him a smile that was as cold and distant as only a Daoine Sidhe could offer. "Oh, yes, I am."

Under the bright noonday sun, Zeb watched Geert Tiwasson and Hathu Aremeer fight for third place in the All-Out.

Zeb affected alert interest, but he could barely manage to concentrate on the fight. Every part of his body hurt. Alastair's medical devisements had in fact worked wonders on his nose, restoring it to its proper shape by morning, but they hadn't stopped it from hurting. His ribs hurt, his arms hurt, his joints hurt, his back hurt.

He managed a smile. Hurting wasn't bad. It was much better than one of the alternatives.

Tiwasson put Aremeer in a hold the man from Donarau could not break. Aremeer tapped out, an expression of disgust on his face.

"Congratulations," Zeb told Tiwasson when the big man returned to the sidelines.

Tiwasson afforded him a faint smile. "I would rather be where you are. Facing Förster."

"It's not that much fun."

A referee approached Princess Edris in the royal platform. He held a pocket watch and shook his head, speaking. She spoke to him briefly. He came to the edge of the platform, to the microphone set up there, and addressed the crowd in Burian.

"The appointed time having passed," Tiwasson translated, "and Conrad Förster not having presented himself—"

The crowd, having already heard the last words in Burian, groaned.

"—Förster is disqualified from this competition." Tiwasson cocked his head. "It looks as though I am second instead of third." He extended Zeb his hand. "And you are first. Congratulations."

Zeb shook it. "Thanks."

"Think of me fondly now. Soon enough, I will take the title from you."

"I welcome a fair challenge, man."

They called Zeb, Tiwasson, and Aremeer up onto the platform. Princess Edris smiled as she placed the

wreaths upon their heads—gold on Zeb's, silver on
Tiwasson's, bronze on Aremeer's.

The athletes turned to face and wave at the crowd,
and the band began the royal anthem of Novimagos—
a song as tediously old-fashioned and predictable, Zeb
decided, as Weseria's.

He found the corner of the field where the Sidhe
Foundation stood and waved to them. Most of them
were bandaged beneath their clothes, especially Doc,
and Ixyail still looked a little disoriented—what she'd
been through, iron poisoning and overuse of her own
special gift, had left her that way. But she was smiling, too.

Swana was with them, and the Bergmonk Boys. And
out in the crowd he saw Kobolde and other duskies—
not many, but more than there had been in the audience during his first bouts.

Okay, he told himself, *you're not Jesse Owens. But
you're doing your part.* He sought out Noriko again.
And you didn't let anyone down.

"Coming with us?" Doc asked.

Rudi shook his head. So did his brothers. "We're
going to watch the Games until the end. In fact, I think
we'll use the Foundation's rooms. If you've a mind to
let us."

Doc took the key from his pocket and passed it over.
"Don't do anything I have to pay for. I don't want to
have to come after you."

"I expect you might . . . someday. If we're not smart
enough. But, no, I won't make it soon. Why are you
leaving before the Games are done?"

"Personal business to take care of."

Chapter Twenty-Six

She was fair of skin and fine of build. Once she had been called beautiful. Even today, many still pointed to the delicacy of her features, the luminous quality of her eyes, the purity of the whiteness of her hair, and accounted her a beauty. But time had set its stamp on her long ago. She wore the lines and frailty of age, and it had been some time since anyone had written songs exalting her features.

Her name was Maeve, and since before the birth of most people now alive she had been Queen of Cretanis, the proud island kingdom of western Europe. She had always ruled alone; her husband, now long dead, had been Consort and Prince, never King.

Today she wore clothing of varying shades of green. The top was the precise color of rich grass that was closely tended. The skirt was made up of alternating horizontal bands of that color and a darker green, and its hem swept just across the polished surface of the floor. It was not too extravagant a dress in appearance, but it was costly of make, with devisements bound into it to keep it light so that wearing it did not tax her.

She moved along the marble gallery in one of the few areas of the palace where she could find privacy. Guards stood at the doors leading into this portion of the complex but could only come within in response to an alarm. The gallery, all of Panhellenic marble, with stone benches upon which she never sat and a small blue pool in which she had never waded, connected the display room, with its banks of glass cases and the treasures they held, with her private library.

She never spent much time in the gallery, but its serenity and its simplicity always soothed her. Today, as for the two days before, she needed soothing.

Maeve swept into her library. It was, by comparison with the two chambers before it, a plain room. Two stories in height, its walls were all concealed by bookcases, map cases, and scroll racks. The furnishings were simple—a sofa, a stuffed chair sagging in the middle from too many years of supporting even her slight weight, chairs, tables, desk lamps. Everything was in various shades of brown—all but the spines of some of the books. Only among the books themselves, and in her garments, were there exceptions.

And in the fire, of course. It blazed in its reds and oranges and yellows in the fireplace, set in the one portion of wall not occupied by bookcases.

She hesitated, looking into the fire. It should have sprung to life as she entered, rather than being ablaze already.

"Hello, Maeve."

It wouldn't do to start, or to whip around to look at the intruder. Maintaining her composure, she turned, slowly and regally, to look up. "Hello, Desmond."

Doc stood upon the walkway above, a volume in his hand, his pose suggesting he was surprised to find her here. It was a charming act, of course. Only she was allowed to be here. His very presence, uninvited, could lead to his execution.

His clothes were no more appropriate than his manner. He wore dark brown pants, riding boots, a long-sleeved black shirt with an open neck and flaring sleeves. It was rather subdued for him, and she realized, somewhat distantly, that he had probably chosen it because it was difficult to see at night. It was likely that he had worn some sort of cap over that white hair of his, so like his father's in length and texture.

"You're dressed to skulk," she said. "Are you here to kill me?"

"I'm here to talk to you." He put the book back in its case, then straddled the nearest ladder and slid down to the floor.

"How did you get in?"

"Oh, a way my father showed me. Long, long ago. I've been saving it. I knew I might only use it once." Without invitation, he moved to take one of the highback chairs, twirling it to face it toward her before sitting.

Primly, she sat upon her comfortable stuffed chair. This situation afforded her no sense of menace. "You are here to talk about Casnar," she said.

"Casnar, and other things. By the way, is he home yet? We could not find any sign of his escape from Bardulfburg. He was, I imagine, too experienced to leave a trail."

"Escape? The Crown Prince of Cretanis need not escape."

Doc shook his head, dismissing the matter. "I will simplify matters by saying that I know you were part of his collaboration with General Ritter and Doctor Niskin."

"Speculate all you will. But I do not collaborate with gangsters."

The comment brought a smile to his face. "How about that? I do. But this is no speculation. Which I'll prove presently." He lost his smile and leaned forward, all amusement gone. "Before I do what I have to do, I should tell you this. All my life, at least in my youth, it was my hope that you would accept me. Not as a son, but as a member of your family. As a boy, I thought you kept me at a distance because I meant that Father had desired, and had, other women. But eventually I learned that was not your reason; had it been, you would have brought your indignation to bear on some of those women, or my mother, as well. You never did. You saved it for me. As a youth, I thought it was because you considered me a threat to your own children—and this was before you'd borne any. But your dislike of me persisted even when it had to be clear to you that I had no intention of seeking the crown of Cretanis." He shrugged. "As a man, I gave up wondering. I always kept my hand outstretched, in case you ever chose to take it. You never did. Now I withdraw it."

"I am devastated," Maeve said, and gave him the faintest hint of smile. He wasn't amusing her. It was time for him to go.

"But now I think I know why you always disliked me."

"Do tell."

"Because I'm Daoine Sidhe and you're not."

She did not move, did not allow a single muscle to twitch, but she felt as though she'd suddenly been plunged into water as cold as ice. She could not breathe for a long, helpless moment. She did manage to cock her head and look puzzled. It helped her stall for time, for her voice to return. But the panic that gripped her said that her delays would gain her nothing.

"The Reinis wanted me for my seed," Doc

continued, "to begin a breeding program. A silly notion. And I, like my father, am a bit old-fashioned about the way I choose to dispense it. But the question it begged was *why*. With Casnar a willing member of their plan, why not use his seed to breed a new generation of Daoine Sidhe and raise them on the soulless words of the Reinis? There were only two possible answers, of course. Either he had no seed to offer—and the bastards he's left around Europe are ample evidence that this is not the case—or his seed was unsuited to the task. Because he is not Daoine Sidhe."

"You are ridiculous." It did her no good to offer denials, and every word she spoke cut her like an icicle being dragged out of her. But pride demanded that she bow not even a little to this man.

"I am Daoine Sidhe because my father and mother were. Casnar and I share the same father. Therefore, if he is not Daoine Sidhe, it is because you are not. Can logic be simpler than that?"

"It is not true."

"I cannot imagine being so devoted to a matter of race that you would lie about it for so many years and suffer to conceal some wayward drop of blood in your ancestry."

"I have never had to do so."

Instead of answering, Doc took an object from his pocket. Maeve recognized it from her tabletop. It was a wooden paperweight, glossy with lacquer. Embossed on it in gold were the rounded hill and eagle atop it that were the centerpiece of her family's coat of arms. The front edge featured indentations, a little small for Doc's fing squeezed his hand into the den fairly sure when I read so at the site of the b manual, being on the care and feeding of little Daoine Sidhe—part of a lecture series, actually. Guidelines for expectant mothers. The Cretanis portion was not signed, but the voice seemed very like you. Still, I wasn't absolutely sure until I found this. *Bitte*," he said.

With a mechanical creak, one of the bookcases swung open. In the niche beyond stood an aluminum cabinet topped by elaborate glassworks.

Maeve stared at the cabinet as though she could will it out of existence, then turned the same look on Doc. But he remained resolutely in place. He set the paperweight on the near tabletop.

"What are you going to do?" she asked.

"I'm going to tell the press. They might not be shocked by your collaboration with the Reinis . . . but when they print the story of the shame you felt about your ancestry, you'll be the laughingstock of much of the world."

She let a long silence fall between them. She knew what she had to say, but the words constituted a surrender, and she had almost never surrendered in her life. Finally she managed to utter them. "What must I do to convince you otherwise?"

"Abdicate Tonight. To Sanborn or either of the girls, but not ⌐snar. My one bit of meddling with Cretan⌐ will be, must be, to deny the throne to ⌐ ⌐ports the Reini philosophy."

⌐ to ask what would happen if ⌐ ⌐ie. She could call her guard, ⌐ ⌐d with which every mem- ⌐ ⌐; she could not count ⌐ ⌐ his associates not ⌐ ⌐it in the event of

⌐st genuine.

[text partially obscured by folded page corner, reading from the overlapping page:] four ⌐ ⌐ers, but he ⌐ ⌐s anyway. "I was ⌐ ⌐ documents. They were ⌐ ⌐ program. They found ⌐ ⌐eding into Burian from Cretanis ⌐ ⌐translated

"I'm glad."

"This one is at an end. I should not like to endure another one. Ever."

He rose. "Farewell, then."

He moved to another bookcase and whispered a word to it. The lower section of it, only a pace and a half high, swung open. He had to duck to enter the gap it revealed. He pulled the case shut on his way out.

It was some time before he could make his way back to the airfield. Sneaking back out through the royal complex, even with the knowledge his father had given him, was laborious. Making his way unseen across the city of Beldon, which had been denied to him by an order of exile for many years, took time and effort.

As he entered the hangar where the plane waited, bells began ringing in the distance. He frowned; it was not yet six bells. And yet the peals reached six in number and continued.

The associates were alert for his return. Harris and Gaby moved out from the hangar's small office. The rest descended the plane ladder. Their faces were grave.

"What has happened?" he asked.

They hesitated and looked at one another. It was Ixyail who spoke. "Doc, it was on the talk-box. Maeve has abdicated. She said it was time. She bestowed the throne upon Prince Sanborn."

Doc nodded.

"And then she climbed to the top of Beldon Tower and leaped to her death. The bells are tolling for her."

Her words hit him like a blow. He must have let some part of his feelings show. She came forward to wrap her arms around his neck. "Doc, I'm sorry."

He held her. He forced words past the stone that had appeared, full-grown, in his throat. "So am I. But here's not the place for it.

"Let's go home."

MERCEDES LACKEY
Hot! Hot! Hot!

DAVID DRAKE RULES!

Hammer's Slammers:

The Tank Lords	87794-1 ◆ $6.99	☐
Caught in the Crossfire	87882-4 ◆ $6.99	☐
The Butcher's Bill	57773-5 ◆ $6.99	☐
The Sharp End	87632-5 ◆ $5.99	☐

RCN series:

With the Lightnings	57818-9 ◆ $6.99	☐
Lt. Leary, Commanding (HC)	57875-8 ◆ $24.00	☐
Lt. Leary, Commanding (PB)	31992-2 ◆ $7.99	☐

The Belisarius series with Eric Flint:

An Oblique Approach	87865-4 ◆ $6.99	☐
In the Heart of Darkness	87885-9 ◆ $6.99	☐
Destiny's Shield	57872-3 ◆ $6.99	☐
Fortune's Stroke (HC)	57871-5 ◆ $24.00	☐
The Tide of Victory *(forthcoming)*		

The General series with S.M. Stirling:

The Forge	72037-6 ◆ $5.99	☐
The Chosen	87724-0 ◆ $6.99	☐
The Reformer	57860-X ◆ $6.99	☐

Independent Novels and Collections:

The Dragon Lord (fantasy)	87890-5 ◆ $6.99	☐
Birds of Prey	57790-5 ◆ $6.99	☐
Northworld Trilogy	57787-5 ◆ $6.99	☐